All's Fair in

LOVE

and Cupcakes

All's Fair in LOVE and Cupcakes

Betsy St. Amant

ZONDERVAN®

ZONDERVAN

All's Fair in Love and Cupcakes
Copyright © 2014 by Betsy St. Amant

This title is also available as a Zondervan e-book.
Visit www.zondervan.com.

Requests for information should be addressed to:
Zondervan, *Grand Rapids, Michigan 49546*

Library of Congress Cataloging-in-Publication Data

St. Amant, Betsy.
  All's fair in love and cupcakes / Betsy St. Amant.
      pages cm
  ISBN 978-0-310-33845-1 (softcover)
  I. Title.
  PS3619.T213A8 2014
  813'.6--dc23

                                                  2014011397

Cover design: Sara Wood
Interior design: Lori Lynch

Printed in the United States of America

---

14 15 16 17 18 19 20 / RRD / 20 19 18 17 16 15 14 13 12 11 10 9 8 7 6 5 4 3 2 1

To Jennye, my fellow cupcake-eater-in-crime, who
also happens to be my best friend, my sister—and more
importantly—someone who understands that eating cupcakes
for breakfast is perfectly acceptable.

one

There was more to life than vanilla buttercream. Or at least, Kat Varland used to believe so.

Once upon a time, she created magic with flour and sugar and eggs. With cinnamon and nutmeg and vanilla. Every measured cup was instinct, every whisked ingredient inspiration. Baking held promise, potential. Power.

Now she could make the simple cupcakes filling the Sweetie Pies shop display in her sleep—in fact, one morning after she'd been up late experimenting with new recipes, she very nearly had. But Sweetie Pies had a reputation, and the owner, her aunt Maggie Mayfield, kept that even more sparkling than the tiny sugar crystals adorning the otherwise plain desserts. *Fancy* didn't have a home at Sweetie Pies, and neither did *gourmet*. Or, as Aunt Maggie usually put it, *weird*.

The display lights caught the clear sprinkles and the miniature cakes seemed to wink, as if knowing Kat could do so much more. Or maybe they were just begging her to try. Who was satisfied with a vanilla identity, anyway?

She wasn't.

The door to the shop swung open, letting in a burst of crisp autumn air. Kat straightened on instinct, like a child caught day-dreaming in school. The bell on the knob tinkled as a smattering of crimson leaves followed Aunt Maggie inside, skittering across the black-and-white checkerboard floor. Little did they know they'd be swept out within the hour—or else.

"I'm back, finally." Her aunt attempted a smile as she bustled behind the counter to join Kat, but the lines around her eyes appeared to be etched deeper than usual, sabotaging her effort. "Tuesday afternoon already. Did I miss anything Saturday? My, but I hate being sick." She tied her trademark white ruffled apron around her round waist, but it didn't fit nearly as snugly as it used to. She glanced around the spotless work area. "Where's Amy?" Then she must have caught sight of the leaves in her peripheral vision, because she frowned and marched toward the storage room door before Kat could catch up—figuratively or literally.

"Amy left early to study for her test since business was a little slow." Not that it was ever technically busy, but at least having Amy's part-time, high school help allowed Kat some days off and picked up the slack when Maggie was sick. Which was more and more frequent these days.

Kat sidestepped to make it to the storage room first, unwilling to let her aunt, who clearly didn't feel much better than she had last weekend, do more labor than necessary. Maggie was her mom's much older sister in the first place, and now that she'd been sick so often, Kat wanted to protect her strength even more than usual.

"I'll handle the leaves, Aunt Maggie."

Her aunt didn't argue, which proved how poorly she must still be feeling. Once again, Kat fought a burst of guilt from her internal, ongoing frustration over her aunt's baking restrictions. Maggie owned the shop—not Kat. It was her choice what products they sold, and if Maggie liked vanilla, strawberry, and chocolate, then vanilla, strawberry, and chocolate it was.

Even if Kat had just perfected a raspberry lemonade torte recipe that could very likely bring world peace.

She grabbed the broom and began to sweep the leaves back to their rightful place outside as Maggie opened the register and riffled through receipts. "Don't worry, you didn't miss much Saturday. We had the usual stream of customers, is all."

Kat could predict them like clockwork. Right on schedule, Heidi Mann had shown up for the single chocolate cupcake she routinely bought each Saturday as a reward for making it through another week of teaching preschoolers. And then there was the group of stay-at-home moms, including Kat's friend, Rachel Cole. As usual, they wanted to distract their husbands with chocolate cupcakes so they wouldn't notice the piles of laundry they hadn't been able to get to all week. There was Mrs. Lucille, Kat's father's secretary at the Bayou Bend Church of Grace where he pastored, who needed her weekend indulgence. And of course, Kat's best friend, Coach Lucas Brannen, with his standing order of two dozen strawberry cupcakes for his high school football team's weekend practice. If Kat had been given free cupcakes every weekend in high school, she might have gone out for a team too.

Most of the other Bayou Bend regulars seemed to suddenly realize the shop would be closed for two days and had to rush in for their favorites before they missed their chance.

But Kat knew the business could be so much more than what appealed to the regulars. She had so many ideas for marketing that got lost in the oppressing aura of routine at Sweetie Pies. Ideas that could expand Maggie's business, allow Kat to bake the recipes of her heart, draw in customers from surrounding counties—the works.

But not with strawberry, chocolate, and vanilla.

Kat lowered her voice, nearly muttering to herself. "Nope. Didn't miss much at all." She swept harder, as if attempting to scrub the black off the black tiles. As if effort and hard work made a difference. As if one could create color from darkness.

"That's nice, hon." Maggie didn't seem to be listening anymore, immersed in the contents of the register from that day's sales. But Kat knew she didn't really care about profits. As long as she kept her shop in beloved Bayou Bend, Louisiana, and made enough to cover her bills, Maggie was content. No, she probably just didn't want to think about the doctor's appointment she'd had that morning, and if she wasn't telling, Kat wasn't asking.

She'd learned two things since coming to bake for her aunt almost five years ago. One—less is more, unless sugar is involved, and then you should be exact. And two—privacy equals respect. If you don't allow someone their privacy, you don't respect them.

That perhaps explained why Kat was twenty-six years old and still in the exact same spot in life since graduating college with her bachelor's degree in Business. No one asked her what she wanted.

Her ex-boyfriend, Chase, surely hadn't asked when he suddenly decided he preferred blondes.

But that was a lifetime ago.

She worked a rhythm with the broom, watching the leaves swirl back into the late afternoon sun, wishing she could capture their exact color in her piping bag. She could make an autumn harvest cupcake, maybe apple and cinnamon with an apricot icing and a sugared date on top, or a caramel apple cupcake with generous dustings of brown sugar and—

"Hey, watch out!"

The warning came a split second before she swept straight into a jean-clad leg. The stick of the broom bounced off the victim's shin, and bristles coated the unsuspecting navy-and-gray athletic shoes with clods of dirt and dust. Very familiar athletic shoes. She couldn't hide her smile as she lifted her gaze to meet Lucas's. "Hey, your shoes are dirty."

"I guess that's what I get for keeping the boys late at practice." His eyes, the color of the cocoa she mixed into the chocolate cake batter every morning, warmed, and she knew he didn't really care.

Lucas wore those shoes to every team practice, and they'd long since seen better days. His gaze darted over her head toward her aunt, and he leaned in and lowered his voice. "Do you have any of the good stuff in the shop today?"

A red flush heated Kat's neck, and she pretended to smack him with the broom. "Hush. My aunt will hear you."

"Good. Then maybe she'll realize there are some people in Bayou Bend who enjoy *weird* cupcakes." He winked, his broad shoulders filling the door frame of the shop.

"Not weird. Gourmet." The retort flew off her lips before she could process that he was teasing. How many times had she held that reply in around her aunt, wishing she could just speak her heart?

She glanced over her shoulder, but Aunt Maggie must have gone into the kitchen. Come to think of it, Kat probably did have some rejected recipes in her file at home that could only be defined as weird. But how did you know unless you tried? That was the best part of baking—getting to experiment and figure it out as you went. If it didn't work, you just poured out the batter and started over.

There was always a second chance.

Lucas must have taken her sudden silence for insult. "I'm teasing, Kat. I would never speak ill of Maggie. The town loves her."

Rightly so. She was a wonderful woman—just not a visionary. "I know. She's . . . vanilla. A staple. Classic." Sort of like everyone else in her family in Bayou Bend. Between her father's pastoring, her mother's committee heading, her aunt's cupcake shop, and her younger sister's pageant wins, Kat was the only expendable one in the family.

Figured her family, who had options, didn't even want out of Bayou Bend, while she remained stuck. Permanently.

"Nice observation." Lucas crossed his arms over his chest, the sleeves of his dark gray T-shirt pulling across his biceps as he studied her. He leaned against the door frame. "So what flavor are you?"

Her breath hitched in her throat as she met his steady gaze. She knew right away what Lucas's flavor would be—dark chocolate with cherry ganache filling. A deep, bittersweet taste that lingered long after it was gone.

But no—she didn't know her own.

She drew a tight breath, eager to break the unintentionally heavy turn of the conversation. "Hey, I'm so busy baking for you on the side . . . I don't have time for taste tests."

Lucas might be her best friend, but he didn't need her dumping her self-analyzing psychobabble on him. After all, he came for cupcakes. She should save the rest of her drama for Rachel. Somehow, even while knee-deep in PTA forms and stacks of baby onesies to monogram, her friend always found the right thing to say when Lucas couldn't.

Or when the topic was *about* Lucas, which had been happening way more than it should lately.

Kat gestured with the broom inside the shop, ignoring how sweaty her palms suddenly felt against the handle. "You coming in, or are you just going to stand here and let more leaves inside?"

Lucas stepped fully inside the shop and the door swung shut. "Actually, the guys were especially hungry Saturday, so I didn't get my strawberry cupcake then. Going to need a replacement."

"You should have told me. I'd have snuck you one at church on Sunday." It wouldn't be the first time she'd passed him a bag of homemade treats after the morning welcome or in the parking lot. Lucas was a great sport about tasting her experiments. Only once in the two years she'd started daring to bake her own recipes had he spit one back into his hand.

Apparently licorice and Greek olives didn't go together after all.

"I should have. I think I was still in denial that I'm this addicted." Lucas rubbed his jaw, his five o'clock shadow scratching under his fingers. His eyes roved over the display behind her, though Kat wasn't sure what he was expecting to see. It hadn't changed in the decades since her aunt had opened Sweetie Pies. "Too bad you don't have any of those raspberry things you made me try last week. That one had medicinal qualities—should be a prescription for a bad day."

"You're corny." She swatted at him, but the compliment attempted to fill the nooks and crannies inside—the hollow spots that still whispered fear into her heart. At least if nothing else, she knew Lucas loved her creations—all of them, exactly for what they were. Not only the simple cupcakes filling the racks inside Sweetie Pies, but the ones she baked from her heart. Of Lucas, she was certain.

It was the rest of the town that had her guessing.

"Not corny. Cheesy." Lucas grinned, then his expression sobered. "Seriously, Kat, my mission is to make you less humble. You're good."

She clutched the broom like a life preserver, simultaneously wishing his words didn't carry so much weight and wishing he would keep speaking them forever. "Good, huh?" She swallowed, her throat dry. She wanted to think so. But she wanted so much more than good. She wanted great.

She wanted to be seen.

"Very good. You just need to believe it already."

He reached out and ruffled her hair, and the feeling of fullness leaked away at the brotherly gesture. The best friend line blurred more often than she cared to admit, but Lucas was good about yanking her back from the edge of that particular precipice when she veered too close. Even if it stung—and even if he was unaware how often she teetered.

Hopefully, he'd stay that way.

She moved to put the counter between them, pausing to lean the broom against the far corner of the wall. Under the framed photo of her sister, Stella, from last year's win, tiara perched snugly atop a mass of perfect curls. Blonde curls.

But Chase wasn't Stella's fault.

No, putting all her hopes and dreams into a very flawed man was completely her own fault—though maybe she wouldn't have done so if she'd imagined she'd ever have a chance of more than a friendship with Lucas.

With a resigned breath, she took her place behind the cupcake counter. "So what'll it be?" She tugged on a clear glove and let her hand hover above the trays of desserts. "Oh, strawberry, right?"

She knew what she'd choose.

But dark chocolate cupcakes with cherry ganache filling were definitely *not* on the menu.

celeo

For someone used to calling plays for a living, he sure was seeing a lot of penalty flags.

He'd actually ruffled her hair. Good grief, it was a shock he hadn't gone ahead and slapped her on the shoulder or called her "buddy." Lucas wrinkled the white pastry bag in his hand and tried to keep his expression neutral as he waited for Kat to close out the register so he could walk her home. He'd apparently spent way too much time on the field with his football players and not enough time dating.

Though he certainly spent more time than he should imagining what it'd be like dating Kat.

Talented, beautiful, completely oblivious Kat.

Lucas pulled his cupcake from the bag and took a bite, less from impatience and more from needing to mask the flood of embarrassment over his fumble. He'd just placed a bid on Roger Johnson's old farmhouse on Highway 169 and the accompanying ten acres of land—land he pictured strolling with Kat. Curling up under the live oak that spread its massive limbs halfway to heaven and back. Tossing a football to their children over the wheat-colored fields every autumn. Maybe planting their own pumpkin patch.

He wasn't going to see his dream come true by ruffling a woman's hair. Kat Varland needed a hero, and heroes didn't act like immature high school boys every time they came around. What was wrong with him?

He couldn't help watching her work behind the counter. Hmm. Maybe he was addicted to more than the cupcakes.

"All done." She shut the register drawer with a solid click, reminding Lucas it was time to stop staring at those shiny brown strands of hair still tousled from his idiocy. "Let me just check on Aunt Maggie and see if she wants me to take the deposit tonight or if it's okay to wait until tomorrow." She disappeared into the back, where Maggie's office was tucked off the corner of the small but efficient industrial kitchen.

As the swinging door shut behind her, Lucas dropped the uneaten half of his cupcake back into its sack and folded the bag closed. The strawberry cakes were great, but man, Kat could do better. *Did* better, in fact, every time she went home, put her hair up, and baked to a background of Sinatra. How many times had he watched her do just that over the years, while he sat on the walnut bar stool and offered suggestions, prompting her to take it to another level?

Somewhere along the way, one batch of cupcakes along the way, he'd tripped right over the label of Best Friends they'd worn the majority of their teen years and landed upside down on the field of Love.

And suddenly, he had zero plays to call.

"Ready?" She pushed back into the front of the shop, shouldering the strap of her oversize turquoise bag. He'd teased her last year about the size of her previous purple one until she bought the bigger turquoise just on principle. He wisely kept his mouth shut after that, in case he pushed her into toting around an actual suitcase for a purse. He knew when to prod and when to shut up, when to encourage her to take it one step further and when to dial it back. No one knew Kat better than him.

Some days he wondered if he knew her better than she did.

"Lucas? You ready?" The pinch of her brow reminded him she'd already asked that question once. Ready? Well, no. But *yes*—the main problem being he had no idea if she was.

He straightened his shoulders. "I'm always ready." His trademark retort rolled easily off his lips, bringing a smile and erasing the confusion that lingered on her expression. He offered his arm. "To the bank?" He hoped not. He hoped he could walk her straight home and she'd invite him in and they'd cook stir-fry or something else delicious.

"No, I'll take the deposit tomorrow. They're about to close, and Maggie said it wasn't worth the rush."

Win. He struggled to hide his victory smile as she came around the counter and linked her arm through his, exactly the same as they'd done a hundred times over the years. But nothing with Kat was the same anymore. It was exhilarating and frustrating all at the same time.

She craned her neck to peer up at him, her wide blue eyes inquisitive. "I have some stir-fry at the house. Want to stay for dinner?"

Another win. "Only if you promise to make dessert."

She tried to plant her free hand on her hip, but the giant purse got in the way and nearly swung her off balance. She lifted her chin, apparently in an attempt at indignation instead. "Hey, now. I'm not cooking dinner *and* dessert after baking cupcakes here all day."

He tugged her toward the door, laughing. "Then I'll handle the stir-fry. You just do what you do best."

Her responding smile made him want to offer to do the dishes too. "Nice play, Coach."

She had no idea.

two

Lucas looked way too much at home sitting in the tiny kitchen of Kat's rental house, elbows propped on the bar countertop as he rocked back and forth on two legs of the stool, mouthing along to the Sinatra song drifting from the portable stereo. She'd always warned him one day he was going to fall, but so far, she hadn't been proven right.

About a lot of things, actually.

Kat filled a measuring spoon with water from the sink, wrinkling her nose at the dirty dishes filling one side. Leftover stir-fry lay congealed in the pan he'd forgotten to clean after cooking, and she'd have a time of it trying to scrub it off. She should get Lucas to do that now, but he looked so comfortable at her bar, paging through a sports supply magazine, that she hated to ruin the cozy image she was sure to daydream about later.

Besides, part of her still hoped he'd fall.

She poured the water into the mixing bowl, dried her fingers on her favorite Parisian dish towel, and began to whisk the ingredients together. She always liked to hand mix, though sometimes she ended up resorting to the electric beaters. Something about staying personally connected to the batter made the end result more satisfying, though. Like she'd earned it.

"Coconut or chocolate chips?" Her bicep burned from mixing, but she kept at it, humming along to the music warming the room.

Lucas turned the page of his magazine. "Both."

She glanced at the miscellaneous ingredients she'd gathered on the counter in hopes inspiration would strike. "Strawberry or orange?"

"Both."

Kat stopped stirring and shot him a look. He lowered his magazine with a smirk. "I'm kidding. Orange."

Coconut, orange, chocolate chip. She could work with that. She resumed mixing despite the ache in her hand. "You should know not to kid about cupcakes by now."

"One would think." He closed his magazine and leaned forward, giving her his undivided attention. Suddenly, she couldn't remember what to do next. Oh yeah, coconut. She sprinkled the shredded fruit into the mix and stirred again.

"Let me do that. Your arm is shaking." Lucas hopped up and reached around her for the whisk, his firm chest brushing against her back. Was it just her, or had Sinatra started singing louder? Her heart beat a heavy rhythm in her ears, and she held on to the whisk, unwilling to let go until he finally pried it from her fingers.

Which remained in a clamped position.

She had a claw.

He shook his head in amusement and dropped the whisk back into the bowl. "Use the beaters next time, Martha." He reached for her hand.

She allowed his touch. "As in Martha Stewart?"

"Or the one in the Bible. Both work too hard." He winked as he began to massage her fingers, his touch sending a shiver of electricity up her spine. Feeling began to flow back into her hand, bringing both pain and relief. His football-calloused palms were rough but gentle against hers, his nails short and practical. She studied her own hands, her lighter skin a stark contrast to his year-round tan. They both had work-worn hands, born of doing what they loved.

Except Lucas was living his dream out loud, while hers had to stay hidden in her private kitchen.

She reluctantly pulled her hand away, averting her eyes. "Better keep mixing. You don't want the batter to gel before the coconut is fully incorporated."

He obeyed without arguing, probably because of the sign she'd bought from a craft fair last summer and hung above her oven range just for him: "Don't mess with Texas, mama bears . . . or the chef." She'd almost bought the one that said she kissed better than she cooked, but that might be a lie.

The familiar wave of insecurity left over from Chase and his selfish choices began to seep around the edges of her heart, healed now but scarred. Sometimes they still pinched. She'd pictured forever after with the man—boy, really, if she got honest about his maturity level. Who tried to switch over to his girlfriend's sister midcommitment?

Not that Stella had fallen for it. She'd been smart enough to see it for what it was, but that didn't change the facts—that Kat might have been the firstborn, but she was clearly everyone's second choice.

That wave of insecurity grew into near tidal force, and she drew a deep breath to remind herself she wasn't drowning anymore. That particular season of her life was over, thank goodness. Chase was over. But man, it'd been a long winter.

She darted a glance at Lucas as visions of spring danced through her head.

No. Not yet.

Maybe not ever.

She took a much-needed step away from him and began to wash the oranges, their conversation replaying in her mind. Martha. He thought her a Martha. It niggled at her, but really, what was so bad about hard work? Someone had to get things done—and she knew how to do it. Besides, there were a ton of Bible verses about the positive qualities of work.

One difference, though—she doubted Martha ever wondered if she had what it took.

Kat turned to zest fresh orange over the bowl as Lucas kept mixing. Their shoulders bumped, their elbows brushed, and the churning in her stomach had nothing to do with the amount of stir-fry she'd consumed.

"Don't forget the chocolate." Lucas handed her the bag of miniature chips, and she measured a careful cupful over the bowl. Right when she dumped it in, Lucas snatched the bag from the counter and tossed in another handful.

"Hey! I didn't measure that." Panic bloomed in her chest, and she moved the bag out of his reach. She wasn't working with a set recipe because she was experimenting, but she still knew which ingredients tended to take over a recipe and which got completely ignored. Which ones enhanced other flavors and which ones demanded the spotlight for themselves.

Which ones complemented, and which ones contradicted.

"Trust me." Lucas handed her the whisk, eyes steady on hers. "Sometimes the best things in life are born of chance."

Very funny, coming from Coach Play-by-the-Rules. Kat took more chances in her baking than Lucas ever took, on or off the field—their lifelong friendship attested to that. So he was going to start preaching today in more ways than one. First she worked too hard, and now she played it too safe?

Sudden frustration bubbled, and Kat plucked a few chips from the top of the batter and shot them into her mouth. She was so tired of vanilla. "Good idea, Coach. But maybe you need to take your own advice." Then she began to stir.

She was going to need a bigger sign.

⊂⊰⊱⊃

Sinatra had been booted in exchange for the television. It currently blasted a cooking reality show featuring several chefs, red-faced and angry as they alternated tossing something resembling salmon in a pan and making snarky comments about the head judge.

Lucas had finished cleaning the wok about three minutes ago, but he kept the hot water running and his hands buried in dish soap in hopes of looking busy—and staying out of Kat's range of fire.

The cupcakes, when they'd been taken from the oven a little while ago, had been so full of melted chocolate they'd turned into a mushy, clumpy mess. They tasted excellent, of course, like a volcano of chocolate lava had erupted in Lucas's mouth. But for Kat, presentation was half the package, and well—epic failure there.

Which was his fault.

Which was why he was doing dishes while she alternated between dejectedly tossing each cupcake into the trash can with a thud and shooting him looks that could have branded his flesh. Something had upset her before the cupcakes had gone into the oven, though, and he knew enough to realize it wasn't just because of his adding extra chips to the batter.

Thud. Another cupcake landed in the can.

Maybe he had overstepped his bounds. After all, the kitchen was her turf. He wouldn't want someone who wasn't a professional coming on his field and directing his boys. Come to think of it, he wouldn't want that even if they were a professional. He knew best for them.

Thud. Another cupcake met its odor-contained, plastic grave.

Kat baked without reservation at home, free of the box Sweetie Pies trapped her inside every day. Free to create. Free to be wild within the security of her comfort zone, which was shaky, at best.

Bottom line, he'd taken her control.

Thud.

He shut off the water. "Kat?" He'd almost slipped and said Martha again, but his gut informed him this wasn't the best time for more teasing.

Even if it was true.

He grabbed a dish towel to dry his hands, and at her silence, he turned to face her. She froze over the trash can, caught red-handed with the last of her failed cupcakes half in her mouth, chocolate smeared across one cheek. Her eyes widened behind the evidence covering her face. "What? I never said they didn't taste good."

Oh, he wanted to laugh. Hard. But he had to apologize first. He tried to stifle his smile as she dropped the remaining cupcake portion into the trash can and he handed her a paper towel. She scrubbed her face, but missed a streak of chocolate near her lips. Before he could think twice, he reached out and rubbed it with his thumb.

She stilled under his touch, and he wished he had the right to kiss her. They'd kissed before—friendly pecks on the cheek after he picked her up from the airport one summer, or a reassuring kiss on the forehead when she cried in his arms when her favorite dog died her junior year.

But friendly and comforting wasn't at all what he was feeling right now.

He lowered his hand and stepped back, wiping his still-damp hands on his jeans. "I'm sorry."

She lifted one eyebrow, a trick he had always coveted. "For ruining my batter?"

"For interfering."

Kat's bravado seemed to crumple, and she sagged against the end of the counter. "I overreacted. Just stressed today." She momentarily hid her face, then lowered her hands, vulnerable. A smile quirked the corner of her lips. "But you should always obey the sign."

Her pointed gaze rose over his head toward the oven, and he grinned at the implication. "How could I forget?" He knew that sign well, had almost bought her one that said she kissed better than she cooked. But he didn't want her to get the wrong idea.

Make that the right idea, but the wrong time.

Maybe he'd waited longer than he'd needed to. Maybe she felt the current between them as strongly as he did now. It was more than just the come-and-go chemistry that occurred between friends of the opposite sex, though. That had flared occasionally over the years, but never taken dominance—especially after Kat dated that dirtbag Chase for almost two years.

To her credit, she hadn't known he was a dirtbag for a long time. But Lucas had an eye for these things, which was only proven after the jerk promised Kat the world and then came on to her own sister—and ended up taking off to see it with someone else after Stella rejected him. After Kat was free, her heart was too spent for Lucas to jump in with more promises she wouldn't believe. Talk about bad timing.

Besides, neither of them would have wanted to mess up the security of their friendship then, a friendship that remained steady throughout high school and college, even though Lucas was two years older. He even came back to Bayou Bend High to be Kat's prom date her senior year.

But this wasn't a limo ride and a corsage. Or an influx of teen-age hormones. This was Kat. *His* Kat.

And lately, the thought of her baking cupcakes for any other man made him throw a football a whole lot harder.

He inhaled, then let it go, blowing away the thought. "Seriously though, I won't butt in again."

"Yes, you will." She tilted her head, still in reach though she'd shifted slightly away. "That's what you do. You push me to try bigger and better."

Maybe. He trailed one finger over the trim on the bar, the chipped Formica rough under his skin. "Sometimes I push too hard." Or sometimes, not hard enough.

"Yep." She smirked. "Even when you're wrong."

And that's what it was really about, wasn't it? He was afraid—no, *concerned*—that he was wrong. That any gesture toward her would ruin a lifetime of friendship that he needed more than he needed air. Food. Football.

Time to man up. But not here, not after he'd screwed up her trust. Kat deserved something big. A real gesture. She needed to believe him.

He needed to believe himself.

One thing was certain. If his offer on the land and house was accepted, he wanted Kat with him. And that meant a ring. He wouldn't dishonor either of them by settling for less.

He needed a game plan. But his mind felt stuffed with sweetgrass. He never operated without a game plan, not for the important things. Football. Real estate. Love. He opened his mouth, unsure what to say, but realizing if he didn't say it, he might explode all over her kitchen. "Kat, I—"

"Round two?" Kat nudged the package of flour still on the countertop, and the hope in her eyes made him bite back the words begging to release. Another time. Besides, he owed her.

And if this . . . *thing* was going to happen, then he probably should get used to baking cupcakes in his free time.

A commercial blared from the television, distracting him from watching Kat grab a clean mixing bowl out of the dishwasher. *Cupcake Combat*, a popular reality show, was accepting applications for their new season. The slick-haired host looked like he'd smeared cooking oil into his hair, but the judges on the panel this year were names even Lucas recognized from previous cooking shows he'd endured with Kat. This one seemed like quality.

He noted the deadline date for applications, which was that upcoming weekend. Kat should apply. Talk about proving to the world what she could do. He started to suggest it, but Kat clicked off the TV, shot him a shy smile, and turned Sinatra back on.

He'd tell her later. Definitely later.

three

"Tyler, I said *grip* the ball. Not hand it over to the other team with an engraved invitation for a touchdown." Lucas bit into his chewing gum to keep from harping further, and clapped Tyler Dupree on the shoulder as he jogged off the field. Sometimes less had to be more.

"Sorry, Coach." The teen's muddy uniform and grass-stained knees showed testament to his effort, but the boy had butterfingers the past few practices. He shuffled to the bench and shucked his helmet, then tossed it at his feet.

Lucas debated between giving him space and doling out a lecture. He had to rag the guys a little—they needed to stay tough, learn how to listen to it and channel it into their game—but he always stopped short of being condescending. A little sarcasm, a little reproof, and a lot of high fives made up his style.

It was just that, lately, Tyler had pushed him to the edge of that style.

Still, these boys were like family, and Lucas was more than a coach. For some of them, he was the only authority figure they had in their lives. That made it tricky to find the balance in his role, and more than once Lucas had to remind himself what was most important. Unfortunately, that answer wasn't always football.

Though it usually was.

The afternoon sun warmed Lucas's neck, and he adjusted the brim of his baseball cap to block it as he called for fifty jump-ups. He'd wanted to let the guys go home early, but it was nearly five o'clock now and they were still goofing up basic drills. His assistant, Coach Kent, had grilled the defensive line earlier, too, accusing them of picking dandelions. Hopefully not literally.

What was the deal?

Not that Lucas hadn't struggled to keep his own head in the game, especially since last week's baking session with Kat. Round two had led to perfectly edible, perfectly awesome chocolate-chip-coconut-orange cupcakes, which they'd enjoyed on the bar stools as they talked late into the night. About nothing. About everything.

Their usual.

All while a diatribe of unspoken truths paraded through Lucas's head with every half-smile she'd shot his way.

Lucas popped a bubble in his gum. "Crunches next!" He ignored the resounding groans as the boys obediently rolled onto their backs on the grassy field and began their stomach work. He'd stop them at seventy-five. The last time he pushed to one hundred, three had thrown up.

All things in moderation.

Maybe he should apply that theory to Kat. He'd been spending more and more time with her lately, but instead of her getting the hint about his changed feelings, all he'd managed to accomplish was torturing himself. She seemed perfectly content to keep their friend-ship exactly where it was. Maybe he should be the one to take the hint.

But he really didn't like losing.

He clamped his jaw. "Bear crawls!"

To their credit, the boys didn't complain, just arched over and began bear crawling toward the fifty-yard line. Last time he'd talked about that particular exercise with Kat, she'd thought he'd said bear *claws*, and well, the most confusing of conversations ensued.

Man. She was everywhere.

As his good friend, Darren Phillips, would say—he had it bad. But his fire department chaplain buddy liked to say a lot of things, such as "you know, God created Eve for a reason," or "it's not good for man to be alone." Darren had been trying to marry off Lucas for a while, even since before he learned of his buddy's change of heart toward Kat, but all his blind date efforts fell short.

None of them were Kat.

On the field, the boys grunted as they finished their laps, and Lucas called them in. Maybe they all needed a water break. Lucas could certainly use a cold splash right in the face. Something had to give, for his sanity's sake if nothing else, and soon. Thankfully, as all coaches should, he'd discovered a master offensive play.

Now to see if it worked—before Kat could pull a defensive move of her own.

His boys crowded around the watercooler faster than Coach Kent could pass out cups, and Lucas noted Tyler didn't argue as Ben pushed ahead of him in line. Apparently defense wasn't on Tyler's mind either. The kid looked downright defeated.

Which probably meant one thing.

He nudged his way through the thirsty, sweaty throng to Coach Kent's side and lowered his voice. "Dismiss them 'til Friday's pre-game warm-up. I'm keeping Dupree after." He headed toward Tyler as Coach Kent nodded and blew his whistle.

Tuning out the barked dismissal behind him, Lucas landed one hand on Tyler's padded shoulder and ushered the boy down the side-lines. "What gives?"

"What do you mean?" Tyler swiped a grimy hand under his nose then planted his hands on his hips, but he didn't look Lucas in the eye. The kid was too good at heart to lie to his face, so he usually went for the denial method.

Lucas tended to do the same.

He braced one foot on the sideline bench and rested his forearms on his lifted knee, hoping to appear casual, approachable. Tyler needed someone to confide in, and if Lucas had three guesses what was on the kid's mind, the first two wouldn't count and the third would involve Mr. Dupree and his favorite long-necked bottles.

"Your head's not in the game. It's pretty obvious, man." Lucas gestured for Tyler to sit, and he grudgingly obeyed, balancing his helmet in his lap. Lucas lowered to the bench beside him, not wanting to tower over him. This wasn't coach-mode. This was buddy-mode.

He waited, but Tyler didn't offer any more details.

"Your old man?"

Tyler shot him a sharp glance, but the truth was in his glassy eyes. He blinked and finally conceded. "How'd you know?"

"Hazards of a small town." Lucas leaned forward and plucked a long strand of grass from the ground, ran it through his fingers. That, and personally knowing the chief of police.

Tyler stared across the vacant field as the rest of his team laughed and shoved their way to the locker room some yards behind them. "He was drunk last night."

"How's your mom?" Mrs. Dupree had dealt with more than her fair share of drunken husband, and he hoped Tyler's dad hadn't gotten physical again. The last thing that family needed was another jail sentence, not when Tyler's reputation at school had barely survived the first one. But if they were in trouble . . .

Tyler shook his head quickly. "She's fine. It wasn't like that." He lifted one shoulder in a shrug. "He passed out. But he had some not-so-nice things to say first."

"About your grades?" Tyler wasn't exactly a straight-A student. More like a scrape-by-to-stay-on-the-team student. Between the Saturday tutor Lucas had found him and his recent diagnosis of dyslexia, however, things had been improving. But nothing was ever quite good enough for Mr. Dupree.

"Grades. My room. Friends." Tyler kicked at the grass with his cleats. "Football."

Ah. There it was. Well, Lucas might not know a lot about deadbeat dads, but he knew plenty about absent ones. All too similar, except Tyler had to absorb the spray of barbs while Lucas had gotten to miss them entirely.

He chose his next words carefully. "Pretty hard to tell you anything about a sport he doesn't understand, though, huh?" Meaning, don't listen to him. Don't take him seriously. But he couldn't actually say that flat out.

Not that the old man didn't have it coming, trying to psych out his own kid.

"He knows more than I thought." Tyler shrugged like he didn't care, but Lucas knew better. "He asks around. Knows all the mistakes I made last game."

"Well, he obviously didn't hear about that awesome pass you made during the Panthers game two weeks ago." Lucas nudged Tyler with his knee. "Or how you had three completed passes."

Tyler turned to look at Lucas, and noticeably brightened. Good, maybe his words were sinking in. It was so important to speak truth to these guys—

"Ms. Varland!" Tyler grinned as he stared past Lucas.

Lucas jerked his head around and spied Kat strolling toward them, a giant bakery box hugged against one hip like a woman carrying a toddler, the setting sun providing a streaked backdrop of crimson and orange fire. So it wasn't his pep talk that helped, after all.

Well, Kat tended to have that same effect on him too.

He stood, and Tyler jumped to his feet, dropping his helmet. The teen brushed his hands against his uniform pants and suddenly resembled a freckled, eight-year-old boy who'd just picked his mom a handful of flowers and was eagerly awaiting approval.

He could relate.

Lucas smiled and greeted Kat with a one-arm side hug. "What's the meaning of this, bringing cupcakes to the field?" He purposefully used his gruff coach voice and winked at Tyler over her head. "This is a no-baking zone."

Kat held the white cardboard box up under their noses and waved it side to side, as if to tempt them with the aroma. "Vanilla leftovers. Aunt Maggie said to give them away. So naturally, I went where the hungriest people would be."

"Wow. That's really nice." Tyler beamed, a flush working its way up his neck, and Lucas felt the sudden urge to cuff some sense into the back of the boy's head. Though to be honest, he felt the urge to babble and blush and act like he was starring in a 1950s sitcom too. He better be careful, or one of them might actually say *swell*.

"Thanks, Kat. I know some guys in the locker room who will be happy to see these." Lucas took the box, and at the gleam in Tyler's eye, flipped open the lid. The kid eagerly plucked one out and took a bite, icing smearing across his cheek. "Take these to the rest of the guys, okay?"

"Sure. Thanks, Ms. Varland." He didn't even bother to wipe his mouth. He just grinned at Kat.

Her eyes softened. "Anytime."

"Man, I hope so." Tyler snorted.

Lucas stepped in before the guy could completely embarrass himself. "If you want to talk later, man, you have my number. Just shoot a text my way, all right?"

Tyler met Lucas's gaze head on. "Thanks, Coach." Then with another goofy grin at Kat, he hurried toward the locker room.

"Well, that wasn't awkward." Lucas shook his head with a laugh as he turned back to Kat. Flour dotted the hem of her long-sleeved red top and smeared across the hip of her jeans. She must have forgotten her apron again, or maybe took it off when it got too dirty to wear.

"Nah." Kat tucked her hair behind her ears, and he noticed flour there too. "He's a good kid. Looks up to you."

"He's had it pretty rough. He's a fighter, though." He crossed his arms over his chest, wishing he could tuck his arm around Kat's waist. Not yet. Not until he knew if his offensive move had been a success. When would he hear back from *Cupcake Combat*?

On second thought, since he'd signed up with all of Kat's information, she'd be the one receiving the acceptance letter—or email. However they did it. The idea had been genius. Foolproof, really. If they didn't select her to be a contestant, she would never know the difference and he could protect her from the rejection. But if they did . . . well, then she'd *know* how much he believed in her. How much he wanted the best for her. Wanted her to grow.

How much he loved her.

"All your guys are great. And I wonder why." The admiring spark in Kat's eye as she playfully slapped his arm accelerated his heartbeat. She was good for him. But why didn't she have that same strong confidence in her own ability? Hopefully *Cupcake Combat* would call soon, with positive results. Kat needed proof of how great she really was.

Both in and out of the kitchen.

 celeo

At least Tyler seemed sincere about her cupcakes. But he was a football player *and* a teenage boy—didn't they eat anything?

Kat slowly followed Lucas to his office inside the school, where he left his keys and jacket during practice. Her father's words sounded in the back of her mind, as they often did when the familiar doubts assaulted. *Don't waste your talents, Kat. Use them for the glory of God.*

Hard to do when God didn't eat cupcakes.

Her dad preached. Her mom gave of her time, energy, and money to the entire community, while her college-aged sister sang like one of heaven's angels offering free earthly concerts. Easy for them to say.

Lucas's athletic shoes squeaked on the linoleum floor as they made their way through the dim halls she'd traveled a hundred times in his wake. Baking was all she had. All she knew. All she was good at it.

But what if she wasn't as good as she thought? What if she was just pacified because of her last name? Or worse—out of the community's obligation to beloved Aunt Maggie?

She forced the thoughts away as she stopped in the door frame of his office. "Looks like you won't get a cupcake again today if the team has anything to say about it." Maybe Maggie did have a point—she couldn't see the team devouring any recipes she concocted at home with hazelnut or ginger.

"There's always Saturday." He shot her the half-smile that always twisted her stomach as he grabbed his keys from the top desk drawer. She turned away from the feeling and hid her face, eyes sweeping the room.

It looked the exact same as it did when he started this job almost five years ago. Photos of former graduating classes hanging crookedly on the planked wall. The rickety desk with one leg propped up by a dusty math textbook. The computer that looked way too new compared to the rolling chair and dirt-streaked window behind it.

The room smelled faintly of Lucas's spicy cologne and leather, and a photo of her and Lucas nestled in a frame near his desktop inspirational calendar. The fluorescent lighting reflected off the glass box his team had mounted their championship football inside as a surprise gift. Besides the football field, this was one of Lucas's favorite places. He belonged here.

Like she belonged in the kitchen.

Right?

"Want to grab some sushi?" Lucas shrugged into his jacket, pausing to adjust the flipped collar.

They hadn't eaten together since their impromptu stir-fry last week, the likes of which her wok had never seen, nor was it the same. She hesitated. Sushi sounded good, but she felt . . . off balance. A little mellow. Maybe she just needed to go home and get her head straight. Bake alone, and reassure herself she wasn't wasting her life.

Or her talents. Whatever they were.

"I don't know if—" Her phone dinged then, alerting her to a new email. She scanned it as they walked back down the hall, using the excuse to delay her answer. She clicked on her in-box. Food Studios? It was probably just another coupon-related advertisement because she subscribed to the TV network's newsletter. She almost hit delete, but then she realized from the subject title that it wasn't a mass mail-out.

CONGRATULATIONS, BAKER!

She punched Open.

And couldn't breathe.

"Lucas." She stopped walking, reached for his arm for support. He half-turned as he pushed the hallway door open for her, supporting it with his back.

"What? What's wrong?" The evening shadows sent sharp planes across his face, which pinched as he frowned.

"I've been selected to be on *Cupcake Combat*." She stared at the message, then at Lucas, then back at her phone. She blinked, but the words didn't rearrange into an order that made sense. She held her phone in Lucas's face for proof she wasn't crazy. "See. How? I didn't—"

"I knew they'd choose you!" With a whoop, Lucas grabbed her around the waist and spun her in the hallway. The door clanged behind him as he turned quick circles and hollered. Now she was confused *and* dizzy, and her smartphone went skittering across the floor.

He lowered her to the floor, almost in slow motion, and she scrambled to grab her phone as Lucas backed out of her way. The message was still on the thankfully uncracked screen. Good thing she'd bought that protective cover—though this circumstance would have been impossible to predict. She shot him a narrow-eyed look. "You knew about this?"

"I did this. I signed you up." Lucas beamed as if he'd just been awarded another championship. "I saw the commercial, and the deadline for applications was coming up, so I thought I'd surprise you. That way if you didn't make it, you wouldn't . . ."

She could only imagine what her face looked like as his voice trailed off. If even a portion of the shock, confusion, and well, to be honest, fear, was registering, it couldn't have been pretty. She shook her head and scrolled through the message. "I'm going to LA. In two weeks."

Two weeks. Two weeks, and her entire life could be different. What if she won?

What if she didn't?

"Walk with me." Lucas helped her up and ushered her outside, and the evening chill nipped at her cheeks, grounded her back to reality. This couldn't happen. She wasn't a big-city girl, worthy of national television. The closest she got to winning contests was watching Lucas's football games. As much as she hated the label, she was small-town. Destined for small things.

Everyone knew it.

And told her regularly.

"I can't go." That was the bottom line, really. She raised the phone again in trembling hands and sucked in a sharp breath. "It says they loved the video. What video?"

Lucas let out a cough, which might have been a laugh. Or a muffled grunt of fear. "Um, remember last summer when we were horsing around with my team's new video equipment?"

He didn't.

She squinted up at Lucas, at the blowing tufts of hair curling beneath his hat, at the heated flush at his throat and the glimmer of victory and guilt in his eyes, and yeah. He had.

She wanted to toss her phone right back on the ground.

"Don't be upset, Kat. I wasn't trying to embarrass you. It was good footage—fun stuff. They obviously loved it!" Lucas leaned against her driver's side car door in the parking lot, blocking her escape. And any attempt to run him over.

"I danced in a chef's hat." She closed her eyes, desperately trying to remember what else was on that video, and desperately hoping to forget. "I sang into a wooden spoon."

"'Do You Know the Muffin Man?' I believe it was." She opened her eyes to Lucas's broad grin.

"You're loving this." She couldn't tell if she was offended or flattered. Lucas signed her up for *Cupcake Combat*. He believed in her. The thought sank in deep.

Lucas might be convinced of her ability. But now she had to convince a panel of professional judges. On national television.

In two weeks.

She needed her Sinatra CD.

She groaned, wishing the paved parking lot would swallow her up. She'd never been on TV before. Not even in high school when they made DVD bonuses for the yearbook. She'd purposefully skipped out that afternoon, despite being president of the cooking club. That time she fooled around with the football team's video equipment with Lucas was the only time she'd ever purposefully put herself on camera.

And that was while believing that tape would be erased immediately after.

"This is your chance, Kat." Lucas's voice warmed, melting through the fissures of self-doubt as he gently cupped her shoulders with both hands. His touch heated through the sleeves of her sweater, sending a spark of awareness down her spine. She dared a glance into his eyes. "You've always said how stifled you are here in Bayou Bend. This is your chance to break out."

She did say that. But it was a lot easier to complain from inside one's comfort zone. Besides, breaking out always meant starting her own shop one day—outside Bayou Bend. Playing by her own rules for once.

Not signing up for more rules and public judgment—and potential humiliation.

She nibbled on her lower lip as leaves skittered around the parking lot at their feet. Her stomach growled, and she remembered she hadn't eaten since she'd had a granola bar that morning. Back ten hours ago when life was still normal. Safe.

But wasn't that what she'd been wanting? An opportunity to shine? Here was her handwritten invitation to glow amidst the stars . . .

And all she could think about was falling.

"You're so much more than vanilla, strawberry, and chocolate." His voice dropped an octave as he leaned toward her. "Isn't it time to show someone besides me?"

Yes. No. She edged away as his hands slipped from her shoulders. The crestfallen expression on his face only made her feel worse. He'd done this big thing for her, believing in her, supporting her— as always—and she couldn't even get excited about it.

"Lucas, I'm sorry. I really appreciate the gesture. I'm just not sure I can do this." Not sure she had what it took. The only thing worse than being ignored was being made a fool.

Only thing worse than wondering if she had any talent was being handed proof that she didn't.

She glanced down at her phone, scanning the email one more time, almost hoping there was some fine print that made her ineligible. That could make this whole thing go away. That could fix the gap she suddenly felt between her and Lucas.

> Contestants are responsible for providing their own baking assistant. No recipe cards, books, or other personalized notes or tips of any sort are allowed at the kitchen site.

Lucas tugged his hat off his head and ran his fingers through his hair. "It's my fault."

Contestants receive two complimentary rooms at the Hotel Francesca in downtown Los Angeles, approximately five miles from the studio. Cab fare will be reimbursed on site.

"I should have asked first. I just thought you'd be happy."

Grand prize winner to receive a one-year, paid internship baking for New York City's famous bakery, Bloom.

Kat jerked her head up. There it was. Her ticket out of Bayou Bend. All she had to do was suffer through the competition, win, and never look back. Leave Bayou Bend and vanilla cupcakes behind for good. Leave her assigned identity and create one of her own. Outside of her sister's shadow, her mother's capability, her father's requirements.

Outside of her doubts.

Hope sprang in her heart like spring's first flower shooting through winter's frost, and she sucked in a deep breath.

"I'll do it."

four

Kat stared at the batter dripping off the electric beaters into the stainless steel bowl, each tiny release of the dense pink liquid conjuring a new worry.

Drip.

What was she thinking?

Drip.

She had nothing to wear to LA.

Drip.

What if the judges laughed her off the kitchen floor?

Drip.

She still had to find an assistant.

"Kat?"

She jerked away from her hypnosis to the bowl and blinked at the voice suddenly ringing through her quiet sanctuary of a kitchen.

"We need to order napkins again." Amy, Aunt Maggie's part-time employee, sagged against the door frame of the kitchen, iPod earbuds dangling from her ears. "We're down to one pack."

"We're supposed to order when we're down to three." Some days, Kat swore people took seventeen napkins per cupcake. She'd suggested cutting back a dozen times, or keeping them behind the counter and providing a napkin with each cupcake transaction so people didn't waste handfuls at the tables, but to no avail. Aunt Maggie, and her God-given ability to believe the best in people, handed out napkins like some churches handed out tracts. Money-saving tips—and baking recipes—were not Kat's domain. Not at Sweetie Pies.

Not ever.

"I know. Sorry." The teen's apology sounded sincere enough, but she'd been here six months or longer. She knew the routine. There really wasn't an excuse.

Maybe she wasn't the only one getting bored at Sweetie Pies.

"Stick a Post-it on the register for me. I'll handle it." Kat lowered the beaters back into the mixing bowl, needing to blend the clumps the drips had made before allowing the batter into the cups. She didn't have time to worry about napkins, anyway. At least if they ran out, they'd quit losing money on them. She needed to focus on the fact that she was—supposedly—going to LA in less than two weeks. On the fact that she had less than two weeks to find an assistant willing to suddenly traipse across the country to—

She raised the beaters again, peering at Amy through narrowed eyes.

The teen straightened and tugged the earbuds from her ears, the wires tangling in her long blonde hair. "Um, yes?"

Maybe not. Amy wasn't exactly the brightest candle on the cake. And she had school. Still, what parent wouldn't give permission for an opportunity for their daughter to be on national TV? They could share the same hotel room, since Amy was a minor, and . . .

"I mean, yes, ma'am?"

Kat softened her analysis at the uncertain twinge in Amy's voice. She wasn't so far from her own minimum-wage days that she couldn't sympathize with the girl's sudden fear of being lectured. Or let go.

She sighed. "Amy. I'm twenty-six. Don't call me ma'am." Or

remind her of her age. And the fact that she still, at closer to thirty than anything else, had yet to accomplish a single, satisfying, long-term thing in her life. Her résumé attested to as much.

So did her left ring finger.

"Oh, okay. Sorry. Again." The younger girl's shoulders slumped slightly in relief, her fingers hovering the earbuds near her ears as if she hated to miss the next song and was totally over the conversation, but couldn't tell if she was out of the "you're fired" woods yet.

She couldn't resist. "Does Aunt Maggie know you wear those at the counter?"

Amy stared blankly. "Yes. She steals them when my shuffle comes around to the Spice Girls."

Nope. Definitely not going to happen. Kat lowered the mixers again. "Don't forget the sticky note."

"Yes, ma'am." The door swung shut behind Amy, leaving a nearly tangible wake of relief and the faint strains of something Bieber-related.

As the pinky-red batter swirled together into beautiful rivers of burgundy and rose, she pondered all the ways she would make Lucas pay for his interference in her life. He just thought he'd interfered last week when he'd been helping her bake at home—

Helping her bake.

Her finger slipped as the germinating idea took root, jerking the mixing speed to high. Batter splattered the sides of the bowl and speckled her apron with edible polka dots. But she couldn't contain her grin.

Or her plot for the perfect revenge.

❧

Lucas stared at the spreadsheet of player stats on his computer monitor, one foot tapping an unsteady rhythm he couldn't contain as he scanned Tyler's latest performance. Practice had ended almost an hour ago, yet here he was, still stuck on whatever was paralyzing Tyler on the field.

And trying not to feel paralyzed himself over Kat's lack of response so far to his Big Gesture. She'd been upset yesterday—and in hindsight, *maybe* rightfully so—when she received that winning email notification. He probably should have thought twice about the video, but then again, her charm with the wooden spoon was probably what had won her acceptance. Like he told his boys, sometimes you had to put yourself out there and take a risk to win.

Just like he'd done with Kat.

Talk about a backfire.

The numbers in the spreadsheet before him blurred as he narrowed his eyes. His best move yet, and her only reaction had been anger. Shakespeare had it wrong. Hell might know no fury like a woman scorned, but it really didn't know any fury like a woman manipulated.

Too bad he hadn't read *those* CliffsNotes in high school.

He punched a few keys on the keyboard just to relieve frustration. Here he was, supposed to be figuring out Tyler's problem, and all he could think of was how he'd seemingly just made his own problem bigger.

He deleted his impulsive addition to the spreadsheet. And what was with the sudden way Kat blurted out that she'd do it? Zero to eighty in two seconds flat. Then she'd shoved him aside and got into her car before he could figure out how many hormones equaled a hissy fit, and they hadn't talked again since. Was she still mad? Should he call, or just wait and pretend like his Big Gesture hadn't blown up in his face?

He kneaded his temples in an attempt to rid the headache that had crept up during practice. Man, he was out of his league. There was *no* playbook for this.

"Here. Try this on." Kat materialized in his doorway, and he jerked, banging one knee under his desk as he automatically reached up to catch whatever object she'd just lobbed at him.

An apron.

"For the show?" That had to be a good sign, right? That she was going, at least. And that she was looking forward to it, hopefully. He held up the baby blue fabric to see the words screen-printed across the front in a flowing black script: Not Your Mama's Cupcakes. Ha. Or her aunt's, for that matter. Nice.

He threw it back at her. "You'll look cute." Understatement of the year.

"Don't be silly." She tossed it back, all business, the ties of the apron upsetting his state championship mug that held all his pencils. They scattered across his desk and rolled onto the floor. "That one's yours. This is mine."

She held up a matching apron, this time in pale pink, and the grin she finally released read even sassier than the printed words.

He snorted, then stared as she held his gaze and quirked that eyebrow. Oh no. She wasn't joking. He really had an apron.

Someone had just thrown a flag on his master play.

❧

"I can't cook, Kat." Not anything beyond freezer meals and stir-fry anyway. Though, on second thought, he could create a pretty mean grilled cheese. He forced another sip of his too-bitter coffee, unable to help comparing it to the way Kat made it, and set the paper cup on the rickety table between them.

Behind him at the front counter, the bean grinder churned, temporarily overshadowing the muffled chats of the conversations from corner booths. From the looks of it, those people were actually enjoying their conversations. Of course, he doubted they had to explain why they wouldn't don an apron on national television.

"Oh, come on. Give the idea a chance." Kat still held her mocha, which she'd ordered with too many adjectives to count and dolloped with whipped cream. Dessert in a sleeve, just the way she liked it.

Did she know he knew exactly how she liked it? Or was he the only one who paid attention to the details between them? If her buttons were still stuck on Best Friends mode, maybe that stuff didn't matter even if she knew. He couldn't tell anymore, and he figured he probably shouldn't care this much. It wasn't masculine. Football—that was masculine. Finally putting an offer on the land he'd been eyeing forever—that was masculine. Mowing his own acreage. Drinking bitter coffee.

Not debating relationship what-ifs as if he were thirteen and wearing a training bra to a slumber party.

Yet something about Kat made him feel more like a man than he ever did on the field.

"Besides, it's not cooking. It's baking." She had whipped cream on her lip, and he wasn't going to tell her.

He shrugged. "Fine, then. I don't *bake*."

"You could. And you have before, every time you've helped me at home." She pointed behind him, in the general direction of her house, despite the fact it sat at least three miles from the coffee shop.

"That's not baking. That's advising. Taste testing. Occasionally stirring." He crossed his arms, unwilling to down another swallow of that brew the owners deemed coffee.

And just as unwilling to fly to LA to tape a reality show in a faux kitchen. No way could he take off work for that long, leave his players, and leave Tyler in the midst of family drama and low self-esteem to trek across the country to mix batter. That was Kat's thing. He'd done his part.

And it hadn't really helped.

"Exactly. You'd be the perfect partner." She narrowed her eyes, and he hated what he knew was coming next. "It's your fault I'm doing this, anyway."

The bustling of the shop around them faded as those words

sank in. *Fault.* Not credit, but blame. He inhaled stiffly. "You still think this is a bad thing to do." Had he really been that off in his play?

If that was any indication of his instincts these days, Tyler and the guys wouldn't stand a chance.

"No." She sighed, pushing her coffee away, then pulled it back for a swig that doubled the whipped cream on her lip. This time she must have felt it, because she scrubbed it off with her sleeve that was already slightly smeared with flour. "I mean, I'm going to do it anyway."

"It's not the guillotine." It might be for him, at this point, but not for her.

"I know that." She ran her finger around the lid of her cup. "But I've always wanted to *see* the world—not fail in front of everyone *in* the world."

"Understandable." He threw her emphasis back at her. "But what if you *succeed* in front of everyone in the world?"

Her eyes brightened slightly at the suggestion, and he at once hated and loved how easy it was to lift her spirits. Loved that she received it from him—but hated she had nothing to give to herself. "Maybe."

"Never know until you try. Besides, what do you have to lose?" Besides his heart, anyway, and she didn't even know she had that. But maybe if he went . . . maybe if he was there, every step of the way, not holding her hand but giving her strength and confidence— maybe she'd see.

Maybe she needed him more than his players did right now. Maybe this was the comeback after halftime.

The game definitely wasn't over yet.

She hesitated. "So in that same vein, what do *you* have to lose?"

Plenty. But she wasn't ready to hear that, and he wasn't ready to say it. So he took another sip and grimaced. "My dignity."

"The apron's blue."

Oh yeah, that definitely fixed it. He wished he could do her eyebrow trick at her about now. He settled for rolling his eyes. "I can see that."

"So what do you say?" Her eyes sparked with hope, and something a lot like guilt pressed upon his shoulders. He really didn't like the thought of Kat in LA for days, uncertain and alone. And she had to have someone assist her as part of the show's rules, and it definitely didn't need to be that nice, yet mostly clueless kid that helped at Sweetie Pies. Besides, Kat had said she wanted him, not Amy.

His stomach clenched. He better not regret this. "I say . . . pass the apron." Sigh. Darren would never let him live it down. Ever.

Kat's squeal and impromptu hug across the table was almost worth it. Bittersweet.

Sort of like a man's last meal before the guillotine.

five

"LA? Really, Kat?" The disapproval practically dripped in tangible lumps from her mother's perfected Southern accent. Kat considered making a face at her cell phone, but the display of immaturity would only prove her mother right.

That she wasn't ready to go off on her own.

She settled for taking her aggression out on her suitcase zipper. *Zzzzip.* "It's a great opportunity. Once in a lifetime, even." *Zzzzip.* Funny how she now defended the same idea she'd initially been against herself.

Her mother sighed, the sound bringing back memory after memory of disappointment. The look on her mom's face when Kat didn't make the honor roll in elementary school. Her expression when Kat didn't make the dance-line team at Bayou Bend High. Her under-the-breath mutterings about getting out of the kitchen and doing something like Stella did. Yet she barely noticed or commented when Kat won the fifth-grade dessert bake-off or when she delivered food on a mission trip to Mexico with the church. Things *Kat* had been interested in didn't fall into her mother's perfectly laid out plan. Stella was the one who had somehow managed to follow the plan.

Kat just wanted to puree the plan into something edible.

"I know you've always wanted to travel, but your lifestyle just doesn't allow for that. Besides, once in a lifetime doesn't automatically make something a good idea, Katherine."

Katherine. Her stomach knotted. She shouldn't have even called. Should have just let her mom find out through the Bayou Bend grapevine. Or better yet, once the show aired. She grasped at straws, hating that she had never outgrown that method of interaction with her mom. "Well, Lucas believes in me."

"Lucas wears blinders, sweetie."

Zzzzzzzzzip.

The zipper tore away from the fabric. Great, now she'd have to take her biggest case. At least she hadn't filled it yet. She traded them out in her closet and hefted the larger suitcase onto her bed. The wheels made indentions on the sage-green comforter, and she smoothed the wrinkles as her mom prattled on. Claire Varland was nothing if not persistent. Probably why she was able to convince half the town to donate money they didn't have to causes they didn't necessarily care about.

"Honestly, that boy would eat anything put in front of him, especially if you made it."

That *boy* was a man, and one of the most respectable ones in the entire town. But to her mom, Lucas was still the college kid who took her to prom and jabbed them all with the corsage pin before relinquishing the honor. "What are you trying to say, Mom?"

But she knew. She'd always known. Her parents didn't believe in outside-the-box any more than poor Aunt Maggie did. Which meant they didn't believe in her ability. They went from pushing her into attempting something bigger and more "meaningful" with her life to finally believing she was doing all she could baking mundane recipes at Sweetie Pies.

She didn't know which was worse.

"Now, don't get defensive, dear."

How else was she supposed to feel? She unzipped her suitcase, carefully this time, and stared at the contents of her closet.

Yuck.

She began tossing in socks instead as her mother continued.

"I'm just saying that Lucas isn't always the best judge of character."

Right. Because he wanted to be her friend more than Stella's? Because Lucas might be the one male in the entire county within a ten-year-age radius of her pageant queen sister who hadn't asked her out at some point in her life?

"He's a great judge of character." *He* liked her cupcakes—and not just because he was her friend. He liked them enough to put her on national TV.

But what if he was the baking equivalent of tone-deaf? Maybe her off-the-wall recipes really didn't belong in Sweetie Pies or anywhere else in the world. Maybe she was better off with a vanilla, chocolate, and strawberry lifestyle.

Maybe her mom was right.

"I'm just saying that a random opportunity and Lucas's approval don't mean the world."

Underwear went in next. "But yours does?" Oops. She hadn't completely meant for that to be out loud.

She could almost hear her mother's teeth grind, could almost picture the automatic responses rolling through her polished brain. *Stella never argues like this. Stella never goes against my wishes. Stella never makes rash decisions that cause a preacher's wife to look questionable.*

Well, Kat usually didn't either. But this decision had all but been made for her, and sometimes, despite Claire Varland's opinion, opportunities could be a good thing.

Of course, she *could* also fall on her cupcake-padded rear end.

Doubt made her unpack her socks.

Her mom's accent thickened into a full-out drawl, which meant she was past frustrated and borderline mad. "I'm just saying you should think carefully about the consequences."

She had.

Which was why the socks were going back in.

"Mom, I'm not moving to LA or anything crazy." Yet. Though New York was certainly on the table—a detail she'd share with her mother only if it ever came to pass. She tried to keep her tone casual. "I'm just going to participate in a competition that happens to be aired on TV."

A long silence followed. And just when Kat thought she'd finally won . . .

"Hollywood is no place for someone like you."

That burned. "But maybe for someone like Stella?" Hardly. As pure as Stella might be now, Hollywood would eat her up and spit her out like yesterday's bacon. But Stella had never been wrong when they were children, and her mother would be more likely to misplace her favorite string of pearls than to break tradition now.

Some battles weren't worth fighting.

"You know what? Don't even answer that. This is my choice, Mom." She was an adult, whether or not anyone treated her like it.

"Of course it's your choice." Her mother's voice turned to sugar, then crystallized. "Just be sure to make the right one."

In other words, her mom's choice. "I've got to pack. Tell Daddy I'll call him before I leave." Kat mumbled what could pass for a good-bye and tossed her cell on her pillow. Maybe her father could talk her mother off the ledge. Or maybe not. He might wear the starched and pressed suit pants in the family, but he avoided confrontation like the plagues of Egypt he had preached on when Kat was ten. She still remembered the way Andrew Hoffman had set a frog loose during the climax of the sermon, how the boys had giggled and the girls had squealed and the blue-haired ladies had yanked up their feet.

How her father had kept on preaching as if absolutely nothing was happening.

He wasn't going to be much help, but he'd at least pray for her while she was gone. Oh, her mother would pray too, but Kat hated to peek at the ulterior motives behind those prayers. *Dear Lord, please let Kat fail miserably so she sees her place is right here in Bayou Bend forever. Dear Lord, please allow all of Kat's cupcakes to burn the mouths of the judges so she isn't lured away into the sin of Hollywood.*

Did she even stand a chance?

She lobbed a pair of socks at the bedroom door just as her friend Rachel knocked on the frame.

She ducked just in time to avoid the flying socks, which landed in the hallway. "You really should lock your front door." Rachel straightened, her silky brown bob swinging along her jaw in that easy way Kat had always envied.

"Why? This is Bayou Bend." And wasn't that the entire problem? Kat rearranged the leftover socks in the corners of her suitcase. "*Mi casa, su casa*, and such." She'd rather that casa be in New York. Or Dallas. Or Chicago. Or anywhere that offered a taste of real life sprinkled with freedom.

"Good thing." Her friend handed over a fountain drink from the gas station and slurped from her own extra-large one. "Cherry coke."

She accepted it with a thank-you. "Where are the munchkins?"

"School and Mother's Day Out. Mama's free." Rachel grinned and toasted Kat with her drink. "Need help packing?"

At least Rachel supported her decision to go—and Lucas. So who cared what her mother thought? Maybe her mom had it backward. Maybe it was *her* opinion that didn't matter at all.

Then why the rock of dread permanently lodged in Kat's stomach?

Rachel shot a pointed look at her mostly empty suitcase and then the socks in the hallway. "I'm thinking the answer to my question is a hearty *yes*."

Kat shrugged. "Good luck getting any further. I have nothing to wear to LA."

"You have that apron for the show, though, right? What are you going to wear with it?" Rachel set her drink down on the dresser, then began pawing through the contents of Kat's closets. "Why so many T-shirts?"

"Asked the stay-at-home mom? Really?" Kat grinned. "I bake all day. I'm the walking flour lady. I don't have much reason to buy dress clothes."

Rachel considered a pair of gray slacks, then kept rummaging. "Some of the girls on that show wear ball gowns, you know. Or overalls."

"And some people jump off bridges. Your point?"

Rachel snorted. "Want to borrow my black dress?"

"The one you wear on anniversaries? No thanks. I've had a few too many cupcakes for that one." Kat patted her hips.

"You're only a size bigger than me. It'll be cute."

"Maybe." Kat hesitated, trying to picture herself in that little black dress, strolling LA after taping, sitting across from Lucas at a candlelit table. Her stomach fluttered, and this time the feeling wasn't born of doubt or insecurity or worry.

It was born of something much, much worse.

Rachel shut the closet door with a click. "I've solved your clothing dilemma."

"Stay home?" It could solve a lot, actually. She could get her mother off her back. Avoid the glaring opportunity to fail publicly. Miss out on embarrassing herself in front of Lucas. They'd never been out of town together before, not like this. Of course they would have separate rooms, but they would know only each other there. Except for when they slept, every airplane ride, every meal, every minute in and out of the studio would be spent together.

Two years ago, that notion would never have been enough of a point to cross her mind. Or if it had crossed her mind, it would be only in regard to the happy realization that Lucas could maneuver extra peanuts from the flight attendant for her and help carry her shopping bags around LA.

Now her palms were as sweaty as a preteen's, and she was more concerned about what Lucas would think of her in Rachel's dress than what she would wear on national television.

"No, silly." Rachel grabbed her drink, and tossed Kat her purse hanging on the bedroom doorknob. "Get your keys. We're going shopping."

Kat hooked her purse on her arm and cast one last glance at her suitcase. "You sure about this?"

"It's time to branch out, girl." Rachel jangled her keys. "You deserve this."

"The show or the new clothes?" Or Lucas. Now, where did that thought come from? She pressed her fingers against her forehead.

"Both." Rachel grinned. "And you know what? I retract my offer of loaning you my dress. It's time you found your own perfect fit."

Like that could be found in the depths of a clearance rack. Kat followed Rachel outside, careful to lock her front door behind her. Maybe it *was* time for some changes.

Too bad Lucas didn't think so too.

 celeo

Lucas drummed his fingers on the display case at Sweetie Pies, yanking his hand back as Kat repolished his finger smudges on the glass with a rag. They left in two days. Two days, and he'd be on an airplane with Kat, headed into what could possibly be the best or worst trip of their friendship.

Could end their friendship.

Or could turn it into something even better.

Not that there was any pressure.

He watched as she continued cleaning, his mind racing through his checklist of all he'd accomplished and still had to accomplish before leaving work and his team for a week. How exactly had he gotten roped into this, again?

46

Oh yeah. His Big Gesture . . . and Kat's blue eyes.

He cleared his throat. "You got our plane tickets?"

She kept wiping down the counters, and he wondered briefly why Amy hadn't done that before she left for the day. "I've got the tickets."

"And all the show information?"

"And the show information."

"Did you buy the trip insurance?"

"No."

He frowned. "Why not?" Everyone always bought trip insurance. He did, anyway. Kat didn't travel much, though, except for those few mission trips she took in high school. This might be a bigger deal to her than he'd originally realized.

Now there was *really* no pressure.

"Because one, the show is paying for the flight, and because two, if we miss this trip for some reason, there is no other trip. It's not like I go to LA to be on TV every year." Kat snorted as she tossed the rag aside and reached in the case to pull out the tray of leftover strawberry cupcakes. "It's now or never."

Was it? He considered that a minute, hating the innuendo she probably didn't even realize she offered. Maybe it was now or never for the show. But what about for them?

No. Enough of that. He'd been coaching himself the past few days on bracing against his personal feelings for Kat. That wasn't what this trip was about, and if he didn't get a handle on it soon, he'd wind up following her around LA with googly-eyes and a trail of drool that would make Hansel and Gretel feel incompetent.

He picked a safer question. "Have you packed?"

The tray of cupcakes clattered against the top of the counter, and Kat shot him a look that could have deep-fried a turkey. "Don't ask."

So much for safe. He tried again. "Where's Aunt Maggie today?"

"Sick." Kat looked over her shoulder, as if the older woman

could somehow still materialize in her office. "Which makes me feel bad for leaving."

"She'll rally before two more days, I bet. Doesn't she usually?" He plucked a strawberry cupcake from the tray. "And she has Amy to help while you're gone."

Kat quirked her eyebrow.

Yeah, true. That didn't really console. He licked the top of the icing. "She'll be fine. So will Sweetie Pies. This is about you." For once. He didn't say that part, though, because he figured Kat didn't need a lot of extra reminders about the obvious.

She pulled out the tray of chocolates, eyeing him in her peripheral. "Don't forget to take the wrapper off this time."

Man, he really needed to figure out how to do that eyebrow trick at her. "That was *one* time."

"You ate paper, and you expect me to just let it go?"

He opened his mouth to argue, but the door chimed behind him. He turned around, straightening from the counter as Aunt Maggie shuffled in, a blue sweater pulled tight around her chest.

"Aunt Maggie! You should be in bed!" Kat rushed around the counter and went to her side, as if she expected the woman to fall down on the floor. She didn't look that frail to Lucas, though he didn't see her as regularly as Kat did. Still, what was with the overreaction?

Unless Kat was trying to find a reason to stay in town after all.

He narrowed his eyes.

"I left my Bible here, and I decided I might as well grab the latest statements to work on the bills while I'm laid up for a few days." She coughed into her elbow, and Kat steered her toward one of the pulled-out chairs. "Katherine, really. I can walk."

"I shouldn't go." She nibbled on her lower lip, the debate evident in her eyes as she hovered over her aunt. "You need me here."

"No, you should go, dear. Besides, I have Amy."

A pulsing silence hung in the room. Lucas could have sworn he heard crickets.

"Anyway, I'm fine." Maggie coughed again, then rubbed the base of her throat with her hand. "You'll be back in a week, and then everything will be just like usual."

Kat's expression dropped toward the floor, a flash of pain flickering in her eyes before she pasted on a smile that, to anyone else, would have seemed perfectly ordinary. But she was hurt.

And rightly so. Even her aunt didn't think she had a chance of winning—the same aunt who ate Kat's cupcakes on a regular basis. If Kat won—*when* she won—nothing would be the same. That was the whole point. She wouldn't have to keep working at Sweetie Pies. She could use whatever prize money she was awarded to open her own shop or start an online business. She'd be free. How could Maggie assume she didn't even stand a chance?

Lucas suddenly felt torn between wanting to get the woman a cough drop and pull her chair out from under her.

The worst part was, he didn't think it was malicious or intentional. In fact, it seemed as if Maggie, just like Kat's mom, was completely oblivious to the way she came across—as if what she said was so truthful and obvious that there was zero shame or consequence in saying it. Kat's father, Pastor Tom, might have been a father figure to Lucas as a teenager, but they weren't so close that Lucas couldn't decipher the truth. Maybe Pastor Tom wasn't as bad vocally as the others in Kat's family, but his passivity might be an even cheaper shot.

Lucas had always known Kat carried insecurity issues over her career and her dreams, but this encounter with Maggie opened his eyes to exactly how bad it had gotten—and why. No wonder she was so torn about going and trying to talk herself out of it every other hour. How could she believe in herself when everyone who should love her the most seemed determined to convince her otherwise?

Well, he believed in her. He might not be a famous bakery owner or cupcake expert, but he was a man with a healthy appetite who knew a good thing when it was put on a plate in front of him. And Kat's ability went beyond good. She deserved the chance to prove them all wrong, and he was grateful now that he'd get the chance to stand by her side while she did it.

"Did you hear me?" Maggie rose unsteadily from her chair. "Will you check my desk for that Bible?"

"Right. Of course." Kat's voice held a hint of monotone that he was sure Maggie didn't catch. Like a champ, she grabbed her aunt's Bible and a binder of what he assumed held financial information and tucked them both into the older woman's purse. "Call me if you need anything."

"I'll make some soup, take it easy, and be back soon. Don't you worry." Maggie patted Kat's cheek. "Have fun on your trip. You deserve it."

That was nice, but a little late now. The damage had long been done. Kat held her wobbly smile until Maggie left, then headed back around the counter. Lucas debated between bringing it up and letting it go. What did she need most?

From the way she banged trays around as she finished her closing duties, he decided to let it go. Help her focus on the positive, just like he persuaded his guys after a bad play. "Just think, Kat. You'll get a whole week of absolutely nothing vanilla, chocolate, or strawberry." A whole week of no negativity, away from those who were supposed to be helping her fly.

That earned a smile, though still tainted with disappointment. "There might be *some* chocolate. As in, German. Or dark."

"That works."

She wiped the corner of her eye, and he changed his mind. He couldn't let it go. He reached across the counter and brushed his fingers against her arm. "You know you're going to win, right? And give your aunt some stiff competition when you get back?"

Her smile turned sincere, and the knot in his stomach eased a bit. There. He'd done it. Mission accomplished.

"Maybe." She frowned a little. "Though I don't see how Sweetie Pies will be competition with Bloom."

"Bloom? You've already named your shop?"

She closed up the bakery boxes of leftover cupcakes. "What do you mean? Bloom is in New York City. The grand prize."

Panic seeped in a slow bleed, his vision blurring around the edges as his thoughts raced to catch up. "I thought the grand prize was cash. To start your own place." No. No. How could he have missed that? Winners got money. It was the rule of television. Or any contest, really. She had to be mistaken. Hadn't they seen enough episodes together for him to have caught this significant detail?

"It has been in episodes past. But you didn't read the fine print, apparently." She stacked the boxes on top of each other. "It said for this show, the grand prize is an internship at Bloom. That's better than cash, trust me. After someone works there a year, they can do anything they want. Their résumé is golden in the baking industry."

A year.

The knot returned and doubled into a noose. New York City. That might be even farther away from Louisiana than LA.

And he'd just all but sent Kat and his heart there on a jet plane.

six

Puffy white clouds interrupted the brilliant blue sky—a sky the same color as Kat's eyes. Lucas slapped Tyler a high five as the boy ran past, breathless, from the football field. Last practice before LA, before his assistant coaches took over.

He drew a breath tight with stress. It was only for a week. No biggie. He could use the vacation, though that much time alone with Kat right now wouldn't be relaxing. Especially not if she actually won.

If she actually moved to New York.

He pointed Tyler toward the water table, grateful for the temporary distraction. "Good job today, man. I see improvement." Thank goodness. Maybe things were finally better at home and his focus had cleared a little. He wouldn't ask right now, in case it hadn't. No need to remind the kid of his struggles.

"Thanks, Coach." Tyler's face lit up as he shucked his helmet and grabbed a paper cup. Compliments meant so much to the boy. Lucas hated he couldn't do more for him. But he'd be okay while he was in LA. Unnerving sometimes how much people depended on him. Tyler, his entire team, Kat . . .

A sliver of doubt cast a long shadow. They might be able to do without him for a week, but what would they do if he ever really failed? If he called the wrong play?

He adjusted his ball cap. No, Kat's insecurities were rubbing off. He was strong and capable. He could carry it all, just like he'd always done. As a fourth grader, mowing lawns to help his single mom make rent. As a tenth grader, scaring off the sharks who circled his mother like she was easy prey.

As a college student, laying a rose on her casket.

He knew what it was to be alone, to have to be strong whether or not you felt the strength. He'd figured that out by the grace of God and the influence of a couple of godly men over the years who stepped up at church to help him navigate a fatherless existence.

And just like those men had filled the gaps for him, somehow he'd help Tyler get through this rough season and prepare for college and help Kat win this competition and gain what she needed. He'd step in for those who lacked, substitute for those who couldn't give. Protect. Assist. Provide.

It was what he'd always done, and what he did best.

If he didn't, who would?

His cell vibrated in his pocket. Probably Darren, since he forgot to text him back about grabbing a pizza before he left for LA. He cast a quick glance at the display screen. Nope. It was the realtor who was helping him acquire his land. His heart pounded in anticipation as he jabbed the Accept button. Maybe they'd accepted the offer. "This is Lucas."

"Lucas, it's Tony."

His grim tone doused Lucas's hopes, and he gripped the phone tighter. "What's up, man?"

"Bad news. They countered your offer again, and I hear through the grapevine there's now another bidder who isn't playing around."

That *was* bad news—actually, a lot of bad news for one day. He rubbed his hand down his jaw, mind racing with figures. He could counter back. *Again.* But not with a lot. Would it be enough to stave off the second bidder? "Go up another five grand."

Papers rustled. "Are you sure?"

Sure? About finally having his own permanent spot in Bayou Bend, about a house and land and the restoration of his childhood spent penny-pinching to afford a two-bedroom rental with no central heating and air?

Sure about a future with Kat?

He tightened his grip on his cell. "Sign the dotted line, man. Whatever it takes."

New York would just have to stay where it was.

ое

Kat debated sitting on her suitcase to zip it, but then she'd only wrinkle the new tops Rachel had talked her into getting, and the little black dress that had taken Rachel, the sales clerk, and an unbiased third-party customer to convince her to buy.

Her credit card hadn't seen so much action since before her student loans had been paid off.

"We're going for a week, Kat. Not for a month." Lucas shoveled another handful of popcorn into his mouth. "Come on, you're supposed to be taking notes." He gestured to the TV, where they'd been watching reruns of *Cupcake Combat*, trying to read between the airwaves to glean as much as they could about what happened behind the scenes.

So far, all they'd concluded was the host desperately needed different hair product.

Kat looked up from where she knelt beside her suitcase on the living room floor and squinted at the TV as another contestant panicked over the rapidly ticking clock. "I'm watching *and* packing." And trying not to freak out over the fact that in a few days, that would be *her* on camera scrambling around like a headless chicken. Would she bark orders at Lucas like that one girl had done to her mother? Would she nearly run into another contestant with a hot tray on the way back to her station from the industrial ovens?

Would her cupcakes make that one judge's lip curl in distaste like that last baker's?

"Packing's done. Your suitcase is closed." Lucas threw a kernel at her, wrenching her from her fears.

She ducked. "Closed, but not zipped. There's still time to switch something out."

"As long as you don't add to it." He hesitated. "I assume I'm supposed to wrestle that monster around the airport?"

She grinned, and he changed the subject.

"I really don't like that one judge." He was ignoring her suitcase now, which was fine. It gave her permission to change her mind about that dress—though Rachel would kill her. If she found out . . . no, she'd find out. Because she'd ask. Forget the show—the dress and Lucas's opinion of it would be the first thing out of her friend's mouth after their plane landed and they were home.

"I'm serious." Lucas pointed a buttery finger at the judge, the gray-suited one who always sat at the end of the panel. "Thad, or whatever his name is. He's . . . he's so . . ."

She followed his gaze to the screen. "Well dressed?"

"No, more like—"

"Attractive?"

Three more kernels flew her way. "*No.* I was going to say—"

"Clever?"

He glared, and she couldn't help the giggle that escaped. It was after ten o'clock, she'd worked all day, packed all evening, and their plane left in fewer hours than she'd like to count. She'd slipped right past exhausted and was barreling headfirst toward delirious.

She fought a yawn. "I should get to bed." Watching *Cupcake Combat* hadn't helped prepare either of them. All it had done was make her doubt which recipes to take along to study on the plane and wonder if the supply shelf of ingredients on the show was really as thorough as it appeared to be. Would they have sweet potatoes and maple syrup there for her favorite autumn buttercream? Should she smuggle some in herself? Was that even allowed?

The information she'd received hadn't helped much. Though maybe that was intentional, and the constantly panicked expressions on the contestants' faces weren't exaggerated for ratings after all.

"You don't want to see who wins?" Lucas stood up and brushed popcorn bits from his jeans, then knelt and began plucking them from the floor. Good man. He'd learned.

"Let's pretend I win." She might.

Maybe.

A fresh batch of nerves seized her stomach, and she rubbed her finger over the polka-dotted pattern of her suitcase. Aunt Maggie didn't seem to think she'd win, and her mom—well, enough about that. Her dad had seemed sincere about wishing her well, yet cautious, as if she might accidentally stroll into some sort of sin-coated avenue just because she was leaving the Bible Belt. Stella had just asked if she was getting her hair done before she went. When she'd reminded her sister this was work, not a pageant or some college party, she'd gotten a half-sigh, half-snort in response.

Funny how it was possible to sense someone rolling their eyes from the other side of a phone line.

She flopped open the lid of her suitcase and stared at the dress, peeking between the sleeves of a heather-gray sweater. Stella would love the new dress, which was reason enough to leave it behind.

But what if Lucas loved it too?

The dress stayed.

She dropped down on her suitcase and wrenched the zipper around before she could change her mind. There. It was done.

Lucas tossed the spilled popcorn into the trash can. "In a week or so, we just might be able to say that you won for real." He walked over and offered his hand. "If I was a betting man, I'd put a wager on you."

"What do you mean, if? I recall stories of a certain first grader making more than his fair share of jelly beans off the playground." She welcomed his help to her feet, though she wobbled once she regained her footing. The spicy scent of his cologne sent her senses reeling, and she backed up a step. Whoa. She must be really tired. She'd smelled Lucas how many times a day over the course of their friendship?

"I'd bet on you any day." His voice lost the teasing tone and took a serious nosedive that sent her stomach reeling.

"At least someone would." She shook her head. "Sorry. Didn't mean to send an invite to a pity party. Just . . . it's hard to be misunderstood." And underestimated. And undervalued.

Unless they were right.

Lucas stood her suitcase upright and began wheeling it toward the front door. "I really love your dad, but, Kat, your family's crazy not to be supporting you better than this."

Or maybe *they* were normal, and *she* was crazy.

He strolled back over to her, closer than before, and tucked a strand of hair behind her ear. She looked up into his eyes and saw the same Lucas she'd always seen. Stoic. Dependable. Trustworthy.

And capable of sending her hormones into a frenzy.

"I need you to do me a favor." He dropped his hand to his side, but held her gaze with his own. "I'm serious."

"What, you want me to promise to bake extra cupcakes for you after taping?" She offered a laugh she didn't believe, partially because that was what Lucas always said before cracking a joke—and partially to break the tension between them she wasn't even sure he felt.

He didn't smile. "No. I need you to give yourself a break, and really go for this."

Oh. He *was* serious.

He took a half-step closer, and his fingers brushed the length of her arm. "Forget what your family thinks. You have to believe in yourself if you expect the judges to."

She nodded, rolling in her lower lip and averting her gaze to the TV to hide her reaction to his proximity. Right. The judges. Because that's what this was about.

"I'll try." She edged away, moving to the kitchen to start throwing away trash from their fast-food dinner and to take a breath that wasn't laced with his cologne. Would things ever feel normal between them again? What if he picked up on her feelings while they were gone? It wasn't as if Lucas was thinking about the next level—not when he'd signed her up for a show that meant potentially living half a country away for a year or longer.

Though on second thought, he'd seemed a little surprised by the internship grand prize. Had he really not known?

Did it matter?

Not really. She was foolish for thinking a new dress would make an ounce of difference. Lucas saw her as a friend, nothing more. Best friend, for that matter, which was a vital status she wasn't willing to lose. As much as her heart thudded a contradiction, she couldn't risk anything more between them, even if he ever did show interest.

Because if she lost Lucas, what would she have left?

❧

Thirty thousand feet above the ground, and all Lucas could think about was his own lack of courage.

And it had nothing to do with flying.

His heart was throwing out so many contradictions that he didn't recognize truth anymore.

He leaned his head against the back of the airplane seat, then removed his hat that got in the way and dropped it in his lap. From the aisle seat, Kat dozed, mouth slightly open and one leg curled underneath her in what had to be a surefire way of putting her foot to sleep. The slight strains of Sinatra's "Come Fly with Me"—fitting—drifted through one of the earbuds that had fallen from her ear and dangled across her lap. She'd literally talked nonstop, as she always did when

58

she got nervous, until she stumbled into a nap. He'd tucked her hoodie around her like a blanket before leaning against the window to try to sleep himself.

But the thoughts wouldn't let up. Neither would the low drone of the two businessmen sitting behind them, discussing stocks and other things that Lucas should probably know more about. Somehow, though, he doubted either of those Suits knew when to call a screen pass or a flea-flicker, so . . .

So . . . wow. Kat's insecurity was *really* rubbing off on him. Lucas pinched the bridge of his nose and exhaled slowly. He'd never been threatened by the intellectual type before—or any type, for that matter. He knew his strengths and weaknesses and played accordingly. What was wrong with him? Why the sudden need to compare?

He cast another look at Kat, whose hair had fallen halfway over her makeup-free face as she slept, and he knew the answer deep in his gut.

Guilt.

He felt guilty—not for signing her up for the show, but for the train of thought careening out of control in his mind. For all his pep talks to her about believing in herself, for all his grumbling about her family's lack of support, he didn't want Kat to win.

He wanted her to lose.

Talk about a scumbag.

Clouds obscured his view out the window, so he pulled the shade and cracked the tension out of his neck. He had to quit projecting. Trying to feel superior to some random guys behind him just to make himself feel better about his secret hopes wasn't the answer.

The businessmen's conversation turned from stocks to sports. Great. One of them coached peewee hockey, and the other was a former college football sensation he would have recognized had he heard the guy's name sooner.

God had to be chuckling.

The attendant wheeled by with her cart, and Lucas shook his head at the offer of overpriced chocolate, then thought better of it and shelled out a ridiculous amount of cash to secure Kat a package for later. She loved anything she deemed "souvenir food." Maybe she'd find a way to work it into a recipe.

Lucas sipped on the Coke he'd brought with him from the airport and then tucked the bottle into the back of the seat in front of him. Chocolate and Coke. Pretty unstoppable combo—surely Kat could do something amazing with that on the set.

His mood lightened. See, he could do the right thing. He was already thinking of ways to help Kat during the competition. He could be trusted to carry this burden on the sidelines and give her his best on the field. Or rather in the kitchen.

Maybe there was hope that once they got settled in the studio and started taping, he would see it all differently. Feel differently. He *had* to support Kat, regardless of his personal desires for the outcome. Whether she won or lost, he had to do everything he could to be her rock.

He couldn't let her crumble.

Hopefully, her cupcakes wouldn't either. Kat never had to work under that kind of pressure before—all of her baking outside of Sweetie Pies had been in the comfort of her own kitchen, without a ticking clock and judging eyes. He had to make sure she didn't bomb on national television, or this entire plan to bring her out of her shell and push her ability—and self-esteem—into the limelight would backfire miserably.

Not to mention the sub-plan of winning her heart.

Though if she won the competition, she'd be moving. And in his gut he knew that if Kat left Bayou Bend, she wouldn't be back. She'd been dreaming of escape for far too long to ever return. That caged bird would fly.

And he'd be left surrounded by a lot of land, too many empty rooms, and a flurry of feathers.

He shifted in the uncomfortable seat, accidentally knocking into Kat's arm resting on the bar between them. She turned toward him, hair still covering half her face, and licked her lips before settling back into sleep. She had to be exhausted after yesterday's hectic pace of preparing for the trip. He should have left her house sooner, but he couldn't shake the thought that that night was their last. Before everything changed, one way or another.

He brushed Kat's hair off her face and let his knuckles linger against her cheek a moment longer than necessary. Things were definitely changing, for better or for worse.

Unfortunately, right now it didn't seem possible to have one without the other.

seven

She really should have worn makeup.

Kat gazed over the top of the taxi at the rows of palm trees lining the median of LAX as Lucas and the driver shoved their suitcases into the trunk. She'd seen palm trees before, of course, when on the beach in Alabama as a teenager. But this was LA. Even their palm trees had a glamorous edge to them—though the cloudy sky seemed foggier than she'd expected. She'd kept a close eye out for celebrities as they funneled through the airport, collected their baggage, and hailed a taxi outside the terminal, to no avail. But really, would she even recognize any if she saw them? That was more Stella's thing. Besides, she didn't really want to run into her favorite actor without makeup on.

One thing was certain. "We are so not in Kansas anymore."

Lucas snorted as the driver slammed the trunk lid and went to his side of the car. "Okay, Dorothy. Time to quit drooling and get in the cab."

"Sure thing, *Coach*." She stressed the title to remind him as she always did when he was teetering on the edge of bossy, then slid into the backseat first. She fought the urge to press her nose against the glass like a child.

She'd woken up as soon as the plane had begun its descent, and it seemed like she hadn't shut her mouth in wonder since. Hopefully, the awe factor of being in California would fade a little before she got on set tomorrow, or she'd make an idiot of herself. She might be small-town, but she didn't have to act like it. At least she'd gotten a good nap on the plane, so the time difference shouldn't be an issue later.

Assuming she could sleep tonight at all. Her orders were to be at the studio by seven a.m., and from the parade of nerves prancing through her belly, she had a feeling counting sheep wasn't going to cut it.

Speaking of naps . . . She glanced sideways at Lucas's stoic profile as he gazed, seemingly unimpressed, out his window at the traffic. He'd been grumpy ever since they landed—too bad he hadn't snoozed like she had.

Or maybe it was something else. Lucas was usually only in a bad mood after losing a game. Was he worrying about his team? A seed of guilt began to sprout. Maybe she shouldn't have coaxed him into coming if he was going to be that distracted. In fact, he could hurt more than help if he wasn't focused in the kitchen.

She tried to ignore the part of her that wanted his complete attention. His team was important—he loved those kids. They weren't just students; they were closer to family. It wasn't like Lucas had any family of his own anymore.

Sympathy coated the guilt and doubled its size. He'd done this all for her, and here she was feeling jealous over a bunch of sweaty boys and bemoaning his lack of concentration. What kind of friend was she?

She tapped the leg of his athletic pants, nearly losing her balance as the driver swerved around another cab. "You okay over there?"

He shot her a smile she didn't believe, and followed it with a nod before propping his elbow on the window edge. His hair peeked out from under the edges of his ball cap, like he'd mussed it before replacing the cap earlier. "A little tired, is all. Long flight."

Liar.

But if he didn't want to talk . . .

She turned back to her own window, barely seeing the eclectic group of sports cars, beat-up vans, and shuttle buses that zipped past. Maybe he was just worried about being on camera. He wasn't used to that kind of limelight, either, though he handled it better than she did.

The parade in her stomach turned into something more closely resembling a conga line. She couldn't think about being nervous, or dropping cupcakes, or forgetting her recipes, or any of the other thoughts that had plagued her dreams on the plane. If she wanted to get out of Bayou Bend, wanted to actually live in the real world and make a contribution, then she had to blot out those what-ifs and focus on the main goal—winning. Blowing the judges' minds. Nabbing the grand prize.

And never looking back.

She glanced over her shoulder at Lucas, and her heart twisted at all the unknowns.

Maybe just a few looks back.

cele

This hotel room was hers for five nights.

For free.

Kat contemplated spinning in a tight circle with outstretched arms like they did in the movies, but settled for tossing her carry-on on the floor and collapsing on the king-size bed. The soft down comforter swallowed her up like a marshmallow, and she bounced a few times for good measure.

Oz had a whole lot on Kansas.

Maybe she belonged here after all—in a little piece of her own fairy tale. Maybe her family was wrong. Maybe she did have what it took.

But only if she proved it tomorrow on camera.

She sat up, struggled to get free of the mattress's embrace, and straightened the rumpled, satiny striped pillows. The entire room appeared to have been dipped in luxury, from the chocolate on the nightstand, to the shimmery threads in the heavy drapes, to the massive desk stationed in the corner—that still left plenty of floor space.

Oh, she could get used to this.

She should unpack, or take a nap, or *something* productive before having dinner with Lucas that night, but she couldn't concentrate long enough to even unzip her suitcase. Who could hang shirts in a closet when her entire life was in the process of potentially changing forever?

Although she really should get that new dress on a hanger.

She unzipped her bag, removed the dress, and smoothed the wrinkles before hanging it in the middle of the generous closet. The steam from her shower that night would take care of the rest—if she remembered to hang it in the bathroom in time.

Kat glanced at the remaining clothes in the now-open suitcase, at the dresser drawers, and then at her watch. She was on vacation. Yet what would her mother say?

She knew exactly what Claire Varland would advise, and that helped make the decision much easier.

She toed off her shoes, climbed back on the mattress, and rested against the trendy, chocolate-brown headboard that seemed to float above the bed. She'd only seen those on the home decorating channel, usually on those shows where the homeowner had a ridiculous amount of money to spend on their house and wanted to do it publicly to get a discount from endorsing appliance and paint brands. Still, the effect was even better in person than on TV.

What else had she missed in the real world while stuck in Bayou Bend?

Not that she could afford to see anything else "real." It wasn't like she could travel and spend her life like this—she wasn't even paying for it. And never could working at Sweetie Pies. If she won the competition, though, and moved to New York . . .

Her thoughts trailed, imagining life in a loft overlooking Central Park. Strolling through the shops she'd only read about, sipping coffee from a diner, and splurging on giant cinnamon rolls once a week before church. Finding inspiration for new recipes in the taste of the street vendors' wares, the aroma of blooming greenery in the park, the sound of children's laughter at FAO Schwarz.

She had to win this competition.

✑

Kat really had to lose this competition.

Lucas tossed his toiletry bag on the sink in the bathroom, hefted his suitcase on the bed—which looked way too soft for his taste—and began methodically removing everything inside. Socks and underwear in the top dresser drawer. Workout clothes in the second. Jeans in the third.

He hadn't meant to have an attitude on the taxi ride over, but nothing about this felt right. In fact, it felt a lot like losing.

He tossed his dress shoes on the floor of the closet and zipped his suitcase. He couldn't do this travel thing long-term. All the flying back and forth, the fancy hotel rooms with the miniature soaps that were more of a tease than an amenity. The complicated shower faucet and the bed with way too many pillows. How could Kat want this to be her life? Not that she wanted to live on the road, exactly, but she wanted to travel. See the world. Bake her way around it.

What was wrong with roots? With the same bed every night, sans decorative pillows? With plumbing he could install and repair himself?

New York would be more of the same. Who wanted smelly subways, disgusting street-vendor food, and the constant bustle of people? Too much concrete and not enough grass. Too much hype and not enough substance.

People needed dirt beneath their shoes.

He shut the dresser drawer and moved on to hanging up his button-down shirts. He'd brought a few nice ones at Kat's prompting, reminding him they'd have some free time tonight and after taping each day to hit the town. He didn't see why he couldn't hit it in a sweatshirt, but this was Kat's deal. He'd play along.

For now.

What about forever?

He tossed his ball cap on the striped armchair across the room and shoved his suitcase under the bed. He was getting too far ahead of himself again. The trip was just a few nights—not forever. And even if she won and went to New York, it was for a year. Not forever.

Yet he couldn't help but notice the increasing time span of each step. A few nights, a year . . . wasn't forever made up of days and weeks?

He wrenched back the multiple layers of burgundy curtains and looked out over the seven-story view of Los Angeles. Their hotel was only a few miles from Sunset Boulevard, where the producer had told Kat the studio was located. Well, off Sunset Boulevard, anyway, which was still enough to make Kat squeal at the prestige of it all. Man, he was out of luck. She didn't just have stars in her eyes as their plane had taxied the runway into LAX—she'd had entire galaxies.

Did he even stand a chance?

The sun glinted across the horizon, preparing for its nightly descent from the city. Too bad he couldn't escape as easily. Must be nice to disappear for a while and recharge. He personally wanted to turn on the sports channel, or maybe go run a few miles in the hotel gym—anything to pretend like he was still at home. Pretend like he wasn't hovering at a crossroads with Kat, holding his breath to see which road she'd choose.

Pretend like he could follow her regardless of which one she picked.

But the truth was he had about an hour until he had to meet Kat in the lobby for dinner. Hopefully, they'd find somewhere in town with a decent burger, though he had a feeling Kat was going to be in an uber-gourmet mood. So far, she'd seemed to be in live-it-up mode, and normally, he'd be right there with her. If this was a real vacation, he'd enjoy experimenting, watching the way she lit up at new discoveries, reveling in how beautiful she looked when she dared to branch out.

But it wasn't a real vacation. And the weight of what was potentially coming hung like an anvil over his head.

His cell beeped from his back pocket, and he pulled it out. A text from Darren.

Can't wait 2 see u in ur apron.

Loser. He snorted and typed back a response.

Just wait. ur time is coming.

Pretty sure it's not since I'm already married.

Lucas shook his head and grinned. *Rub it in.*

What's up w/blue? Thought real men wore pink.

Hilarious. I'll be sure to have Kat make you a spare.

Thanks Buddy. Have fun in the Golden State.

Easier said than done. But he didn't want to get into anything heavy through a text message. Will do. Don't start any fires while I'm gone. With a fire department as small as Bayou Bend's, even as chaplain, Darren still worked the line.

Same to you.

Ha. Words to live by. And knowing Darren, he'd said them with innuendo on purpose. He knew about Lucas's evolving feelings for Kat. But Darren was the one who had pushed Lucas toward getting married and settling down for years now . . . so what did he mean? He zipped back another text with a question mark. He had to know.

Song of Solomon 2:7

There was the chaplain he knew and loved. He was going to make him look it up.

Lucas sat down in the horribly uncomfortable, fancy armchair, then remembered he'd thrown his cap there and pulled it out from under him. He pulled up his phone browser, connected to the hotel's free WiFi, and Googled the reference.

"Do not stir up nor awaken love until it pleases."

Ha. Good one.

He turned off his phone.

eight

The wind was stronger than she'd expected. Kat tugged her coral-colored cardigan around her as they climbed out of the cab, grateful she'd opted for skinny jeans instead of a dress tonight. She still might regret the high heels, but she couldn't spend her first night in LA in her practical work shoes. Some blisters were worth it.

Lucas looked perfectly unaffected strolling beside her toward the restaurant, the wind threatening the bill of his cap and slightly ruffling the sleeves of his button-down shirt. When she reminded him to pack some nice clothes before they left town, she didn't think she'd need to remind him to leave the cap behind. Oh well. It was trademark Lucas.

Sort of like the smell of his cologne. The breeze kept wafting it right up her nose and straight into her heart. The memories of that scent could last her well into the night.

She turned her head to gain some distance physically and emotionally, wishing she could slip her fingers into Lucas's or at least hold on to his arm while they walked. They'd just done that a few days ago, as they'd always done, yet suddenly . . . it felt different. Forced.

Or worse, inviting.

Did he feel that awkwardness too? That shift? What had happened—nothing tangible, besides this trip together.

Maybe that was it.

"Kat?" The question in his tone nudged her, and she stopped as she realized he'd lagged behind. Maybe he felt the tension too. Maybe it wasn't a bad thing like she assumed, and she'd been holding back for no real reason. Maybe it was worth acknowledging, even worth a chance . . .

"You passed the restaurant." He gestured to the shiny gold-plated door he held open.

Oh. Right.

She followed him inside the dimly lit lobby, nearly stumbling into the hostess desk as she misjudged the distance. Maybe mood lighting wasn't as cracked up as she'd imagined it to be.

"Two?" The black-clad hostess—no wonder she hadn't seen her—smiled a straight white smile and gathered menus. "Right this way."

She followed the woman through the maze of tables, mostly set for two, toward the back of the restaurant and fought a swell of panic. Here it was. The candlelit table she'd been imagining since before they'd left home. She wasn't in her new dress—she'd save that for later in the trip, assuming she gathered the nerve to wear it in the first place—but the rest of the scenario was so far playing out exactly. The white linen napkin that it seemed a shame to spill anything on. The rosebud centerpiece. The uncomfortable, trendy chairs. The low murmur of other couples sharing intimate moments.

After they sat down, Lucas tugged his ball cap off his head and folded it into his back pocket. "Didn't realize this place was so fancy."

She set her clutch on the floor near her feet. Did he look uncomfortable because of the implied dress code or because of being alone with her? "It was a shot in the dark. The concierge at the hotel recommended it."

Not to mention it wasn't but a few miles from the hotel, so the cab fare was reasonable. She wasn't sure how this would play out—who paid for what. She fully intended to cover her own meal, but it didn't seem fair to let Lucas keep paying for the taxi rides, even if they were being reimbursed later. They were here for her, after all.

Well, they were here *for* her, but *because of* him. Maybe that was enough reason to split the difference.

If they were a couple, these questions wouldn't be nearly so complicated.

She spread her napkin on her lap, almost afraid to open the menu for fear the prices would match or supersede the environment.

No need. Lucas's eyes were already bugging. "The salad is fifteen dollars."

She shrugged. "That's not too bad."

"The *side* salad."

Oh. She flipped to the next page. *Definitely not getting the steak. Or the fish. Or the pasta.*

Maybe a small water and they could share that side salad.

The waitress came and brought their water—which looked to be sparkling—and rattled off the specials that sounded amazing but included buzzwords like *wine sauce* and *lobster* that Kat knew were too far out of reach for her checkbook. They asked for a minute to go over the menu and then went back to staring at the overpriced options.

"So are you excited about tomorrow?" Lucas leaned forward in his chair, accidentally bumping the table and sending Kat's fancy water dribbling over the side of her glass. She dabbed it with her napkin and waved off his apology.

"I'm sort of ready to just get it done so I don't have to be nervous anymore." She placed her napkin back in her lap. "But yeah, I'm a little excited." Maybe. Down deep, below the fear, the insecurity, and the full-out horror.

Why couldn't she tell him that? She used to be able to tell him anything—and did. She had zero secrets from her best friend.

Now she had a huge one. And he could never know.

"Good." He nodded, picking his menu back up before turning it over and setting it back down.

The awkward silence morphed into some kind of monster between them, and suddenly, Lucas didn't look like Lucas. He looked like a complete stranger sitting on a ball cap. The usually easy camaraderie between them seemed doused in vinegar. The candlelight cast strange shadows across his face, illuminating the five o'clock shadow he had yet to shave and highlighting his uncertainty.

He was miserable.

And so was she.

Yet he was enduring this for her. Always for her.

What kind of friend was she?

Enough of this. She grabbed her clutch and stood up, accidentally knocking into the tiny table. Lucas's glass tipped and righted itself, but not before a river of sparkling water doused their candle.

She refused to take that as a sign.

"What are you—" Lucas stared at her like she was crazy, and maybe she was. But she wasn't going to do this to either of them any longer.

She threw her napkin over the mess and pointed to the door. "Let's go."

She didn't have to tell Lucas twice. Somewhere between the table and the lobby, he donned his ball cap, then snagged a handful of mints from the hostess stand and held the door open for her.

He was back.

ceee

The second Kat spilled her water, Lucas fell in love all over again.

He fell a third time when she instructed the taxi driver to take them to the nearest McDonald's and bought them both Big Macs— large sized.

They stood outside, using the top railing of a black iron fence as a table, and laughed as they fought the Santa Ana winds threatening their french fry wrappers.

Lucas stuffed the last bite of his burger in his mouth and chewed quickly. "I owe you one. This beats an overpriced side salad any day." Nearby, a car horn honked, followed by a red convertible pulsing a deep bass beat all the way down the street. Two Rollerbladers whisked past their impromptu picnic spot, their neon green skates matching the streaks in their hair. They were certainly seeing a different side of LA than they would have in that stuffy restaurant, and while he still wasn't necessarily a fan, at least there was fresh air. And beef.

"No kidding." Kat's hair tangled across her face in the breeze, and she shook it back, but not before missing her mouth with one last ketchup-laden fry. He used a napkin to wipe the ketchup off her cheek for her, then balled it up and stuffed it in his empty burger container. "And you don't owe me anything. You've been paying for all the cabs." She started to say more but stopped, averting her gaze to follow a middle-aged couple strolling past them hand in hand. Man, he hated that. She used to tell him everything.

What went on behind those baby blues these days? Was she that worked up over the show? Though come to think of it, she'd been like that for a while now—since before the contest acceptance. Maybe her family had been getting to her for longer than he'd realized.

Or maybe she really was that eager to leave town.

He gathered up her trash. "Don't worry about it. You know we high school football coaches are rolling in the dough." He lobbed their garbage into a nearby can and picked up his cup for a last swig of soda.

"Right. Cookie dough, maybe." Kat grinned and slid the edge of her cup, thick with cold condensation, along the curve of his neck.

His heart lifted even as he fought back the involuntary shiver.

She was back. For a minute, anyway, and he'd take it. "I've told you not to start battles you can't finish." He grabbed for her, but she dodged his attempt with a squeal.

"Who says I can't finish this one?" Her eyes sparkled—even bluer than the stripes in her multicolored top—and carried a hint of challenge.

Game on.

He faked a lunge to the right, and as always, she fell for it. He was ready at the left when she sidestepped, and he spun her around and held her against him, ignoring the clawing grip she used on his forearm, and swiped his drink cup over her neck, cheek, and forehead.

She stumbled away, giggling and gasping for breath and dabbing at her face with her sleeve. "Not fair! I have on makeup." She checked her sleeve. "I used to, anyway."

"You don't need it." A standard argument of theirs. Maybe one day she'd listen. Or at least not care enough to have the debate. He grabbed her hand, tugging it away from the compact she fumbled with inside her purse. "I told you not to start something you can't finish."

Or maybe that's what he'd done.

He squeezed her hand, and she responded with the same pressure, sending a chill racing up his arm. Her gaze ran from their connected palms to his eyes, then away. "We should get back to the hotel. Need to get up early tomorrow for the big day."

And that was that.

He let her hand slip away, hating that it felt like he'd lost a whole lot more than the warmth of her fingers. "You're right. Let's head back." Or maybe . . .

They said the way to a man's heart was through his stomach, which was probably true enough, but he knew one surefire way into Kat's.

"Or we could get dessert first."

A slow smile started at the corners of her lips, and she tilted her head. "Cupcakes?"

"Over my dead body."

She snorted. "That can be arranged."

"Brownies?" Lucas didn't even have to hope. She had no idea how predictable she was. Or how adorable she was while being predictable, for that matter.

She licked her lips. "Okay, you've been pardoned. Bring it on."

Oh, he would. This wasn't over.

Not by a long shot.

nine

*Y*ou did finally make a decision on which recipes you would use this week, huh?"

Lucas dipped his spoon into the chocolaty glob, which the nearly deserted diner called a brownie. Kat preferred to think of it as one hot mess plated on the checkered table between them. Brownies should have some sort of form and texture. Substance. Consistency.

This was like fudge soup. With crumbs.

She set her spoon down on her napkin and started to answer his question, but he interrupted with another.

"You don't like the brownie, do you?" Lucas stopped midswipe for his next bite, and studied her, the corners of his mouth teasing into a grin. "And it has nothing to do with the taste."

"What do you mean?" She tucked her hair behind her ear and took a sip of her lemon water. She wasn't *that* predictable.

"You're mad that it's not following the rules."

On second thought, apparently she was.

"I know it doesn't make any sense." She stuffed her spoon into the mess and licked it, just to prove . . . something. "I'm the baker who experiments with new and crazy recipes almost every day."

"But you're also the baker who nearly had a panic attack when I

77

threw in those chocolate chips last minute. There's still a lot of order to your creativity." Lucas dug back into the so-called brownie, and she slowly followed suit. He had a point. She hated the confines that others constantly put her inside.

Yet she was terrified to leave them.

Talk about a hot mess.

She took another bite. The brownie tasted great, especially considering it came out of a hole-in-the-wall diner on the outskirts of Los Angeles. Who cared that it wasn't traditional? She, of all people, should appreciate that. And yet . . .

Sometimes she just wanted what she expected.

She darted a look at Lucas, who seemed too immersed in their dessert to notice anything odd lingering between them. Maybe it was just in her imagination. Once they'd started eating their burgers, they'd found their usual rhythm, even horsing around with their cups, and she had hoped that everything was normal. That their relationship hadn't actually tumbled down the rabbit hole à la *Alice in Wonderland.*

Yet she missed him. And on top of that, this strange part of her heart missed the parts of him that she'd never known.

"You never answered my question about the recipes." Lucas used his finger to steal the last drizzle of chocolate off their shared plate.

"You never let me." She quirked her eyebrow at him, just because she could and just because he hated it when she did.

"I think you're procrastinating now." He wiped his hands on a napkin and leaned back in his chair, pushing two legs up from the tiled floor. "You don't have a clue what you're going to bake, do you?"

"I have ideas." She finished her water to procrastinate further. She knew what her specialties were, knew which recipes she felt the most comfortable with, and knew which recipes were the safest.

She just didn't know which of those categories the judges would most appreciate.

"Besides, it seems like the rules vary from show to show." She signaled the waiter for their check, determined to pay for this—ahem—brownie, even though she'd also bought their dinner at McDonald's. She wasn't sure what she needed to prove, but she really didn't want to leave LA owing Lucas a thing.

The *why* of it all was what she refused to dwell on.

"Yeah, that one episode had the Mardi Gras theme." Lucas rocked back and forth slightly in his chair. How did he always do that without falling? If she even tried it, she'd be on her back on the greasy floor. She debated raising her eyebrow again just to even the score. "Which would have been perfect for you, representing Louisiana and all."

She wrinkled her nose. "Maybe. I don't do King Cake cupcakes, though. I'm not into people breaking their teeth on ugly plastic babies." And she hated anything with green icing. St. Patrick's Day was not her friend.

"Then there was the wildlife benefit episode." Lucas landed his chair on the floor as the waitress brought their check. "And the opera."

That could have been a fun one; she enjoyed music. "Don't forget the literary episode." The winning contestant had whipped up cupcakes representing *Jane Eyre*, several Jane Austen novels, and other classics that had inspired Kat to dust off her hardback copy of *Pride and Prejudice* and take a bubble bath.

"You'll figure it out. Don't worry." Lucas reached for the fake leather folder with the check on the table between them, and she lunged to intercept.

"I've got it."

He pulled it out of reach but not before she snagged the end with two fingers.

He tugged on his side of it. "Don't be ridiculous. You had dinner."

"You had the cab rides so far." She pulled harder.

"So what? This isn't a competition." He smiled, but it didn't quite reach his eyes. "That's tomorrow."

She refused to let go, unsure or unwilling to acknowledge why a knot of anxiety clogged her throat. "Let me pay."

"Seriously, it's a nine-dollar brownie and free water. It's all right." He tried to pry the folder from her hands and snorted back a laugh as she held on. "Kat." His brow furrowed as the struggle continued. "Kat?"

"I need to do this." Why did her voice sound so strangled? And were those tears? She swallowed, and the knot shifted slightly. "Please."

His grip lessened but didn't release as he lowered his voice. "Why is it so important?"

The panic swelled into a wave, and she hung on to the folder as though it were a life preserver. "Because."

Because . . . because the brownie wasn't really a brownie. And Lucas wasn't really Lucas anymore. Nothing was what it seemed or should be, and tomorrow would be even weirder. What if partnering in the competition caused even more strain between them? She already got the vibe that he didn't even want to be there.

Or what if she somehow, during the stress of taping and during the course of all their alone time over the next few days, revealed her feelings for him and lost her best friend? She couldn't *owe* him on top of that. She already depended on him too much as it was.

And as long as she did, he'd never see her as anything other than Kat, anyway. The girl next door who baked for his football team, had an age-questionable obsession with Sinatra, and spent more time with cupcakes than she did with real people.

The girl who couldn't even convince her own family to believe in her.

Her chest tightened, and she inhaled sharply. "Just let go."

And he did.

❧

Lucas couldn't sleep, and it wasn't because the bed was so soft.

He woke up for the third time from a fitful doze, pulled on his track pants and running shoes, and pocketed his key card before slipping down the carpeted hallway. Maybe a few miles on the gym's treadmill would clear his head, eliminate the echoes of conversation with Kat from their evening together—or at least make sense of her freak-out over the brownie bill. He still wasn't entirely sure what that had been about, but she'd avoided any further conversation about it afterward, so he had too.

He might not know a lot about women, but he knew enough to take their lead when it came to dodging awkwardness. If she didn't want to talk about it, he definitely didn't.

But he couldn't get the image of that panic in her eyes out of his head. He hurt for her, because something had made her hurt in those moments, and he didn't have a clue how to fix it.

He knew how he wanted to, but talk about increasing the awkward factor.

He swiped his key card to get into the gym, grabbed a complimentary towel, and draped it around his neck as he headed toward the exercise equipment overlooking the adjoining inside pool. He had figured he was the only one who'd be working out near midnight, but a lone swimmer cut laps in the water.

He guessed he wasn't the only one who was stressed and unable to sleep.

He warmed up, then cranked the treadmill speed up to a comfortable jog as he mentally ran through some plays for his team. Before him, through the glass window, the swimmer continued to make laps, one after the other, barely surfacing at each end before diving back under for another. Too bad some of his boys didn't have that same level of dedication on the field. Hopefully, they weren't slacking further in his absence.

He increased his speed to a full run, grateful for the endorphins distracting him from the weird evening. He should be able to sleep well after this—the last thing he needed was to be yawning and groggy on camera in a few hours. He'd give it another half mile, maybe a little more, and call it quits.

Swabbing his face with his towel, he dropped it back over the display screen and looked up just as the swimmer hoisted herself up to sit on the side of the pool.

A very familiar, brown-haired, red-swimsuit-clad swimmer.

His foot slapped the edge of the conveyor belt, and he tripped off the side, almost landing on the floor.

What was Kat doing up?

He sprung quickly to his feet, snagging his towel and shutting off the machine before limping his way to the pool door. His rolled ankle protested, but he refused to acknowledge it. He'd had enough sprains and breaks in his day to know his ankle wasn't either, but there'd be a good bruise reminding him of his blunder for weeks to come.

Not like he needed any more reminders to think of Kat.

She looked up in surprise as he joined her, sitting with his knees pulled up to keep his feet out of the water and making sure to keep plenty of space between the puddle of water forming around her and his own weakness.

"What are you doing up?" she said.

Falling off treadmills. "Couldn't sleep. Decided to run. You?"

She averted her eyes to the water, glistening under the fluorescent lights above. "Couldn't sleep. Decided to swim."

He averted his eyes, too, but not for the same reason she did. "I know you're nervous about tomorrow." Not nervous enough to pull that whole exchange over the diner bill earlier, but he wasn't going to bring that up if she wasn't. Kat knew he was there for her. If she needed him, she'd initiate it.

She always did.

"Not too much right now, but tomorrow, when they say 'action,' that's going to be a different story." She crossed her arms over her swimsuit, her hair sending rivulets of water down her bare arms.

He pulled off the hoodie he wore over his T-shirt and wrapped it around her shoulders—as much for his sake as for hers. "Do they still actually yell action and slap a clapboard?"

She tugged the sweatshirt closer. "Guess we'll find out."

"You're going to shine." He shifted positions to accommodate his ankle. "You always do."

A hint of color flushed her neck, and he relished in the fact he could still make her blush. If he ever lost that, well . . . he'd have lost a lot. She might not return the feelings he had for her—yet—but that telltale blush still meant he affected her, meant his opinion mattered. Meant she needed him.

Maybe he needed her just as much.

The revelation throbbed harder than the pain in his ankle, and he quickly stood up. "I should get to sleep."

"We both should." She stood as well, and started to hand him the hoodie.

"No!" He shook his head rapidly. "I mean, you keep it. For the walk back to your room." Even if she had clothes she'd brought down with her, it never hurt to have an extra layer. Especially the way she looked now, with her hair long and wet across her shoulders and her blue eyes striking against her makeup-free face.

She shrugged. "I'll walk with you. We're on the same floor."

How could he forget?

He returned his gym towel to the bin inside, then followed Kat to the elevator. She'd slipped some gym shorts over her swimsuit and kept the hoodie wrapped tight. "You really think I'll do okay tomorrow?"

He pressed the button to summon the elevator as Kat shivered beside him. "You're going to be so busy that I bet the cameras will sort of fade away after a while. We won't have time to be nervous."

"We?" She grinned as the doors opened and they stepped inside the deserted elevator. She jabbed the button for the seventh floor. "So you *are* nervous."

He crossed his arms, wishing he hadn't implied that hint of truth. The last thing she needed was to feed off the little bit of his anxiety that kept popping up. He wasn't camera shy, but this was actual TV, so it was more like didn't-want-to-do-something-stupid-in-front-of-a-percentage-of-the-country shy. "Nah. Don't think so hard about this."

He should probably take his own advice.

The numbers above the doors ticked toward seven. One. Two.

Kat watched them, and shivered again.

"Come here, you're freezing." Before he could think, he pulled her into a warm hug, just like he'd have always done without a second thought.

Except there was a lot of thought. Like about how she still fit so perfectly into his embrace.

Floor three.

How she let out a little contented sigh as her head tucked against his shoulder.

Floor four.

How the pool water from her swimsuit soaked through the front of his T-shirt in a matter of seconds.

Floor five.

How her hair smelled like strawberries with a hint of chlorine.

Floor six.

He closed his eyes and held her tighter. Maybe the elevator would get stuck.

Ding.

He really hated losing.

ten

The studio was bigger than it looked on television. A *lot* bigger—and brighter. Hopefully she brought enough concealer. Between stressing over the taping and reliving Lucas's extended hug in the elevator, Kat had barely slept.

She covered a yawn with her right hand, peeking at her watch on her left arm at the same time. Seven thirty-five. Her late night swim had done little to clear her head, and Lucas's compassionate attention had only amped up her nerves.

Why did everything have to get so complicated between them?

"Is it bright in here, or is it just me?" Lucas squinted at the fluorescent canned lighting shining down from the metal ceiling. Giant microphones on long sticks—they probably had a more technical name, but she had no clue what—protruded from stands, set up at various intervals around the judges' table and six stainless-steel cooking areas.

Wait. Six? There were usually four. What was that about?

She frowned and turned away from the stations and what appeared to be a sound crew making last-minute adjustments, trying not to imagine herself behind one of those very counters, creating epic failures in hot pink wrappers. "No, it's not just you. It's bright." Definitely needed more concealer.

Now that they'd signed in, the producers were letting them get a peek at the floor before heading to the dressing rooms for makeup touch-ups and preshow interviews. That's also when she and Lucas would finally meet the rest of the contestants. She had no idea which of the other people she'd seen at the hotel might be on the show too. So far here, she'd seen only the back of one girl's head, a mass of curly black hair gathered into two bunchy pigtails.

"They better not come at me with a makeup brush." Lucas shifted Kat's tote bag of personal essentials that he'd insisted on carrying for her to his other arm, his eyes scanning the wide room as rapidly as Kat's.

She tucked the cord of her hair straightener back into the top of the tote where it had escaped. "If you don't let them, then *you'll* be bright."

He smirked. "I'm okay with that."

"You won't be when you see the show. You'll be lighting up like Rudolph once you start sweating under these lights."

"I have no problem guiding a sleigh as long as I'm not wearing makeup." He shoulder-bumped her playfully, and she bumped him back, momentarily distracted by the memory of those arms being around her in the elevator. His warmth had seeped in much deeper than surface level, and despite the pool water still clinging to her suit, she'd heated right up. How did he not feel it? And if he did, why didn't he say anything? Maybe he had his own list of reasons like she did.

Or maybe it was just in her head, and she'd ruin everything if she even mentioned it.

She eased away from his playful touch. "We better find the others." And try to shift her focus to the fact that in a few minutes, she'd be on her way to achieving a lifelong dream—leaving Bayou Bend in her powdered-sugar wake and baking any recipe she wanted for a prestigious bakery. She had to concentrate.

Her future depended on the next few days.

They turned back to the pencil-thin, smiling assistant who'd accompanied them to the studio after they had arrived at the building by taxi. "This way."

They followed her down a maze of hallways to a door with a giant red cupcake hanging on the front. "Go on in. There will be someone to help with your makeup, and you can change if you want to. Plenty of dressing screens." The assistant kept smiling. "See you on the set!"

How was someone so perky that early in the morning without clutching a cup of coffee?

As the assistant strolled away, Kat stared at the door. A red cupcake had never seemed so intimidating, and she'd messed up her share of red velvets before. They were tricky to master, especially texture-wise. Hopefully that wasn't a sign. She gestured to Lucas. "You first."

He somehow managed to frown and grin at the same time. "You know my mama taught me better than that."

It was just a decoration cupcake. Yet hesitancy froze her hand on the knob. Somehow, once she opened this door, everything turned real. Stage makeup. Dressing screens. A different world resided on the other side of this cupcake. A world of glitter and flounce and fame. Padded vanity stools. Multibulb, trifold mirrors. Gourmet hors d'oeuvres.

This was a big moment.

"It's a door, Kat. Not a magic portal." Lucas nudged her in the back, and she reluctantly twisted the knob.

Chaos greeted with all the charm of a disgruntled hostess. Contestants sat on canvas folding chairs in front of square-cut mirrors hanging on the wall above gleaming white vanity tables. The assistants, wearing red T-shirts, dabbed at contestants' faces with fluffy makeup brushes, while behind one solid black dressing screen, a pair of sweatpants suddenly flew over the top and nearly landed on a woman rushing by with a curling iron cord streaming in her wake, her left arm clad in a sleeve of tattoos. On a side table sat a tray of pastries and fresh fruit.

Definitely not a portal.

Though if Cinderella's fairy godmother had a storage room, this might be it. Sort of half-glamorous, half-realistic preparation.

"There's a chair over here." A Red Shirt gestured with a makeup compact behind her. "You'll be next."

At the moment, she wasn't sure she wanted to be at all. Judging by the amount of blush being applied on the blonde contestant's round cheeks, Kat might be better off letting Lucas do her makeup. She clutched her purse like a shield, ducking instinctively as a button-down shirt flapped over the dressing screen from the corner of her eye. She spun just in time to avoid being blasted with hairspray.

"I'm going to wait in the hall." Lucas's voice sounded strangled as he practically shoved the tote bag into Kat's hands. "Too much . . . you know."

She raised her eyebrow. "Hairspray?"

"Estrogen."

He bailed.

Lucky.

She slowly settled into the empty folding chair, pulling out her makeup bag while avoiding looking directly into the mirror. So this was Hollywood. Wouldn't Stella be surprised? Though knowing her beauty queen sister, she'd somehow manage to wrangle her own room complete with gold sequined star.

Enough of that. *She* was here, not Stella. And Kat deserved to be.

Or at least Lucas thought so.

It would have to be enough.

"You ready?" A smiling Red Shirt appeared at her side in the mirror, and Kat dared to look at her reflection. A little pale, and a little shiny. She could use the help.

She took a deep breath. "Yeah. I'm ready."

Ready or not.

⁓

He'd never been tempted to smoke before, but after leaving that hairspray-ladened, female-crowded dressing room, Lucas suddenly considered the appeal. How did those women even breathe in there?

He shoved away from the wall and began to pace, trying to focus on the upcoming show. He was already wearing what he'd be wearing, sans apron, and he sure enough wasn't letting anyone near him with that powdery stuff on a brush. Hopefully Kat wouldn't let the workers make her over into something fake for the cameras. She already shone enough on her own, and he wasn't referencing the Rudolph conversation from earlier. She didn't need all the extra.

He couldn't wait to see her in that apron.

The door opened, and a collegiate-looking girl in a red T-shirt motioned him inside. "We're about to brief."

Hopefully, it would *be* brief.

He followed her inside, sucking in a last gulp of hallway air before succumbing to the inevitable.

He quickly located Kat standing in the back of the room, next to another set of contestants in hot pink T-shirts and jeans. *Good, she got next to some of the few Normals.* He meandered through the crowd and the haze to her side.

"Coward." She nudged him, and he nudged her back on instinct. "Jealous."

She wrinkled her nose, and he laughed out loud. Man, he knew her.

And he was right about how cute the apron looked. At least they hadn't turned her into a clown. Besides some extra brown stuff smeared on her eyelids, she looked like Kat.

With glossy lips.

89

He turned his attention to the suited man in the center of the room—the slick-haired host he'd watched too many times on TV. "Attention, please. I'm Sam Carson—as you all know." He winked. Lucas bit back a groan. The only thing worse than the dude's hair was his arrogance.

And that was saying something.

"We here at *Cupcake Combat* have a surprise for you." He spread his arms dramatically, the sleeves of his black jacket riding up and revealing a shiny silver watch. "You might have noticed in the studio that this episode's setup is for six teams instead of four. Well, I can assure you, it's not because we miscounted."

A nervous chuckle rose from the group, and something cinched in Lucas's stomach. He didn't like surprises—especially not where Kat was concerned. What was this guy up to?

"And as I'm sure you noticed from your itinerary, we're spending five days taping. What you might not have realized is that five days is not usual for our typical hour-long show."

Just get to the point, Slick. Lucas shifted his weight impatiently.

"That's because . . ." He paused for effect, and Lucas swore every person in the room leaned forward an inch. "This is a special, three-hour holiday episode to celebrate our fifth anniversary on the air."

A collective gasp rose from the gathered contestants. Beside him, Kat stiffened like a coiled spring. An anniversary episode—with three times the airtime. Wow. Well, that explained the change in the grand prize. His thoughts raced with the implications, and he could sense Kat's blood pressure rising beside him like a rogue hot-air balloon.

She was going to kill him.

"We'll be taping over a period of five partial days, ending with the big championship round. And just stay prepared. There might be more surprises along the way." Sam's jubilant expression proved he enjoyed freaking out people whose nerves were already on edge to start with. Figured.

Kat's fingers clamped around his arm and squeezed, her nails digging into his flesh. He adjusted her grip with his free hand, squeezing back to reassure her. She still had this in the bag, if she wanted it badly enough. This new element didn't really change anything, right? Except, well, he supposed it did up the prestige of the win a little. And it lowered the odds of winning because of the extra teams competing.

Okay, no wonder she was squeezing so hard. He felt like kicking himself in the rear end. How could he have put them in this position? Of all the times for him to miscalculate a play.

But the game wasn't over. It hadn't even started yet. They were still in it.

And his ultimate goal still had a chance.

Unless, of course, Kat decided she never wanted to speak to him again after this.

"That said, I'd like everyone to introduce themselves. Just your name, team name, and home state is plenty for now." Sam rubbed his hands together and waggled his shaggy eyebrows like an overly dramatic, classic movie villain. "And remember, this is *Cupcake Combat*. This is war. So if you're inspired to create any friendly—or not so friendly—competition for the cameras, even better."

Everyone chuckled on cue, voices still shaky from the shock of the announcement. Lucas tried to force a smile and not roll his eyes at Sam's corny script. He guessed his previous questions about how *real* reality shows were behind the scenes were about to be answered.

He vaguely tuned in as the team at the front of the room wearing bandanas tied around their heads talked about motorcycles and cupcakes from Florida. They stood next to two women who had so many tattoos that it was hard to determine where the ink stopped and clothes began.

"Here."

He looked down just as Kat thrust the apron at him, the blue fabric trembling in her shaky grip. How could he forget? The moment of truth. He slowly began to cinch the thing around his jeans and gray T-shirt, almost wishing he could trade it for a tattoo instead.

She smoothed out the front of it for him as she whispered, "Tie it tight. Don't want to lose it."

No, that would be tragic.

Though her touch across his chest made the whole apron thing a little worth it.

"So we've heard from Chops and Michelle of the team Real Bakers Ride Bikes, and farmers John and Sarah from We Grow Cupcakes, as well as from tattoo artists Hallie and Gemma from Inky Dots." Sam pointed with two fingers to the ladies in hot pink next to Kat. "Next?"

"We're sisters from Mississippi." The ladies spoke in unison, their voices as oversize as their hot pink fingernails. "Tameka and Tonya." They looked at each other and laughed, white teeth a gleaming contrast against their bright T-shirts.

The larger one nudged the other in the side, probably indicating she wanted to talk by herself. "I'm Tameka, and Tonya's acting as my assistant for the show. We own an online business called Classy Cupcakes." The smaller sister then gestured to her T-shirt where the words were printed in a cursive script.

"Welcome." Sam pointed to Kat. "And you are?"

She sucked in her breath, and Lucas put his hand on her back to steady her. "I'm Kat and this is Lucas. We're from Louisiana."

Good girl. Her voice didn't even quiver.

"Not Your Mama's Cupcakes." Sam read the front of Lucas's apron, and the smile in his eyes seemed to turn genuine for a moment. "Nice. Very catchy."

Kat relaxed slightly under his touch, and Lucas felt a twinge of guilt. Maybe the guy wasn't as bad as he initially thought. He probably shouldn't go solely off first impressions—

"But I guess we'll let the judges decide that, huh?"

Kat's smile wobbled, and Lucas wondered what would happen if he decked a host. No, it'd be pointless—his fist would probably just slip right through all that grease in Sam's hair.

"Hey, Sam? Thanks for saving the best for last."

The snarky female tone sounded from across the room. Lucas leaned around the guy in the Harley vest and red bandana to see who had spoken. Oh, yeah—the girl with the curly black pigtails they'd seen briefly in the studio earlier. Kat had pointed out then how cute the girl's hair looked, though Lucas sort of always figured pigtails were only cute on three-year-olds toting lollipops. She was standing next to a thin blonde girl, and they both wore fluffy purple tutus and some kind of weird patterned leg warmers or whatever those things were called. They looked like their combined ages had to be less than his own.

"We're college roommates, from New York." The pigtailed girl jabbed her thumb at her chest, the series of neon bracelets on her arm jangling as she gestured. "I'm Piper, and this is Amanda." The blonde lifted one hand in a tentative wave. "We're the Icing Queens."

"Best for last, huh?" Sam sized them up with a dimpled grin and rocked back on the heels of his shiny dress shoes. "You might have to prove it."

Piper crossed her arms over her sequined black tank top and lifted her chin. She'd have been pretty if not for the too-dark eye makeup and the attitude. "Not a problem."

The room erupted into whispers as the other teams reacted to the sudden shark among them. Lucas rubbed his hands over his face, wishing he could magically transport both him and Kat back to Bayou Bend where they belonged. How exactly had he ended up here, in an apron, surrounded by baking bikers and cocky college students and colors so bright they shouldn't be allowed in public?

"They're either really good, or they are just trying to compensate for being really bad." Kat whispered up at him, uncertainty lacing her voice. She hadn't stopped frowning since Sam's anniversary announcement.

"Nah. Those girls are hardly a threat." He leaned down to whisper back, grateful for the excuse to be closer to her. "Look—they had to reinvent the 1980s because they completely missed them the first time."

Kat snorted and elbowed him in the side, a giggle escaping through her nerves.

He straightened with a smile. He'd made her laugh. That was all that mattered.

He just hoped he was right.

eleven

The stage lights threatened to melt her makeup. A drop of sweat trickled down Kat's back beneath her T-shirt and apron, and she clenched her hands into fists before flexing her fingers and trying to relax them atop her baking counter. This was it. Showtime.

Well, eventually, anyway. The teams were all in place at their stations, waiting on instructions for the first round as Sam held a whispered conference in the wings with a man in frayed jeans, a button-down shirt, and worn flip-flops—a man who apparently held more authority than his wardrobe indicated. The director, maybe?

All around them, cameramen lurked, tinkering with their equipment, downing coffee, and looking bored. So this was showbiz. She'd have to tell Stella, though she sort of had the feeling if Stella were here, the cameramen would no longer be bored.

The judges, perched on shiny silver stools behind a waist-high table at the front of the room, sipped from Coca-Cola bottles and joked among themselves. Easy for them to do—they were about to get free cupcakes and make people cry. The contestants had already been introduced briefly to the panel of judges, whom Kat felt she already knew just from her hours invested in the show.

There was Dave Donaldson, whose belly protruding between

his trademark suspenders gave testament to his love of pastries. But the silver mustache and grandpa-type appearance hid a master pastry chef whose opinion had been sought and respected in the industry for decades. He'd started several successful businesses and had his own show a few years back. His opinion mattered, and while he wasn't as harsh as some of the judges in his comments, he was firm. If he looked Kat in the eye and told her that her cupcakes weren't up to par, she might never recover.

Then in the middle of the table was Georgiana Britt, a middle-aged famous chef and author of multiple best-selling, gluten-free recipe books, including a weight-loss book that had rocketed off the charts. Her fiery red hair and boisterous voice were entertaining to watch—she was definitely the judge who seemed to have the most fun on the show. But her quick wit and honest opinion could slice deeper than a carving knife. Kat would hate for those clever barbs she usually enjoyed on TV to be directed her way.

And of course, at the end of the table sat Thad Holson, the attractive, pinstriped-wearing, preppy judge in his late thirties whom Lucas had joked about not liking last time they'd watched an episode together at her house. Or maybe he'd been serious. The judge was a little cocky, but he was the best in the business. He owned Bloom bakery in New York, so he'd more than earned the right to be confident.

Could she really be potentially baking for his shop one day soon?

The tension in Kat's shoulders doubled, and she arched her neck, wishing for a massage. Or caffeine. Or a headache pill.

Or maybe just a flight home.

"It helps to breathe."

Lucas's sudden voice in her ear tingled, and Kat jumped, gripping the counter before her. She whirled and pounded Lucas on the shoulder. "Don't do that." Her heart thundered beneath her apron.

"You can't win a competition if you pass out." He picked up a blank index card they were allowed to make notes on during the show, and fanned her face with it. "You've got this, Kat."

"You shouldn't lie to your wife." Piper breezed past, so close her flouncy tutu brushed against Kat's arm.

"He's not my—"

"She's not my—"

Kat and Lucas looked at each other, then at Piper, who raised her dark eyebrows and smirked. "Whatever. Bottom line is, he lied. You don't have this. We do." She gestured to her teammate—Amanda, if Kat remembered correctly—who just stood there and spun a strand of her blonde hair around her finger, smiling as if they were all best friends. Apparently Piper hadn't filled her buddy in on the mean-girl game plan.

It would have been almost funny if Kat didn't fear so badly that Piper was right.

"Back off, Pigtails." Tameka—or Tonya? One of contestants from Mississippi in the hot pink bustled her way between them, towering over Piper. "You ain't being very classy."

Piper didn't flinch. She just crossed her arms and looked up in the bigger woman's face with a cool smile. "You focus on being classy. I'll focus on winning." She leaned around Tameka and pointed at Kat. "Which means beating you first."

Before Kat could react, all three women had gone back to their stations, Amanda still twirling her hair and Tameka huffing about "some people."

Lucas rubbed his hands over his eyes, then looked down at Kat and blinked. "What just happened here? That was worse than high school."

Maybe *his* experience in high school. This fit hers just about right, but Lucas hadn't grown up in the shadows of the family tree that she had.

Kat snatched the index card from his hand and began fanning herself faster. "Who knows? Women can be catty." To put it mildly.

At least Tameka had stood up for her, though the fact that someone had to rubbed Kat a little raw. Why couldn't she be the girl who always knew what to say, always had the right timing?

In her head, she was so much more than she was in person.

She just never seemed able to pull it out at the right time.

"That wasn't catty. That was ridiculous." Lucas paced behind their workstation, his voice low. "Who does she think she is? Some college-aged punk—"

"Let it go." She fanned faster. No point in dwelling on it. She wasn't here to make enemies; she was here to make a good impression. With cupcakes. Not with clever retorts.

Then why did she feel so slighted? And small?

Lucas persisted, his voice rising. "But she's trying to get in your head. It's not fair. That's such an unsportsmanlike way to compete."

She shushed him, and he lowered his voice an octave. "Sorry. I'm just saying—"

"Lucas. I'm fine. Seriously." Always her protector. She loved him for it.

And hated that she needed it so badly.

She dared a glance across the room at Piper, who was already staring at her. Kat looked quickly away, determined to ignore the girl's pathetic attempts to psych her out.

Attempts that were maybe working just a bit.

"Sorry if I made it worse. I just don't get people like that—and I'm as competitive as they come." Lucas leaned against the counter beside her, effectively blocking her view of the Icing Queens. "Once we start baking, everything should settle down."

"If we ever do." She fanned herself again with the note card. Why wouldn't the director hurry up already? They'd been standing here at least an hour waiting for the taping to start. And earlier someone on the Red Shirt staff had mentioned candid interviews before they broke for lunch. At this rate, would they even tape before lunch? Her stomach growled, and she pressed her hand against it to stifle the noise.

"She got to you, didn't she?" The question came out more like a statement, like Lucas didn't even really have to ask. Just knew.

Was she that transparent? That obvious? If so, no wonder Piper had pounced on her. She was like a walking, apron-clad target.

She couldn't answer honestly without giving herself away, or at best, without tearing up. And she couldn't lie to Lucas; he'd never believe her anyway.

Thankfully, at that moment, Sam broke away from the man in flip-flops and called for everyone's attention. "We're about to start taping. Thanks for your patience, guys."

Someone from the back of the group snorted, and someone else giggled as if Sam had made a joke. Clearly, nerves were shot through-out the room. Kat struggled to take a deep breath, and avoided glancing at the cameras that began rolling into position around them. Hopefully not every day would be this nerve-racking. Once she got into baking mode, would she forget about the cameras? Or would they remain a constant, nagging presence in the back of her mind?

"Welcome to *Cupcake Combat*. I'm your host, Sam Carson, and tonight is a special three-hour episode celebrating our fifth anniversary." Sam breezed through the intro on the first take, plastic hair and smile firmly in place as he clasped his hands in front of him. "Our theme today in honor of our anniversary is We Love Cupcakes. Each round will feature a different element of love, and what better way to start than by acknowledging how love is all too often a circus?"

The cameras panned back, and focused on a display table to Sam's left, where a red tent and mini stuffed animals sat encircled inside a striped hula hoop.

"In this round, our contestants will use inspiration from the Big Top to represent how love is a circus. Ready teams?" He grinned, and Kat's heart raced into overdrive. "Everything you need is here in the stocked kitchen to my right. You may use anything you find on these shelves to help you create your masterpieces. Remember, in this round, decorations are scored the highest. So don't hold back."

Kat's heart constricted as Sam gestured to the giant ticking clock mounted on the wall above the judges' table. "On your mark . . . get set . . . go!"

The teams ran simultaneously toward the kitchen area as one big, cupcake-fueled herd. Lucas stayed at Kat's side as she began frantically pilfering through the shelves. "What am I even looking for?" She couldn't think. Could barely talk. Her fingers fumbled on the boxes of supplies.

"Stop and think, Kat." Lucas's low voice briefly grounded her. "What's your plan for recipes? Think about the theme first."

The theme. What was the theme? Circus. Yes. And love. Her thoughts scattered as her eyes roamed the contents of the shelves before her. Maraschino cherries. Pickles. Radishes.

This wasn't helping.

"What about peanut butter?"

She heard Lucas talking, making suggestions, but his words came through as if from a tunnel. Around her, the other teams had already gathered ingredients and were heading back to their stations. The beep of ovens being heated up filled her ears like a warning bell. She couldn't freeze up now. But what happened to her creativity? All she could picture was a burnt, naked cupcake on a plate before a scowling judge.

"Kat." Lucas grabbed her shoulders and spun her to face him. She closed her eyes, unwilling to see the disappointment on his face at her failure—or maybe afraid of finding pity instead.

"Look at me."

She couldn't ignore him. She opened her eyes, wishing whoever had put that cement block on her chest would take it off. It was hard to breathe.

But there was no condemnation. No judgment. And no pity.

Just Lucas, smiling, like he had every time he'd eaten any of her cupcakes.

"You're in your kitchen, and I'm sitting at the bar. You're asking me what you should put into this next batch."

His words washed over her, and she could immediately picture the scene. She closed her eyes again, this time to focus. Lucas, with his pile of magazines, rocking back on two legs of the stool and teasing her about ingredients. Pushing her. Making her consider combinations even she hadn't thought about putting together.

The panic subsided, and the answer came. "Peanut butter. You're right. And animal crackers." She opened her eyes and began pulling supplies from the shelves as images of the circus filled her mind. "And caramel. And chocolate chips."

Lucas's smile widened, and his evident rush of pride toward her sent her sailing on air back to her workstation, arms almost as full as her heart.

She became briefly aware of the cameramen taping Sam's entire intro a second time, probably from different angles, but managed to tune them out as she began measuring flour into a cup and dumping it into the mixing bowl. No time for distractions. They only had forty-five minutes to make three identical, super cute, super impressive cupcakes—one for each judge.

Lucas jumped in beside her, handing her utensils before she even asked and anticipating her next move as they prepared the batter. She darted a glance at him from the corner of her eye as they worked.

Maybe she really did have this.

ceees

Lucas had a new respect for his chaplain friend Darren, and a new understanding of what the guy went through daily—putting out fire after fire and trying to smile the entire way through it because everyone looked to him for strength.

He peeked inside the refrigerator, tested a cupcake with the back of his wrist, then shut the door with a thud. Still too warm for the icing. He signaled Kat across the room, who was busy sorting animals from the package of crackers they'd nabbed from the kitchen. Apparently it was harder than they'd thought to find ones with all their hooves and paws intact.

He leaned against the side of the fridge, eyes warily raking over the room as contestants finished decorating their creations, every muscle in his body tense and ready to react. He couldn't relax. First there'd been Piper's flare-up of jealousy, or pride, or whatever the heck that had been before they started taping. Tameka had helped douse that one, thankfully, since Lucas had been too shocked initially to respond. Then again, there wouldn't have been much he could have said that would have been appropriate in the first place. Too bad this wasn't the football field, where you could take your aggression out in the form of a legit tackle.

Piper would have been flat on her tutu in no time.

Then there'd been Kat's near panic attack in the stockroom. He knew she'd been nervous, but he hadn't expected a full-out episode. She'd been too close to losing it—which just showed winning this competition meant more than it should. Of course, Piper had only contributed to her stress, which wasn't fair.

Man, he needed to get out of this estrogen-laden kitchen. He and the other two males on the teams did not make enough testosterone to counteract all this.

He pulled the cupcakes from the fridge and turned just in time to avoid hitting the Harley guy's arm with the tray as he rushed past. "Sorry, man." The bandana-wearing biker smiled as he jumped out of the way. "My fault."

Lucas apologized in return as he toted the tray of cooled-off cupcakes to Kat's workstation. Something was definitely wrong when a biker and a football coach could get along better than two women.

It was going to be a long week. He really hated to admit that he had a feeling the fires weren't out yet.

And he really, really hated to admit that all of this was his fault. He'd put them there, and it hadn't even accomplished what he'd hoped. If anything, it had made Kat even more insecure and unsure of herself, and it was causing strain between them because of their proximity to each other. He could only continue to hide his intentions for so long.

What would happen when *that* particular buzzer sounded?

A horn honked, and Lucas jumped, nearly dropping the tray of cupcakes on the workstation in front of Kat as Sam waved a bicycle horn from the front of the studio. "Ten minutes!"

Kat mumbled something that sounded an awful lot like a word he'd never heard her say and then grabbed the icing bag. "Quick, make sure the crackers are ready for the top. When I finish icing, stick one upright in the middle and put the caramel corn around him."

Right. He could do that. He grabbed the bag of crackers. "Rhino or elephant?"

She shot him a look that not only proved she could not care less but that he was less than genius for asking. Fair enough. Moving on.

"What about the flag?" He'd cut those out of red fondant and assembled them on toothpicks.

"Flags go last. Right in the middle."

He was grateful she had skipped past the panic mode she'd been stuck in earlier, but this bossy mode was starting to wear thin too. He'd tease her about it later, though, and they'd laugh. Only Kat could go from insecure wallflower to instruction-shouting diva in the space of forty-five minutes. But she'd apologize, and he'd be reminded for the thirteenth time that minute why he felt so much—

"Lucas? Today. Today would be great." Kat looked up from her death grip on the icing bag, jerking her head toward the cupcakes still cooling between them.

Right.

He quickly passed the cupcakes to Kat, and after she swirled buttercream icing on each one, he stuck them on the judges' plates.

She dropped the icing bag on the counter and wiped her hands on her frosting speckled apron. "Grab the crackers. I've got the caramel corn."

103

"Wait. The rhino lost his leg." He held up the decrepit animal and its missing limb in both hands.

"Then find an elephant." Kat began pawing through the remaining crackers that lay on a napkin on the counter. "Or a monkey."

"There aren't any monkeys." He helped her search, wincing as a sheep head broke under his thumb. "Camel?" Her anxiety was getting contagious, as was the ticking clock and their mostly naked cupcakes.

"Here's a tiger. No, wait, it's a bear."

He fought the delirious urge to add "oh my" to the end of her sentence, figuring all he'd get for his wit would be leftover icing shot into his face.

Piper drifted slowly, intentionally, by their workstation, hands clasped behind her back, humming the *Jeopardy* theme song.

Kat's eyes darted to Piper, then to Lucas, and the anxious sheen in her gaze shot right through to his stomach. The diva had exited stage left, and the wallflower had returned. "Hurry."

Any frustration over her earlier bossiness drifted, and Lucas focused on the cupcakes before him. Forming an assembly line, they finished decorating with one minute to spare.

He slapped her a high five, wishing he could just pull her into a hug instead, but if he did he might not let go. "You did it, Kat." She'd pulled off the first round—against all odds, considering her shaky start.

She sagged against the counter, shooting a careful glance back at the judges' plates, and offered a weary grin. "No, we did it."

A smile broke through his hesitation. *We.* His personal favorite pronoun of the day.

He squeezed her hand and tugged her away from the counter. "Go line up. It's all you."

For now.

twelve

*W*ould the judges deduct points if she threw up on camera?

Kat clenched her fists at her sides in an effort to avoid clutching her churning stomach, wrought with nerves as she stood before the judges. Just moments ago, she'd been so proud of her circus cupcake creation—largely because of the pride lingering in Lucas's eyes when he'd smiled at her and told her she'd done it.

She wouldn't have made it without him. As evidenced by her near breakdown in the stockroom. If he hadn't pulled her back from the edge, she'd have likely wound up lying unconscious in a heap on the floor, a can of pickles in one hand and a peanut butter jar in the other.

Piper circling like a shark around Kat's finished product hadn't helped her confidence level, nor did the catty glances the younger girl blasted her way from down the line of contestants.

Kat glanced over her shoulder at Lucas, who stood with the other baking assistants in front of the deserted workstations, and drew in the warmth of the lazy thumbs-up he shot her. How did he do that—exude confidence and security? They radiated from him in waves. Part of her wanted to follow him around and absorb the confidence.

The other half just wanted to knock it out of him with a rolled-up newspaper so he could understand what it was like to be her.

She turned back to the judges, intentionally ignoring the laser-beam stare Piper kept shooting into the side of her face, and waited for someone to yell "action." Once again, each step was taking forever to shoot. No wonder they'd allotted five partial days of taping for a three-hour show.

And if Sam had the makeup team powder his face one more time, she might be tempted to shove a cupcake in it.

The judges seemed used to the delays, though, as they chatted back and forth and laughed easily. Georgiana's trademark chuckle seemed to begin in her toes and rise upward, and the warm sound eased a bit of the tension in Kat's neck and shoulders. They were just people, people who loved cupcakes and had made a living involving their passion. Wasn't that what Kat was trying to do too? Accomplish and live out her dream?

It had worked for them. Maybe it could work for her.

Hope rose like a fragile blossom, desperate for sun. She closed her eyes and took a deep breath.

When she opened them, Thad's eye caught hers from behind the judges' table, and his smile broadened. Blushing, Kat looked away, embarrassed to be caught daydreaming. He probably found her nearly tangible nerves amusing, though surely she wasn't the most anxious contestant they'd ever had. She'd seen one episode where a contestant had stumbled forward, nearly fainting during this portion of the show, and been caught by the baker next to her. And that one time when the male contestant had stuttered so badly during his description of his cupcake entry that Sam had to ask him to repeat himself.

On second thought, why hadn't they edited that part out? Clearly they allowed time for double or even triple takes on everything else.

Sam's words from earlier in the dressing room repeated in her ears. *So if you're inspired to create any friendly—or not so friendly—competition for the cameras, even better.*

If competitive banter was encouraged, then embarrassing moments must be downright coveted for ratings.

Great.

She shifted her weight on her feet, peripherally glancing at the other bakers. Maybe that was Piper's angle. Trying to get more camera time, her fifteen minutes of fame, by stirring up drama and tension. But why pick on Kat? Why not target one of the other contestants? Was she truly Piper's biggest threat?

The thought simultaneously filled and drained her hopes.

She looked back at the panel once more, hoping to catch something else from the judges' expressions to ease her thundering heartbeat.

Thad was still watching her, eyes narrowed in consideration as if sizing her up.

Great. Her hope blossom slowly withered and died.

"And, *action!*"

Finally, the magic words that stilled the set and straightened the judges' shoulders. Sam introduced the next portion of the show, and motioned for Tameka, the first one in line, to present her cupcake.

The bigger woman flashed what was quickly becoming her trademark grin. "The circus always makes me think of peanuts, so we concocted a peanut butter, dark chocolate cupcake with almond buttercream icing and peanut brittle on top." The cameraman zoomed in on the cupcake sitting in front of Georgiana. "We decorated it with a fondant bear and a hula hoop, juggling peanuts."

Juggling peanuts? How in the world? Kat squinted, grateful for the TV screens off to the side of the set that showed what was currently being taped for the segment. Oh, cute. She'd used clear plastic toothpicks to hold up peanuts in staggered heights around the bear.

Her awe faded into uncertainty. Would her animal cracker topping be enough to impress?

The judges forked off a piece of the cake while everyone in the room held their collective breath. Kat's stomach dipped into her shoes, and it wasn't even her invention on the line. How would she survive potentially five days of this?

Then again, how would she survive if she got sent home and didn't even get to survive five days? Her mind darted in circles like the dang hula-hooping bear.

"Judges?"

Dave wiped his mouth with a napkin and nodded heartily at Tameka. "Well done, sister. The peanut brittle was a delicious extra touch. I found your decoration to be fun and right on target with the theme."

"My only suggestion is to be careful with the consistency of your chocolate cake." Thad leaned forward in his chair, skipping Georgiana in order to speak next. "It wasn't quite moist enough. Almost dry, really."

Georgiana slapped the table with her hand. "Whatever! That cake texture was perfect, and you know it. Ignore him, Tameka. I know what I'm talking about." Then she good-naturedly elbowed Thad, who rolled his eyes.

Thad would be the hardball this episode, apparently. As per the usual. Still, was that his honest opinion, or did he exaggerate for the camera's sake? Suddenly, everything Kat thought she knew about the show seemed null and void. Whom could she trust?

Thad shoved his plate farther away from him, as if the not-moist-enough cake was his new archenemy in life.

Yeah, apparently she should only trust Lucas.

"A little division in the ranks. But we'll fix that up during the break." Sam laughed. "Next up, We Grow Cupcakes. Present your cake, please, Sarah." He motioned for the shy woman to step forward.

A nervous smile fluttered across Sarah's freckled, makeup-free face. "We've never actually been to the circus, so we had to imagine a little. We decided on a chocolate buttercream icing on a lemon zest cupcake, and designed a clown for the top using fondant, chopped up cherries, chocolate chips, and sprinkles."

The camera panned back to take in the creation, and Kat winced. The clown had been thrown together pretty sloppily, as if they'd run out of time or simply had overshot their decorating ability.

The judges went down the line again, complimenting the cake this time but harping on the decoration. Dave even called it lazy, which started Sarah blinking rapidly.

The Icing Queens, Piper's team, went next with a confidence that even tempted Kat to vote for them. The judges, especially Thad, raved over the texture of the cake, the taste, *and* the decorations, which featured a tiny giraffe on a pogo stick and a real miniature striped tent made of fondant.

The biker team didn't get as rave a review, but seemed to pass well enough compared to We Grow Cupcakes. Then it was Kat's turn.

Sam motioned for her to start, and she licked her dry lips, wishing Lucas could stand behind her. She desperately grappled for the intro she'd written in her head while she waited. "Love is a circus, and for us, nothing speaks circus more than animals, peanuts, and popcorn." She cleared her throat, wishing Thad's consistent stare would level elsewhere. "We created a peanut butter chocolate cake with peanut butter caramel icing, topped with caramel corn and animal crackers, complete with a fondant red flag."

Her voice shook on the last word as the judges' forks cut into her creation. This was it. The only moment that mattered for the rest of her day.

Sam's voice cut through the pounding in her head. "Dave, tell us what you think."

"Love the peanut butter. It's a good blend with the cocoa." Dave cleared his throat as he set down his fork. "Nice consistency throughout. And the animal crackers were a good, not-too-sweet addition to the cake. Well done."

A dull roar started in Kat's ears. One down. Two to go.

Georgiana smiled at Kat, as if sensing her fear. "I liked the caramel corn the best. Unique addition, but not too weird, even for this gal." She pointed her fork at Kat. "You did good, honey. I want another one of these."

A seed of confidence nestled into her heart, and Kat returned the woman's smile. "Thank you."

"Thad?" Sam raised his eyebrows. "What did you think?"

Thad, who had been propped on his elbows, leaned back in his chair and sighed as if he'd just been interrupted from deep thought. "I'm getting a little tired of peanuts, to be honest."

A brick slammed into Kat's stomach and pushed her backward a step. She nearly stumbled into one of the tattooed team members next to her, the dull roar becoming a deafening soundtrack. She should have known it wouldn't be that easy.

"But this combination was refreshing. Nice job."

Kat exhaled a breath she hadn't realized she'd been holding. The brick disappeared, leaving her light-headed and exhausted from the sudden lapse of weight.

So much adrenaline coursed through her body that Kat couldn't even concentrate on what the judges said about the last entry from Inky Dots. It took every ounce of her focus to remain upright until they were dismissed to the contestants' lounge, where they'd wait while the judges debated.

Lucas appeared at her side, gripping her arm and tucking her against him as they filed in a silent line to the lounge. "You did great."

"I almost had a heart attack." Kat tried to ignore the camera following them to the lounge, and kept her attention on Lucas's face. His stubbled, tanned, ridiculously handsome face.

Well, that might not be a safer choice after all.

They squeezed onto an oversize purple couch next to John and Sarah from We Grow Cupcakes, who whispered their concerns to each other. Across the room, Piper and Amanda spread out on the green couch, taking up more than their share of the available space, while the biker team stood against the wall, tapping an anxious rhythm with their boots.

Tameka clapped her hands from her position on a stuffed armchair, making everyone in the room jump. "I think we did fantastic, y'all." She glanced at Piper, who raised a challenging brow in return. "Even you, Miss Thang."

The younger girl's brow furrowed into a deep frown, but Tameka kept going before she could retort. "We should all be proud, regardless of which team they send home here in a minute. And I mean that."

Tonya nodded, supporting her sister. "That's right. I was impressed by everyone's entries."

The room erupted into hopeful chatter as the sullen mood lifted and morphed into one of hope. How did the sisters do that? Kat found her own spirits lifting, and she leaned across Lucas to speak reassurances to John and Sarah, who were worried about their clown decoration.

Lucas's hand landed on her back, offering comfort, pressing lightly to reassure her of his presence. His steady, rock-solid presence. What would she do without him? Gratitude swelled, and she squeezed his jean-clad knee before straightening back into her spot.

Then reality tapped her on the shoulder.

If she won, she'd be leaving Lucas behind for a year. What was she thinking, even being on this show in the first place? For the sake of her heart, it would be helpful to have a break from him. But that same heart that threatened their friendship would break into a hundred pieces if she was away from him for a year or longer.

It was one thing to spread her wings and fly on her own.

It was another to be pushed out of her safety nest before she'd even read the flying manual.

The door opened, and a Red Shirt assistant directed them back onto the stage for the first round reveal. Kat's fingers anxiously found Lucas's and held on tight as they walked what felt like a path to the guillotine. Her traitorous thoughts kept drifting from the upcoming elimination to the dread of her apparent no-win situation. She could get sent home this round, and then the chance she'd be leaving Lucas wouldn't even be on the table. It'd be back to chocolate, vanilla, and strawberry day in and day out.

But if she won . . . if she kept going in the competition . . . the threat—opportunity?—would linger for at least another twenty-four hours until the next round.

Palms slick, Kat joined the rest of the bakers on the taped line to await the verdict. Thankfully, this time the torture wasn't stretched out. Sam must have powered up while they were in the lounge.

The judges offered steady smiles that Kat struggled to return, noticing how they didn't meet anyone's eyes dead-on. Beside her, Hallie from Inky Dots fairly bounced from one foot to another, while the biker on her other side rubbed his left arm so hard she thought he might scrub off his American flag tattoo.

"Bakers, you all did a great job creating unique and edible cupcakes featuring how love is a circus." Sam paused for dramatic effect. "But one of you didn't live up to the high standard the judges demand from decorations in round one."

Tension thickened the room until Kat struggled to take an intentional breath, just to make sure she still could. She didn't know if she was really in danger or not, having zoned out during the last of the first round judging, but she knew in her gut her decorations hadn't held up in comparison to a few of the other entries. Anything could happen. How many times had she watched episodes at home and yelled at the judges for being blind to what was clearly the cutest cupcake?

"That team is . . ."—Sam stretched out the one syllable until it sounded like eighteen—"We Grow Cupcakes."

Kat exhaled with relief even as dismay over what the other team must be feeling nudged her heart.

"John and Sarah, I'm sorry, but your clown didn't pass the test. You've been eliminated from *Cupcake Combat*." Sam offered a fabricated, almost-sympathetic smile as Sarah and John hustled off the stage, heads down, fingers entwined.

The cameras cut off, and Sam smiled more naturally at the remaining bakers. "Contestants, we'll meet back here tomorrow, same time and place, for round two. Everyone, stick around for a brief post-elimination interview, then you can all head to your hotels. Good luck, and get some rest tonight."

Rest. Right. That was a laugh. Like she'd think about anything tonight other than the disappointment on Sarah's face when Sam announced the judgment, and the mixed feeling of relief and regret in her own head that she and Lucas weren't going home.

At the moment, she wasn't even sure anymore where home was.

thirteen

here's no place like home. There's no place like home."

Lucas pulled another slice of pizza from the cardboard box on the bed in his room and nodded toward the remote control, which Kat had conveniently placed just out of his reach. "How much longer are you going to make me watch *The Wizard of Oz?*" They'd come back to the hotel after being dismissed from the studio, and quickly agreed to crash in front of the TV and order a pizza. Forty-five minutes later, they were set.

Except for the chick flick. Or it seemed like a chick flick to him, anyway. Compared to the *Terminator*, which she'd flipped quickly past a few minutes ago.

"There's nothing else on." Kat wiped a smear of pizza sauce from her chin and leveled the control at the television, cranking up the volume as a dark-haired Dorothy clicked her red shoes together.

Not true. There was always a football game on this time of year. "*Nothing* is relative. And subjective." Lucas reached for the remote, but Kat twisted away, holding it behind her pizza slice. He could have gotten it, but not without knocking her—or the pizza—off the bed. Besides, it was kind of fun watching her mouth the lines of the movie between bites. Sometimes she'd do the voices of the characters without even realizing she was mimicking.

"Subjective to the person holding the remote control, you mean." She wiggled the black rectangle from her spot at the foot of the bed and grinned a challenge.

"Whatever." He'd fight that battle later, if needed. Right now, he was too comfortable. And he was enjoying watching her relax for the first time all day.

"Those pigtails of Dorothy's remind you of anyone?" Lucas folded a pillow and propped it between his back and the headboard, stretching out his legs. Speaking of relaxing, here he was a football coach, always moving around the field, but somehow, standing on that set today had coiled his muscles tighter than springs.

Kat shoved the last bite of her pizza in her mouth and pulled her sweatpants-clad legs up underneath her. "If you're talking about Piper, let's not. She was more Wicked Witch today than Dorothy, anyway."

"Want me to drop a house on her?" Lucas grinned at Kat's exaggerated expression of consideration. If Kat only knew how badly he'd wanted to intervene on her behalf all day long—with Piper, and with Thad, that preppy judge he especially didn't like now that he'd been around him in person. He'd witnessed the near heart attack Thad had given Kat with his proclamation about being tired of peanuts. He could see the reasoning behind drawing things out for the sake of the show, but these were real bakers with real feelings and real careers on the line. It wasn't all that entertaining in person.

He'd never watch reality TV the same way again.

Kat brushed pizza crumbs off her fingers and onto her pants. "Tomorrow will be better."

"In general, hopefully. With Piper? Let's be realistic." Lucas opened his second Dr Pepper, not even caring. He'd get back on his food and exercise regime after they returned to Bayou Bend.

At this point, sooner would be much preferable to later.

Though he wasn't sure if he could handle the disappointment in Kat's eyes once Sam told her she'd baked her final cupcake or said some other dramatic garbage.

"Hopefully we don't run into her here at the hotel." Kat wrinkled her nose at the very idea. "Why do you think she's so awful?" She turned down the volume on the TV, and Lucas fought back his grin. He apparently had just crossed the threshold into official Girl Talk time. Where was Rachel when he needed her? This was her and Kat's specialty.

But the scary part was, he really didn't mind.

"Everyone has something they're dealing with." Lucas shrugged before taking another swig of his soda.

"Wait. Are you defending her?" Kat stretched across the foot of the bed to grab her diet drink from the desk. "I have to say, I'm a little surprised."

"Well, sure. Just look at the movie." Lucas struggled to keep a straight face, hiding his mouth partially behind his aluminum can. "Dorothy, for one, is struggling with wanting to go home. The lion, for another example, needs courage. So he's clearly struggling with fear."

Kat frowned, trying to follow, clearly not used to him waxing philosophical. "So you're saying you think Piper might be homesick, or afraid of losing, or something?"

Man, she was adorable. "Close." He nodded seriously, desperately hanging on to his stoic demeanor, unable to look directly into Kat's eyes for fear of ruining his performance. "I was actually thinking she was more like the Tin Man."

"Really? How so?" She leaned forward, as if he was about to reveal a deep, psychological truth.

He prepped for the punch line. "She has no heart."

WHACK.

The pillow came out of nowhere, knocking his nearly empty Dr Pepper can onto the floor. He tried to sit up to grab it, but the attack kept coming.

"I can't believe you! You totally had me going." Kat's face flushed red as she beat him with the pillow a second and third time, giggles erupting between hits. "You are such a dork."

"And you're more gullible than you used to be." Lucas wrestled the pillow from her grip and knocked it lightly against her shoulder. "Someone's got to toughen you up."

She looked anything but tough at the moment, in her messy ponytail, pink sweatpants, and rumpled hoodie—though fully capable of beating his heart to a pulp.

"Whatever. I'll show you tough." She grabbed for the pillow again, and he released it on purpose, loving the joy in her eyes when she realized she'd actually gotten it from him. She went to hit him, but he blocked it with his forearm, effectively knocking her flat on her back on the bed, her head nearly landing in the grease-stained pizza box. She giggled again, and he leaned over and grabbed for the pillow before she permanently stained it with tomato sauce.

She refused to let go, holding on with a grip tighter than he expected, and ended up pulling him down beside her. He laughed, the pillow smashed between them, and scooted the box out of the way of her hair before propping up on his elbow. "I'm still waiting to see tough, by the way."

She grinned up at him, all long lashes and aqua eyes, and his breath hitched. She had no idea the power she wielded, which was part of the charm. But the way she blinked at him, two parts innocence to one part sass, made his propped fist tremble.

He wanted to kiss her.

Needed to.

But what would it change?

Everything, one way or another. For better or for worse.

Maybe 'til death did them part.

His eyes darted from her gaze to her lips, to her flushed cheeks, to the inch of her stomach peeking from between her top and sweats.

He squeezed his eyes closed. He needed to move. Get up. Off the bed. Away from the potential that might not even be potential.

And Lord help him if it was.

His cell phone buzzed from the bedside table and his eyes flew open. Text message.

Yet he couldn't make himself move.

His gaze found Kat's again, and time suspended, his decision to act or not to act hovering over the two of them like a wisp of a cloud that was both foggy and transparent all at once—just tangible enough to distort, yet not present enough to possess. This moment—it mattered. It counted.

And he had no idea what to do. *God* . . . the prayer froze in his thoughts, crystallized. Slammed against an invisible ceiling between him and heaven.

His phone vibrated a second time.

Kat sat up so fast her forehead almost clipped his chin. He ducked out of her way. "Should you get that? It might be one of your football boys."

Might be. Or it might be the president of the United States, and it still wouldn't matter enough to drag him away from her side.

But the spell had broken. Answered prayer? Or Murphy's Law?

With a muffled groan, he shoved away from the bed and stood, his back to Kat, and picked up his phone, reaching up with his free hand to massage the tension in his neck.

Two incoming messages. Both from Darren. Perfect timing, as usual.

He jabbed the envelope icon on his screen.

DID UR APRON FIT?

He snorted. Hardly worth the interruption. He dared a glance over his shoulder at Kat, who had sat up and was sipping on her Diet Coke, engrossed in the ending of the movie. Maybe it wasn't too late to recreate the moment. Give himself a second chance.

He scrolled down to the second message.

DON'T 4GET. SONG OF SOL. 2:7

He tossed his phone back on the end table, palms slick. The verse was burned in his brain. *Do not stir up nor awaken love until it pleases.*

Definitely not Murphy's Law.

But God knew his heart for Kat, knew the sincerity of it. So why the red light? He clenched his hand into a fist. Maybe because of the direction his thoughts had been slipping . . .

Kat, looking oblivious and completely unfazed, continued to watch the movie and nurse her soda, none the worse for the wear. He should be grateful she didn't realize the battle that had just been warred over her. But the lingering what-if settled on his shoulders like an itchy wool jacket, a constant irritation he couldn't scratch.

He couldn't stay here.

He snuck a peek at his watch. It was too early to call it a night, but he couldn't be in this room with her for a minute longer, not in this mood. Not with the truth of Darren's reminder pounding in his ears like Bayou Bend's marching band drummer.

Not with Kat in those pizza-stained sweatpants.

"Let's go work out."

Kat turned, midsip, and raised one eyebrow. "Now? We just ate."

"It's been long enough." It hadn't been, really, but they weren't swimming. Oh no. *Not* swimming. That was the last thing he needed to see before going to bed.

He pulled one arm in a stretch, then the other while bouncing on the balls of his feet. "We'll go jog." Or walk. Or bear crawl. Or do a thousand burpees. Anything to burn off the what-if circling his head like a vulture, a vulture with terrible, terrible timing.

Kat slowly stood and reached for her shoes, continuing to stare as if he'd lost his mind, but that was okay. He'd rather she think him crazy than recognize the true train of thought he'd been fighting. The train that Darren—and the Holy Spirit—had derailed.

He ushered her out the door, barely remembering to shove his key card in the pocket of his athletic shorts. Crazy was definitely better than humiliated.

Or rejected.

୧୧୭

Kat supposed rejection was better than being humiliated—though the two felt sort of the same at the moment.

Her feet slapped a rhythm on the treadmill, a steady punctuation to the drilling of her thoughts. *Los-er. Los-er. Los-er.*

She'd thought they'd had a moment there, with the pillow fight, and the pizza box, and the laughing over his *Wizard of Oz* prank. Clearly she'd imagined it. Clearly she'd landed in some form of Oz reality herself, thinking the entire exchange had been anything other than what it was.

Re-ject. Re-ject. Re-ject.

How embarrassing. Her stomach shifted into a knot cinched with regret. The flirty eyes she'd thrown at Lucas, the way she'd held her breath hoping and waiting for a kiss that never came. How pathetic and obvious could she get? No wonder he'd suddenly decided to leave the room. She'd probably scared him half to death. First she dragged him across the country to be her baking assistant, of all things, then she'd practically thrown herself at him.

So-dumb. So-dumb. So-dumb.

She ignored her racing heartbeat and cranked up the machine's speed, pushing herself in a desperate attempt to drown out the haunting beat.

Just-friends-just-friends-just-friends.

Still not fast enough. Her feet thudded against the belt, spasms shooting up her shins.

Hopelesshopelesshopeless.

Enough.

She jumped her feet onto the stable sides of the treadmill and bent over, gasping for breath as the conveyor belt churned beneath her. Maybe there was hope. Maybe she hadn't been as obvious with her feelings as she thought. But why else would Lucas leave their cozy dinner and a movie setup so suddenly if she hadn't given off a vibe he hadn't returned?

She never thought she'd be jealous of Dorothy. But a tornado spinning her off into a land full of wicked witches and singing peers and cotton-brained sidekicks sounded halfway appealing at the moment.

On second thought, she was sort of already there just by being on set in LA.

She watched the treadmill eat up the belt between her feet. Maybe there had been a spark of chemistry between them. Maybe she'd imagined it. Either way, she had to push past this. It was probably just the trip throwing them together in such constant proximity that had her hormones whipping like the exercise conveyor.

She inhaled deeply, heart begging for oxygen, her side cramping into a stitch. They were friends. Best friends. Closer than that, really. This was Lucas—the man who knew her best and wanted to be her friend anyway. The man who had cleaned her kitchen sink almost as many times as she had. The man who had once brought toilet paper and Sprite to her door when she'd caught a stomach virus and her parents were out of town. The man who'd nursed her back to emotional health after Chase had hit on her sister behind her back—not that she didn't have a way to go to becoming the strong woman she really wanted to be.

No, she had no business entertaining these thoughts and feelings of more—even if they had set up camp and refused to leave. She was in charge—she could boot them out. There had to be a way.

God . . . She tried to pray, but the words choked in her throat. Her poor divided heart. She wanted more, so much more, so badly—but Lucas didn't fit in with her dreams for herself. That had to mean something—the fact that they didn't mesh. They weren't meant to be.

But one day, someone *would* be the right woman for Lucas, and their relationship would change forever. There was an inevitable end careening toward them, regardless of how hard she tried to protect their friendship now. One day, reality *would* collide with the present, and everything would be permanently different.

She needed to win. Needed New York. Needed to prove herself.

Because Lucas wouldn't always be there to lean on. Not like this. Not like she needed.

It was time to stand on her own two feet.

She jumped back on her machine, punching the Down arrow to slow it down slightly. The last thing she needed tomorrow was sore muscles on the set.

Lucas, his iPod earbuds in, didn't seem to notice her internal debate from a few machines down. He ran hard, chest heaving, his typically perfect form almost sloppy. In fact, it looked like he ran as if something was chasing him.

Maybe her?

She risked a second glance at him from the corner of her eye, but he only ducked his head and increased his stride. Fine. She quickened hers to match his, concentrating on her breathing, refusing to allow worry and fear to interrupt her focus. If Lucas was running, she wasn't going to stand still. Somehow, they had to set their pace to work together on the show.

One thing was certain. For all her previous doubts earlier, now she knew for sure—she *had* to win *Cupcake Combat*.

Because there was no way she could keep up this pace forever.

fourteen

There wasn't strong enough coffee in the world to get him through this round.

Lucas groaned and wished he could take back the past half hour he'd spent griping to Kat and anyone else who would listen—not that there had been many—over how long it took to get any kind of action rolling on this set. He'd give anything at this point to go back to being bored and antsy.

Because shifting his weight from one sneaker to another, counting the tiles in the floor, and playing about thirty-seven games of tic-tac-toe with Kat—and three with one of the bikers—remained preferable to actually participating in round two.

Thanks to Sam Carson—or whoever was responsible for dreaming up this crazy love theme. And he thought the circus concept was bad . . .

"Think *love is romance* in this round." Sam wiggled a red rose— it looked fake—from his spot near the judges' table, then stuck it between his teeth and snagged Georgiana's arm. Before the boisterous woman could protest, he'd spun her in a quick twirl and dip. She snatched the rose from his lips and waved it at the contestants as Sam righted her and sent her back to the panel.

He brushed the lapels of the tuxedo he was wearing today and picked up as if nothing had happened. "In this round, taste is key and will be scored the highest. But the judges still expect quality decorations to go with the love theme of your cupcake selection. Be creative, be bold, be romantic—and most importantly . . ."—his voice trailed off and lowered into a loud stage whisper—"be on time." He pointed to the clock, which had quickly become every contestant's archenemy. "You have one hour to impress the wings off Cupid. And . . . go!"

Lucas watched Kat run with the other contestants to the supply closet, dodging an overeager Tameka and nearly getting shoved by Piper along the way. Probably not an accident, though Kat had managed to avoid the cheap shot.

He started to follow after her, for bodyguard duty if nothing else, then hesitated, choosing to give her space to make her choices alone for this round. He wouldn't mind throwing a few elbows in Piper's direction—or at least teaching Kat how to do so. But he refused to be one of those "do as I say, not as I do" coaches when it came to sportsmanship.

Still, something about that younger girl rubbed him raw. It was cupcakes, for crying out loud. Not worth losing one's integrity or character over.

Or sanity, for that matter.

His gaze found Kat again as she flitted around the shelves, snatching items and then rummaging through the giant refrigerator, brows furrowed with concentration. So far, so good. It looked like she had a plan, at least. Would she pull through, or freeze up under the pressure again?

Speaking of frigid—she'd all but ignored him in the exercise room last night, after that terribly awkward—and terribly wonderful—moment they'd shared in his room before Darren's texts interrupted. Judging by the way Kat had attacked that treadmill as if she held a personal vendetta against it, she apparently wanted to avoid the subject as badly as he did. He'd never seen her run like that—not without something chasing her, anyway.

Had she been trying to burn off stress from the taping? Burn off her doubts, burn off her memories . . . burn off him?

This stupid show was going to be the death of him.

And not just because he was still wearing an apron on national television.

Kat returned, loaded down from the stockroom—meltdown free—and he quickly moved to help her dump the items on their workstation. She'd done it alone, but he wouldn't point that out right now. That would just backfire and remind her of yesterday.

Neither of them needed to relive *any* part of yesterday.

"What's the vision, boss?" He needed her to smile. Needed to know their usual camaraderie was still alive and well beneath the junk he'd piled on top of it last night.

Needed to believe nothing had changed—but that the possibility for change still lingered.

Really, he just needed a football field and a chance to clear his head.

"I'm getting the impression the cornier the better for this round." She jerked her head toward Sam, who had started waltzing around the judges' table with an invisible partner. "So I was thinking of going all-out romance. Lots of red and pink." Her lips pursed as she studied the materials on the counter in front of them.

He looked away from her mouth. Red. So . . . "Strawberry?"

"Raspberry lemonade torte."

His stomach growled on cue. "The one that can bring world peace?"

"Exactly." She turned her full smile on him, and for a minute, the drama disappeared. The awkwardness that had lately colored their vibrant edges gray vanished, and she was Kat, and he was Lucas, and there was no almost-kiss. They were just baking cupcakes like they'd done a hundred times in her kitchen.

They could do this. He could do this.

He just wouldn't think about the consequences until later. He'd cross that bridge—or jump off it, rather—when the time came.

He picked up a lemon and a handheld grater. "I'll start on the lemons."

She nodded. "I'll start the batter."

Teamwork.

Like usual.

Nothing to see here.

He grabbed a mixing bowl and began to zest, only slightly embarrassed anymore that he knew what that term meant. His boys on the team loved to tease him about his kitchen knowledge, but after he'd cooked for them once or twice, they'd shut up fast. Especially Tyler, who thrived on anything that felt like home.

He sobered as he moved on to blending the raspberries. He should have texted Tyler by now, checked on him. Just in case. He'd only been gone a few days, but in Tyler's world, a lot could change overnight. And often did.

He shot a glance at Kat, who paused from using the electric mixer to brush a stray wisp of hair out of her eyes. She'd had to resort to the mixer because of their time restraint on the show, and he could tell she hated it.

He definitely needed to be here—as Kat had reminded him, this whole thing was his "fault." But he couldn't ease the nagging sensation that he needed to be back in Bayou Bend too. His team needed him, and not just for the upcoming game.

If he'd stayed home, he wouldn't be tormenting himself with this proximity to Kat, with these thoughts of the future that wouldn't go away. His dreams involved her on his soon-to-be-acquired (hopefully) ten acres, but clearly, this wasn't the right time to pitch the idea. Not with Kat all over the place, distracted with the show, and not with his own roller coaster of emotions.

He really needed to get out of this apron.

He shut off the blender and finished measuring the other icing ingredients. "What's next, boss?"

She glanced over her shoulder at him, then back at her mixer, using a spatula to scrape the batter from the sides of the bowl. "I'll add the butter. You can come pour this batter into the tins."

He changed places with her and dismantled the bowl from the mixer stand. "What's our decoration?" Raspberry lemonade torte cupcakes with the fruit whipped icing . . . that had to win. The thought tied his stomach into a knot any Boy Scout would be proud of.

Odd in his profession to realize that, for the first time, winning was not equivalent to victory.

"What do we have here?"

Lucas jerked, missing the muffin cup and spilling a clump of batter onto the edge of the pan.

Thad smirked across the counter, where he stood near Kat. A little too close, in Lucas's opinion. "Sorry there, man. Didn't mean to scare you."

He didn't scare him. There was nothing remotely scary about the guy—except maybe his ability to have a say in Kat's future. "No problem." Lucas grabbed a paper towel and cleaned the drip, keeping one eye on the preppy judge and his conversation with Kat. What was he doing walking around, anyway? Yesterday the judges had stayed put.

As they should.

He frowned over at the panel. As Georgiana and Dave still were.

"It gets boring at that table for an hour, watching all of you prepare to wow us." Thad crossed his arms over his striped suit jacket, which he had rolled up to his elbows and worn with dark denim jeans. Skinny jeans? Lucas didn't want to look close enough to tell for sure. Man, the guy was metro, and today the black wire-rim glasses he wore only added to the costume. "Though some are more entertaining to watch than others."

Kat blushed under his attention as she poured the remaining ingredients into the icing he'd started. Flustered? Or attracted?

No way. Not a single way possible.

Lucas filled the remaining empty muffin cup and picked up the pan. "Twenty minutes?"

"Eighteen." She didn't miss a beat in her conversation with Thad, just tossed the number over her shoulder at Lucas and kept listening as the judge went on about humidity and baking environment factors.

But all Lucas could hear as he headed toward the oven was the voice of Charlie Brown's teacher. *Wahhh wahhhh . . .*

ﻌﻠﻌ

She really needed to be concentrating on piping roses and creating lace out of fondant. Not trying to psychoanalyze every word that came out of Lucas's mouth. Not trying to read between the lines of his every gesture and expression.

Not trying to decide if she should demand he explain what he was actually thinking last night.

She drew a deep breath and let it out slowly as she piped another rose. Focus . . . focus. This icing bag tip was tricky, and she'd messed up three roses before this one. They were running out of time, and if she didn't figure this out, their cupcakes wouldn't look anything like a valentine.

Speaking of . . .

"How are the hearts coming along?" She'd assigned Lucas's heavier hand to cutting out red hearts from fondant, instead of the more delicate work of the roses and lace, which she'd left lying on wax paper at the end of her workstation.

He looked up from the end of the counter, first at her, then at the clock. "They're coming." His paring knife slipped and he winced. "Oops."

"What's wrong?" Maybe she wasn't the only one having trouble concentrating.

Lucas shot a glance toward the judges' panel, then resumed his cutting. "Nothing." He bit the word off like a kid chomping into a crisp cookie.

She started to argue, then knew better. The time restraint had to be getting to him, was probably all. He wasn't grumpy a little while ago.

In fact, he had been acting as if nothing odd had gone on last night. Which was both good and bad; it just made her a little crazy. Like maybe she had imagined it all. Like maybe they really had just been hanging out, eating pizza, and jogging. Nothing more dramatic than that.

She bit back a groan as she messed up another rose. Of all the times to be dealing with a romance-themed round . . . *God, I could use some help here.*

"Uh-oh!" Piper's loud voice sliced through the buzz of last-minute preparations on the set, punctuated by a loud clatter. "Oh no. I'm so sorry."

The room stilled. Even the hand mixers shut off, the incessant whirring on set ceasing as everyone stared.

No. *No.*

But her heart knew the truth even before Piper slowly moved her muffin tin away from Kat's pile of carefully crafted lace—now crunched and smashed into broken fragments.

"How clumsy of me. To trip and fall over nothing like that." Piper's broad smile only widened as she sauntered away with her tray. "I do apologize . . ."

For the cameras. And for the judges, maybe. But not for real. She was downright gloating.

Across the counter, Lucas's mouth opened in shock. He looked as frozen as she felt. She slowly, with a heavy arm that felt half-numb, reached up and tucked loose strands of hair behind her ear.

She could barely breathe. She pinched the bridge of her nose and tried to draw in oxygen. Not exactly the kind of help she'd meant when she'd prayed. What now? And how could one girl be so cruel for no reason?

"Oh, I *know* she didn't!" Tameka's voice rose loudly over the muffled din that had slowly increased to a dull roar as reality sank in across the set. "Piper! Where do you think you're going?"

"It was an accident," Amanda protested, sticking up for her friend, her hands on her tutu-clad hips. "Mind your own business." Apparently Amanda had finally gotten the "time to be mean" memo. Better late than never. Beside her Piper smirked and draped her arm around her friend's shoulders.

Continued murmurs reached Kat's ears, even as she let the pieces of lace slip through her fingers like sand. Her eyes began to water, and she couldn't look away from the shards of fondant. All that work . . . and the clock. Oh no. Her chest tightened. They were done here. It was too late now. They'd never be able to redo that delicate work.

"Deep breaths." Lucas's voice in her ear warmed her through, but it couldn't undo the damage. Not this time.

Not even Lucas could fix this one.

It was over.

"Stay with me, Kat. One thing at a time." He pointed to the clock, all traces of his own previous frustration vanishing in light of the new challenge. "We can do this. You remake the lace, because you know how. I'll finish the roses." His eyes searched hers, his own eagerness to help, to fix, to restore, nearly tangible in his gaze. "Okay?"

She wanted to argue, but numbness had set in. Besides, Lucas hadn't waited for her agreement anyway, but was already heading around to the other side of the workstation toward the piping bag of icing. Always a leader, on the move. Why couldn't she concoct game plans as quickly?

Other than her default plan B to give up.

That one probably didn't count.

"Fifteen minutes, bakers!" Sam bellowed.

Oh, he had to be kidding.

"Everything okay over here?" Thad appeared at her side, much like he had done earlier in the segment, and Kat squeezed back a tear as Lucas joined them, his brow furrowed. Thad looked back and forth between the two of them. "I heard that noise. Like metal hitting metal. What happened?"

"We're fine." Lucas's tone, heavier than her black boots, broke the expectant silence. Was he ending the conversation because of the time? Or was he afraid that admitting there was some drama would hurt their chances?

Either way, he was probably right. This wasn't the time to tell the story. She flashed a smile at Thad and shuddered back a breath. "We just need to finish up. It'll be fine." The words tasted sticky and uncertain, but she held her smile and stiff back until Thad murmured his encouragement and headed back to the panel.

She quickly salvaged two pieces of lace that were still intact and large enough for a cupcake, then began measuring the sugar and corn syrup to make another batch of fondant for the others. Her thoughts churned, and she avoided looking at the clock. Piper had clearly done that fake fall and smash on purpose, but why? Why hadn't she bothered the other contestants?

Why was she so threatened by Kat and Lucas?

She snapped her gaze over to Piper's station, then reached over and tugged Lucas's apron tie to get his attention. "Look at that." She barely remembered to lower her voice, but Piper and Amanda continued putting the finishing touches on their pink decorations as if they hadn't heard.

Lucas pulled the string free from her hand as he made a 180 in an obvious attempt to spot what she was gesturing toward. "Look at what?" He accidentally squeezed the icing bag he held, and a glob of red dripped onto the floor.

She pointed discreetly. "Piper made lace too."

"And hers looks—"

"Second-rate to ours?" Kat turned her hopeful gaze to Lucas's face.

He considered for a moment, then looked away and shrugged as if in defeat before a half smile teased his lips. "I was going to say 'awful,' but that works too."

She play-slapped his arm, relief and hope laying a much desired but still shaky foundation in her heart. "Well, that explains the sudden clumsiness, anyway. She feels threatened by our design plan, I guess."

"As I've been trying to tell you for two days."

"Do you think she sabotaged us because she saw that our lace looked better and was jealous? Or do you think she decided to make lace after we did and she stole the idea?"

Lucas kept working on the roses, with a surprisingly light touch. "Is either way less diabolical?"

She almost forgot her question; she was so focused on his work. She probably should have put him in charge of the roses from the beginning. Had he always been that talented? "Um, no." That's right. Piper. "No. Not really."

"Then let it go and get back to the fondant and the lace." He looked up long enough to send her a confident smile that sank into her toes. "We're going to make it, you know."

And if she held his gaze long enough, she could almost believe him.

fifteen

*L*ucas thought he'd been nervous when Kat stood before the judges' panel the first time. But that had been nothing compared to the nauseating churning going on in his stomach right now.

He braced his hands against the cool edge of the workstation, wishing he could stand beside Kat and prevent her from facing the guillotine alone. But the assistants weren't allowed "on the front lines"; they had to join their teammates in the lounge while the judges decided and then hang back at the workstations while waiting to know whether they were to congratulate or commiserate.

This show just continued to make less and less sense.

He let out a sharp puff of air, rocking back on his heels and refusing to make eye contact with any of the other team assistants at their counters. He wasn't up for putting on a mask and pretending like he wasn't worried about the results of this round, and he *definitely* wasn't up for any expressions of self-pity they might send his way. He and Kat had finished placing their decorations literally as the buzzer sounded—but one cupcake only received half its edible adornment. It was missing the lace border that made Kat's valentine creation actually resemble a valentine.

The completed cupcakes on the plate looked amazing, of course.

Kat had gone all out, and even a football coach like himself could appreciate the feminine, artistic, even girlie touches.

But it might not be enough. It might be over for them.

And wasn't that okay?

Guilt gnawed like a mutt with a T-bone, and he slapped it away. He had to stop convincing himself it mattered. The results were out of his hands, and the verdict from the judges would determine what happened next—not him. Nothing was his fault, and he had no reason to hope for one particular outcome or another.

If he didn't hope, he wouldn't have to feel guilty.

Because he sort of knew which direction his feelings would slide if he set them completely free.

"All right, bakers, prepare to present your cupcakes." Sam's voice boomed over the set, and Lucas straightened so quickly his back popped. Finally. The moment of truth.

He schooled his features into what he hoped resembled comforting reassurance just as Kat looked over her shoulder at him, eyes wide and nervous. Her smile shook almost as much as her hands, and he gestured for her to cross her arms over her apron to hide the telltale trembling. If she couldn't actually be confident, she could at least look the part.

Go out in style.

As Sam slid the first plates of cupcakes—from Real Bakers Ride Bikes—in front of each judge, the tension in the room tangibly heightened among the contestants. Tameka's sister, Tonya, cleared her throat loudly. Then a second time.

He glanced at her, then did a double take as she pointed a hot-pink tipped nail at him. "Don't you worry, now, son. I saw what that pretty little thing did to y'all's decorations."

Ha. Son? The vivacious woman *might* have five years on him. He saluted to show he wasn't worried, and turned back to the action on the set. But she wasn't finished. "The good Lord's got you," she hissed in a stage whisper. "And that sweetheart of yours over there too."

The reluctant protest came automatically. "She's not my—"

Tonya simultaneously lowered her chin and raised her drawn-on eyebrows, and Lucas knew it was pointless to argue. Especially with a woman.

Especially with a woman who was now quoting Scripture.

"'Vengeance is mine; I will repay, saith the Lord.'" She jerked her head toward Piper's tutu-covered backside. "You believe that?"

"I—well . . ." He never really thought about it, but if it was in the Bible, then it would be true. He shrugged. "Sure."

The bad part was, he wasn't all that concerned with whether or not Piper got what was coming to her, because her interference might be a blessing in disguise—might send them home early.

Home. Where he belonged—*with* Kat. Not with her holding his heart in one hand while she whipped up cupcakes with the other in New York City.

"Next up, we have Not Your Mama's Cupcakes, from Louisiana. Tell us what you baked." Sam reeled back in exaggeration and pointed to the camera zooming in on the half-naked cupcake in front of Thad. "Oh, man. And tell us what happened here, exactly."

A muscle in Lucas's jaw started to twitch. Sam knew what happened. He saw the whole thing, and so did the cameras. But that part might or might not make it on air. On the one hand, Lucas could see them using the "accident" for conflict and drama, but he could also see them leaving out the explanation entirely to focus on the conflict of Kat simply not having her cupcakes completed.

It could go either way. One viewpoint would make Kat look incompetent, while the other would make Piper look like a klutz. It would probably come down to whichever the producer thought would receive the highest ratings.

The question now was how Kat would answer Sam's question.

Lucas held his breath, wishing he could will strength into her, but her voice barely even trembled as she lifted her chin. "We ran out of time on that last cupcake's decoration because of having to remake our fondant lace to counter a last-minute incident." She quickly changed the subject before Sam could interrupt, running through the components of her cake, and even Sam looked like he might start drooling by the time she finished describing the raspberry lemonade torte.

Attagirl.

The judges began tasting the offering, and exchanging expressions of surprise before scraping their forks against the muffin cups, gathering each crumb. Even the normally reserved and stoic Thad didn't hesitate to lick icing off his finger.

The winning smile he shot at Kat, however, wasn't reserved or stoic.

Lucas's fist clenched, and he quickly flexed his fingers before shoving his hands into his apron pockets. What was wrong with him?

Or better yet, what was wrong with Thad? Was his jealousy radar just blitzing, or was there something legitimately inappropriate about the judge's interactions with Kat? He hadn't been hovering over any of the other cooking stations earlier during taping. If the same accident had happened to another contestant, would he have come over to inquire?

There was no way to know.

The judges continued through the rest of the entries, stopping occasionally for Sam to reshoot takes of his corny clichés, and then finally the contestants were dismissed to the waiting lounge.

Kat tugged him to the far corner of the brightly lit lounge. Away from the rest of the bakers settling on the couches, she lowered her voice to a whisper, her crestfallen expression proving she was predicting the worst even before she vocally confirmed it. "Everyone else's cupcakes were great."

It was so unlike her to be sad over someone else's success that Lucas had to bite back a smile. "So was yours. I thought Dave was going to bite into the wrapper."

"Maybe so, but I was the only one without all the decorations." She twisted her fingers in front of her, the bold woman on the set replaced once again with one riddled with insecurity.

He instinctively pulled her into a hug and rested his chin on top of her head, inhaling the mixed aroma of flour and sugar and lemon. "You can't change it now. You did your best."

She pulled away, eyes narrowing with suspicion. "It sounds like you agree that we're probably going to be eliminated."

No. Well, maybe. He fought the urge to tug her close again. "It doesn't matter. Either way, you did what you could with what you had to work with."

"Is that what you would tell Tyler? Or the other guys on your team?" The spark was back in her eyes now, fiery and dangerous, which would have been great had it been pointed at anything other than him. "That they did their best, so losing was okay?" She wasn't being quiet anymore. Or timid.

Or huggable.

"Piper sabotaged you." He remembered to lower his voice just in time, grateful for the sound of the air-conditioning kicking on overhead to help drown out his words. "It wasn't like you had a lot of options afterward. You should be proud of yourself."

He didn't mean for his words to sound so negative in context, but he couldn't stop their flow. Maybe he really was hoping they lost, despite his previous efforts to curb that train of thought.

What a great friend he was.

But that was the problem. He didn't want to be a friend. He wanted to be a lot more.

If he really loved Kat, though, would he be hoping for something so contradictory to her hopes?

His head throbbed.

"It's not about being proud. It's about advancing to the next round." She glanced over her shoulder at the other contestants on the lounge furniture. "If Piper actually gets away with what she did . . ."

Her voice trailed off, but the message was clear. She didn't want a pep talk. She wanted to win. She wanted it all to be fair.

Unfortunately, Lucas had been in the competitive industry long enough to know that a lot of people just didn't play fair at all. And sometimes justice prevailed and sometimes it didn't. "Look, Kat . . . I'm just saying you did an amazing job. You're the best cupcake chef I know, regardless of what happens here in a few minutes."

She nodded slowly, and gratitude flickered through her eyes, followed by a hint of another emotion he couldn't identify.

But that mystery look of hers turned his stomach, because for one of the first times in his lifetime of knowing Kat, he got the feeling that his opinion wasn't enough.

celos

Never again would Kat take for granted standing in a line when her stomach *wasn't* giving salsa lessons to the butterflies fluttering inside.

Just when they'd been ready to announce the loser of the round, Georgiana had asked to excuse herself, probably for the restroom. Then when she returned, there was a sound issue so they had to wait another fifteen minutes for the repair before they could proceed with taping. Apparently the producer was adamant about results being recorded only while they were actually being announced. Part of the "integrity" of the show, though Kat would blink twice about several other elements she'd seen so far in contradiction to that goal.

Finally, Sam stepped up on the set and got into position, which she now knew involved him clamping his hands behind his back and straightening his shoulders until his tux coat pulled taut.

Did she have a chance? Or would her poor, naked cupcake send her home? Thad had still seemed to enjoy it despite its simplicity, and decorations weren't the highest scoring factor in this round. But still—an unfinished cupcake was a negative strike. In fact, she could only think of one episode where a contestant with an unfinished cupcake didn't get sent home.

And that was only because a competitor had happened to burn their offering to an iced crisp.

She exhaled slowly. As hard as she'd tried to fight Lucas's dose of reality in the lounge, she should probably just prepare herself for the worst. They were going home. And she'd be back to her usual strawberry, chocolate, and vanilla existence.

The butterflies switched from salsa dancing to a conga line, and she pressed her hands against her apron-covered stomach. Would she ever be set free from her box? And more importantly, did she even have what it took to justify breaking free?

What if her destiny, God's plan for her life, was to remain at Sweetie Pies? What if she was already living out her calling and just needed to be content where God had placed her? Put aside her dreams, put aside her desires, and bloom where planted?

But if that were true, why did she feel so wilted?

"This round wasn't an easy one for the judges." Sam's eyes swept across the contestants' faces, and Kat struggled to keep her hands from shaking. It was just a contest. Just a contest. Just a—no, it wasn't. It was more than that, and her heart knew it. Hence the uncontrollable tremors. This contest represented more than just a chance to prove herself. It represented the opportunity to finally *identify* herself. Outside of expectations, outside of her family, outside of resignations.

Even outside of Lucas.

She forced her eyes to remain on Sam's face and not seek Lucas's support. He wasn't any more convinced they were staying than she was, so it wasn't as if she'd find what she needed on his face anyway. Not this time. Besides, if by some miracle she did win, she'd have to figure out how to live without Lucas in her daily life.

She might as well start the process now.

"There were a few technical issues with almost everyone in the round." Sam continued, pacing before the contestants like a drill sergeant while the judges remained expressionless from their table behind him. "But it finally came down to sending home the team who produced a bare cupcake . . . or the team who produced a cupcake the judges deemed simply not up to par."

He paused for effect, and Kat squeezed her hands into fists, her sweaty fingers slipping against her palms. *Come on, come on.* It was clearly between her and—who? In the last round of judging, she'd been so distracted by her own failure, she hadn't paid enough attention to be certain who Sam was talking about.

"But this particular round scores taste higher than decorations, so the decision was finally made." Sam pointed at Kat, and her heart slipped into her shoes. "Despite your bare cupcake, you're safe." He swiveled in his shiny shoes. "Inky Dots, I'm sorry to say you have been eliminated."

Relief rubbed a balm over the slash of panic in her heart, and Kat nearly collapsed from the letdown of adrenaline. She was here. They'd made it. Another round . . . another opportunity.

Another chance.

Joy surged with a fresh burst of energy, urging her toward Lucas, who waited in the back. She rushed into his hug, her frustrations over his realism earlier long gone. "We did it!" She bounced, nearly catching his chin with the top of her head.

"*You* did it." Lucas caught her and held her back so he could see her eyes. Kat warmed at the pride beneath the surface of his gaze. "This is your show."

He was proud of her. Again. It made her giddy. "Whatever. I couldn't have even gotten two of the three cupcakes decorated without you." Kat gripped his firm arms in both hands and jumped up and down, shock and hope driving her feet to move. "Remember that. We're a team, Lucas."

Then she stretched up on her toes and kissed him.

The studio tilted, then faded away as their lips lingered against each other's. Kat leaned into his whisper-light touch, his mouth gentle against hers, and a shiver danced up her spine. The butterflies in her stomach exited an abrupt stage left as warmth seeped through her stomach, crawling up her chest until her face flushed. She was kissing Lucas.

She. Was. Kissing. Lucas.

Lucas was kissing her back.

And from the way his hand moved up her neck to cup the back of her head, he didn't intend to stop anytime soon.

sixteen

He'd seen Kat move pretty fast before. Once in high school when a bee had landed on the shoulder of her denim jacket outside the mall, where she had begged him to take her picture by a flowering bush, before she'd become so shy and insecure. Then again, when she'd been on her laptop at one end of her house and thought her new recipe was burning in the oven at the other end. And there was that time they'd been washing his truck, and she'd attempted to dodge his sneaky attack with a water hose.

But he'd never seen her move as quickly as when she moved away from him after one of the cameramen let out a wolf whistle.

Even now, strolling the breezy streets of downtown Los Angeles by her side, the memory of that kiss made his lips burn. She'd tasted even better than that magical torte of hers. Lemon, with a hint of raspberry—and a lot of extra sweetness.

He missed her warmth, had felt the loss to the core of his gut the second she moved out of reach. The kiss had taken him off guard, though apparently not as much as it had taken her off guard. Realization had dawned with a vengeance, all because of an immature potbellied guy with a video camera.

Still, it had been one of the best ten seconds of his life to date.

And if anyone had ever preached on "best friends not having chemistry," well, that argument was out the window. Gone.

Out the window, over the river, and deep into the woods *gone*.

He glanced down at Kat, subtly, as he'd done a dozen times already in the minutes it had taken them to abandon their cab and walk Main Street. She'd wanted to see the renovated area, laden with historic buildings. She had talked about it even before they left Bayou Bend—but she remained unusually quiet.

Two guesses why, and the first one wouldn't count.

He matched his pace to hers, wishing she'd tuck her arm in his like she often did when they walked. But she didn't. And then somewhere deep inside, foreboding crept in like a fog, took up residence, seeping through the cloudy edges of his subconscious. Dark and heavy. Sort of like the tension between them.

Yeah, silence wasn't good here.

Torn between breaking the ice with a corny joke and forcing the topic between them to the surface, Lucas ran his fingers through his hair, opening his mouth, then closing it before he could decide the best play. He just couldn't get the image of his ten acres out of his mind. As she always had, Kat filled center stage in the visual. Those two dreams went hand in hand, and after that connection, after that moment they'd shared a few hours ago, he couldn't separate them if he tried. It'd be like trying to yank apart two pieces of paper that had been taped together without ripping them.

Impossible.

He had to say something. The silence was getting to be more unbearable than his fear of the reason behind it. Was she embarrassed?

Or did she regret it?

He had no idea guys actually wondered these kinds of things. He never had before, anyway, not with any girl he'd ever dated or kissed. He'd just gone with the flow, not worrying one way or another about what happened next or who was thinking what. He'd definitely never obsessed the way he did with Kat now, trying to read between the lines and interpret every nuance of her expression, shoving down his stuttering heart that stammered every time she coughed or indicated that she might be about to speak.

If this was what women went through on a regular basis, well, he'd start a mass apology letter ASAP.

She stopped suddenly in front of a boutique store window that was decorated with glittery pink material and filled with jewelry, and gawked. "Look at the size of that diamond."

He was so relieved she'd said actual words out loud that he didn't even care what they meant. "Yeah, that's pretty big." He guessed. He wasn't exactly an expert on jewels, but he sort of figured he couldn't afford much in any window in downtown Los Angeles. But hey, they were talking. He'd talk about cupcakes or diamonds or panty-hose or anything else she wanted.

"I don't think I could wear that thing even if I could ever buy it. I'd scratch myself up." Her voice sounded a little strained, as if she were trying to shove her words around the boulder lodged between them and each syllable barely slipped through the crevices. Well, if she wasn't going to force the topic, he wouldn't either.

Yet.

"Yeah, you wouldn't want to lose that one in cupcake batter." Inwardly, he cheered at her responding chuckle. Progress toward normal.

Then his eye caught a dangling charm on a silver necklace in the display, a cupcake, right there on a chain. It was small, pink with a blue wrapper and a red cherry on top . . . yet apparently valu-able, if the price tag hanging from the chain was any indication of its worth. Or maybe it was just an indication of the shop owners' opinion of their store.

Either way, it'd look great on her, especially if she won the com-petition. It could be a congratulations gift . . .

No, wait. What was he thinking? She couldn't win.

He couldn't lose her.

But the what-if in the back of his mind wouldn't go away. They'd come close to going home today after Piper's petty attempt at sabotage. Talk about low. He'd been happy the unsportsmanlike ploy hadn't worked, of course—but if he were painfully honest, he wasn't exactly thrilled that they were one step closer to winning.

Though more than likely, if Piper hadn't made this particular round so difficult, Kat's exuberance at making it through the session wouldn't have ended the way it had.

He blew out a slow breath. What a double-edged sword. That kiss had given life to his hopes for them, but at the same time, it threatened to turn him into a villain. How could he love Kat but want her to fail?

And why couldn't he get several specific ideas of how Piper *should* have sabotaged the round out of his head? There were so many more surefire alternatives if she really wanted Kat to bomb . . .

No. *What?* He wasn't that guy. He refused to entertain the idea a second longer. He supported Kat, no matter what.

Even if it meant gritting his teeth and banging his head against a wall.

He glanced at her to see if she'd somehow noticed the war raging in his head, but she seemed fixated on the rest of the window display. Either that, or she was simply zoned out in thought too. Maybe her default thought process went back to that kiss every time she hesitated as well.

He hoped so.

But what would the kiss change if they never talked about it?

What would change if they did?

He swallowed hard, noted the price on the cupcake charm one more time, and then coaxed Kat away from the window. They needed to move. Walk. Stir his brain away from the dangerous ground it seemed determined to tread. "Come on, you promised me another dessert that you didn't have to cook."

She finally grinned, the light from the street lamps above

highlighting her hair and the purple knit cap she'd thrown on before leaving the hotel. It made her eyes pop, and when their gazes finally collided for the first time all evening, he took a step back. He couldn't risk repeating history right there on the sidewalk in downtown Los Angeles.

Not until he knew where she was with it all.

Then it was game on.

She fell into step beside him, shoving her hands in the pockets of the jacket she called a peacoat. "So what do you want?"

He nearly stumbled, then realized she was talking about dessert options.

"I'm thinking apple pie." He was thinking about a whole lot more than pie, which was the problem. He shoved his own hands in his pockets, feeling like one of his awkward teenage football players instead of a coach with a wise head on his shoulders. He sort of wished someone could tackle him and knock some sense into him. Where were Darren's texts when even Lucas realized they were needed?

"I could go for pie." She nodded, her hat slipping down on her forehead. She stopped walking and reached up to adjust it, but he beat her to it.

"Hang on. Hair's in your face." Why was his voice so raspy? He cleared his throat, reaching up gently to tuck the wayward dark strands under the purple covering. Her cheeks were soft under his calloused fingers, and he winced at the contact. "Sorry. Hope I didn't scratch you."

She reached up and covered his hand with hers, gently tugging it down and away from her face. "Not at all." Her fingers held on a little longer than they needed to, and he fought the urge to cling to her hand like it was a life preserver. It would be so easy to pull her back into his arms and kiss her until they both forgot all about dessert.

But what if she didn't kiss him back?

Or what if she did, and that step dictated the rest of their trip together, one way or another?

Such dangerous territory, full of too many unknowns. He needed a game plan, needed a play to call, and until he had one, it was probably best to do nothing.

Her eyes searched his, full of silent questions, and unfortunately, he didn't have a single answer. If he opened his mouth now, he'd mumble something incoherent about ten acres and toddlers with footballs and probably just end up tossing her over his shoulder like a caveman.

Man, they needed to talk this thing out.

But he hated the idea of putting words to whatever floated between them, afraid a conversation would shoot sniper rounds straight into it and never give it a chance to breathe.

As much as he wanted "next," they needed to breathe.

Because "next" was too important to sacrifice.

He squeezed Kat's fingers, then let go, putting his hand lightly on the small of her back and ushering her down the sidewalk draped in street-lamp shadows. "Let's go find that pie." Their silhouettes formed before them in an inaccurate picture of reality, tall and oddly thin and misshapen.

He refused to take that as an omen.

❦

If mirrors could talk, hers would probably tell her to shut up.

Kat squinted at her reflection, shoving her hair back from her forehead and then fluffing it forward with a ragged sigh. It was no use. No hairdo helped eliminate the stress lines by her eyes, the new, seemingly permanent wrinkle between her brow, nor the bags under her bottom lids that could hold a week's worth of groceries. Short of attending that morning's taping segment as Cousin Itt from the *Addams Family*, she was out of luck.

Maybe the proverbial ten pounds the camera added would distract from her puffy, tired eyes.

And was it any wonder? Between the stress of the show itself, the pressure of the end result looming before them, Piper's sneaky, immature attempts at playing dirty, and her constant proximity to Lucas, well—it was just short of a miracle that she could stand upright and not stay curled in the fetal position under the hotel bedsheets.

She ran a brush through her hair, determined not to think about Lucas and that kiss. The kiss that had—

No.

She brushed on a little more blush to counter her paleness and fatigue. Still not helping. She looked as tired as she felt. Sort of how Lucas had looked yesterday when they'd come back to the hotel.

Hopefully he hadn't noticed how strained things were between them last night. Strolling Main Street should have been a highlight of her trip, and while the apple pie they'd found in a little bakery off a side street had been a delight, and some shoe shopping afterward had been fun—at least for her—it hadn't been enough to cover the awkwardness hovering between her and him like a—

No.

Oh, what was the use? Sort of like her hair and that one kinked spot by her ear, it was just as inevitable that she replay that kiss over and over in her head. Maybe it would go away if she gave it attention for a little while.

She turned off the bathroom light, mentally reliving each moment of their lips pressed together in vivid replay, and perched shakily on the edge of the bed to put on her shoes. Her jeans were too long today, the ragged edges fraying over the tops of her sneakers, but they were the only shoes that didn't kill her feet after hours on the set. Hours she would shortly spend baking, hovering, stalling, and killing time beside Lucas.

Funny how his name today made her want to simultaneously swoon and snarl. Why hadn't he asked her about the kiss yet?

There'd been a moment last night when she thought he would, and she had held her breath in anticipation, stomach shooting off bursts of adrenaline like the Fourth of July shot off colorful rockets.

But then he'd just nudged her on down the sidewalk as if getting to that piece of pie was the only thing that could possibly matter. She knew the way to a man's heart was through his stomach, but good grief. Lucas couldn't put off dessert long enough to have a discussion about something important?

No, he *could*.

And that was the problem. It wasn't about his eagerness for pie.

It was about his eagerness to avoid that particular conversation.

She yanked the laces of her sneakers tighter than necessary. Great. She'd freaked him out. Again.

Not that it hadn't been worth it, maybe.

But she'd messed something up, let her excitement over going on to round three turn a friendly kiss into something so much more.

He'd kissed her back.

Her fingers fumbled on the laces, and she scrambled to retie them. She hadn't imagined that part. He'd kissed her, too, but the question was, why? Had his excitement about the round just taken over?

Or had he meant it?

And more importantly, what did they do about it now?

Her frustration built as she tied her other shoe. She might have initiated the moment, but he was still the man. Was it too much to ask for him to step forward, speak up, and rebuild the bridge teetering between them?

Maybe it was too much.

Maybe she was too much.

Tears pricked the backs of her eyelids, and she drew a ragged breath. No time to let emotions pile up today. Today mattered toward the rest of her future. Mattered more than Lucas, if she would just let that be true long enough to believe it.

She thumbed a quick text to Rachel, asking for prayer for God's favor. She sort of had the feeling she'd need it today.

‿◦‿

The set was exactly the same as they'd left it yesterday. Except this morning a dark expectancy hung over the air that hadn't been there before. The remaining teams seemed almost gloomy, a feeling as thick and heavy as the fog that hovered over the studio and frizzed Kat's hair until she finally white-flagged the entire mess into a ponytail.

She waited on the set near her workstation, wishing she could just get the assignment for the day's baking already and get on with it. Her hands itched to hold a wooden spoon, her arms ached to stir icing and pound dough and cut fondant. She needed a project. Needed to be busy.

Needed to channel everything stirring in her heart into a creation, into something edible and desirable, into an inverse version of how she felt. She shifted her weight, grateful for her sneakers already that morning, and bounced anxiously on her toes with the knot of her flour-streaked apron pulling taut against her back. She wiped them down each night after taping, but somehow, the flour always came right back. Across the room, Piper and Amanda whispered furtively with furrowed brows, while Tonya and Tameka paced their cooking station and talked in hushed tones. Chops and Michelle drummed their fingers on the countertops and murmured, their black-and-white handkerchiefs tied low on their biker foreheads.

Even Lucas seemed on edge, performing push-ups off the side of the counter. Yet she couldn't be sure if it was the unresolved tension between them or the text he'd read in the taxi that had elicited a heavy huff and a long pause before he finally responded to it.

Lucas, not wanting to talk? *Shocker.*

She held back the sigh begging for release. The sarcasm wasn't fair—even internally—but this was getting ridiculous. If he would just tell her how he felt, she could feel secure enough to do the same. Hadn't she sort of laid it all out there in kissing him in the first place? The least he could do was step up now and show some masculinity.

She darted a glance in his direction, at his five o'clock shadow that just wouldn't shave away, at the way his muscles corded in his arms with each push-up, the way his dark hair fell over his forehead with every rotation.

Even in a stinkin' apron, the man broadcasted more masculinity than an old-fashioned Marlboro ad.

That was definitely not the problem.

No, if she thought about it long enough, the problem actually resided in the fact that she wanted Lucas to do what she herself lacked the courage to do.

She still wasn't as strong as she wanted to be. Meant to be.

Needed to be.

And that was the most maddening part of all.

How could one man complete her and destroy her all at once?

"Bakers ready!" Sam clapped his hands as he approached the set, all gloss and shine and fake tan. "Let's do this."

Yes, by all means, let's. She avoided Lucas's eyes as he straightened from his impromptu workout and adjusted his apron. This one baker was most certainly ready. Ready to bake. Ready to win.

And ready to run.

seventeen

He might never appreciate the scent of vanilla again.

The smell of raw eggs made his throat close.

And if he had to dig flour out from under his fingernails one more time, he might run screaming onto a football field like a bat out of—

"Lucas! Did you hear me?"

Kat's frantic cry interrupted his mental train wreck of complaints. No, he hadn't heard her, because the set was alive with panic. It was nearly a tangible pulse at this point. And the tension between him and Kat wasn't helping his nerves, already shot from keeping a wary eye on Piper and trying to turn a deaf ear to Tameka's louder-than-our-inside-voice protests to her sister.

"The cupcakes. Did you turn them?"

No. He'd almost forgotten. Scratch that, he *had* forgotten. Like a robot on auto-command, he quickly turned an about-face and rushed to the ovens. Because of the cheesecake cream center, this particular creation of Kat's needed to be rotated halfway through the baking time to cook evenly. Something apricot and pear and cinnamon—autumn in a cupcake, according to Kat.

At this point, he was almost ready to miss vanilla, strawberry, and chocolate.

He'd always been her biggest fan, but the stress was getting to him, making him miss the time when Kat wasn't so focused on her career and had more time for him. Needed him. Needed his compliments and support as much as she needed her paycheck. Maybe more so.

Despite the chaos, Kat was blossoming under the set lights, and it stung a little more than he'd anticipated. Well, no, he hadn't anticipated it, to be honest. She was surprising him, and he was two parts proud to one part disappointed.

Great, now he was even thinking in cooking measurements.

He had to get out of this kitchen.

He remembered an oven mitt seconds before he grabbed the scorching hot trays and shoved the cakes back into the oven after a half-turn. Leave it to the show to make this round the "love is war" round—with the scoring focused mostly on creativity. Kat was busy cutting tiny cannons out of gray fondant, her collection of black fondant bombs with yellow hard-candy fuses already spread across the decorating table.

Talk about timing—and weapons of mass destruction. Things were still up in the air between them, after the kiss and the lack of discussing it. And on top of that, Tony had let him know the other buyer had countered once more. If Lucas's most recent offer wasn't accepted, he was going to lose his land. His plan.

His dream.

The thought of those ten acres belonging to someone else made his chest tight—sort of like the way he lost oxygen every time Thad's pinstriped-suited-self looked at Kat longer than necessary. There was something inappropriate about that man's attention, but at this point, he had no idea if Kat noticed or if he was possibly blowing the entire thing out of proportion because of his own inner chaos.

At this stage of the game, anything was possible.

He shucked the oven mitt and tossed it on the counter, turning to punch in a few minutes longer on the oven timer. They'd be ready in about seven minutes, but would the icing? And the decorations?

Did he even care anymore?

What was he doing?

He just wanted to go home. Back to the football field, back to his boys, and back to Bayou Bend, where he could at least feel like he had some control over what was happening to his desired property. He'd lost home-field advantage by traipsing off across the country, and his competitor probably knew that. Whoever he or she was.

Kat was making him crazy. Turning him into some sort of dough-speckled sous chef.

This wasn't him.

What if it was her?

What if he just let the cupcakes burn?

The thought snuck in like a cornerback blitz, and he jerked, tried to shake it off. Too late. The idea might have blindsided him, but it was in his sights now.

Kat was busy; she'd never notice his mission. She'd never assume he let it happen on purpose—it would look like an honest mistake.

Except it wouldn't be.

Still, one slight misdemeanor for the greater good? He didn't belong here, and if he didn't, then Kat didn't. Because they belonged *together*. Not in LA. Not in New York.

In Bayou Bend.

Kat wouldn't really be happy in New York, anyway, away from everything she knew, away from him. Sure, it'd be a break from her family and their drama, but that would follow her long distance. No one could fully escape blood.

Unless they died.

And even then the ghosts lingered as memories, as potential regrets and what-ifs that were more haunting than any creaky door or flickering light. What if he'd failed his mother as a son? What if he'd not done enough to take care of her over the years? What if he'd let her down?

The doubts could hang around for days, if he let them.

But no, this wasn't about his mom. Not anymore. This was about him and Kat.

And about him making the right choice.

He glanced at the cupcakes, then away, their gooey edges teasing him from inside the tiny window.

Could he do it? A few jabs of a few buttons on the oven and this whole ordeal could be over. Done. They could get through the elimination, he could dry Kat's tears, and they could go back home. She'd get over the loss quickly enough, once he told her about his plans for their ten acres, his plans for her heart.

His heart rate quickened as the roots dug deeper and began to sprout. Didn't Kat always tell him that he knew her better than she knew herself? And didn't she trust him to make good decisions for her? That's what he was doing here.

The excuses sounded petty, even in his own head, but he couldn't stop the drumming of his pulse, the adrenaline coaxing him to the dark side. Not *that* dark, though. He wasn't cheating—it was his own team. What Piper had tried was inexcusable, but was self-sabotage still considered poor sportsmanship?

His head stuttered off an immediate answer, but he shook it back. The kitchen and the football field were two totally different elements. You couldn't compare them. Besides, this wasn't about cupcakes or a competition anymore. This was about his future— and Kat's. What was more important? Clearly, the bigger picture.

He inched toward the oven, which was counting down the seconds, and glanced over his shoulder at Kat.

Flour smudged on her cheeks, food dye staining her fingers, and hair tousled in a haphazard ponytail, she darted around the work counter like a bee around a hive. Focused. Determined. And graceful as always. His heart twitched. What was he doing here, he had wondered earlier? Easy. He was helping her. Like he'd done for years.

Like he'd always do.

Regardless of the cost.

Even the cost of losing her.

What had he almost done?

He darted away from the oven like he'd already been busted, guilt a heavy-handed companion. That had been close. Too close. At least Kat would never know the level to which he'd almost stooped. He disgusted himself.

And yet . . . resignation weighed like a tackling dummy on his back. Sabotaging the round wasn't the answer. But helping her all the way to New York for a year didn't feel any better. Talk about a no-win situation.

The timer ticked down the minutes, as did the clock on the wall ushering the contestants to the end of the round. Kat looked up, panic in her eyes, and then her gaze collided with his. *Help*, she mouthed.

He stood frozen a moment longer than he meant to, unable to convince his body to betray his heart. Then he took a deep breath and hurried to her side. "I'm here."

Where he belonged.

No matter what.

Someone had set the clock on the wall to fast-forward, she was sure of it. Kat tried to ignore the numbers ticking away and focus on her decorations. Replays of the last round and Piper's sneaky attempt—and near success—to eliminate her paraded in her mind, destroying her concentration. She gripped the icing bag tighter in her sweaty hands as she finally scooped the rest of the buttercream inside. She was ready to ice, just as soon as Lucas got the cupcakes out of the oven.

Which should have been several minutes ago. Where were they?

She scanned their workstation, but all she could see was Lucas, busy finishing up the white fondant angel wings they would pair with a set of crossed pistols for the cheesecake cupcakes. The effect would hopefully be enough to impress the judges. It wasn't easy trying to make a war theme attractive. What was edible and fun about weapons?

And speaking of war . . . this had been the hardest round yet, maybe because the entire set seemed on edge. They were nearing the finish line, and this round mattered. There was only one more before the final event. Everyone knew it, and the niceties seemed to be over. Everyone was looking out for number one now, even Tameka and Tonya, who had so far been the most encouraging contestants on the set. It was an inevitable shift, but the atmosphere had plummeted all the same.

Where were her cupcakes?

She smelled them at the same time Lucas's head jerked up from his workstation. A sugared pair of wings slipped from his fingers as his eyes widened. "Oh, no."

Her nose told her the truth before her eyes confirmed it. She wrenched open the oven door and a thin stream of smoke seeped from the edges. Her should-be-golden-brown cupcakes were the color of charcoal.

Her apricot, pear, and cinnamon cheesecake cupcakes, the only recipe she'd been completely confident in this entire round—burned to a literal crisp.

She grabbed a mitt and yanked them out, despair and anger fighting their own war in her thoughts. She dropped the hot tray on her workstation and crossed her arms, the warmth from the mitt seeping through her apron and heating her skin. But she was already flushed. "How did this happen?"

The room stilled, even the judges hushing as they shifted on their stools to watch the unfolding drama. Somewhere in the back of her mind, her conscience urged her to reel it in, to take a step back. It wasn't Lucas's fault. But he'd been the last one at the oven. The last one to touch the cupcakes or mess with the timer at all. He wouldn't have burned them on purpose. She knew better than that. But still—she had burned cupcakes, a ticking clock, and a tightening chest.

Something had happened, and she wanted to know what. Before she had a complete meltdown on national television.

Lucas stared at her, unmoving, like a deer in front of an oncoming eighteen-wheeler. "I set the timer. For seven minutes." He blinked rapidly, his eyes darting from her to the ruined cupcakes as if he couldn't register what they were. "I never even heard it go off."

"It didn't." Tonya piped up from her workstation. Her sister nudged her in the side, but she shrugged. "I'm just saying, I didn't hear it either. Those alarms drive me batty, and there hasn't been one to go off now in a good ten minutes or so."

Lucas's face waxed pale, and Kat frowned. Why did he look relieved? Had he felt responsible after all? Though she had given him the evil eye . . .

"The last cupcakes out of the oven before yours were Piper and Amanda's." Tameka pointed to the friend duo across the room, who were icing their cupcakes as if they couldn't care less what had happened to Kat's. Well, they probably didn't. Not surprising. Still, it was like pulling your car over on the side of the road when a funeral procession drove by. Basic show of respect by acknowledging someone's pain.

And this one hurt.

But there wasn't time for that. Not yet. She could wallow later.

And wallow she would. First, though, she had a batch of cupcakes to remake.

She pulled off the oven mitt and began gathering her ingredients for another batch. Slowly, the remaining contestants around her began slipping back into work mode, too, and she tuned out the bustle. Let's see, she'd have to skip the cheesecake element, but maybe she could add something special to the icing to give it an edge—if they would bake in time. She glanced at the clock and wished she hadn't. Panic clenched her stomach in a vise and she drew a deep breath to counter the squeeze. She could do this.

Somehow.

She glanced up at Lucas for support, but he remained stock-still beside the end of the workstation. "Are you okay?" *As in, move. Do something. Help. Not just stand there like a guilty—*

Wait a minute.

"Me? Why wouldn't I be? I mean, why would I be?" Lucas cracked his neck, the resounding pops making her stomach cringe. He slid the dry ingredients across the counter to her, and she began measuring them into a mixing bowl. The steadiness of her hands surprised her—but not as much as the shakiness in Lucas's voice. How had their roles just reversed?

"This is bad, Kat. Really bad."

So much for his words of encouragement like after Piper's sabotage. Apparently there would be no pep rally this time. It was up to her to fix it.

And he was talking like a parrot. Short and choppy and higher pitched than usual.

She spoke slowly, to defuse his crazy, her thoughts racing wild at the reversal of their usual roles. This didn't feel good. "You can relax, Lucas. I'm not saying I blame you for this."

"Of course you don't. Why would you?" His voice cracked, and he gripped the edges of the counter with both hands, accidentally tugging on the wax paper that held their fondant cannons. He caught the lot of them just in time and slid the paper back to a safer place on the table. Her heart skipped and she glared at him, the relief of the near miss only skimming off the top of all she felt ready to boil over.

"Because you were the last person to mess with the oven." Her

accusing tone didn't make sense with her declaration of his innocence, but she couldn't stop the onslaught of emotion. "I *should* be
blaming you."

He hesitated, confusion highlighting his features. "But you're
not?"

She couldn't fully determine if it was a question or a statement.
"I don't know yet. You're being weird." And useless. "Hand me the
sugar." Oops. "Please."

She was slipping, forgetting her manners, being rude, turning
into That Girl on the show she swore she wouldn't be. How did any
of the contestants handle this kind of stress with grace on the air? Or
was it all the magic of editing?

Who knew how she'd appear once the show actually aired.

"You can at least line the pan again with muffin cups." The words
snapped off her lips, harsher than she intended, but they spurred
Lucas out of his frozen state and into action.

She didn't like herself much at the moment, but what she didn't
like even more was how she felt, and how much of that was Lucas's
fault. That dang kiss still hung over them, like dangling mistletoe
that wouldn't go away, and even when upset with him over something this crucial, she wanted to kiss him again. Fall into his arms
and hear his reassurance that somehow she'd pull this off.

He'd encouraged her after Piper's sabotage attempt. Why wasn't
he doing that now? Speaking life and truth over her instead of adding to her stress and chaos?

She turned on the mixer, sifting the ingredients off the side of
the bowl with her spoon as it spun, and for the first time in a long
time, didn't miss stirring by hand a single bit. This was faster. And
right now, time was what she needed most of all.

That, and for her baking assistant to get his apron strings out
of a wad. What was wrong with him? She powered down the mixer
and began spooning the batter into the cups he finally finished lining. She wouldn't look at the clock. Wouldn't look at the—oh man,

these cupcakes better bake fast. Now they were at risk of the icing melting off before plating them for the judges. Maybe she could use the freezer for just a minute . . .

"Here, I'll put them in."

Lucas reached for the pan, but she found herself snatching it away as if on autopilot. "I've got it."

The hurt in his eyes before he briefly closed them registered deep, but she almost didn't care. No, she did. Just not enough to change her mind. After all, he'd left this to her to fix, left her alone in the emergency, and worst of all—left her alone in her emotion over what had happened between them the day before.

How much of this was about burned cupcakes anyway?

She slid the tray into the oven and set the timer, then crossed her arms and waited. Directly in front of the window. No way were these cakes burning. She looked at the clock again, then at Lucas, and her heart sank for two different reasons.

They might not make it.

eighteen

They'd made it, but barely. Kat paced the contestants' lounge while the judges debated, unable to get the image of her melting buttercream out of her mind. The decorations had turned out better than she'd hoped, though, especially the wings and pistols. It was charming in a country-girl-tough kind of way, which reflected well on her home state. Maybe the judges would feel the same.

And ignore the fact that her once-perfect cupcakes were cheesecake-less and more like glazed instead of iced because of the drizzles sliding down the still-warm sides.

"You're about to wear a hole in the carpet. Just calm down." Lucas's hands brushed her arms, but she shook him off, afraid if his touch lingered too long she'd cling to him forever. "Calm down? Easy for you to say." She forgot to lower her voice, and she was awarded with curious stares from Piper, Amanda, Tameka, Tonya, Michelle, *and* Chops—all of the remaining contestants.

"Besides," she went on in a whisper, "you were more on edge than I was earlier in the kitchen, practically leaving me alone to deal with all that. I would imagine it's my turn now."

"If we're going to do this, we're doing it outside." Before she could protest, Lucas grabbed her hand and tugged her out of the lounge, down a short hall, and to a door marked Exit.

He really meant outside. The breeze felt fabulous against her flushed skin, but still . . .

"Lucas, we're going to get locked out."

"No, we won't." He jammed his shoe between the door and the frame and braced it open, crossing his arms across his apron-clad chest. "Now, what's going on?"

She threw her arms to her sides, feeling any edge of control she'd managed to hang onto slip away. From the distance, a car horn honked, and the sounds of nearby traffic did little to ease her anxiety. "Besides the fact that once again, something random and awful happened that might be sending me home?"

"*You* home?" A shadow flickered across his face, despite the sunny afternoon streaming around them. "Don't you mean *us*?"

"Us. Me. Whatever." She paced the concrete walkway, unable to stay still, unable to look directly at him for fear of what she'd do. What he'd do.

Or not do.

"We're a team."

"You're right. And teams don't bail when one member needs another the most."

"I didn't bail. How did I bail?" Lucas jabbed his thumb at his chest. "I was right there the entire time."

"You didn't hear the oven go off."

"You didn't either!"

"Don't yell at me."

"I'm not yelling!"

"It's your coach voice. It's close enough." Kat shook her head. The conversation had just taken an immature spin, and if someone didn't put it back on track . . . "I'm just saying you weren't as there as you usually are. And you were being weird. Almost—"

163

"Almost what?" Lucas raised his eyebrows. "You were going to say guilty, weren't you?"

There was that shadow again, dancing across his expression like a winged admission. "You did it on purpose?"

"Kat! Are you serious?"

She leveled her gaze at him, and the fight fled his stance. "I didn't burn the cupcakes." He ran his hands down the length of his face, and the weariness on his features sent a twinge of sympathy across her heart. She knew he couldn't have done it on purpose, but if she were honest, the cupcakes weren't even what she was mad about in the first place.

She'd needed him to stand up for that kiss, and he'd been silent. And Lucas reacting to the emergency that way in the kitchen today—as if he almost hoped they didn't win—made his first offense all the bigger. And more personal.

Like it was about her.

Her fight left then, too, dissolved into a thousand tiny droplets that went up in a puff of steam. She let out a sigh, leaning against the rough side of the building. "If you didn't burn the cupcakes, then why are you so upset?"

"Because I *thought* about burning the cupcakes."

She pulled his hands away from his face, gripping his fingers so tightly her knuckles whitened. "You didn't just say that."

"I'm serious, Kat. I thought about it. And decided not to, and then it happened anyway, and I didn't know what went wrong, and I felt bad. Like it was still my fault, somehow." He tugged his hands away, and she let them go, reaching up to touch her cheek like she'd been slapped by his words. How could he—

"I didn't do it, Kat." He stared her in the eyes, as if the truth would somehow make it hurt less. "That's all that matters. I made the right choice."

No. *No.* She took a step back, away from him, clenching her hands over her heart. "What matters most, Lucas, is that you even had to make it in the first place."

Fear branded his gaze, and she forced herself to look away. This was done. She was done. With the conversation. With the truth. With the lies.

Done.

"Just go."

"Kat, I'm not leaving you out here alone—"

"Go!" Now she was the one yelling, and not in a coach voice but in a woman-scorned voice. "I can handle myself. Just watch me." Anyway, the only one threatening to hurt her right now was Lucas.

He gave her a long stare, then disappeared inside with a slow shake of his head.

She forgot to catch the door behind him. Gave it a tug, and— yep. Locked.

Perfect.

She leaned against the side of the building again, crossed her arms, and closed her eyes. Just breathe. One breath at a time. Someone would let her back in. Lucas would realize soon enough if nothing else, and she'd have to go stand in line for the big announcement of who was continuing on to the next-to-last round all windblown and sweaty.

And heartbroken.

How could he do that? How could he even think of sabotaging her like Piper? And after all he said about Piper being a bad team player. Lucas was on *her* team, and he'd considered—actually considered—making her lose. On purpose.

Why?

The unknowns made her want to kick the brick wall.

The door banged open beside her, yet she refused to open her eyes. Let Lucas wonder if she was okay. He should have propped the door behind him when he went inside. Apparently he was worried about leaving her alone, but not all that concerned with locking her out.

"Excuse me, I didn't realize anyone else was out here. Do you need a minute alone?"

Not Lucas. Her eyes flew open. Thad.

Oh, great. She wiped her eyes, grateful the building tears hadn't actually cascaded down her cheeks yet, and nodded. "Fine, just getting some air. The lounge was getting a little . . . intense." So was the outside, but that was a different story.

Thad shoved a door prop—where had that come from?—into the frame, then lit a cigarette and leaned against the wall beside her, a respectful distance away. "I hear you. I'm here for my own version of air." He saluted her with the cigarette. "We're about to start taping, though. Ten-minute warning."

Ten minutes to turn into a human again. Great. She pushed off from the wall. "I better go put myself together."

"Don't worry. You look great." The compliment rolled easily off his lips before he pulled another drag on his cigarette. Kat hesitated, unsure of the conversation's direction. Lucas's odd behavior around Thad jumped to the forefront of her thoughts, but she shook it off. How could she trust Lucas's judgment or advice now, knowing he'd actually struggled with the idea of getting her eliminated? Clearly his discernment was far from spot-on.

Thad was probably just trying to make her feel better. After all, he'd caught her outside alone, crying, against the side of a building. Who wouldn't offer a compliment? She smiled. "Thanks. But I could stand some touch-ups."

"You're actually one of the prettier contestants I've seen on the show so far." The line on anyone else would have felt awkward, and cheesy, but somehow from Thad, it just seemed matter-of-fact—not sleazy at all. "You sure you're okay? You've had a rough couple of rounds. With the tray dropping, and now the cupcakes burning."

"I had hoped you weren't paying that much attention." Kat felt a blush heat up her cheeks, and she fought the urge to fan her face. At this point, embarrassment was just a given. She should get used to it until she got home.

Which, after this round, might be sooner than she'd hoped.

"Oh, I'm paying attention." His voice lowered an octave as he flicked ash from the butt of his cigarette. "Trust me."

That line churned her stomach a little, but she brushed it off. Why would Thad be hitting on her, a nobody, apron-wearing baker from a small town in Louisiana? He was just checking on her, is all. Trying to cheer her up. He'd be saying the same thing to Piper or Tameka if they were out here.

"I hope I get a chance to prove myself and what I can do." Kat reached for the door, but Thad came behind her and tugged it open first, nudging the doorstop out of the way. His proximity kept her from turning to look him in the eye, but hopefully he could sense her determination. "I won't let you down."

"I never had a doubt." His hand bumped against hers—by accident?—as he passed her in the hallway. "See you on the set." He winked, and disappeared down the hall.

She turned in the opposite direction to go to the ladies' room, unsure why her heart was pounding so hard she struggled to breathe. Had he hit on her? Or was she paranoid after Lucas's earlier comments? Or just nervous about the judging coming up?

Thad's comments had been encouraging in that sense, though— if he didn't doubt her letting them down, then that meant she would get the chance she needed to prove herself.

Had he just given her a heads-up as to this round's results?

She washed her hands in the bathroom sink, then dried them with a paper towel and smoothed her hair back into a ponytail. Something about the conversation didn't sit right, but it might just be because of the drama with Lucas.

Who hadn't come back for her after all.

༺༒༻

She'd done it.

All by herself.

An addicting sensation, however unfamiliar it might be. She could get used to this.

Kat opened her laptop on the hotel bed and leaned back against the nest of pillows she'd created. Her cupcakes had come through, despite the lack of cheesecake, and impressed the judges with their simplicity. Thad even commented how the ingredients shone individually and weren't compromised by too many extra flavors. Maybe the cheesecake elimination had been for the best after all.

The bikers had been sent home for their less-than-creative decorations, so now it was an all-girl competition. Except for Lucas.

Ugh.

She shifted the pillow behind her head, and took a deep breath. Time to relax and *not* think about Lucas, cupcakes, or competitions.

Though two of those three seemed downright impossible.

Lucas had congratulated her after the results, though his demeanor during the cab ride back to the hotel had been stony at best. Even Thad's encouragement after the show had been stronger than Lucas's. What was his deal? Whatever it was, he wasn't volunteering the information, and she sure enough wasn't going to ask.

Not yet, anyway. Not while she was still this mad. And hurt.

No, just mad. Mad was better.

She booted up the computer, popped a lemon cookie in her mouth, and waited for her mail to load. Ten new emails, mostly spam, one announcing she was the random winner of a Nigerian bank account inheritance, and one from her mom.

Great.

Get it over with or procrastinate? She hesitated, then kept skimming the list in her in-box.

The last email was from her sister.

She almost choked on her cookie. What in the world could Stella have to write to her about? The mouse arrow hovered over the entry, and she finally double clicked. Her eyes scanned the words, an odd mixture of trepidation and anticipation building inside. Maybe she and Stella could reach a new level of friendship long-distance this week. At least they had something to talk about at the moment, which was rare for them.

The email started casually enough, and Kat reached for another cookie.

Hey, sis. Hope you're having fun. Have you seen any celebrities yet?

Not that she'd know if she had.

Not that you'd know if you did. Queen Oblivious.

Kat frowned. Whatever.

I know there's all those rules about not being able to tell the results before the show airs, but maybe you can give me just an idea of how it's going? You're not home yet, so you must not have been booted the first round. LOL!

Kat shoved another cookie in her mouth. Hilarious.

I don't even know if you'll read this before you get back, but I wanted you to know Aunt Mags isn't doing so hot. She's been in the hospital again, but don't worry, she's already home now, and that girl at the shop kept things running while she was gone.

Oh dear. They'd left Amy in charge? For longer than a single shift? Was the shop still standing, or had it burned to a crisp around her while Amy swayed along with her earbuds?

Just letting you know you're needed around here.

169

That was nice. Sort of. Needed—or wanted? Her throat closed, and she forced herself to swallow the rest of the cookie. Didn't matter. She was on the fast track here, had proven she had what it took so far—even without Lucas's support—so who cared?

Well, she did. But she could pretend a little longer that she didn't.

What would happen if Aunt Maggie didn't improve? If her health kept getting worse, she might have to shut down the store.

The only thing worse than baking the same cupcakes over and over might be not baking any at all.

If she won the competition, though, it would be a moot point. She wouldn't be involved with Sweetie Pies regardless of what Aunt Maggie decided. Right now, Kat was still in the running in the competition, so the opportunity for change lingered. She felt like a stuffed animal in a toy vending machine, jumping around, begging to be chosen, for the claws to reach down and pluck her up into a new life.

Preferably one where best friends didn't betray and families believed in each other and kisses actually meant something.

She went back to Stella's email.

Dad says hi. He's worried about you, but won't admit it outright. I don't know what he thinks is going to happen to you—you're Kat, after all. Predictable to a T. I assured him you were fine, don't worry. ☺

Hmm. She wasn't sure she entirely enjoyed being predictable. Predictable was what had kept her immersed in vanilla, strawberry, and chocolate cupcakes. Still, she was here in LA doing something about it, and that was pretty unpredictable.

Except Lucas had been the one to make it happen.

She didn't like to remember that part.

Anyway, I better run, almost late for my highlight appointment. Gonna go a lighter blonde this time. What do you think? Well, have fun taping, and tell Lucas I said hi. I haven't seen him much lately. Now that I think about it, we haven't talked much in person at all since that time he asked me out! I guess I never mentioned that to you, did I?

The text on the screen suddenly blurred into squiggly lines. Kat blinked, but the image didn't clear, the letters didn't rearrange into an order that made sense. Lucas and Stella? No. Impossible. He'd never.

Keep an eye out for celebrities. Try hard, okay? If you ignore Gerard Butler on the streets of LA, I swear I'll disown you.

She squeezed her eyes shut. This wasn't happening. No. Way. She'd open her eyes, and there would be rambling about movie stars and hot actors and nothing at all about her best friend. The only man she'd ever truly loved. The only person in her life who hadn't gone behind her back.

Until today.

Though he had gone behind her back to sign her up for the show, right?

And maybe on another day too, that she had yet to know about but might discover if she kept reading.

Did she want to know?

It didn't feel like she really knew anything about anything at the moment.

She exhaled slowly, opened her eyes, and then skimmed the previous lines again. But the lead weight in her stomach only grew heavier as the realization sank in deep. The truth was right there before her, in black and white. Lucas had asked out Stella.

She shut her computer with a snap, took a deep breath, carefully closed the bag of cookies, plumped her pillow.

And burst into tears.

nineteen

The treadmill couldn't contain him. The weights didn't hinder him. And the water in the pool just slowed him down.

They had to talk. Lucas had to fix this, somehow. The woman he loved thought he was a notch lower than an ogre, and until he smoothed things over, he wouldn't be able to sleep. Or eat.

His stomach growled. Well, maybe eat. But not enjoy it.

He rubbed his hair with the towel he'd snagged from the hotel gym and paced the carpeted floor in front of Kat's room. Maybe he was an ogre. How could he have ever debated something like that? No wonder she'd been ticked.

Their conversation from earlier replayed through his head, in vivid Technicolor, and he wished he had handled the entire ordeal better. But she'd taken him off guard—the whole thing had, really. How had those dang cupcakes burned?

Surely he'd have realized he had those kinds of superpowers before now.

No, it'd probably been an accident—a glitch of the oven timer. Though ironic didn't even begin to cover it.

And Thad—man, that guy bugged him. The judge's hearty congratulations after the show had seemed too familiar, too . . .

exuberant. He didn't give more than an obligatory handshake to the other finalists. What made Kat different?

Well, Lucas knew what made her different. What made her shine. What made her unique.

But Thad had no business knowing.

He paused in front of her door and raised his hand to knock, then lowered it, then raised it again. He ran his fingers through his damp hair. Man, this was stupid. He should just knock on the door. It wasn't like he was scared of her.

Kat was more hurt than angry, despite the front she'd put on outside the studio. He'd only seen Angry Kat a few times, and she would have him locked inside his own room, deadbolt on and chair under the knob.

But he could handle Hurt Kat.

He just couldn't stand the fact that he'd hurt her in the first place.

He finally tapped on the door with his knuckles, slung the towel around his neck, and held on to both ends as he waited.

And waited.

"Kat?" He knocked again. Had she gone to find something to eat? Surely not without him—though, no, he couldn't exactly blame her if she had. He wouldn't want to eat with him either, if the roles were reversed and he only had the same puzzle pieces she did. Maybe she was downstairs in the hotel restaurant or had run to one of the nearby cafés they'd discussed trying.

He started to turn away, wondering if he could actually stomach dinner without her, when a telltale sob sounded through the door.

No.

His heart plummeted onto the patterned carpet.

"Let me in." He knocked harder, jiggling the metal handle. Those tears would do him in if she didn't quit. A protective surge welled inside, and he shoved harder against the door. "Kat! What's wrong?"

A pointed cough sounded behind him. He turned and saw Tonya in his peripheral, ambling slowly down the hall with a giant purse tucked over her shoulder. She raised her eyebrows at him, and he groaned. They'd made it this far without running into any other contestants in the hotel, and Tonya chose this moment to make a debut?

At least it wasn't Piper.

He acknowledged her with a dip of his head, willing her to keep going.

But no, she stopped, tucked her thumb through the strap of that giant purse, and stared at him like she could burn a hole in his soul if he so much as blinked.

He didn't dare.

"Trouble?" Her tone suggested there better not be, and he was suddenly torn between rolling his eyes and begging for help. Something about the woman on the set rang true, and right now, he could probably stand some truth.

Tonya took a step closer, waiting for his response. Then she must have heard Kat's cries, because her suspicious expression morphed into compassionate. "Oh, sugar." She frowned at him and shook her head. "That doesn't sound good."

He swallowed the knot welling in his throat and looked between the door and Tonya and back again. No kidding. He just wanted the tears to stop. Now. At any cost.

Even his cost. Maybe especially his.

What had he done?

"Three words, sugar."

Now, it was his turn to raise his eyebrows at Tonya, knowing she really did care even if she was technically the enemy. Knowing she probably had a lot of wisdom she was preparing to tick off on those brightly painted long fingernails she held up.

Knowing he should probably listen.

"Say. You're. Sorry." The nails popped up one by one in emphasis. "Don't worry. She'll be fine."

Before he could answer, she kept on toward the elevator, pushed the button, and disappeared.

Hadn't he tried apologizing already?

He knocked again, louder.

Had to keep trying. He had no other game plan.

He lowered his voice and his hand, heart pounding so hard it might escape his chest. "Kat, open the door. We have to talk." He knew she'd been upset over his confession, but to be crying this hard, this many hours later? That wasn't like Kat.

Then again, he'd never admitted to anything so awful before.

The urge to protect transformed into the urge to grovel. Anything to stop the tears. Hurt Kat was one thing, Angry Kat quite another, but Crying Kat . . . He shuddered. "I said I was sorry."

Tonya was right. But it wasn't enough, apparently. Desperation surged.

"Kat—"

The door swung open under his hand, propelling him forward. He stumbled and caught himself against the frame, his gym towel slipping off his neck and landing at their feet in a flash of white.

Kat's mascara-streaked cheeks rang the first alarm in his head.

The pillow she hurled rang the second.

He ducked, and it sailed into the hall.

"Kat?" The tears didn't go with the violence. Now he was just confused—and to be honest, a little nervous. He didn't know whether to laugh, run, or join her in crying. "You've got to help me out here."

He grabbed for the pillow on the floor, but by the time he straightened and turned, she lobbed his chest with a second one. "Help you out?" Her laugh of disbelief rang hollow, completely devoid of humor. She hit him a third time in the shoulder. *Whack.* "I don't think so."

Good grief. He grabbed the pillow she wielded, used it to push her forward, and secured the door shut behind them. At least whatever this was could be handled privately. He released the pillow and put his hands on his hips. "Now, what the—"

Whack. Right across the cheek. It didn't hurt, but the disrespect element of being slapped across the face—even with a feather pillow—caught him off guard. He stilled, and the pillow dropped from Kat's fingers and hit the floor. The fight fled her stance, and she crumpled down beside the pillow. "I can't believe you."

She couldn't believe *him*? He was the one who had just walked into a sneak attack.

He shoved aside his pride—whatever trembling mess was left of it—and sank onto the floor beside her, cross-legged between the bed and the wall. She lay facedown on the pillow, head buried into the soft case. "I'm sorry."

He drew a deep breath. "For what?"

Her muffled words were almost unintelligible, but he caught most of them. "For . . . face . . . pillow."

He felt like he was calming a child. Or maybe a wild animal. He brushed her hair off the pillowcase and nudged her shoulder. "Look at me."

She shook her head, staying hidden. Hiding. From him. And it made his stomach hurt. He nudged again. "Kat." He let out his breath in a slow exhale. "Listen, I said I was sorry about the cupcakes. I promise I didn't burn them on purpose. The only reason I even thought of it was because I'm just—I'm ready to go home." *With you.* But he couldn't force the words out, couldn't make himself take the plunge when she was clearly not even on the same ledge he was on.

And if she was, if that kiss proved they were indeed standing on the same cliff—she wouldn't jump. And he couldn't make her. Not while her heart was focused on her dreams.

Dreams he'd actually considered sabotaging.

He really was an ogre.

His chest tightened, and his fingers absently played with the dark strands of hair splayed across the floor. "I'm sorry. For whatever that's worth. But I didn't do it. That dang timer—"

"This isn't about the cupcakes." She lifted her head then, revealing two black smudges on the white case.

"It's not?" News to him. What else had he done? He racked his brain, but came up with nothing. "You've lost me."

She pushed herself into a sitting position, facing him, and leaned against the side of the bed, their bent knees touching. She pulled the pillow into her lap and hugged it. "That's the problem."

His confusion was the problem? Great, feminine mind games at their finest. Darren used to warn him about these, but Kat had never been that way, had never been the type to be "I'm mad at you but want you to guess why." Maybe he screwed up and should know, but he didn't, so here they were. And here they'd stay if she didn't give him at least a strong clue.

"Kat, I'm exhausted. I've felt like crap ever since we left the studio, and I'm sorry, but I have no idea what else happened or what I did." He ran his hands down the length of his face, his growling stomach frustrating him further. He just wanted to scoop her up, dry her tears, and go eat. Put everything back to normal.

But normal wasn't enough anymore.

Maybe *that* was the problem they both felt.

He held out his hand, a peace offering. "I'm confused." And she was hurt. Neither of which was fair.

She stared at his outstretched palm, tentatively reaching, then suddenly pulled her hand back. The fire in her eyes reignited, and she held her drawn-up legs tightly to her chest. Distancing from him. Protecting her heart. Removing contact between them.

"I didn't say I expected you to know." The ice in her voice was a chilly contrast to the spark in her gaze.

He had nothing to say to that. So he waited, ignoring the ache in his gut that started the minute she pulled away from him and probably would continue to grow until she agreed to marry him.

Unless she killed him first.

He shifted under her intense gaze, his frustration mounting—mostly at his inability to defuse the situation. "Kat, I'm not up for games. What the heck are you talking about here?"

She raised an eyebrow, a mask shading what was really going on in her eyes, making her appear a stranger. "I'm surprised you forgot. Most people don't."

"Forgot what? What did I forget?"

"Who."

He frowned. "What?"

"Forget *who*, not what."

He let out a huff. "Kat, I swear . . ."

"You asked out my sister!"

And there it was.

But it wasn't over.

She launched forward onto her knees, pushing against him with all the strength she could muster, pounding him with doubled fists. The surprise of it all kept him motionless, leaving him open for her attack. The blows landed on his shoulders, his chest, his biceps. He took the hits, letting her finish, his mind racing to catch up. Stella. He had asked out Stella? Why didn't he remember that? And why did it make Kat so crazy?

Well, no, he knew why it would make her crazy, if she actually believed it to be true.

Once again, he wished he could beat up Chase. That idiot left more residual damage than anyone he'd ever met. But he couldn't beat up Chase, because at the moment, he was busy being beat up himself.

The brunt of Kat's attack finally slowed, tears now pouring down her cheeks. He caught her fists in one hand and pushed, gently, holding her away from him but close enough to see her face.

She struggled limply in his grasp and then gave up. "You asked out my sister." The repeated accusation floated from her lips like the last gasp of air from a woman on death's door. She sagged against him, shaking, and he released her wrists to wrap his arm around her.

He started to speak, then stopped, terrified of saying the wrong thing, of somehow making it worse instead of better. But he had no idea what Kat was talking about. When did he ask out Stella? He had never been interested in Kat's younger sister—she wasn't his type. Sure, she was beautiful, but in a model thin, try-too-hard kind of way that worked for some guys. He, however, preferred his women like he preferred his cupcakes—sweet, unique, and round in all the right places.

"I've never dated your sister. You know better than that." He smoothed her hair away from her forehead.

She shrugged. "Maybe you didn't date her. She didn't say anything specific. But you still asked her out." She shifted, burying her face in his shoulder. "Same difference."

Same diff—how was asking someone out and dating them the same?

Girl World was such a scary place.

He tightened his arms around Kat and racked his brain again, knowing his window of time to fix this was rapidly sliding shut. He had to figure this out, had to make this right, or it would be forever before they got past it. This, on the heels of the cupcake burning incident, would be too much for the tension already throbbing between them on this trip.

He thought, rocking Kat slightly in his arms, wishing he could make it go away. All of it. But no, he had to try. Stella. He would have never asked Stella out. Not for real.

Wait.

He abruptly stopped rocking. "I didn't ask her out on a date. I asked her to meet me for coffee—about two months ago. But then I changed my mind and canceled."

Kat pulled away to look at him, her red-rimmed eyes even more suspicious than the hotel housekeeper's had been in the hallway. "Why? Why did you ask her?"

To talk about Kat. To talk about ten acres, and dreams, and the future, and his heart. He'd needed an ally, needed someone on his side as he pursued this. Pursued Kat. He'd realized after further discussion with Darren that Stella wasn't the right confidante for the job. They'd never even gone to get that coffee.

But could he admit all that? How would Kat take it? He hesitated, unwilling to play his whole hand without knowing what other cards Kat had up her own sleeve. "Secrets."

She sniffed, wary. "It's not Christmas."

"Wasn't Christmas secrets."

"Why did you want to tell my sister secrets at all?" The defense was back in her voice, scraping another layer of concrete between the bricks she kept building between them.

He didn't blame her for any of it. Betrayal was betrayal, and this one had Essence of Chase spilled all over it, in all its reeking glory. Man, he needed to punch that guy. But Chase wasn't here. He was, and Kat's laser beam of distrust was aimed right at his own heart.

"Did it ever occur to you that you ask too many questions?" He teased, knowing it to be dangerous in her current mood, but he couldn't tell the truth. Not the whole truth. Not yet.

The fight edged back into her eyes, subtle, but nearly tangible. He'd rather see fight than tears any day. "Did it ever occur to you not to go behind my back with my sister?"

"Go behind your—I didn't go behind your back." Why did she insist on making this harder? He was torn between wanting to pull his hair out and kiss her senseless.

Probably both.

She stiffened, defensive. "Maybe not exactly, but you still didn't tell me."

"For good reason!"

"Well, I'm sure Chase thought the exact same thing!"

She jumped up before he could respond, threw the pillow on the bed, and walked—more like stomped—toward the bathroom.

Nope. Not happening. He might be guilty of some things, but he wasn't about to start taking all the blame for a loser in her past.

He reached behind him and grabbed Kat's ankle as she passed. She shrieked, and he caught her in his lap as she tumbled down. "Lucas! Are you crazy?"

He didn't answer, just wrapped one arm tightly enough around her to discourage any ideas about leaving, and brought the other hand up to lightly cover her lips. "That's the last time you compare anything I do to Chase. Got it?"

Her eyes widened, and he pulled his hand away, allowing her the chance to talk. She didn't take it. Smart girl. He loosened his grip, and as she stood, she whacked him with the pillow again. "And that's the last time you manhandle me. Got it?"

She didn't wait for an answer. She just marched into the bathroom and slammed the door.

Lucas leaned back against the wall, breathless, unsure if he was chagrined or impressed.

Probably both.

twenty

Maybe she'd overreacted. But so had Lucas, going all caveman on her. It wasn't his typical style, yet then again, she wasn't usually the crazy, jealous, pillow-throwing type, either.

What had happened to them? This trip was driving them both insane. Once upon a time they'd both been functioning, mature adults.

Or at least faked it well enough.

Kat really didn't want to come out of the bathroom. She'd stared at herself in the mirror for five minutes, hashing out her own internal debate, hoping Lucas would take the hint and leave.

And hoping he would stay right there and not give up on her.

She'd given some kind of ultimatum by hiding out in the bathroom, some sort of battle-of–the-wills, manipulation thing that Lucas was calling her bluff on by refusing to leave—and by refusing to come after her.

Now she had to play it out. Or look even more foolish than she already did.

Why had she snapped at him like that about Stella? She should have known better. But that email, and her mood, and his betrayal from earlier about the burned cupcakes . . . She'd panicked. For those few moments in time, it seemed as if she had no one to trust, no one on her side at all.

She was tired of distorted half-truths.

At least she knew Lucas wasn't lying. His story made a lot more sense than what she'd first thought, and if Lucas and Stella had never even talked about why he was asking to meet with her, then obviously Stella would have taken his invitation to be what it sounded like—a date with her sister's *friend*. She didn't know any different, and she didn't seem to care that Lucas had changed his mind. Her sister's entire life was spent either turning down or accepting dates, and she had too many men in her life to worry about one canceling on her.

She'd say it must be nice, but it really wouldn't be. Kat didn't want a lot of men pursuing her.

Just the one.

She sagged against the counter by the sink and frowned at her reflection, at her own immaturity and neediness she couldn't seem to tame. She hated these relationship games. And she and Lucas weren't even in a relationship.

Which was largely part of the problem.

But he remained too blind, even after that blasted kiss, to do anything about it.

Which wasn't entirely fair, maybe, because in her heart she knew even if he did, it wouldn't stop her from going to New York for a year—or longer—if given the opportunity.

Talk about a no-win situation. She squinted at her reflection, sighed, and swiped her fingers under her eyes to remove the smeared mascara. Was she really mad at Lucas for not taking the initiative on something she couldn't even accept in the first place? Mad at her best friend for not pushing their boundaries and throwing himself out there to be rejected by her?

She just wanted to be wanted.

Wanted him.

But at the cost of her dreams?

Ugh.

She leaned forward, propping her elbows on the counter and burying her face in her hands. Her brain hurt. Too many options, too many possibilities, and all of them currently outside of her immediate control or choice.

What if she lost the competition and remained in Bayou Bend for the rest of her days? Would Lucas decide to step up and change things between them *then*?

And could she ever be content with that life? It wouldn't be hard at all to be content with Lucas. But the rest of it—well, marriage, wouldn't be enough forever. Not when she had all this stirring inside her, all these longings and this sticky need to prove herself, to push herself, to *be* and *do*.

If she didn't find her niche, her spot, her purpose, how could she be the wife Lucas would need in the first place? She didn't want to be a burden, another mouth to feed or person to entertain and keep happy. She wanted to contribute, to flourish, to expand.

She wanted to play the game *with* him, not stand on the side-lines and cheer.

Part of her wanted to be content in Bayou Bend. But God had put these dreams in her heart for a reason, right? So what did that mean? Was she supposed to find contentment in the mundane, ignore her gifts and desires, and somehow find a way to bloom where planted?

She really just wanted to bloom at Bloom.

So if she lost . . . the outcome didn't look good. She'd have to find a new route out of Bayou Bend on her own. Which was about two shades short of terrifying.

But if she won . . .

What if Lucas came with her?

The idea floated just out of reach, like a butterfly flitting from flower to flower. There, and beautiful, yet uncatchable. She knew it wasn't actually possible for Lucas to leave everything he had in Bayou Bend for her—but what if he did? What if he cared enough about her to follow *her*, for once, instead of her always being a step behind him?

She didn't need him as much as she thought she did. She'd proven that already on this trip, having to step up and take care of things herself, having to pep talk herself into victory. She really was capable. She could figure it out on her own, could survive on her own. She knew what she was doing.

Realizing she didn't *need* Lucas, however, only served to remind her how much she *wanted* him.

Which was way, way, way worse.

Knock knock knock.

She jumped. Lucas.

She'd won?

"Kat." His voice radiated through the thin door, as if he'd pushed his lips close to it. "Get out of there, already. I'm hungry."

There was the Lucas she was used to—borderline demanding coach voice and grumpy when he hadn't eaten. She checked the time on her cell phone, which she'd stuck in her back pocket. No wonder he was hungry; they usually ate an hour or two earlier.

"Kat!"

"I'm coming." She'd won. He'd come to her. She smiled at her reflection, but the victory didn't feel as good as she'd hoped.

In fact, it made her feel a little silly.

She opened the door, embarrassed. "You pick. Anywhere you want to go."

"I vote whatever is closest." He handed her the room key card she'd left lying on the entry table, shoved her purse at her, and ushered her out the door. It clicked shut behind them, and Lucas made an immediate beeline for the elevators.

While she rushed two steps behind, trying to catch up.

 celeo

She'd teased him after he asked their taxi driver to take them to the nearest McDonald's. But after they'd eaten double cheeseburgers and grabbed milkshakes to go, he'd put them back in a cab and instructed the driver to head toward Santa Monica—and he hadn't heard a single complaint since.

Now they were strolling on the famous Santa Monica Pier, and all previous tension between them had completely dissipated, right into the brisk October wind blowing off the Pacific. He watched Kat sip from her strawberry milkshake, grateful that for the moment, at least, everything was normal. No drama, no tension, no unanswered questions. No cupcakes or recipes or timers. No football stats or obligations or pressure to win.

Just him, Kat, and a quarter mile of tourist-trap heaven.

If they couldn't find a way to breathe out here by the ocean . . .

Kat shifted the pink bear he'd won for her to her other arm and tossed her cup into a nearby trash can. "Probably would have been cheaper to buy the bear outright."

"Hey, watch it." Lucas sipped from the large root beer he'd bought after a dozen or more attempts at Skeeball, relieved she could tease him again and even more relieved that it didn't offend him. "I finally made a decent enough score for a prize." Sort of.

She neatly dodged a little boy running toward them with a cone of cotton candy. "That, or the carnival worker felt sorry for you."

Definitely that. "Well, it's not like they had a bunch of footballs lying around."

"Because you'd have nailed it."

"Exactly." He laughed, then nudged her. "Glad we understand each other." Again. Finally.

They stood in a short line for the Ferris wheel, and as their car climbed toward the top, providing a stomach-dropping view of the shore and the waves below, Lucas opened his arm to Kat.

She immediately nestled against his side, his arm draped around her shoulder, the stuffed bear in her lap.

Here he was in such a hurry to get home, and home was already tucked right against him.

Kat pointed out a street show of mimes down below, leaning slightly away to peer over the side of their car, and laughed. The sound danced on the wind, reminding Lucas of a hundred memories gone by and about a hundred more he wished to make.

But there was something different about Kat on this trip, especially in the last few days. She was stronger, sharper—harder. More confident, more vocal.

Louder.

In some ways, it was a good thing, yet in others . . . not *bad*. Not exactly. Just not . . . right. Different.

He didn't like it.

Didn't like her being more independent, not needing him as much. But hadn't that been his goal all along? To help her stand on her own two incredibly capable feet and spread her wings? Bloom?

Bloom. Man, there was that blasted bakery again, creeping into his thoughts. Interrupting every peaceful moment he'd almost captured. Threatening to steal whatever hopes he dared to hope.

He still didn't like Thad. Didn't trust him. The man sent out a certain vibe, one Lucas couldn't ignore any longer. And Kat would have no idea about a guy like that, not with having been so sheltered in Bayou Bend her entire life. She to this day had zero idea how strikingly beautiful she was.

And how much of an idiot Chase had been. Stella might be a pageant winner, but Kat—she was the kind of woman a man wanted to spend his life with.

And she could stop traffic all at the same time.

"This was a good idea." She leaned her head back against his shoulder, craning her neck to watch the star-studded sky above them.

Lucas relaxed, despite the wind rocking their Ferris wheel car as they ascended, and he halfway wished the thing would get stuck for an hour or two. Down below, the mimes continued their performance, drawing a crowd of giggling tourists. Children shrieked from far away, and somewhere up the pier, music blared faintly from another carnival game. But up here, reality couldn't touch them. They had their own world, one void of rules, expectations, and confusion. Just the two of them, like it used to be. Like it should be.

Like it *would* be, if he could just get Kat home again.

Despite the fact that kiss of theirs had messed up so much, he couldn't help but want a repeat.

In slow motion.

He leaned forward, subtly inhaled the scent of her hair instead, and closed his eyes. Ran his lips across the silky dark strands. Wishing he could bury his hands in it, hold on. Hold her.

"I just realized I never said I forgave you."

Her words cut the stillness of the night, and he pulled away, stiffened. Why had she brought it up again? But that was Kat, needing to know. Needing closure.

He didn't really blame her. Especially considering how their fight earlier had ended-but-not-really with a pillow fight, a locked bathroom door, and a growling, hungry football coach.

"So, do you?" He tried not to hold his breath, but he couldn't help it.

She nodded against his shoulder, snuggled an inch closer. "How could I not?"

Good question. He exhaled and squeezed her briefly, then joined her in looking up at the sky. Maybe it was the roar of the ocean waves, or the wide expanse of the blackness above him, or the feel of her hair brushing his chin, but something sort of put him in a retrospective mood too. "I shouldn't have left you outside at the studio earlier. Even though you pretty much demanded it."

He still didn't know why he'd let that door shut between them. He figured it would lock, and part of him hoped it would and that

Kat would realize how immature she was being by running away. Yet the other half of him couldn't venture farther than just around the inside corner, so that he'd be the first one to hear her knock for reentry.

But someone else must have let her in, or maybe it hadn't locked after all, because she'd come barreling inside right on time, no worse for the wear.

"It was okay. I wasn't out there alone anyway."

His double cheeseburger did a forward roll. "What do you mean?" But he already had a pretty good idea.

She shifted slightly to look up at him. "Thad joined me. He was taking a smoke break."

Perfect. "What'd he say?"

She absently twisted the leg of the pink bear in her lap. "He just asked if I was okay. Saw that things had gotten . . . hectic."

Hectic. Talk about an understatement. "What else did he say?" There was more. He could tell by the way she began plucking fur off the bear's leg.

"That he believed in me."

An unbiased judge, huh?

She plucked faster. "And, you know . . . that I'm . . . pretty."

Now he just wanted to strangle the teddy bear. Thad. Outside, with Kat, alone behind the studio, complimenting her. Winning her over. Boosting her confidence.

Man, the guy was slick. Slicker than Sam's blasted hair.

Their car jerked into a descent, sending the horizon into a momentary, dizzying blur of lights. "I told you I didn't like that guy from the beginning." His voice was stiffer than he meant it to be.

"What do you mean?"

"I mean, I warned you about him." He shook his head with a humorless laugh. "And I was right."

"Right about what?" Kat pushed against the side of the car, twisting to face him. "He didn't do anything wrong."

Now she was defending him. "It's not appropriate, *Kat*. How can you not see that?"

"I only see one thing, *Lucas*." She bit off his name as sharply as he'd spoken hers. He hadn't meant it to sound condescending, but apparently it'd been worse than that. And apparently she hadn't forgiven him as thoroughly as she'd thought.

She squeezed the teddy bear with both hands, and he briefly wondered if she'd send the thing flying off the side of the Ferris wheel. "I see you overreacting, because, for once, someone else stepped in where you were supposed to."

His temper flared, hotter than the rush of indignant heat creeping up his neck. "What do you mean, *supposed* to? I've been your number one supporter from the beginning. And I'm pretty sure my motives behind that are a whole lot purer than that slimy judge's."

"Thad is slimy now? Real mature, Lucas." Kat raised her eyebrow at him, and he wished he could take a Sharpie and draw the thing back in place where it belonged. "He would have done the same thing for any contestant in my position."

"Right." So, so naïve. "You really think he'd have been out there telling Piper or Tameka how pretty they are and that he believed in them?"

She averted her eyes, calmly placing the teddy bear in a choke hold. "That's not fair."

He snorted. "Yeah, you say that because I just shot your theory full of holes. Why can't you just listen to me? Trust me? I know what I'm talking about with this guy."

"No, you don't. Believe it or not, you're not always right, Lucas."

Not always. But pretty close to it. He had to be right—he'd always been, his entire life, because people depended on him. If he wasn't right, people got hurt. Like his football players, or his friends. Like his mom.

Like Kat.

He mentally counted to ten. First in English, then in French.

Then again in Spanish and pig latin. "I'm right on this one. I can see it coming a mile away. You need to listen to me."

"Oh, I'm listening, all right." Their car jerked to a stop as people climbed into an empty car down below. "I'm hearing you loud and clear. You're just upset that you can't control me anymore."

"Con—" He cut himself off with his own hand fisted against his mouth. Had she really just accused him of that? He lowered his hand slowly, wishing he knew any other language to count in. "Kat. Seriously? When have I ever controlled you?"

"When have you ever not? You're always giving me *suggestions*." She air-quoted the word, letting go of the bear, which slid dangerously close to the front of the open-ended car. "Suggestions that are more like demands."

She was exaggerating. Yet a portion of her words pricked his heart with truth. Truth he couldn't handle. "It's not about control." Was it? No. He wasn't like that. He was a coach. He liked being in charge. He was *good* at it. People needed him to be good at it. Kat had always needed him to be good at it.

Apparently that had just changed.

He let out a sharp sigh. "I wasn't trying to control you. Ever." Maybe sometimes he had, by default. It was all for her sake, though. No one would ever take care of Kat like he would. No one would ever protect her like he would.

No one would ever love her like he would.

But wasn't his making plans for their future without even telling her a prime example of being controlling?

Now he couldn't turn off his own conscience.

Kat's steady gaze burning into his own didn't help, like she could read his thoughts. Like she knew them better than he did.

She snatched the bear back from the edge of the car. "I'm not one of your players, Lucas. You're not my coach."

Thank goodness, or they'd have killed each other long ago. But . . . "What are you trying to say?"

"I'm saying, back off. Let me do this." She pushed her hair from her eyes with both hands and tucked it behind her ears. Hard to believe just moments ago he'd been inhaling the heady scent of it. Why did everything between them have to be so extreme all of a sudden? He missed Kat's consistency. Missed knowing that if he could ever count on anything, it was her. Them.

What was happening?

"You *are* doing it." He lowered his voice, hoping to defuse the fight, but it only seemed to rile her up more.

"Exactly!" Her eyes lit with a light he couldn't quite place. One he didn't recognize anymore. "You've always pushed me to try harder and reach further and put myself out there. Now that I'm doing it, now that I'm making it happen, you're trying to hold me back."

He started to defend himself, started to run through his go-to list of automatic plays, but stopped cold. Was she right? He shut his mouth, pressed his lips together.

There was absolutely nothing he could say.

The Ferris wheel creaked into motion again, jerking them forward, back to the ground below. Back to reality.

Back to an unpredictable future he couldn't see.

twenty-one

"Love is blind."

Kat fought the urge to roll her eyes at Sam's overly dramatic presentation of round four. He stood solemnly before the cameras, hands clasped behind his suit-clad back, rocking slightly on the heels of his shiny shoes, delivering his monologue with all the seriousness of a Shakespearean actor.

She stole a glance over her shoulder at Lucas, who stood at the ready at their empty workstation as she, Piper, and Tameka manned the front lines, ready to grab their ingredients as soon as Sam stopped droning on. Love might be blind, but it also opened one's eyes to a *lot*.

Such as how stupid one could be when in it.

Her stomach churned, and she wiped her palms on her apron, wishing she hadn't bought those blasted aprons in the first place, wishing she could just bake already, distract her runaway thoughts, and channel her hovering aggression into something tangible.

Wishing she could dunk Lucas's face into a bowl of cupcake batter.

How in the world could he not see how he'd controlled her all these years? Maybe the motivation behind his actions wasn't a negative one, but the facts remained the same. All this time, she had doubted her own ability, doubted her talent, felt trapped in the binds of her insecurities and fears . . .

All while Lucas held the ropes.

Maybe love was blinder than she realized. After all, she'd never noticed the truth before, and apparently Lucas still couldn't see it. If he was still blind, did that mean he was in love too?

Or was he just that oblivious?

With men, it could go either way.

Her eye suddenly caught Thad's from behind the judges' table, and he offered a subtle wink. Feeling a flush creep up her neck, she looked quickly away, feigning interest in Sam's never-ending soliloquy. Hopefully, Lucas didn't catch that, or else he'd blow it up to ridiculous proportions.

"Today, bakers, you're going to create three different cupcakes that demonstrate the beauty, pain, and blindness of love." Their exaggerating host paused for effect. "All in two hours."

Great. What could she make that represented the beauty, pain, and blindness of love? She couldn't ask Lucas's opinion on what to bake, that much was certain. Not after she railed on him last night on the Ferris wheel about his backing off and her doing it all herself. In fact, she was halfway surprised he'd even gotten out of bed this morning and come to the show in the first place. Probably because she'd have been eliminated if he hadn't.

But wasn't that what he essentially admitted to wanting in the first place?

Focus, Kat. She shook off the negative, distracting thoughts of Lucas and crouched slightly, ready to run to the shelves of ingredients at Sam's word. She could do this. She *had* to do this. She'd just figure it out when she got there—with or without Lucas.

Probably without.

"This round will be scored on a combination of both taste and decorations, so don't hold back, guys." Sam clapped his hands. "Start the clock! Ready, bakers?"

She stiffened, felt Lucas's eyes on her back, felt the challenge, the loaded question. *Could* she do this? Could she prove herself once and for all? She squared her shoulders, lifted her chin. Of course she could.

That nagging feeling in her stomach—fear? regret?—would dissipate eventually. Right?

"Three . . . two . . ."

And if not, well, she'd gotten what she came for. Self-respect. Self-esteem. Self-pride.

The nagging feeling intensified, and she swallowed.

"One! Go!"

Ready or not.

∾

This wasn't working. Her meringue was more sloppy than fluffy. Her rhubarb filling was so chunky it looked as if she'd only considered the blender instead of actually using it. And her black fondant sunglasses appeared more Johnny Bravo than Johnny Cash.

Meanwhile, Lucas hovered just out of reach, following the instructions she tossed at him but taking no initiative. When he finished a task, he stood and waited with expectation for his next mission rather than looking around to see what needed to be done and just doing it as he always had before.

She apparently had just graduated to being both chef *and* sous chef.

And the pressure was about to make her shove her apron into the blender and hit puree.

She gritted her teeth. "Lucas. The filling on the stove."

"What about it?" He asked calmly, rocking back on his heels like Sam continued to do over by the judges' table. Was that just a guy thing? Was Lucas mocking Sam? She didn't know anymore. Didn't have time to care.

Besides, if someone didn't prevent that second batch of rhubarb compote from burning, she was going to do some fancy footwork of her own. Like kick her tennis shoe straight up—

"Bakers, forty minutes!" Sam barked from the front of the room, appearing way too gleeful at the grim announcement. Kat bit back a rush of panic and cast a frantic look at her competition. Tameka and Tonya, faces grim, lips pressed into straight lines, bent over their decorations as they cut pink fondant into shapes she couldn't recognize from this far away. Piper and Amanda, who had been strangely quiet all day, worked steadily as well. Maybe even they were tired of the cattiness and had decided to just concentrate on winning.

Which just made Kat all the more nervous.

She swung her attention back to the stove. "Lucas! Take the compote off the burners." Please. She couldn't make herself say it. If she showed any hint of compassion or friendship, she'd crumble faster than the coconut in her chocolate cake. She had to stay mad or she'd never make it through this round.

"Aye, aye, boss."

Well, at least Lucas wasn't making her angry goal hard.

He ambled to the stove, wrestled an oven mitt onto his hand in seemingly slow motion, and removed the pan from the top. He stood there, then, holding it like a programmed robot that could only hear and absorb one comment at a time and waited for his next prompt.

Frustration balled in her throat. She couldn't swallow it back, couldn't breathe. She flapped her hands at her sides, tried to inhale around the tennis ball of anger that lodged there so tight. She couldn't explode. She knew why he was doing this, and deep down, beneath the ball, she knew it was her own fault. She'd asked for this, and pretty rudely, at that. What did she expect? Lucas to ignore her childishness and schemes and be the bigger man—again?

Yes, actually she had.

But she couldn't depend on that. On him. It was all on her.

She had to make her dreams come true. No one else was going to do it. At this point, no one else seemed to even support her dreams in the first place, much less be willing to help her achieve them.

Maybe not even God anymore.

The ball widened, and she choked back an unshed tear. Maybe God wanted her to prove herself too. Maybe she'd been dependent on Lucas for too long, and God was giving her the reins to do this herself. Make it happen herself and prove that she didn't need anyone.

Or maybe he just wasn't all that interested either.

Maybe she was on the wrong path, and he'd given up on her already.

No. The panic swelled. She could—no, *would*—make this happen. No matter what.

And if not, then, well—she'd go down trying.

With a deep breath that dislodged the ball, she snatched an extra oven mitt from the counter, grabbed the pan from Lucas's hand, and took it to the mixer. She stared unseeing at the concoction bubbling into the bowl, gave it a brisk stir, and loaded the piping bag.

Then realized she hadn't cored the cinnamon cupcakes yet.

Deep breath times two.

She grabbed the corer and began hastily cutting out the centers, then poured the filling inside.

All while Lucas stood beside her, arms crossed, watching. Waiting.

She'd almost rather go home than play this game with him—and lose.

But not quite.

"Would you finish the fondant sunglasses? Less animated, if you can. More legit." She didn't look at him, proud of the way she kept her tone in check. Not even a hint of the indignation she felt bubbling inside hotter than that compote. She licked her lips. "Please." She didn't want to be a complete bear, though she couldn't seem to figure out how to retract her claws.

"Sure." He swung around the work counter to face her, and went to work on the fondant glasses.

She hated that he made them perfect. Did what she couldn't.

Again.

Deep breath times three.

She quickly creamed some extra butter into the stubborn meringue, and it stiffened right up. Ha. See? She knew what she was doing. She could do this. She was capable.

Had to be.

She iced the remaining cupcakes, ignored Lucas standing motionless near the finished sunglasses, and then placed the completed decorations atop the cinnamon cakes. The caramel apple cakes were already decorated with red fondant, split-down-the-middle broken hearts, and the chocolate coconut cakes boasted little books with tiny sugar crystals pressed inside to represent Braille.

"Ten minutes." Sam's joyful alert didn't strike panic in her heart for once, because for once she was ahead of schedule. Now she could stand back and watch Piper and Amanda scurry around in a frenzy.

Not a drop of sympathy to be given there.

Kat untied her apron and leaned against the counter, exhausted. She did sort of wish she could lend Tameka and Tonya a hand, as they'd been consistently friendly to everyone for the duration of the taping. They were still scrambling to finish their decorations, which looked amazing so far, but that wouldn't matter if they didn't actually make it on the cupcakes in time.

She closed her eyes briefly, then jerked them open to double check that their cupcakes were plated and ready to go before closing them again with a sigh of relief. Funny how this round—the round in which she'd had the least help—had gone the smoothest. No shady tricks from Piper. No accidents in the kitchen. No possible sabotage from her own team member.

"Good job." Lucas's quiet words of affirmation in her ear, probably intended to soothe, just rubbed irritatingly raw. What was he trying to do here?

"No thanks to you." The words fell from her lips like miniature missiles, and she wished she could swallow them back. But then she'd blow up inside, and that wasn't any better.

He nodded slowly. "I deserved that. Don't worry."

"What's your deal, Lucas?" Kat tried to keep her voice low but struggled. "You barely did a thing today. This is the round that determines the finals, and I had to practically babysit you."

"You told me to back off, give you space. Not hold you back." He shrugged, then crossed his arms over his blue apron, which still made him look way hotter than he'd ever know. "Just doing what you asked."

She had asked that, yes, but—since when did he listen to her? She shook her head. "Whatever, Lucas. I'm just tired of this." Tired of herself. Tired of him.

Tired of the unspoken currents between them that kept carrying them away into no-man's-land.

"So am I, Kat. I came all the way out here to help you, and it's been one attack after another." His words sounded sharper somehow at low volume, more intimate and intense. More sincere. She tried to dodge their pointy barbs, but they landed in her heart anyway. "You know, you're so obsessed with winning and with this dream of yours."

"*I'm* obsessed? You pushed me out here. You made me come!" Kat yanked her tone back to a whisper as Piper's gaze rose and her head tilted their direction. She turned slightly to put her back to the opposing team.

Though lately, it seemed more like her own teammate was the real opposition.

"Exactly." Lucas leaned forward, his warm peppermint breath wafting against her hair. "I wanted to help you make your dreams come true, Kat. Not turn them into an idol."

She reeled backward, heart somehow simultaneously in both

her shoes and in her throat. "Get out." Leave. Go. Go away. She couldn't hold back the tears pressing, burning, about to consume her. An idol? How could he say that?

Could it be true?

"Gladly." He untied his apron and tossed it at her. "See you in the waiting lounge."

Her eyes narrowed as she balled the apron in her hands.

No. He wouldn't.

◦◦◦

There was just no pleasing a woman.

Lucas, careful to keep his phone angled toward him and away from the chatting women perched on the couches near him in the lounge, punched in a text to Darren. Deleted it. Then tapped it in again and hit Send before erasing it a second time.

He had no idea what to say, how to sum up what had just happened over the past twenty-four hours. He just knew that everything was different, and he hated it.

He leaned his head back against the couch and sighed. Maybe Darren had been right. Maybe he had been trying to stir up or awaken love before it was time, and this was the disastrous result. Maybe he should have just been Kat's friend and supported her and left it at that. Left it for God to work out instead of taking over himself and messing it all up.

Well, that was a pretty good start for the text.

He keyed in the realization, then sat back and waited, hoping his friend had some words of wisdom to share before the decision for this round was announced. Kat had yet to come into the lounge to meet him. Was she avoiding him?

Could he blame her?

He'd called her dream an idol. Not even just labeled it, but accused her of making it that way, no less.

What was it about this show that made the worst of each of them jump out and claw at the other? They'd spent more time fighting each other lately than banding together against the other competitors.

Speaking of, Piper had been laying low this round—a fact that made him more nervous, as Kat's Aunt Maggie would say, than a long-tailed cat in a room full of rocking chairs.

He stole a sideways glance at the snarky younger girl, and realized with a start she was boring her gaze right back into him. Unashamedly staring, with a smirk.

Angling that rocking chair leg right toward him.

His phone beeped, and he jumped. Piper laughed. He glared back. That striped-sock witch in the movie he'd watched with Kat the other day had nothing on this chick.

Incoming text from Darren. Finally. WHAT'D U SAY 2 HER?

Well, no turning back now. He started typing. CALLED HER DREAM AN IDOL.

OUCH.

Lucas snorted. I KNOW. JUST HATE HOW BLIND SHE IS, MAN.

LOVE IS BLIND, RIGHT?

Well, that was ironic. Darren didn't even know about the theme of the round. Lucas thought a moment, then keyed in a response. SHE'S LET THIS CUPCAKE DREAM BECOME EVERYTHING TO HER.

EVERYTHING HOW?

U KNOW. IT'S ALL SHE WANTS. ALL SHE THINKS ABOUT.

HMMM.

Man, he really hated Darren's "hmmms." That noncommittal, I'm-not-going-to-say-anything-until-you-realize-stuff-for-yourself-first trick. Made him almost as anxious as Piper was making him now as she whispered with Amanda over in the corner. Where was Kat, anyway? He should go look for her.

But she didn't really seem to want to be found.

He hesitated, then continued typing. IT'S THIS OBSESSION THAT'S

CROWDING OUT ANY HOPE FOR REAL HAPPINESS. FOR OTHER DREAMS.

U MEAN, YOUR DREAMS?

Ouch.

He powered his phone off.

လူလ

Once again, she was outside behind the studio, fuming—except this time, she'd propped the door with the same wooden doorstop from inside the door Thad had used.

She did learn *some* lessons.

How dare Lucas tell her she'd made her dream an idol? Talk about hypocritical. Here he'd been shoving her *toward* her dreams all these years, taking the final steps to help launch her into her desired future—and now he wanted to pull the rug out from under her and say never mind? To cast judgment?

Easy to say to someone who didn't have any dreams because they were already living theirs out. Lucas had everything he wanted—dream job, dream career, small-town fame. He had a purpose and a plan every day. He had obtainable goals and had already won a championship to prove it. He didn't know what it was like to feel like you were constantly missing the mark, like everything you hoped for was always just a step out of reach. That, worse yet, everyone who knew you the best didn't believe your dreams were even possible for you.

Yet he wanted to point fingers at *her* motivation and *her* goals? Men.

She texted a quick summary of recent events to Rachel, who wrote back with a brief OMG and sympathetic MEN in all caps.

Not entirely helpful.

She lifted her face to the breeze blowing through the alley, trying to inhale peace. Catch her breath. Not think about the fact that here in just a few minutes, her entire fate would once again be determined by three assorted, famous bakers sitting behind a metal table.

Was God involved in this process at all? Or had she kicked him out?

Sure felt like she was alone.

Her phone beeped again. SORRY, DIAPER EXPLOSION.

Kat wrinkled her nose. NO PROB. Rachel definitely won the pity party battle of the day with that one.

LUCAS IS JUST PROJECTING. IGNORE HIM.

Ignore him? How? He was her baking assistant. Her best friend. And the only other person she currently knew in Los Angeles. EASIER SAID THAN DONE.

HIS OPINION MATTERS 2 U. REMEMBER THAT.

Ugh. TRYING TO FORGET.

THAT'S THE POINT. IT MATTERS ANYWAY.

Kat frowned. WHAT'S UR POINT?

MY POINT IS: HAVE YOU WORN THE BLACK DRESS YET?

Oh good grief. She powered her phone off.

"There you are." The male voice wasn't Lucas's, as she halfway expected, but Thad's. He had been looking for her?

Which she hadn't expected.

"Nervous?" Thad grinned around the cigarette in his mouth as he clicked on his lighter.

"Not at all." Chin up. Head high. She wasn't requiring any sympathy or pep talks this time—not from Lucas or any man. Confidence would be her new mission. Fake it 'til she meant it, anyway.

Anything to keep the tears at bay that still sprang at the ready from Lucas's verbal assault.

She blinked rapidly and looked away, down the alley, as if the Dumpsters and piles of abandoned cardboard boxes held the answers she so desperately sought.

"I wouldn't be nervous. Pretty little thing like yourself."

That jerked her head around. She watched as Thad took a drag on the cigarette and exhaled away from her, the wisps of smoke curling into the air. The resulting aroma floated around them, and she took a step back, already feeling nauseated in the pit of her stomach. "Well, thanks for the compliment, but that has nothing to do with my baking."

"Doesn't it?" His eyes narrowed, and she never realized how gray they were up close. Probably because she'd never been this close to Thad before, and shouldn't be. Was this even allowed, her talking to a judge during the show, before the results were announced? It seemed . . . shady.

Maybe Lucas had a point.

Man, she didn't want that to be true. But Thad was definitely pushing the boundaries of what was appropriate here.

Especially now that he'd taken another step closer to her.

"I really don't know what you mean." She edged toward the door, wondering how to make an escape that wouldn't leave them both feeling awkward. He *was* still a judge, after all—and the owner of the shop where she was hoping to bake for the next year. She needed to keep a level of professionalism between them even if he'd forgotten that. Surely he wasn't coming on to her—just enjoying his spontaneous smoke break company, attempting to encourage her, give her a compliment.

Stella would know what to do. This was practically her life.

"I think you know exactly what I mean." He exhaled another puff of smoke, and then brushed the back of his hand down her arm. His knuckles grazing her bare forearm sent a shiver down her spine.

But not the pleasant kind.

"Don't make me spell it out, Kat." He grinned, then flicked his cigarette on the ground at their feet. "I was always better at math."

She crossed her arms, effectively moving her arm from his touch even as her head raced to catch up to his implications. She sidestepped toward the door, stomach fluttering with indecision. Run for it and embarrass them both? Play dumb? Call him out on his misbehavior? "You're a judge."

"Exactly, Ms. Contestant. And the owner of Bloom." He tugged at a strand of her hair, and then brushed her cheek with his hand as he moved another inch closer. "Sure wouldn't mind baking with you every day." Now he had her against the brick wall, not blocking her movements, but too close for comfort.

Way too close. His eyes were darkened with subtext, and his hand—now he was trailing it back down her arm, tugging at her fingers, pulling her toward him. "Could make that happen, you know. Real easy."

Was he actually propositioning her in exchange for a win?

Indecision over, she shoved Thad away from her with both hands on his shoulders. "I'm going to pretend you didn't say that." Her heart thudded heavily in her chest, and she blindly reached for the doorknob, unwilling to turn her back on him to leave.

He pulled another cigarette from his pocket, eyes hard and cold as he lit it. "I don't have a clue what you mean."

So it was going to be like that. Figured. "Then we're in agreement." She wrenched open the door and stalked inside, kicking the small wooden prop out of the way and letting it click shut behind her in pointed exclamation.

She'd barely looked up before barreling straight into Piper.

"Watch it." Kat bounced off the girl, surprised at the aggression in her own tone, then even more surprised at Piper's lack of catty response.

The younger contestant simply backed up a step and raised both hands in the air in innocence. "Oh, I'm watching." She grinned, which didn't exactly make sense, but Kat didn't have time for childish mind games. Piper wouldn't psych her out this close to the judges' announcement. She was too late—Kat had enough on her mind already. She could handle that task herself.

She clenched her hands against her chest as she hurried to the lounge, her thoughts replaying the unlikely events of the last ten minutes, hating that she hadn't done or said more sooner. Hating that she might have just ruined her chances of proceeding to the final round.

And hating most of all that Lucas had been so very, very right.

twenty-two

"$\mathcal{D}$on't judge a book by its cover . . ." Lucas's voice trailed off as he held the taxi door open for Kat. "But I thought we both could use a taste of home." He pointed to the lettered sign above the restaurant.

She slid carefully out of the cab, careful not to wrinkle her black dress, and joined him on the sidewalk, her gaze finding the tired words scrawled in cursive against weathered wood. "The Gumbo Bowl." She snorted. Then bit back a snicker, then let loose with a full laugh. "That actually sounds fabulous."

"Figured we could use a change." Lucas smiled down at her, the blue of his dress shirt doing dangerous things to his eyes, and offered his arm. She hesitated, then curled her hand around his bicep as she'd done a thousand times in Louisiana. Tonight would be perfect, if only because they'd already agreed to avoid any controversial, argumentative discussions. If that meant they discussed nothing but the weather and the new shoes she'd bought with Rachel to go with this new dress, it'd still be just fine.

Because they were together, they were going to the final round of *Cupcake Combat*, and in a few days, this entire nightmare of a dream would be over.

And now, there would be gumbo.

The outside of the restaurant had seen better days, likely due to the proximity to the ocean winds coming off the Pacific, but the inside showed creativity and promise. They ducked inside the dimly lit lobby and made their way to the hostess stand, which held a tea light candle that barely illuminated a stuffed crawfish perched atop the seating chart. Mardi Gras masks and beads hung from the wall above the stand, along with a bulletin board that boasted scenic postcards from Baton Rouge, New Orleans, and Shreveport.

It wasn't Bayou Bend, but it was as close as they were going to get in California. The college-aged hostess smiled, silver alligator earrings dangling from her ears. "Two?"

At their nods, she led them to their table, near the raw, wood-framed window at the back of the restaurant, currently void of other customers. Either it was early for dinner or this place wasn't as promising as Lucas had hoped. But Kat was so relieved the day was over, as long as she didn't get food poisoning, she almost didn't even care.

Lucas pulled her chair out for her, and she settled in, tugging the hem of her dress over her knees. She didn't remember it being quite this short. Rachel would be proud. She pulled her napkin into her lap self-consciously as Lucas took the seat across from her. The hostess handed them menus. "Enjoy."

"Thank you." Kat took a breath of hope as the hostess left them alone. They'd try to enjoy themselves, anyway. As long as the awkward factor that kept circling her and Lucas like vultures didn't actually land, they'd be fine. All they had to do was stick to the script. Nothing about dreams, nothing about their kiss, and definitely nothing about the show or Thad—

"I'm really glad you made it through to the finals."

Her gaze collided hard with Lucas's, and he offered a sheepish grin that hitched higher on one side than the other. She shook her head. "Wait a minute. We said no—"

"I know, but seriously. I was sort of a jerk today in the kitchen, and I'm glad that didn't hinder you." Lucas leaned forward, toward the table, toward her. "You really came through—all by yourself. You earned this round, Kat."

No, no. She smiled her acceptance of the compliment, but inside, her stomach shifted. He was doing it again, weaseling beneath her guard, warming her with his words and assurance and compliments that still mattered—too much. How could she ever be truly independent and free of her need of him if her insides tangled up with every word of his approval?

The worst part was, he didn't even know he did it.

"Nice night out. Not too windy." She was actually resorting to discussing the weather, but those were the rules, and they'd set them for a reason. Someone had to play by them.

Leave it to the coach to bend them.

Lucas narrowed his eyes at her before plucking his menu from the tabletop. "I know what you're doing."

"Is it working?" She couldn't resist the flirty edge to her voice, the one that sprang out of nowhere but exactly on cue, like a cast member waiting in the wings.

He shook his head at her, but couldn't contain his smile. "No."

"You getting steak or gumbo?" She stared at the menu so she wouldn't have to remember to avoid his eyes, which kept threatening to suck her in and make her forget all the reasons she was supposed to be on guard. Stay distant. Keep her wall up.

"Gumbo."

She nodded. Safe enough. "Me too."

"Dessert?"

"Cheesecake." They said it at the same time, and she relaxed. They were back. Somewhat. Close enough, anyway, for now. It would have to do.

The waitress took their drink orders and then returned with their sodas and a basket of toasted bread. While Lucas placed their orders, Kat fiddled with her napkin, covering more of her legs, halfway thinking she needed to grab a picture of the evening at some point to prove to Rachel she actually wore the dress.

"Kat?"

"Yeah?" She looked up then, right into his eyes, and regretted it immediately. His gaze warmed as hot as the flickering tea light on their table.

"You look really beautiful tonight."

No, no, no. Her heart couldn't take it. She calmly smiled, as if the simple sentence didn't swell to capacity and rip her insides apart. "Thank you." The dress—that awful magic Rachel had sensed but Kat had denied—must be working somehow. Had to be the dress; she didn't get compliments like that without it.

Though there had been Thad . . .

Speaking of. She let out a reluctant sigh. She owed Lucas the truth. He was all-in tonight, putting himself out there, trying to reinstate their friendship and get them back to normal, and yet she was the one holding back. Refusing to admit he'd had a point. It wasn't fair.

She gathered her courage and shoved away her pride. "I need to tell you something."

He leaned back in his chair, eyebrows raised, no visible sign of anxiety over her pending announcement except for the steady tapping of his index finger against the tabletop. "What's wrong? Did I say something wrong? Because you do look great. I meant it. That dress . . ."

Well, that at least cleared that up. Her heart sank a little. "No, it's not about the dress." Which she would promptly burn after tonight. "You were right about Thad."

He straightened suddenly in his chair, elbow nearly knocking his bread off his plate. "What do you mean?"

"You're surprised you're right?"

"Surprised you're admitting it. If you are, something must have happened. What happened?" He leaned forward, his dark-brown eyes a mixture of suppressed anger and compassion. He was already checking out, though, the anger taking over. She could clearly see him imagining what had gone on, and what he was going to do about it.

She had to stop it.

"It's nothing major, relax. He just . . . let on that he was interested." Hey, if Lucas got a little jealous during the confession, all the better. Maybe it'd be good for him to know someone found her attractive in regular clothes.

"Interested how?" His eyes narrowed, and she was saved from answering by the arrival of a couple at a nearby table.

She fiddled with her napkin again. "It was nothing."

Lucas waited until the couple's chairs finished scraping and the hostess left before pinning her down with a lowered voice but the same steady gaze. "How, Kat?"

There was that voice she knew not to argue against. Completely no point. "He was outside smoking again, and—"

"I wondered where you went. Did you meet him out there?" His voice was rising, his tone more intense, and the obvious surge of jealousy ignited a spark of something dangerous in her stomach.

"Keep your voice down! Of course not! Not intentionally. He came after me." True enough. Thad had sought *her* out. How about that? Pride lifted her disappointment a notch. So rare.

"This isn't something to brag about, Kat. This is serious."

Bubble burst. Now she got the condescending tone, the coach voice that silently screamed, *I know best so don't even try!*

"It's nothing. He came on to me a little, I shot him down. The end." Sort of. There had been that gleam in Thad's eyes that alluded to worse things, things like revenge.

Lucas braced his arms against the table, muscles tense. "Are you going to report it?"

"Like what? File for sexual harassment?" At his serious nod, she laughed, but it rang hollow. "That's ridiculous. He didn't touch me." Well, no, he had, just not aggressively. Did that still count?

She shook off the doubt. "He didn't push me past what I couldn't handle. Trust me. I think he was just being flirty and took it too far. That's probably just his personality."

But it'd been more than that. He'd had an obvious agenda: his vote in exchange for her . . . attention, or whatever you wanted to call it. Not to mention that when she'd survived the round and Classy Cupcakes had been sent home, Sam had made sure the contestants knew that the decision hadn't been unanimous. Had Thad voted against her because she hadn't fallen into his trap? Or was she overreacting, or overthinking the entire exchange?

She had no proof.

And she sure didn't want Lucas snooping around to find it.

"Let's just let it go. I only brought it up to apologize to you for not believing you about Thad." She reached across the table and rested her hand on Lucas's wrist, hoping the contact would calm him.

Nope, all it did was stir *her* up. She brought her hand back to her lap. "Everything's fine. We're going to the finals." She forced a bright smile, hoping he would too, but his expression remained grim.

"I still don't like it, Kat. I think you should tell someone."

"Why make everything awkward? Now I know to keep my distance. After the next round, I won't have to see him again."

"Unless you win."

So he did think her still capable of it. She nodded. "Unless I win."

The statement stretched before them, an endless timeline of opportunity and possibility, both negative and positive.

They stared at each other across the flickering candlelight, and Kat wished Lucas would put into words what even just one of his changing expressions meant. Regret? Longing? Could he even consider coming with her if she moved to New York?

Could she even consider asking?

He opened his mouth, head tilted, considering her, and she held her breath, hoping. Expecting.

Needing.

"Gumbo for two?" The waitress interrupted the moment, clanging down bowls laden with crawfish, shrimp, and sausage floating in a dark roux.

Kat stared down at her bowl as the waitress deposited crackers on their plates. She wasn't nearly as hungry as she'd been moments before. Because as surely as she knew how to peel a crawfish, she knew there was a distinct possibility that her immediate future would require gumbo for only one.

Unless . . .

She risked a glance at Lucas as he unwrapped his napkin, picked up his spoon, tested a bite of the gumbo, and reached for the pepper. There was no way she could go an entire year not sitting across from him at dinner, not barking orders at him in a kitchen, not fighting over the remote control. There had to be a way to convince him to come with her if she won.

Wasn't she worth it?

Is he worth staying in Bayou Bend?

Ugh. That voice again. Was it God's prompting or her own conscience? Maybe both. Maybe neither. She just knew in her heart that she could never be truly content unless she exhausted every possibility to break out of Bayou Bend and show herself—and her family—what she could do. What she was made of. What she was worth.

So there was really only one solution.

Convince Lucas that New York held just as much—if not more—opportunity for him than Bayou Bend.

⁂

She'd come clean with him, and now it was his turn. Kat deserved to know about his dreams, the land, the offer he'd placed and increased twice now because it was too important to let go.

Like she was.

He hadn't told her yet because he wasn't sure how to tell her the things of his heart without admitting she was its very beat.

But at the rate this was going, if their friendship was headed down in a fiery crash anyway, he might as well put it all out there. What was the point in holding back? Things were changing between them, for better or for worse, and he couldn't stop it. Couldn't hold it back. It was like trying to lasso a hurricane. Impossible—and dangerous.

No, they had to ride this storm out and see where it deposited them. And after Kat's confession and all the drama of the last few days, it probably wasn't wise on his part to keep anything a secret anymore. If she found out his plans before they came out of his own mouth, well—by now he'd learned enough to know she didn't like secrets. Or secondhand information, for that matter. She deserved the truth.

It was just up to him to determine how much of it he doled out tonight.

The cheesecake had come and gone, another hit had been made on his credit card, and now they were strolling on the beach. Kat's shoes were dangling from her fingertips, and the hem of her dress fluttered around her legs as she walked barefoot. He'd left his shoes on, a choice he was now regretting. But they were already full of sand, so taking them off now seemed sort of pointless.

They walked in silence, listening to the wind, the lights and cries of the Santa Monica Pier fading behind them as the crowd thinned and the roar of the waves took ownership.

"The gumbo was good." Kat's voice, thin against the crash of the ocean, barely registered in his ears. She was reaching now, desperate to fill the silence between them, same battle he'd been fighting. It was like, lately, if they weren't bleeding their hearts out to each other, they couldn't communicate at all.

"It was great—for California, anyway." He nudged her, and she laughed, but none of it felt sincere. It was all a façade, a fabricated version of reality to hide the undercurrent that kept dragging them both under.

Enough.

"Kat, stop."

She did, surprisingly, without fuss, and turned, her body inches from his, face lifted. Man, he could kiss her again. But that wasn't what he'd meant. Was that what she wanted?

No. It had messed up too much before.

Darren's reminder rang like a warning bell in his ears. *Do not stir up nor awaken love . . .* Had he learned nothing? He wouldn't make that mistake again. Not yet. There was still too much unsaid, too much yet to be determined to keep putting either of their hearts in that vulnerable state.

"Now I need to tell *you* something."

She stiffened a little, the wind tossing her hair in her eyes, and he reached out to tuck it behind her ear before he could stop himself. "It's not bad. Just news."

The anxiety in her eyes faded, and she shook her head. "Then don't. Let's just . . . walk. And talk. About regular stuff." Hope filled her gaze. "Like we agreed before dinner."

Regular stuff. Right. Was that even possible for them anymore?

He hesitated, then shoved his hands in his pockets. "Sure. Let's go." They began walking, sand kicking up against the back of his slacks and sliding into the heels of his shoes.

She must not be over her confession about Thad from dinner if she was still trying to avoid any serious or heavy conversation. He'd thought he'd done well, hiding his anger, when it'd taken everything in him not to turn the table over and go running to the studio to find the preppy punk's address. Kat wasn't taking the issue as seriously as she should, but he could see her point in the awkward factor. If she didn't win, it would become a moot point.

But if she did, how could she go to New York to work for him?

What if Thad tried something more aggressive on his own territory? Or . . . what if he somehow actually won her over?

The thought threatened to make his seafood gumbo return to the sea.

"You miss your team?"

Kat's quiet question thankfully redirected his thoughts, and he shook off the lingering doubts. "Yeah, a bunch. I'm constantly wondering if my coaches are remembering to do this or that with the boys. It's like I've been gone a month instead of less than a week." He laughed, picturing the headache his guys must be giving the assistant coaches, then sobered at the thought of Tyler and all the unknowns. "Just hope I don't go back to a mess."

"Your assistants have learned from the best." It was Kat's turn to elbow him in the ribs, and he basked in relief at the simple gesture. She was trying. "They'll be fine. All of them."

"And Tyler, and his dad . . ." His voice trailed off, and he ran his hand over his jaw. Was the kid's old man behaving himself? Would he be coming home to more drama, more fires to extinguish?

Or had everyone somehow survived in his absence?

He wasn't really sure which scenario he considered worse. "It's just a lot at one time."

"For everyone," Kat agreed, looking off to the ocean, the wind whipping her hair around her bare shoulders. He started to wrap his arm around her to warm her, then thought better of it. The less physical contact right now, the better. He kept his hands shoved in his pockets.

"You really love what you do, don't you?" The words came out of Kat more like a statement than a question. "You practically light up when you're talking about your team."

He smiled down at her, grateful for the upbeat change in conversation, the natural flow between them slowly returning. Smart move, getting him to talk about his boys like this. Somewhat of a default safe topic—one of the things they'd never argued about.

"I guess I do, huh? Sort of the way you do when you talk about cupcakes."

⌘⌘⌘

Like she did about cupcakes.

Like she did about cupcakes?

Kat's heart squeezed in a vise, pulsing, pounding, throbbing to escape . . . all of it. All the stress of the last few days, all the changes, all the unknowns swelled inside her rib cage and pressed. She was going to burst. Right there in the sand.

She stopped walking, panic gripping her voice tighter than her sudden hold on Lucas's arm. She didn't even remember grabbing him, but she held on for dear life. "I don't get it, Lucas. What's wrong with me?" The sand swirled beneath their feet, and she choked in air. A panic attack, on the beach? She was losing it. Had lost it.

Gone.

But they were right. What if they were right?

"What do you mean?" Confusion clouded Lucas's face, and he gripped her arms in return, as if afraid she might fall over if he didn't. And maybe she would. His simple statement had driven her to a terrifying realization that left her wobbly. Light-headed.

Were her parents right? Was she that . . . hollow? Like a cored-out cupcake?

She struggled to put words to her fears, to pass air through her lungs. "You're passionate about a sport and teamwork and kids . . ." She sucked in another gulp of oxygen, the salty wind taking her panic down from Code Red to a shade of burgundy. "Some of those kids are even underprivileged. They need you, depend on you. And the comparison in my life is—*cupcakes*?"

His head dipped low, brows pinched. "No. I mean, yes. But no. Kat, it's not like that."

But it was. Wasn't it? He couldn't even really say otherwise, or

217

he would have by now, instead of staring at her with that expression she couldn't quite decipher.

Didn't really want to try.

She sank down to the sand, curling her legs sideways beneath her, staring at the ocean. She picked up a handful of the tiny grains and held them tightly, the contact somehow soft and coarse all at once. It slowed her raging pulse enough to think, to process. Lucas knew who he was, what he wanted. What he was supposed to do. He had a flavor—one imprinted deep and not subject to change. He was what he was.

And he was amazing at all of it.

She looked up at him, wishing she could guard her heart—guard *him*—against the storm stirring inside. "You're settled, Lucas. You're exactly where you need to be." A fact that wasn't changing, whether or not she asked him to come to New York. He wouldn't go. It would break her to even try, to set herself up for obvious rejection. "You've found your calling in life."

And who was she to mess that up?

Even for love.

The sand slowly drizzled through her clenched fingers.

Lucas lowered himself to his knees in the sand beside her, his eyes searching hers, confusion still lingering around the edges. No wonder. She'd done a complete 180 on him, but she couldn't help it. Los Angeles, this competition, this constant proximity to Lucas, were all doing a number on her soul. How much longer could she keep this up?

She was breaking—one uncertain crack at a time. Where would she finally crumble? What would be left of her when she did?

"I'm flavorless, Lucas." She didn't mean to say it out loud, or maybe she did. Either way, it was there between them now, embarrassing and honest and real. "I'm worse than vanilla." At least vanilla was a classic, a staple, dependable. Something everyone could count on and default to. "I have nothing real to offer." Lucas opened his mouth, then closed it, probably afraid to even try to touch this one. She didn't blame him. She couldn't quite touch it herself.

But then he spoke. "Kat, you're not flavorless. If anything, you're so full of flavor, there hasn't been a name invented for it yet."

His words stirred a longing she kept futilely trying to kill, and once again, she pushed it aside, desperate to let it grow but terrified that if it did it'd choke the life out of her.

"Look at me." He gripped her chin lightly, just long enough to turn her face toward him, then let go. But the feel of his fingers on her face lingered, just like these words of his would. "Some days, you're like a mocha cupcake with espresso frosting. Driven and productive and on a mission to help someone, to show someone else love. You're jacked up and impossible to stop."

She snorted.

"I'm serious." His face grew thoughtful, and he continued. "Then other days, you're more like a red velvet cupcake with cream cheese. Classic, and rich, and leaving a mark on everything you touch." He was touching her face again, eyes shadowed with an emotion she couldn't quite place. "Red velvet is classy and always unforgettable."

Her breath caught, and her heart ached—physically ached—for those words to be true.

"Then other times, you're a tiramisu cupcake. A little sassy but always elegant, always a favorite." His voice trailed off. "Trust me, Kat. You're far from dull or invisible. You have a purpose."

With the end of his monologue came the rush of the too-familiar insecurity. She forced her tone to sound casual, despite the fear pushing and shoving into the crevices of her thoughts. "Then why does it seem like it's so easy for everyone else to go after what they love but I have to constantly fight for it?" Maybe he really saw her as all those things, but did anyone else? Why did his opinion not mean enough?

Probably because she needed to believe in herself before she let someone else.

He leaned toward her, his shoulder touching hers, and she wanted to grab on and never let go. But she had to let go, whether or not she wanted to. Fate was happening, right now, and she couldn't stop it. Couldn't stop it any more than she could count how many grains of sand she'd just held, or how many she'd released, or how many clung to the folds of her dress. The dress that was supposed to have been magical.

More like cursed.

His voice shook through the fear. "Fighting makes you stronger, Kat. If it was easy, it wouldn't mean as much."

Then why didn't it mean more now? She was *one* round away from getting her dream, from getting to start over in a new city with new people, where she could bake whatever she wanted and begin her career outside of the shadow of her family and the expectations and the disappointments.

But her heart . . . it was listless. Disengaged. Detached.

None of it meant nearly as much as she'd hoped.

Would it ever? Was she chasing the wrong dream?

What else was there?

"We both grew up in Bayou Bend, Lucas. So what's the difference?" She pleaded with him for an answer, knowing he couldn't truly give it. They were different people, after all. Different journeys, different experiences. Somehow, Bayou Bend had become ideal for Lucas, offering security, purpose, and small-town fame, as well as a sense of direction that he couldn't—or wouldn't—get elsewhere. A perfect fit, like a puzzle piece nestled snugly into place.

Yet for her, Bayou Bend meant staying stifled. Unable to breathe. Unable to *be*.

"The difference? It's all what you make it, Kat." He moved her hair out of her face, and she turned her cheek into his palm. His touch lingered for a moment before he planted his hand back in the sand, propping his weight. "You have a history in Bayou Bend. That can be a good thing with the right perspective."

"You know my family, Lucas. It's not a matter of perspective; it's a matter of what *is*." She drew a ragged breath, playing with the strap of her new shoe, knowing if she made eye contact she'd fall facedown in the sand and never get up. "I still have no idea if people would ever actually like my own cupcakes or would feel obligated because of my last name. Because of my aunt. My bloodline."

"Blood is important." His voice sobered, almost lost on the wind as he gazed out at the dark waves, churning foaming whitecaps. For once, Lucas didn't seem to have all the answers. For once, he appeared like he might need a few himself.

Imagine that.

Los Angeles was taking them both through the wringer.

"Not everyone has blood, Kat." He looked at her then, and years of pain and a longing for what he'd never have back filled his eyes. Sometimes she forgot he lost his mom; he never talked about her death. Never talked about how truly alone he was without anyone besides her, a few friends like Darren Phillips, his team, and his coworkers. "Some of us have to make strangers into family, because it's all we have."

Ironic.

"And some of us have family who are more like strangers." Kat shook her head, pushing her hair away from her face with both hands, holding it up into a ponytail as reality crashed like the waves. Overwhelming. Endless. "Guess that's the difference."

And would always be. Whether she left for New York or stayed behind. Whether Lucas came with her or stayed behind.

Some things would simply never change.

Despite her heart's desperate cry for everything to do just that.

twenty-three

So much for no heavy conversation that night.

Lucas walked Kat from the cab through the hotel lobby and into the elevator, leaving a trail of sand along the carpeted path. Her bare legs were still covered in goose bumps from the nighttime breeze, her shoes still dangling from her fingertips as she pressed the elevator button for their floor.

He leaned against the wall and studied her as the elevator began a slow climb. Her pale complexion, makeup all but erased from time and wind and tears. Slight black smudges under her eyes where the conversation had gotten the best of both of them earlier. Yet her eyes, startling blue and just as striking with or without makeup, still had the power to stop his heart in his chest.

She turned the full force of her gaze on him then, her eyes full of the same questions and pleas for assurance that he asked of her. Assurances that he couldn't supply, couldn't answer. Wanted to take. Wanted to give.

Impasse.

At least until tomorrow's competition played out, and they saw what choices were really before them. It would be hard to make a move until then, despite his heart still insisting he come clean, tell her about his land. Tell her about his big plans, and beg her to want the same thing. To give up her dream and marry him instead. Make him her new dream.

Why wasn't he enough? The elevator dinged, announcing their floor, and he walked Kat to her room. He figured the cleaning lady wasn't around this time to see how he'd made it right. But had he, really? Because the lines of defeat around Kat's eyes suggested otherwise.

They'd tried. So hard.

Just to come full circle back to this?

It was beyond depressing.

She fumbled with her key card, then flipped it around before sliding it into the lock. "Thanks for dinner." She wouldn't look at him again, and he was halfway disappointed, halfway relieved. He couldn't stand the pain in her eyes, knowing his own reflected right back.

"No problem." Except, there were a ton of problems, but they'd already talked a useless labyrinth around those.

"Good night." Kat attempted a smile that fell miserably short, opened her door, tossed her shoes inside, and let it fall shut behind her with a solid click.

If only that deadbolt was the only thing between them.

He shuffled toward his end of the hall, his heart as heavy as those tackling dummies he made his guys use in practice, and he reached for his own key card in his wallet.

No.

He turned back toward her room, working into a near jog. He couldn't end things like this between them for the entire night. Not with too much unspoken, with so much said. Neither of them would sleep, and the big finale was tomorrow, and he might not want Kat to win, but he sure enough wasn't about to let her sabotage herself from lack of sleep. Not because of him.

He'd done enough sabotaging on this trip.

He pounded on her door, shifting his weight anxiously from foot to foot. Except he didn't know what he was going to say to fix it, to break the ice, to bring back more than a decade's worth of friendship. There wasn't a sentence in the world that could reverse time, or speed it up, or do whatever the heck needed to be done to get them through this impossible valley.

He'd think of something, maybe, when he saw her again.

The door opened, and she squinted at him, still wearing that dangerous black dress. "You forget something?"

No. More like he needed to remember.

He reached across the frame and pulled her into a kiss.

She didn't even hesitate, just melted into his embrace like butter in a skillet. She pressed closer against him, and he tangled his fingers in her hair, pulling her closer, deepening the kiss. All the anxiety, all the fear, all the doubts, slipped away as he returned her breath and she, his.

Her hands slid up his back, digging into his shirt, a soft sigh escaping her lips that nearly melted him right back. This wasn't an accidental, celebratory kiss.

This was a *kiss*.

This was everything he'd ever wanted, all wrapped up in one little black dress and one big moment in time that he never wanted to end.

But he had to end it.

Because somehow, they were completely in Kat's room now, and the door was shut behind them, and his hands were sliding with her against the wall. He grasped her arms by her shoulders and pushed himself away, just far enough to separate, to breathe, to clear his head before he did something stupid.

Really stupid.

"We can't—just . . . wait. Hold on." He couldn't think, just wanted to kiss her again, and there she was, slipping back into his arms, pressing her soft lips against his cheek. "Kat." The groan in his voice didn't even sound like his own, it was so full of torment.

She grinned, finally taking him seriously, and moved to sit on the edge of the bed.

"Not the bed."

She stood up quickly, leaning instead against the open bathroom door. "Better?"

"For now." He kept one hand on the doorknob leading out of her room, refusing to allow himself permission to let go of it. Clarity was slowly returning, along with a rush of oxygen and a sense of euphoria he couldn't tame.

But he had to. He wouldn't compromise her, or their friendship, or whatever this was called now. Not even for that. Because morning would come, and nothing would look the same. He wouldn't ruin it.

Long as she stayed at the bathroom door.

They stared at each other, and Lucas wondered if Kat felt the same pressure he did, that same unspoken obligation that whoever spoke first would carry.

Since he was the one who pressed her up against the wall, it should probably be him.

"So." He kept his hand on the doorknob. "That was . . ." Well, maybe it wasn't as easy as it looked.

"Yeah." Her grin turned halfway impish, and he tightened his grip on the knob. Heaven help him . . .

"We should probably . . ." He sighed, looked at the ceiling, then at her. Now she was biting her lower lip, eyes wide, and his palm was so sweaty, it was sliding off the knob. "I need to, you know . . ." Leave. Call Darren. Take a cold shower. Pray. All of the above, at least twice each.

"Come here?"

It was a question, not a command. But he couldn't obey it, not even though her eyes *were* as big as a pleading puppy's. Even though his arms actually ached to hold her again. He shook his head, saying no from a source greater than himself. "Not a good idea, Kat."

"That's easily fixed, then. I'll come there." She crept over to him, like one might approach a stray dog or a deer in the woods, and stood directly in front of him before raising up on her tip toes, lips inches from his. She smiled.

"Hi."

Man, she was good.

He wrapped her in another kiss, loving that dress, loving the feel of her in his arms, loving how suddenly, finally, nothing made sense *except* her. This was how it should be, was meant to be. They'd figure out the rest. What was the rest of it again, anyway? Because now it was just them. Him and Kat.

Together.

There was no rest anymore.

His phone chimed from his pocket, and he took the moment to pull apart, catch his breath. Regroup. Return to the doorknob.

"Hold that thought." He grinned and pulled out his cell, figuring Darren and God were at it again with their uncanny timing. He braced himself for a sobering Scripture, which he desperately needed, but the black text peering at him from the screen did a lot more than sober. It wasn't from Darren.

It was from his realtor.

He'd gotten the land.

ﾟﾟﾟ

For once, Kat didn't mind the seemingly endless delays that came with life in a television studio. Absently watching the cameramen yell at each other about various broken forms of technology while Sam got his face powdered just gave her more opportunity to prop her elbow on her baking station and daydream about Lucas and that kiss—okay, *kisses*—one more time.

Because the past five hundred times hadn't been nearly enough.

A tingle worked its way through her stomach at the memories, and she couldn't contain a smile. She could even halfway still feel

Lucas's strong arms around her waist, feel the pressure of his mouth against hers.

Sigh.

She still wasn't entirely sure how they'd gone from their depressing, all-hope-is-lost conversation on the beach to making out in the doorway of her room, but somehow, they'd gotten there, and she for one was not complaining.

Nothing had changed about their situation.

But now, she had the hope that it could.

Although the way Lucas left so quickly after getting that text left her a little unsettled. Kat frowned, threading her fingers through the tie of her Not Your Mama's Cupcakes apron. He'd told her it was just business from back home, and she believed him, but what business, exactly? And why did it have to cut short such an amazing time together?

Well, probably better that it had. She still couldn't believe the gumption she'd possessed, the flirty attitude she'd shown—so unlike her. But Lucas brought that side of her to life, and once it had taken a full breath, she couldn't bear to shove the poor creature back into the ground.

Maybe Rachel had been right about the dress.

"You nervous?"

Kat jumped, knocking her elbow against her workstation with a painful thump. She straightened and forced a smile at Piper, unnerved by the girl's choice of the word *nervous*, the exact same word Thad had used yesterday in the alley. Coincidence?

How could it be anything else?

She was in too good of a mood to assume the negative or let Piper psych her out even unintentionally. "Good luck today."

Piper's eyebrows shot toward her hairline. "Seriously?"

"Sure, why not. We've both made it this far. We've proven we're here for a reason." Kat shrugged, unsure whether to laugh or cry at the shocked expression on Piper's face. Was the girl that desperate for assurance? Or was it all just a catty game to her? Either way . . . "You're a good chef, Piper. Everything you've made has gotten great scores. And the decorations on those key lime cupcakes you made last round were adorable."

Successfully unarmed, Piper mumbled something under her breath and wandered back to her workstation.

Kat shook her head. Good grief. If she'd known it could be *that* easy to get rid of her, she'd have tried doling out compliments three days ago.

Her gaze darted to the judges' table and then back to her mixing bowl. At least Thad hadn't tried anything since yesterday, and he had been keeping to himself at the panel. So far, she'd managed to avoid eye contact, but was still debating on whether or not doing so made everything even weirder. Should she be her normal self since she hadn't done anything wrong? Or cower away like she was guilty? There had to be an in-between somewhere.

If they could just get on with the taping, it wouldn't matter. She'd be too busy to worry about Thad, Piper, or even Lucas, for that matter.

Lucas.

She started to slip back into her daydream when the very star of it appeared at her side.

"Hey, I'm back." Lucas slid his cell into the back pocket of his jeans, which were dark denim and a slimmer fit than he usually wore, but who was noticing? "Sorry, had to take that call. Figured I might as well while we are still on a time-out." He smiled at her, but a slight strain remained evident around the corners of his eyes.

Kat smiled back, wishing she could erase the lingering frown lines. Maybe he was nervous about the final segment too? A lot was riding on the results. Maybe more so for them both after last night.

But no, she refused to think of it that way. She much preferred thinking of it as finally having real options—one way or another.

"Who was it?"

He hesitated, and Kat rolled in her lower lip, plowing ahead before he could answer. Or rather, continue to *not* answer. "Is everything okay?"

He nodded, but didn't elaborate. He just pulled out his phone again and sent another text before putting it back in his pocket.

Kat tried to shake off the hurt as she turned, brushing wisps of flour off her workstation as if she didn't have a single thing on her mind. What was the deal? Why wouldn't he tell her who was on the phone? They didn't keep secrets from each other.

She paused midswipe and frowned. Although, that misunderstanding between him and her sister had sort of been like a secret, or at least something he'd never told her about. And then there were his thoughts about sabotaging her cupcakes because of being ready to get home.

But he'd confessed all that, so none of it was a secret anymore. Right?

She pressed her fingers against her temples. This step—no, make that this crazy, terrifying leap—from best friends to significantly more was tricky, to say the least.

And they hadn't actually even labeled anything yet.

But those kisses . . . how could it not mean that something had changed? It had for her. Had to have for him too. Surely Lucas was at least considering options, possibilities now. They couldn't just share something like that, have that kind of connection at their fingertips and just throw it away.

Because there would be no going back.

The sobering realization sent a shiver racing down Kat's back, erupting into chills along her forearms and shins. She shoved her hands into her apron pockets, wishing for a blanket. A coat. Something to wrap up in and to warm her frigid train of thought.

It was true, though. From here on, regardless of what happened with the contest, there was no going back. They had to go forward from this proverbial line in the sand, and if she knew Lucas, it would be all or nothing.

The all would be difficult to navigate, at best.

But the nothing . . .

She couldn't even begin to grasp the darkness that accompanied that thought.

Lucas leaned over the workstation, his broad shoulder brushing hers, and she fought the urge to lean into his warmth. "What did Piper say?"

Ha. "I think she was going to try to get in my head, but I complimented her, and she left. Quietly, even."

"Really. Wow. I'm impressed." His smile, slow and wide, calmed the barrage of fears bombarding her heart, and she allowed herself to relax. She needed to concentrate on the round, not be constantly analyzing the details of last night or imagining—or fearing—the future.

First things first. And first, she had a contest to get through.

The urge to pray overwhelmed her. *Lord, you know how badly I want to win. But you know how much Lucas means to me. If you could just somehow find a way to fix this . . .* She knew nothing was impossible for God to figure out, but this whole situation she and Lucas found themselves in seemed like it had to rank pretty close. *Your will, God.*

But I really do want to win.

"All right, bakers, we're finally ready." Sam clapped his hands for attention, even as one of the red-shirt-clad assistants dabbed his forehead with a makeup sponge one last time. He waved her away, and she stuck her tongue out before rushing off the set.

"Sorry for the delay, teams. There's a lot going on today." He grinned from Piper and Amanda to Kat and Lucas, head turning back and forth as if viewing a Ping-Pong tournament. "We have some surprises in store for this final round."

Oh, joy. Kat steeled herself, knowing from experience this past week that a surprise and that particular grin on Sam's face could be good, bad, or incredibly ugly.

Maybe a little bit of all three.

"The final round challenge for today has nothing to do with decorations—those will be decided according to the theme of each team, as you'll discover momentarily." Sam offered a cat-ate-the-canary grin. "For this round, bakers, your challenge is to incorporate a secret ingredient into one of your cupcakes. The more unusual or outright weird the ingredient, the more points you'll score with the judges."

Uh-oh. A weird secret ingredient? She'd used unusual elements in her cupcakes before but nothing she would describe as *weird*—even if Aunt Maggie did. What could she throw together that would qualify but not be too big a risk? Her mind raced with the possibilities. Rosemary? Lavender vanilla? Cayenne pepper?

"Finally, as you all know, we've chosen a love theme this episode to celebrate our fifth anniversary here at *Cupcake Combat.*" Sam gestured to the heart-shaped banner that had been suspended from the ceiling near the judges' table for this final segment. "We thought we'd share the love by asking each of our remaining teams to bake cupcakes for a charity event. Regardless of which team wins, each charity will receive the five hundred cupcakes baked here this afternoon to help promote their cause."

Five hundred cupcakes? Kat grasped the edge of her workstation. On a typical episode, the final challenge consisted of baking one hundred cupcakes. That was plenty. But five hundred? How were they supposed to—

Sam continued. "Of course we realize that goal isn't possible all by yourselves."

Well, duh.

"So, we brought in some extra special hometown helpers for you both." He stepped to the side and gestured to the backstage doors. "Helpers, if you please!"

Kat sucked in a surprised gasp as Lucas's entire football team paraded past the judges' table, wearing their team jerseys with jeans and school-logo ball caps turned backward on their heads, football helmets tucked under their arms. *What in the world—*

Lucas let out a little yelp of joy as the guys rushed to their workstation, crowding around the counter, slapping their coach a high five.

"We rode a plane, Coach!"

"Yeah, and Michael got locked in the bathroom!"

"They gave us free peanuts, but Ben tried to pay for his."

"Some guy in a suit threw up in seat 5A! It was awesome."

The guys' voices mingled together as one as they all jockeyed to outdo each other with news.

"One at a time, gang." Lucas laughed as the din only rose.

Then Tyler barreled right through the crowd and bear-hugged Lucas, sending him staggering backward. "So glad to be here, Coach." The boy held on tight, then stepped back, sheepish, as if forgetting where he was. "Hi, Ms. Varland." He grinned at Kat, and she returned the awkward fist bump he offered.

Several of the guys followed suit, as though unsure if hugging your coach's female friend was okay on TV, while a few of the others, red-cheeked, ducked their heads, studied their shoes, and mumbled brief hellos.

This was the help and the will she had prayed for? *God, is this part of your plan or just a little bonus?* She couldn't entirely decide if it was good or bad. "I'm so surprised, guys. This is amazing." And it was. Shocking too—especially for Lucas, who needed this boost. So maybe it was amazing in a good way. Maybe now he would relax, and see that everything had been just fine in his absence. Maybe he'd see that, sometimes, it was a good thing to not be in control.

She nibbled on her bottom lip. She could stand to learn that same lesson.

After she won.

"We have with us today a championship winning team of high school football players from Bayou Bend, Louisiana. They're eager to help Coach Lucas Brannen and their favorite cupcake baker, Kat Varland." Sam introduced the bevy of players briefly and wished them good luck.

Lucas caught her eye over the top of Tyler's head as Sam finished his welcome, his chocolate-brown eyes bright, face beaming. He tapped the brim of Tyler's ball cap good-naturedly, knocking it off center. He mouthed *I can't believe this* to her, all smiles.

She couldn't either. She smiled back. But why the pit in her stomach? Not because the boys weren't capable of following instructions and helping them bake the five hundred cupcakes—though there was that, maybe, a little. She'd have to be on her toes with them, make sure they stayed on task.

No, it was beyond that.

It was because they'd lit Lucas up in a way she couldn't.

Her hopes that those kisses would change anything—everything—extinguished a bit more. How could he leave behind his life, or even consider it, after having it all flaunted fresh in front of him?

She couldn't compete. Not with her sister. And not with an entire team of guys who looked up to Lucas, who offered hero worship and dependency and fed on his strengths. How selfish would she be, asking him to come to New York with her when these guys needed him more than she did?

She'd proven she could stand on her own. She just didn't want to. But Tyler, and this team . . . this was Lucas's element.

He'd shrivel up and blow away in New York City.

"And now, to assist with our other team, we have a group of ballerinas from the Icing Queens' hometown." Sam applauded as a herd of pink-tutu-clad girls danced *en pointe* from the back door to Piper's workstation, hair rounded up in buns, glitter showering off their leotards. "Let's welcome these dancers from the Pink Slipper Academy, where Amanda teaches part-time and Piper volunteers."

Kat struggled to join the applause, struggled to keep the tears that burned her eyes from slipping down her cheeks. No opportunity for makeup reapplication. It was showtime. She had to figure out this secret ingredient, whip up five hundred to-die-for cupcakes, and do it all with the assistance of a dozen teen boys.

She didn't have a choice. She had to do this, for herself. For her family. For Lucas. He didn't sign her up to watch her fail.

And she hadn't put both of them through all of the torture of this past week for nothing. She might not be a sports buff, but she'd heard enough of Lucas's pep talks to his team to know one thing: she had to go down swinging, regardless of the outcome of the show—or it wasn't even worth playing.

twenty-four

Only in LA could jump-ups and bear crawls turn into measuring and sifting.

Lucas wished he could stop and just soak in the moment, maybe snap a few pictures to tease his guys with later—Coach Kent would get a kick out of seeing Tyler with flour smeared across his team T-shirt, and Ben wearing both an apron *and* a helmet—but there was no time. All hands on deck were occupied, stirring, mixing, cutting.

Three of his players, including Tyler, had created an assembly line. After Kat measured out the ingredients precisely—two of which he swore had been cinnamon mixed with chili powder—they dumped them in the bowls, operated the mixer, and filled muffin tins with paper liners. Then, after Kat tasted and approved the batter, three other guys, including Ben, poured the cupcakes into the liners and manned depositing the cupcakes into the oven and taking them out again.

Lucas was in charge of decorations, alongside a few other boys and Kat, who flitted back and forth, checking all the progress like an adorable, cake-battered drill sergeant. Sugar crunched on the floor under her shoes as she paced, barked, and praised. He was glad she remembered to dole out a few compliments in between the instructions and occasional panicked correction.

He was proud of her. Of all of them, really. *This* was teamwork.

And such a great surprise. Seeing those guys parade in like that . . . Lucas couldn't believe they'd shocked him and Kat so completely. The studio had provided airfare for the one-night stay for all the team members and threw in an allowance for several of the parents to tag along as chaperones on the plane and outside of the studio. Wise, since the entire team were minors. The parents got to sightsee while the kids were taping the show. Win-win.

He'd never done anything so cool in his high school days.

"Where are the fondant footballs?" Kat's voice rose in his ear.

He shot what he hoped was a reassuring smile over his shoulder. She was too close to catch it, though, her eyes riveted on the brown lumps that should have been footballs but currently resembled something more akin to roadkill.

He picked one up and winced. "Working on them, boss."

The look she shot him in return would have made him laugh if the stakes weren't so high. But high they were—like the highest pole-vaulting bar at the Summer Olympics.

"I can't have roadkill on my Mexican hot chocolate cupcakes, Lucas."

Uh-oh. He hadn't said roadkill out loud. That wasn't good.

He clapped his hands, in full-out coach-mode. "Jack, let's try to cut the fondant a little more oval, with pointed ends. I'll handle the white grips." He grabbed the paring knife, reaching for the wrong end before catching himself. "Gabe, how are the goalposts coming along?"

The tall redhead held up an example. "Great, Coach."

They were, actually. His kids had more skills than he'd realized. If only they could put that kind of creativity into their game each practice.

He turned to Kat. "We'll get it."

Hopefully believing him, she moved to the end of their assembly line, closest to Lucas, and began heaping the green icing—for the football to perch upon—into a piping bag. Probably through gritted teeth. She'd always hated green icing. "Lucky break that our event to bake for is the Cowboys versus Saints charity football game, huh?" She looked up with a stressed smile.

They planned that on purpose, he was sure, after figuring out which hometown helpers to bring in for each remaining baking team, but it was sort of funny. "Talk about creating what you know. Maybe this time you'll have to consult *me* in the kitchen."

That earned him an eye roll. "At least we weren't assigned the Los Angeles Ballet School's fund-raiser for the homeless. My guys wouldn't be nearly as helpful with tutus."

That got a distracted short laugh out of her, which was as good as it would probably get right now. But he'd take it.

He went back to creating and supervising the decorations, unable to help but watch Kat work and remember those moments last night, the way she fit so perfectly against him. The way that for those few priceless minutes, nothing could keep them apart.

Nothing except a text from his realtor, that is.

The land was his. All he had to do was sign on the dotted line and he was a homeowner. Everything he'd wanted was falling into place, except for the key ingredient—Kat.

Although if she lost today . . .

He shaped another football, forcing himself to look away from Kat, swiping her hair out of her eyes with her elbow as she piped green grass like a crazy woman. A woman crazy about her dream. He couldn't even begin to allow himself to wish she didn't make the cut today. He couldn't go there again.

Because did he really want to be second place to her? Winning by default wasn't a real win. Any sportsman knew that. Despite the score sheets, you didn't ever truly win a game just because the other team didn't show up. Where was the pride in that? The honor?

It was almost like, win or lose, he lost.

Unless he went with her.

He accidentally squished the football in his fingers, and with a frustrated sigh, he crumpled it up and grabbed a new one. He'd considered the idea last night while wrapped up in all things Kat, but could he really do it?

She wanted him to. He could see it in her eyes even though she'd never say it out loud.

"Coach?" Tyler ambled over to their workstation, and Lucas's spirits lifted at the spark in the boy's eyes. For once, he didn't look weary and burdened like a kid carrying the weight of the adult world on his shoulders. He looked carefree and borderline mischievous, like any teen boy should look on a given day. This trip had been good for him.

"Here's another tray, cooled and ready to ice." Tyler presented it with gusto, as if he had baked the cupcakes all by himself. If Lucas wasn't so proud of his boys, he'd be teasing the mess out of them right now.

"Great. Thanks, Dupree." He formed another football, then realized no one had checked on the caramelized pecans. "Hey, Jack, go check on the pecans, will you? Don't forget an oven mitt." Man, Kat had rubbed off on him. He was definitely on his game today. Funny, since he'd never felt more distracted mentally.

Maybe that was the point. He kept pushing away what he really needed to be thinking about in exchange for pecans and toppings.

Kat shot him a grateful, if not weary, smile as she continued to ice the cupcakes. "Good call, Coach." Her soft affirmation sank in deep, and he wanted to hear her whispered reassurances for the rest of his life.

Pecans. Toppings. Pecans. Toppings.

Nope. It wasn't working anymore.

"What's the grand prize, Coach? When we win?" With an emphasis on the word *when*, Tyler straddled the stool next to Lucas and immediately began pressing the white grips on the cutout fooballs—all without even being asked. Nice. Now where was that go-getter attitude on the field? Clearly, Lucas still had his work cut out for him.

Which was more of a relief than it should have been. These guys hadn't arrived, by a long shot. He was still needed.

Even if not so much by Kat anymore.

"Uh, some kind of big deal baking contract in New York." Lucas tried to say it casually, as much for Kat's sake as his own, as if their entire world wasn't revolving around that one line of fine print.

Tyler slowly moved a completed football to the parchment paper on the counter. "New York? Like, forever?"

"It's for a year." Though it might as well be the same as forever, because if Kat went to New York for a year, she wouldn't be back to Bayou Bend.

"What? That's a really long time." Tyler stood suddenly, his stool legs scraping against the floor, the excitement in his eyes replaced with panic. "Ms. Varland, you can't leave us for a year!"

His arm gesture upset the stool, knocking it over behind him. The studio quieted as all heads in the vicinity whipped their direction. Jack stood motionless nearby, the pan of caramelized pecans still in hand. Even Piper and her team across the room stilled and turned to watch, a blur of glittery pink tulle.

Kat sat completely still and openmouthed at the other end of the workstation, icing bag in hand, a steady drip of green drizzling onto the counter instead of the cupcake she'd been decorating.

"Tyler, I—" Tyler didn't wait for an answer.

"What about you, Coach?" The boy's expression twisted into pure anxiety. "You aren't going with her. Right?"

The silence pulsed, like a heartbeat, loud and frantic. Lucas slowly straightened the stool, feeling Kat's gaze boring into his back, knowing his answer to Tyler was more than just an answer for the kid.

It was for her too.

The visible drama over, the room returned to its bustle. Jack set the pecans on the island, Ben went back to the footballs, Gabe the goalposts, and the chatter from the judges' table resumed. Ten ballerinas resumed baking, the clock kept ticking, and everything returned to normal.

Except for the rhythm of Lucas's heart. He flexed his arms, wishing he could tangibly hold the weight rather than it weighing on him on the inside. Untouchable. Unending.

"Coach?" The teen's voice, half-prompt, half-plea, cut through the static, and he knew. Deep inside, he knew. Just like Kat did.

He clamped a reassuring hand on Tyler's shoulder. "Of course not, Dupree. You know my place is in Bayou Bend."

Like a moth to a tiki torch, like a glutton for punishment, he met Kat's eyes.

Pain and resignation registered like a mirror reflection of his own heart, and regret rose hot inside. He'd done it. He'd stirred up and awakened love before it was pleasing, before it was right.

He'd failed.

ceee

She had to win now. All the doubt, all the half-hopes that maybe she wouldn't win, the half-hopes that maybe things could work out for her and Lucas even if she did, disintegrated faster than egg whites into cake batter. She had to go to New York now, because if she didn't, she was lower than second place.

Forget the judges' opinions. Lucas had already cast his vote. He had chosen.

And she had lost.

Tears blinded her vision as she placed the final cupcakes on display before the judges, giving each one a final once-over as the clock ticked off the remaining seconds of the competition. She wasn't enough to coax Lucas to New York. She might not be enough to earn New York in the first place.

What was she even doing?

The room tilted slightly and she bent down, head between her knees, under the pretense of retying her shoelace. She wouldn't lose it in the final round, wouldn't give the producers of the show the satisfaction of airing that kind of drama for ratings. She might not have had much pride in the first place, but she'd cling to what she had left now. Hadn't she said all along she'd go down swinging?

She just never thought it would come to this.

She straightened up, stood tall, and avoided Lucas's concerned gaze as she hurried back to her team. "The cupcakes look great, guys. You did an amazing job." They really had, despite the fact that most of them were teen boys who'd never baked a day in their lives. They might not be used to baking, but they *were* used to teamwork, following orders, and respecting authority. She could easily recognize the good work Lucas had done in each of them in those areas.

She'd tell him that, eventually, when her heart remembered how to beat and she lived through this last segment.

The timer for the round buzzed, and the room erupted into applause. "Good job, teams." Sam clapped louder than necessary from the front of the set. "And right on time."

Not really; they'd actually finished with a minute and a half to spare, which in reality television time was like a decade. But she'd long since realized Sam was eager for a tie-in or voice-over that could lead to any hint of drama.

"He's right. I'm proud, everyone." Kat blew them a group kiss.

"Hey, we learned from the best." Gabe offered a high five, and she slapped him a good one. He grinned. "That is, from eating the best, anyway. We couldn't let down our favorite cupcake lady." The other guys nodded enthusiastically, except Tyler, who still seemed reserved from his previous outburst. Did her leaving really mean that much to him? Or was he still just reeling from the thought that Lucas might have been going away too?

Was it possible that she had more of a significant role in Bayou Bend than she'd realized?

No time now for wishful thinking and imaginary silver linings. Sam was already ushering them toward the waiting lounge. "These charities are going to be blessed, regardless of the outcome of this round, everyone. Remember that."

Now, that actually sounded sincere. Maybe their host had a soft heart somewhere under all that hair gel after all.

Kat clung to the positive thought as she herded the boys into the waiting lounge, standing back as they mingled and flirted with the other team's ballerinas. She should switch her focus off Lucas and the pending future to the fact that she'd just accomplished a lot—on her own *and* with help. She'd proven herself, but she had worked well with Lucas and her hometown helpers too. All of that was worth celebrating, no matter what happened. She'd contributed to a good cause, and she would gain a lot of exposure for herself and Aunt Maggie's shop, even if she lost.

Worst case in the contest from this point on was second place.

It could have been worse.

Her eyes met Lucas's as he perched on the arm of the couch beside Tyler, and she met his slightly wobbly smile with a forced one of her own.

But it definitely could have been better.

❦

"Welcome back, bakers." Sam smiled at both Kat and Piper, who continued to shoot Kat suspicious glances every few seconds. Was she still that concerned over the compliment she'd given her about her cooking? You might get more *flies* with honey than vinegar, but Piper had apparently gotten stuck in that particular dab of honey, a fact that was possibly more annoying than the girl's buzzing had ever been.

But it didn't matter now. The round was over, the verdict was in, and Sam couldn't possibly have any idea that he held Kat's entire future in that hot pink envelope he clenched between his fingers. Piper couldn't sabotage her anymore.

Lucas, either, for that matter.

Or Thad.

Had he voted for her based on merit? Left the entire earlier issue alone? She didn't want to look at him, but she didn't want to be caught not looking at him either. She risked a glance, but the handsome judge's gaze remained riveted on Sam. Was he fighting the same battle about her?

Yeah, right. Like someone of his status would think twice about Kat or even a rejection from her. He could have a number of celebrities on his arm as soon as he made his intentions known. She was overthinking, as always, making things bigger than they were.

But this announcement Sam was about to make . . . it *was* big. Legit. Mattered.

Kat leaned back on her heels, then realized she was making that same move Sam and even Lucas had made earlier. Great, now she was being sucked into the reality television curse, the one that apparently channeled all anxiety and nerves into rocking motions. It was a wonder anyone managed to stand still around here. She stole a glance over her shoulder at the cleaned-off workstations, where their teammates awaited the verdict. How did Amanda do it? Or Lucas, for that matter? Both remained steady and stoic at their stations, as if the next few minutes wouldn't change absolutely everything.

For Lucas, though, maybe it didn't. Not really, not now. He'd already made a decision for himself that would hold, regardless of what Kat did. He could take her or leave her, apparently.

No, that wasn't fair. Or true. She swallowed back the distaste of being an afterthought. He didn't mean the choice personally; she knew enough to be certain of that, knew that if she'd been in his shoes, with Tyler asking that same question in that same way, she'd have given the same answer.

But the answer was honest, regardless of its delivery or timing. And that would continue to sting for a while.

Even if she'd known all along that it was coming.

"It was a tough decision, as has been the case recently, but"— Sam paused for effect, tapping the envelope against his open palm—"the judges finally reached a verdict." He waved the envelope, and Kat's stomach tightened against her will. She pressed her hands against her waist, concentrating on breathing. Every nerve in her body tingled. She won. She knew it, knew it in her heart, in her soul, in her mind. Knew it by the way Sam's gaze kept raking across hers before darting back to Piper's.

She'd won.

She was going to New York. For a year.

Leaving Lucas.

Starting over.

Sam's deep voice continued, nearly vibrating with the intensity of the moment. "And the winner . . ."

Behind her, muffled calls sounded from the waiting teams. The ballerinas squealed silently behind hands pressing against their mouths, and the football players whistled until a cameraman shot them the evil eye.

An unlikely surge of terror and joy collided into a heaping mix of adrenaline. If Lucas didn't want her to stay, then she definitely wanted to go. Needed to. What would her parents say now? She'd done it. Proved herself.

". . . of the special anniversary edition of *Cupcake Combat,* the winner who is awarded a yearlong baking contract at the prestigious Bloom bakery of New York City is . . ."

She was capable.

She was worthy.

Her dreams were about to come true.

". . . the Icing Queens!"

Her dreams were over.

twenty-five

*L*ucas's heart soared and crashed at the same moment.

Kat was staying in Bayou Bend. Staying home. His worst nightmare, avoided.

But she'd lost.

He rushed to catch her, tucking her into his arms moments before she crumbled. He'd seen the expectation on her face, the excitement, the anticipation. She'd believed she had it.

And he had, as well. For a moment, he'd been convinced, even. Had felt it down deep. She'd had it in the bag. So what happened? What had given Piper's cupcakes an edge? The girl's decorations were decent, but not anything superior to their own. Not by far, especially after Kat's idea to feature each football team's logo in icing. It had been a work of art.

Confetti showered from the ceiling above Piper and Amanda and their team, the cries of a dozen excited girls drowning all rational thought. Kat shuddered in his arms, and he leaned forward, shielding her from the colored paper reminder of her failure as best he could, wishing he could protect her from the disappointment.

Her hair tickled his chin. They only had a minute before the rest of their team would swarm them, and he wished as well that he knew what to say. He wanted to say it was okay, but to her, it wasn't.

And the fact that relief was one straw short of knocking him to his own knees in gratitude made him feel like such a pig. How could he be rejoicing when she was heartbroken? What kind of friend was he?

What kind of love was that?

He tightened his grip around her, heard her sniff into his T-shirt. "They're coming." He could hear the rush of the players starting to gather.

"I know. I'm fine." She lifted her chin, sucking in her breath and blinking rapidly to clear the tears. Trouper. Pride surged.

"There's the final interviews to do. Remember? But after that . . . we'll go. Me and you."

She nodded, but she wouldn't look at him as Tyler, Ben, Gabe, and the rest practically assaulted her with hugs. Gone were the awkward, unsure gestures of affection from earlier in the day. Now his boys pulled it together, proved their merit by gathering Kat in a giant group hug and calling out reassurances that ranged from "You're still the best to us" to crude insults about the other team.

He'd deal with reinforcing proper sportsmanship for losers later. Right now, it was making Kat laugh.

And he had questions he wanted answers to.

The judges had already left the set, their job long done, so there was only one fish to catch. And potentially fry.

"Sam." He caught the host's suit-clad arm lightly in one hand, but firm enough to let the guy know he meant business. "Got a minute?" It wasn't a question. It was happening.

"Sure. Sorry about the loss." Sam crossed his arms, sidestepping slightly out of the way of the crowd of squealing ballerinas surrounding Piper and Amanda. "Win some, lose some, right?"

Sam's plastic persona was gone, and it was man-to-man now. Sam better step up. "Listen, I want to know what happened. Just between us." Lucas lowered his voice an octave, even as he stood an inch taller. "Because we both know Kat had this one nailed."

Sam started to protest, and Lucas tilted his head, pinning him with his gaze. The host rolled his eyes. "Okay, you don't have to get all jock on me. I don't get paid enough for that kind of drama."

Lucas snorted. "Go on."

"It's your friend's fault."

"Kat? What did she do?" Nothing that he'd noticed, and he'd helped her bake enough cupcakes to know if something had gone wrong. Had one of the boys somehow accidentally messed up a batter? But no, Kat had tasted everything before it even hit the ovens—and then tasted it again afterward, risking the time element of losing cupcakes in exchange for quality control. They weren't guilty of any mistakes.

Sam practically whispered the revelation. "She actually won."

Now he'd lost him. Lucas shifted his weight, his gaze darting to Kat across the room, still surrounded by his players. "What do you mean?"

Sam shook his head, eyes heavy and serious. "You can't hit on the judges. They don't take bribes—even from contestants as pretty as Kat."

"Bribes? Are you kidding me?" He'd forgotten to lower his voice that time, but the congratulatory noise still sufficiently drowned out his shock. "She didn't bribe anybody."

"Maybe you don't know her as well as you think, then, because she offered Thad—well, let's just say she made him a pretty good deal." Sam smirked, and Lucas clenched his fists at his sides. He couldn't punch the guy until he finished talking. But no, he didn't deserve the hit. Thad did. The lying, cheating—

"Of course, Thad refused," Sam continued, waving his hand flippantly like they weren't discussing the moral ethics of the woman Lucas loved. "We don't take that kind of thing lightly. It hasn't been the first time, let me assure you. And if we'd had found out earlier in the competition, she'd have been disqualified. As it is, we can keep it quiet now to save her the embarrassment. We don't need that kind of negative rating."

Of all the . . . Lucas gritted his teeth. "She didn't come on to Thad. It was the other way around."

"Right." Sam nodded his head, and Lucas vaguely reconsidered knocking the obnoxious, superior expression off the host's face. "Look, it's too late for the he-said, she-said game. Thad has been a judge on this show for years. His track record is impeccable."

Probably because he'd never been caught. Hadn't Sam just said this wasn't the first time? "I'm telling you the truth, here. Why would I lie?"

"Why would you lie?" The host scoffed. "To win the grand prize, of course. I'm not stupid, man. Look, I'm sorry it all worked out the way it did, but someone has to lose. At least this way the reason is private, and Kat won't have to go home with a bad reputation."

No, just with a suitcase full of injustice. Lucas raked his hand through his hair. Frustration welled at the helplessness of it all. He couldn't fix it. Kat had earned this, deserved it, and—now what? Was this God's way of showing them both that Kat's place was in Bayou Bend? It was just so unfair. Of all the ways to teach a lesson . . . there had to be something else he could do.

But Sam was walking away, and short of causing a scene that would embarrass them all, mostly Kat, he couldn't do a thing about it.

For the first time in his life, Lucas didn't have a single play to call.

ceees

Kat had almost forgotten about the postshow wrap-up interviews, the ones that would be clipped and cut and sprinkled throughout the show's airing. Now that she'd been on this side of television, she could only imagine how the contestants' words were twisted or manipulated slightly—or significantly—for dramatic effect.

Great.

She climbed onto the burgundy director's chair and crossed her legs one way, then another. She didn't want to do this; she just wanted to go home. No, not home. Not yet. She wanted to go back to her hotel and hide.

The walls of the small, behind-the-set room were painted beige and boasted the show's logo in bold colors. They seemed to be closing in on her. She rubbed her palms against the knees of her jeans as the camera crew prepared their equipment. A red-shirted staff member appeared with a compact and brush. "Touch-up?"

Wouldn't help. What she really needed was waterproof mascara. She nodded anyway, like her heart wasn't currently in the middle of a free fall. Where was Lucas? Why weren't the assistant bakers required to do this stuff?

Several other people were in the room, including the cameraman and Hal, one of the network's employees who always conducted the interviews off camera, but she'd never felt so impossibly alone.

Sudden laughter and cheers rang from the set, located somewhere behind her and the wall. Celebratory cries from Piper and her team, no doubt, who were being briefed on what would happen next regarding the ballet fund-raiser, the transfer of the five hundred cupcakes, and the start of Piper's internship at Bloom.

That could have been her in there, hugging Lucas with joy, crumpling confetti under her feet and making plans.

Well, maybe not hugging Lucas. He probably wouldn't have been in much of a party mode if she'd won. Still, he'd signed her up for the competition in the first place. How could he be all that upset over the idea of her leaving Bayou Bend, anyway? Or was he just concerned she wouldn't succeed without him? Afraid she couldn't navigate New York on her own or handle men with agendas like Thad's?

She'd already proven she could if she had to.

Now she just didn't have to.

Reality lapped at the edges of her heart. She widened her eyes to ward off the tears barreling toward her lids like a tsunami. It was just a contest—one competition. Not her entire future. That pink envelope had held the results of three people's opinions. It didn't determine her value or worth as a person, or even necessarily as a chef.

So why did it feel like it did exactly that?

The assistant dabbed Kat's face with powder, swept on some subtle pink blush, and then fluffed her hair around her shoulders. "Better."

Doubtful, but the encouragement helped ease her nerves slightly. She smiled her thanks as the girl slipped out of the room and Hal took the chair across from Kat. Too bad they didn't have makeup to completely camouflage her emotions.

"Okay, we're ready. Just act naturally and tell the truth." The scruffy-bearded cameraman angled the giant black camera toward her, pausing to adjust a setting before tilting it slightly to the right. "Don't worry about whether or not you say the wrong thing or stutter. We can edit all that out."

She just bet they could.

Hal smiled at her, but it was businesslike and brief. "State your full name and what round you were just eliminated from, please."

She swallowed, mouth dry. "I'm Kat Varland, and I was just eliminated from the final round." Nothing like ripping off the Band-Aid. Maybe the questions wouldn't prick as bad from here on. Maybe they'd have some kind of postshow mercy.

Hal nodded with approval. "Good. Now, how did you feel when you heard the other team's name being announced as the winner?"

Nope. Kat reeled back against the chair, the question digging deep and scraping a fingernail against her insecurities. Yet Hal threw it out there like he was asking how she liked her coffee. How did she *feel?* Hurt. Devastated. Shocked. "I was surprised."

"Why so? You assumed you would win?" Hal quirked a bushy eyebrow.

"Not assumed. It was a fair competition." Kat shrugged. "I don't know, I just . . . had a feeling. I really thought I had it."

He nodded like he'd heard that a dozen times. He probably had—but did that make it any less true? "Did you have fun? Try to answer in complete sentences, by the way, for the editors."

Sure, because that made her feel a lot more natural. She tossed her hair off her shoulder and thought before she spoke. "I had a lot of fun taping the show." It was definitely the safe answer, if not an entirely truthful one. There had been a lot of fun times, but Piper sabotaging her efforts and finding out about Lucas's near attempt at being a traitor and Thad hitting on her in the back alley hadn't been fun—at all.

"I'll be taking several good memories and pieces of advice from the judges home with me." There. Compliment the judges' expertise for TV. That was a safe way to avoid having much of her wrap-up comments aired. Or if they were aired, at least she would come off as a professional baker and not an overly emotional woman on the verge of bursting into tears.

What did they expect her to do? Rag on how awful Piper was and stoop to the girl's petty sabotaging level? It wasn't how she played the game, and it didn't matter anymore, anyway. Piper had won, and anything Kat said negatively about her now would just reflect badly on Kat.

Hal leaned forward in his chair. "Do you think you deserved to go home or deserved to win?"

Man, these guys didn't play fair. Kat shifted in her seat, avoiding the camera's "eye." That red light on the side was starting to unnerve her. It seemed so unforgiving. "I don't think either of us deserved to go home. But someone had to."

A muscle in his jaw twitched knowingly. "You're happy with the outcome then?"

No. But she wouldn't express the contrary to the entire world at large. No point. "I think Piper is a great chef. I didn't get to taste any of her cupcakes, but her decorations were always top-notch." She offered a half-grin. "And everything she baked always smelled good."

Hal chuckled. "Nice. Most contestants say something along opposite lines."

Kat shrugged. "Not my style." She couldn't stoop to that, though she was beyond curious what Piper would say in her interview.

"So . . . now what?"

She stared at the camera, the question spiraling between them like a smoky mirage. Now what?

Hal tilted his head, waiting for her to pick up the conversation, then tried again as she continued to blink. "What's next for Kat Varland?"

What was next? Wasn't it obvious?

"Vanilla, chocolate, and strawberry, I guess."

twenty-six

She'd slept the entire way to Los Angeles, yet today, when she needed the anonymity of sleep, the bliss of unconsciousness, her eyes were as wide open as if she'd just downed a gallon of espresso.

Kat leaned her forehead against the small circular window of the airplane, staring down at the puff of clouds below, dark and barely visible now in the early evening dusk. The football team had been scheduled on a different flight, and she wasn't sure if she was grateful to be left alone from what would have surely been incessant chatting, or if she'd have welcomed the distraction. Regardless, in a few hours, she'd be back in Bayou Bend. Back to normal. Back to vanilla, chocolate, and strawberry.

As if nothing had ever happened.

But everything had happened.

Beside her, Lucas shifted, struggling to prop his ankle on his knee in the cramped seating arrangement. He'd tried to make small talk earlier, and she'd all but blown him off. She wasn't up for reliving the trip or hearing platitudes that only made her ache worse. She'd lost. That was that.

Now, not only would she have to face her family and her

hometown as a failure, she'd gained—and lost—ground with Lucas that could never be recovered.

Everything had happened.

The plane banked slightly left, tilting them away from the clouds, and she watched them disappear from the window, the glass now framing a navy sky. Behind her, a baby fussed, then quieted after a desperate shushing from its mother. She felt shushed as well.

"You want a Coke?" Lucas leaned closer to ask her, hogging the armrest. She drew her arm against her side and shook her head as the flight attendant approached their row.

"No, I'm fine."

"You didn't eat lunch. And I bet you didn't eat breakfast before going to the studio this morning, either." He nudged her. "Kat. Don't hide."

She wasn't. Though she probably would if she could. "I'm not hiding. I'm right here." She turned to look out the window again. The plane had leveled, and the clouds were back. Darker, and thinner this time. More wisps than puffs.

"I don't know how to tell you this."

She swiveled back to face him. "Tell me what?" Oh no. Tell her that he was glad she lost? Tell her he was sorry she lost? Tell her he regretted everything that had transpired between them on this cursed trip?

Did *she* regret it?

No. Not entirely. Maybe there was a shadow of regret, but only because of what they'd lost in trying to gain more. She'd always have the memories.

Which was both good and bad.

Lucas adjusted his seat back an inch. "Maybe I shouldn't."

"Little late now." She shifted to face him, sliding her purse out of the way with her foot. "You can't do that."

"I know." He sighed, rubbing his hand over his jaw. "I talked to Sam after the show. I wanted to see if I could figure out what happened."

"I lost. That's what happened." Not a whole lot to it—though the look in Piper's eyes after they'd all filed off the set still registered as . . . odd. It wasn't nearly as gleeful as she'd expected. In fact, she'd expected haughty, proud, boastful. But oh well. It didn't matter now.

"Kat, you won."

Apparently the stress of the trip had gotten to him. "No, pretty sure that confetti was dumped straight over Piper's head."

Lucas didn't even blink. He just looked her straight in the eye. "Sam said so."

A sudden gust of turbulence shook the plane. The overhead bins rattled, but not nearly as much as the news rocked Kat. "Lucas. What are you talking about? I just did a loser's interview"—she checked her watch—"four hours ago. Pretty sure they would have told me if all of that was a mistake."

"It's because of Thad."

The plane dipped again, and she gripped the armrests, her fingernails digging into the hard material. "Are you serious?" But she knew. He couldn't—wouldn't—make that up.

"Two of the three judges voted for you, but Thad came out with what happened between you. He turned the story around, Kat. You were technically disqualified, but because it was the final round, they just let you lose and save face."

What? Disqualified? Lucas's words bounced off her ears but didn't compute. "Save face?" The words sputtered off her lips, out of her control. So was her increasing volume. "I didn't do anything wrong! He came on to *me*."

"I know, Kat." Lucas's low-set tone reminded her to lower hers. And breathe. "Trust me, I know."

Now it made sense why Lucas looked so exhausted. He'd been carrying this information ever since they'd left the studio. Why hadn't he told her sooner? Well, probably because she could have very likely, in her state of embarrassment, exhaustion, and indignation, made a scene and humiliated herself or his team.

The overhead intercom squawked. "Good afternoon, passengers, this is your captain speaking. Just wanted to apologize for the bit of turbulence we're experiencing." The plane shuddered on cue, and Kat caught Lucas's eyes.

His gaze held more baggage than the luggage carousel in LAX. "I'm sorry, Kat."

It wasn't entirely obvious what exactly he was apologizing for, since none of it was his fault. Not a single bit of it—except maybe for getting them on the show in the first place. But somehow, she sort of knew.

She nodded, licking her suddenly dry lips. "Me too."

The captain spoke again, his deep voice vibrating throughout the cabin. "I'd like everyone to keep their seat belts on for the duration of the flight. Unfortunately, it looks like we're in for a bumpy ride."

No kidding.

ceeo

Back on the football field.

Like the past week had never happened, like his world for six days had never consisted of arguments and kisses and cheaters and liars.

He really would be perfectly happy if he never saw another cupcake again. His new dessert default could be brownies. Or cheesecake. Or oatmeal raisin cookies.

Except Kat didn't bake those, so that was already an epic fail.

Lucas blew his whistle, interrupting the practice game. "Guys, look alive. I know you're tired from the trip, but we have to get our heads back in the game." Advice he needed to tattoo on his own forehead. "Try that run again. Garrison, your defense needs some strength. Dupree, watch your six on that last play. You had a shadow and never even knew it."

"Welcome back, Coach."

Lucas jumped and turned to see Darren behind him, grinning and chomping on his gum. Talk about having a shadow.

He smiled, feeling relief for the first time all day. "Hey, man." He pulled his friend into a back-pounding hug. "Long time." He stood back, taking in his standard fire department polo and slacks. Then he called to Coach Kent to take over.

"You on call?"

"Just came from the station. Had to debrief the guys after a rough run." Darren popped a hot pink bubble, the gum neon against his cocoa-colored skin. "Fatality on the highway. Wasn't pretty."

Ugh. Lucas turned his eyes back to the field as he nodded, then adjusted the brim of his cap to block the late-day sun. "Can't imagine, man. You do good work, though."

"Those guys don't need me so much as they just need someone willing to listen. Talk them through the experiences so they can begin to deal with them." Darren shoved his hands in his pockets and stood beside Lucas. "It's just being a friend, really. Praying with them."

"Then you're clearly my chaplain too." Lucas snorted.

Darren smiled. "Call it what you want, man. You behaving?"

"If behaving means totally ruining things between me and Kat, then yeah, sure. I've been an angel." He blew his whistle. "Jackson, you fumble that ball again, you're doing ten laps."

Darren crossed his arms, his short sleeves pulling tight against his biceps. Lucas tried not to make comparisons. They really should start working out together again, though. The dude was downright inspiring. "Ruining things how?"

"You know those texts you kept sending me? About stirring up love?" Lucas waited for Darren's nod. "Well, let's just say I didn't just stir, I downright pureed."

His friend's eyes widened. "You didn't sleep—"

"No!" Lucas cut him off before he could finish. "Nothing like that. Not that far." But that night could have easily gone that direction, and then where would they be? He didn't even want to think about it.

He just wanted to put a ring on it.

Speaking of . . . "I got my land." He knew Darren would see right through that abrupt change of subject, but thankfully, his friend played dumb.

"What'd Kat say?"

"Haven't told her."

"Dude."

"I know. It just . . . hasn't been the right timing." He had started to tell her that night on the beach, when they'd walked after dinner, but Kat hadn't wanted to talk. Of course that had just turned into her meltdown in the sand that left them both in near tears and then led to Those Kisses . . .

Great. He'd just come full circle.

"You have to tell her. You think it's going to help smooth things between ya'll if she finds out because you ask her to help you pack?" Darren shook his head. "There isn't any getting around it."

"I will." Eventually.

"Today."

Not happening. Kat had enough on her mind coming home from the trip yesterday. He wasn't about to tell her he got his dream-come-true while hers had disintegrated—and unfairly, at that.

"Tell me what you think about this." He quickly briefed Darren on the final events of the show. "And by the way, that's all confidential, man. We signed agreements that we wouldn't reveal the results before the show airs in a couple of weeks."

"Wow. That's a lot." Darren pulled in his lower lip, frowning. "You sure it went down like that?"

"Positive."

They both stared out at the field as Coach Kent put the boys through their paces. Lucas knew not to push Darren for an answer. When he had a thought worth sharing, he would. It was one of his favorite things about his friend. Pushy to a fault, but when Darren was, it was legit—and Lucas should listen.

Sort of like how he should have listened to him about Kat in the first place.

He should confess the rest. "The worst part is, I was relieved when she lost."

"Of course you were. You don't want her leaving for a year with that scumbag chef in New York." Darren popped another bubble. "That's normal."

"Yes. Exactly." He exhaled in relief. At least his friend understood him, wasn't showing judgment. Maybe his complicated feelings weren't so awful and traitorous, after all. He relaxed slightly, feeling a bit of the burden lift. Not lift completely. Not even halfway. But a little.

He wasn't a complete jerk. He was normal.

Whatever that meant.

"It's not too late, you know."

Darren elbowed him in the side, and Lucas ducked away, holding his ribs. He always did that, and it always caught him off guard. "For the show results? Afraid it is."

"For you and Kat."

He shouldn't even ask, because he wasn't going to like this. Or was he? But he had to know. "What do you mean?"

Coach Kent blew the whistle for the players' water break, and the team piled off the field where they started pulling off their helmets and guzzling from bottles.

Darren turned to face Lucas, lowering his voice though the younger guys' roughhousing and jostling around made eavesdropping impossible. "You love her, right?"

With all his heart. "Can't help it."

"Then prove it."

He blanched. "Prove it?" Hadn't he already? By signing Kat up for the show in the first place, by going to LA with her, by encouraging her and taking her to see the sights, and by kissing her senseless not just once but several times?

"You want her to give up her dreams for you, man. Why haven't you considered giving up yours for her?"

He had, actually, but then seeing his team on the set . . . it had changed things. But now—it didn't matter anyway. "It's irrelevant at this point. She didn't win. She's staying in Bayou Bend."

Darren leveled him with a look. "What if you made a way for her to leave?"

"Made a way—" He sounded like a parrot at this point, repeating everything Darren said. But he was clearly missing a step. "What are you driving at? You think I should contact the TV studio or something? Fight for her?"

"That's the obvious answer. But not the one I'm talking about."

Did anyone know what Darren was talking about at this point? He took off his ball cap, smoothed back his hair, and replanted the hat. "Dude. It's been a long week. Help me out here."

The department-issued walkie-talkie on Darren's hip squawked. He reached down to adjust the volume before meeting Lucas's gaze. "You haven't signed on that land yet, have you?"

"No. I'm supposed to meet for closing in two days."

Darren didn't speak, just raised his eyebrows and waited.

What—oh. Lucas closed his eyes briefly, brought up his hands to cup his neck.

Oh.

Yeah. That would be proving it.

❧

"What did you think, Mom? That I was going to come back with a tattoo on my bicep and a ring in my nose?" Kat rolled her eyes at her mother, perched primly on the edge of one of the chairs in Sweetie Pies as if the back of the chair might soil her white dress shirt. If her mom made one more comment about how surprised she was to have Kat back in one piece . . .

"I'm just saying, is all." Claire Varland crossed her legs and rested her purse on her knees. She looked even more uptight than usual—maybe because Aunt Maggie had been coughing nonstop since they arrived at Sweetie Pies an hour ago. Or maybe because it was driving them all crazy that Kat refused to tell what the results of the show were. "Your father was worried. Well, concerned. Pastors don't worry."

Of course not. This time Kat didn't have to roll her eyes. Stella did it for her, propped across the table opposite their mother while examining her nail polish. "Mom, he was plumb worried, and everyone knows it. Don't even try."

Their mom bristled while Kat sighed. Would overprotective ever feel good? Maybe when it was done out of love and not obligation—or from sincere care instead of believing she would just screw everything up on her own.

Right now, it was just another burden to carry.

Aunt Maggie coughed again from behind the Sweetie Pies counter, hopefully not over the cupcakes. "Well, I still can't understand why you just don't tell us you didn't win. You aren't nearly excited enough to be sitting on that kind of secret."

"You never know. Maybe my lack of excitement is a trick to make you assume exactly that." It was a little fun to mess with them. More fun if it would have been true.

Though it sort of was true, if Lucas was indeed correct. And she knew he was.

But she couldn't explain all that right now. "We really do need to know," her mom persisted.

"Why?" Kat shoved away from the table, unable to take any more speculation and doubt. Not after what had actually transpired.

"So you can prepare to either brag to your friends or make excuses as to why your daughter failed?"

"Kat!" Aunt Maggie scolded, hurrying from around the counter to join them. "That's uncalled for."

Stella hid a smile behind her hand. "Yet accurate."

Their mom cut her a look that could have cracked a time capsule a decade early. "Stella Varland. I'm surprised at you."

"Must be a day for surprises, then." She stood slowly, then turned and stretched. "I want a cupcake."

Kat didn't. At all. Maybe not ever again. In fact, the entire dessert was about to turn into a four-letter word. But she didn't have anything else. She *would* bake them again, and eat them again, because that's what she did even though her own family couldn't fully support her. Why had Aunt Maggie never gotten any flack for baking cupcakes? Was it because she owned a shop and didn't "just bake"?

She left her crazy family and the growing pile of frustrations behind her and went to stand at the front window, choosing to ignore nature's display of autumn leaves and the decorative scarecrows across the street. Instead she stared at the deserted sidewalks.

Everything was the same.

Well, everything was exactly the same—except for her.

She'd figured she'd come back to a sort of *Alice in Wonderland* reality, where nothing made sense or fit anymore.

But it was just her. *She* didn't make sense or fit anymore.

Hadn't ever really in the first place.

And now she'd been robbed of her one chance of escape.

Kat looked down, and the black-and-white tiles at her feet started to smear together as she stared, eyes blurring. And Lucas . . . she just wanted to cry on his shoulder about the whole thing—and hated that she needed to. At this point she was so unraveled about so many things that she wasn't even sure what the root issue was anymore.

But her heart knew. And it stuttered out a single name in every two beats.

Luc-as. Luc-as.

Had Chase messed her up that badly? Was she that damaged with trust issues now? She didn't feel attached to him anymore, but everything that had gone on with Lucas the past few days pointed to her potentially not being over Chase emotionally. Just look at her overreaction to Lucas's innocent interaction with her sister. Maybe she didn't have feelings for Chase, but she definitely had collateral damage from their relationship. Had she healed at all?

Would she ever be healed completely?

Ever be worth doing something worthwhile?

Kat drew a ragged breath. At least she had Sweetie Pies, if nothing else. She knew that wasn't going anywhere, and neither were strawberry, vanilla, and chocolate cupcakes. She could count on those two things like the rising sun.

She just would rather count on pumpkin cupcakes with lemon icing and caramel drizzles.

Or, a dark chocolate cupcake with cherry ganache filling—

A shaky—and thinner than usual—arm wrapped around her shoulders. "We have a reason for asking about the show, dear." Aunt Maggie patted Kat's back. "Quit assuming the worst."

"I'm not assuming the worst . . ." Well, probably a little. But she was done crying and tired of the pity parties. "I'll be okay. It's always hard coming home from vacation, I guess. It's just—it's been a week." Though it wasn't a real vacation, was it?

Aunt Maggie turned back toward Claire's table as Stella dug a cupcake from the display behind the counter. "Stella, I made extra strawberry cupcakes today. Help yourself."

"How did you have time to make extra?" Stella pulled one from the display and peeled off the paper before taking a bite. Icing dotted her chin, and Kat decided not to tell her. It was the little things. "You had that doctor's appointment."

"Another one? Aunt Maggie . . ." Kat forgot her own issues for a moment and stared hard at her aunt. How selfish had she been, lost in her own problems even after Stella had mentioned in the email that Aunt Maggie's health was getting worse? "What's going on? What have I missed this week?"

"Only the inevitable." Her aunt let out a sigh and took the chair across from Kat's mom. "I guess it's time you knew."

"Now? You're going to tell them now?" Her mom stood abruptly, towering over Aunt Maggie. "I really don't think—"

"You think all the time, dear. Overthink, usually. So that's simply not true." Stella nearly choked on her cupcake, and even Kat hid a smile. It was a rare treat for someone to stand up to Claire Varland and live to tell about it—not even their father was that daring. Maybe Aunt Maggie was more used to dealing with her own younger sister than Kat had thought. If only Kat could learn from her, maybe she would do a better job with Stella.

Then she felt the smile slowly fade from her face. Or maybe Maggie was just being brave now because she knew something she and Stella didn't.

"Sit down, girls."

There was no disobeying the command in their aunt's tone. Stella slid into the chair beside their mom, and Kat pulled another chair up beside their aunt.

"What's going on?"

Aunt Maggie folded her hands on the table and lifted her chin. "I know this isn't the best timing, but cancer doesn't really give generous time frames."

"Oh, for heaven's sake. You're not dying." Claire slung her purse strap over her shoulder and huffed. "Don't be so dramatic."

"Fine. I'll work on that while you work on not allowing your fear to come across as anger." The two women engaged in a silent brief stare down before Claire sat back in her chair. "You're right, Mags. I'm sorry."

Kat nearly fell off her chair onto the floor. Maybe everything *had* changed while she was gone. Maybe it hadn't been just her.

An apology from her mom? To someone else? Without even being prompted?

She leaned back in her chair to look out the window, halfway expecting to see a winged pig.

"I'm about to start chemotherapy."

"No! Aunt Mags . . . really?" Stella gasped and reached out for her aunt's arm. "I don't believe you."

Kat swallowed hard as the pieces fell into place. The missed hours of work, the appointments, the lingering illnesses.

"It's true. And it's not stage four or anything completely dire, but it's closer than I'd prefer. My doctor also says it's past time to retire. I can't manage this place and be on treatments. Plus my immune system will be down for a time, and well—like I said, it's just inevitable." Aunt Maggie rubbed Stella's hand before reaching out to take Kat's.

"The biggest change will be around here, obviously." She briefly closed her eyes before meeting Kat's gaze. "Kat, I'm going to have to sell Sweetie Pies."

twenty-seven

The whole town turned out for the football game—which wasn't saying much, except for what Bayou Bend lacked in numbers, they made up for in loyalty.

Kat leaned forward on the edge of the metal bleachers, elbow-deep in a box of popcorn, and breathed in the comforting aroma of the turf spread below her. Green grass, brown dirt, sweat, and energy. Totally different from the smells of her kitchen, but hopes and dreams baked in all different environments.

Her friendship with Lucas made the football stadium a second home to her—well, third after her kitchen or maybe Sweetie Pies. Her gaze naturally sought him out on the sidelines. His hat was turned backward, which meant he was already stressing a little over the game, whistle dangling from his neck, clipboard tucked under his arm.

That was Lucas. Her Lucas.

Past tense?

Time would tell.

She munched another handful of popcorn, then slid over on the bench as Rachel settled in next to her. "Snickers or Twix?" She held out the candy bar choices, and Kat plucked the Twix from her grasp.

"You're trying to make sure I never fit into that black dress again, aren't you?"

Rachel grinned, tossing back her sleek hair as she slipped off her jacket. She draped it over the bench beside her and crossed one booted ankle over the other. "Hey, you're the one who said the dress backfired. What else are best friends for?"

"I'm just glad your hubby stayed home with the kids so I wouldn't be sitting here alone tonight, candy or not." Kat ripped open the wrapper on the candy bar. "I feel like everyone is staring at me."

"That's because they are." Rachel took a delicate bite of Snickers.

"Thanks a lot."

"No, really, I noticed earlier. You're like a celebrity now." Rachel wiped chocolate from the corner of her mouth. "It'll get worse after the show airs. I still can't believe what happened."

"Me either." She'd told her best friend the results of the show, despite the confidentiality clause, because if you couldn't tell your best friend, who could you tell? And since she and Lucas weren't talking nearly as regularly since their return home last week, she'd had to vent the news to someone.

She knew better than to turn to her mom or Stella, though she'd strongly considered Aunt Maggie at one point in recent days. There'd been a softening about her aunt since learning about her diagnosis, a rounding of the hard corners that Kat had known her entire life. For the first time since working for her, Kat actually wondered if she and Maggie could have something in common.

Like feeling trapped. And being single.

And now, no more Sweetie Pies. Unless someone was willing to buy it as is and keep Kat and Amy on staff and running business as usual, there was a good chance the shop would be leveled or remodeled and made into something else. Like a mattress shop, or a climate-controlled storage unit.

Kat never thought she'd live to see the day that she'd actually miss Sweetie Pies, but she'd created a lot of history there. Those walls—and ovens—had seen a lot of dreams bred, born, and baked. It would be weird to see it go—and even weirder to know her entire future was now even bleaker than it was before she left for LA. At least then she had her old standbys, her steady paycheck and routine schedule making up her safety blanket of sorts. That blanket might be worn and scratchy and rub in all the wrong places, but it still provided a sense of security.

Now she had nothing but a head full of gourmet—*weird*—recipes and a lease on a house that required regular income.

What was she going to do?

On the field, the game started, the players bursting through their painted school banner and running out on the turf to the cheers from the stands. She and Rachel stood and cheered with the rest of the crowd, then settled back on their seats. Kat adjusted the scarf around her neck, chilled despite the higher than average temperatures of the evening. She couldn't remember being warm since returning from Los Angeles. She sort of missed those nights on the beach with the ocean wind and the balmy LA, palm-tree-dotted air.

"You know, at least you can hold onto the fact that you won the show on merit. You proved yourself." Rachel finished her candy bar and wiped her fingers down the legs of her skinny jeans, evidently a mom thing. "That's significant."

Kat shrugged. "Not as significant as a contract in New York."

"Working for that sleazeball of a judge? That's hardly a prize. More like a sentence."

True. After the drama Thad had created, could Kat really ever consider making him her boss or respect him—or even tolerate him, for that matter—for an entire year? On the one hand, it'd be worth it because of the reputation she'd earn working at Bloom under its prestigious chefs.

On the other hand, that bordered on ethically unwise.

She bit back a groan. Why was nothing clear-cut anymore?

On the field, the boys moved into formation, then earned a first down. Lucas clapped and barked orders from the sidelines, intense instructions she couldn't quite make out. The other team, a school from an hour south whose mascot was a crawfish, rallied with an interception.

"Lucas must be freaking out." Rachel laughed as she snagged a scoop of Kat's popcorn. "He gets so stressed during these games."

"For sure." Kat loved watching him in that stress, too, trying to decipher the meaning behind the lines in his expression, attempting to read his lips as he talked to the other coaches. Half the time she knew exactly what play he was going to call before he actually called it.

And the best part was, even when he was at his wit's end and the game was tied or his team fumbled the ball, his eyes stayed aglow—the glow that only comes from a man living out his passion.

To think she'd tried to jeopardize that for her own desires. That wasn't love, just selfishness on her part. If she truly loved Lucas, she'd back off and let him live out the life God had clearly called him to.

Even if that meant living her dreams solo.

Not that God was trying to tell her anything about those lately. Her future remained a giant question mark, and the more she thought about it, the more panicked she became.

Halftime.

The majority of the crowd stood and filed down the stairs to the concession stands, laughing and chanting the school's cheer. All of them having a great time, probably because they weren't attempting to evaluate their life's value and progress at a high school football game. What was wrong with her? It was as if she only knew one mode these days—hardcore.

Rachel and Kat remained on the bleachers, unmoving rocks against a flowing sea of people. "Why not start over anyway, Kat, if you're so disappointed about New York?" Rachel turned to face her, as if they were having a private, quiet conversation in Starbucks rather than nearly shouting to be heard over the sound of the cheer-leaders revving up the fans still around them.

"Because money doesn't grow on cupcakes?"

"No, seriously. Why not go to Dallas and open up a shop there? Get a business loan. You could do it."

"No, seriously. I've looked into that."

"And?"

"And I don't qualify. My credit isn't established enough for the amount I would need. I'd have to have a cosigner at best." She sure wasn't going to get that from either of her parents, not with their opinions on her future and her capabilities. They wanted her to stay in Bayou Bend for all eternity; they'd hardly be willing to sign a paper supporting her spreading her wings, especially over something like baking.

"Face it, Rach. This was my chance." Kat moved her legs off the bench in front of them as a young boy scrambled back into his seat, cone of cotton candy held high like a trophy. "Now I'm just as stuck as ever. It's like I've come full circle." As productive as a hamster on a wheel. And she'd actually lost more in LA than she'd had when she left home. A negative score.

"I refuse to believe that." Rachel shook her head so hard her hair swung across her face. "There's always a way. You have the will, so there's a way."

"That's a cliché."

"Aren't clichés stemmed from truth?" Rachel nudged her in the side, and Kat allowed a small smile in response. "Cheer up, gloomy. This isn't the end of the world." She smirked. "If you'd seen the dia-per situation I had to clean up before escaping long enough to come here and support you, you would know what the end of the world looks like." She wrinkled her nose. "And smells like."

Kat snorted as the players filed back onto the sidelines, gearing up for the third quarter. "I'm not trying to be negative, really. Just realistic. I had a chance, and it didn't pan out. Maybe that's a sign."

Rachel's trimmed eyebrows arched in suspicion. "A sign of what?"

That part she was still trying to figure out for herself. A sign that God was changing her path? Narrowing her options? Convincing her to stay in Bayou Bend and forget her dreams?

Maybe forgetting was the best bet. With everything that had transpired between her and Lucas last week, she wasn't just afraid to dream again—she was downright terrified. Because she'd seen up close and personal how dreams could morph into nightmares all too fast. How quickly cracked hearts could shatter.

"We got the ball back!" Rachel put two fingers in her mouth and whistled loud enough to rival the one hanging around Coach Kent's neck. "Go team!"

The glee on the boys' faces as they jumped up and slapped high fives was almost childlike in its purity. Kat was almost envious. They were living out their dreams, right there on the field, in real color.

She frowned slightly, her gaze raking across each player as they huddled around Lucas. How many of those guys dreamed about playing ball in college or even going pro one day? What were the odds of many of them, if any, actually succeeding?

And should knowing the odds change that dream?

They filed back onto the field, and as the clock clicked over to the fourth quarter, the opposing team took the lead.

Rachel deflated next to her. "Are you kidding me? We totally had them. Man, what a game." She leaned forward, elbows on her knees, staring intently at the scoreboard. "I can't believe they pulled that field goal out of nowhere."

Kat could. She had seen it coming, actually, and figured Lucas had too. He was rarely caught off guard on the field.

A whistle blew, and Lucas called for a time-out. Kat wished she was an eavesdropping jersey number in that huddle. She'd love to hear what play he was calling, to hear him talk through the specifics of why he chose that particular one. He always had a reason, usually an in-depth one that she only grasped about half the mechanics of, but she enjoyed hearing him flesh it out. It always made sense— even to a non-sports addict like herself.

Suddenly, chaos erupted on the turf as the play took a wrong turn. The other team intercepted the ball, and Lucas whipped off his cap and threw it on the ground, shoving his hands in his hair in frustration. She could see the vein in his neck from the stands. Uh-oh. That wasn't like Lucas at all. Something else was wrong, more than just the interception.

"Wait, what just happened?" Rachel sat up straight, straining to see around the people in the stadium who stood and called out an overwhelming mixture of *boos* and critical instruction.

Kat squinted, tuning out the crowd and focusing on Lucas's lips as he called in the quarterback, Ben. He clamped his hand on the boy's padded shoulder and talked firmly, directly in his face. He wasn't yelling; she could tell that much. But the vein had yet to disappear. He was holding back his temper, yet she knew without a doubt the boy knew exactly what his coach thought.

"I think the quarterback called a different play than what Lucas told them in the huddle." The longer Kat watched and caught key words via lipreading, the more certain she became. "Yeah, that's what happened. Wow."

"Direct disobedience? That's crazy. Those guys love Coach." Rachel fished in her purse and came up with a pack of gum. "Drama, drama, drama. What a game, though!"

Drama, for sure. How could Ben make a decision like that last-minute, one that was so against the coach's wishes?

The comparison hit her then, square in the face like a banana cream pie from a black-and-white sitcom.

Hadn't she been doing the same thing? Trying to make her dreams happen on her own rather than listening to and heeding the voice of her heavenly coach? When had she actually sought God's will and asked him to guide her to *his* plans, in *his* timing? All she remembered doing lately was complaining. Whining. Throwing pity parties big enough to rival New Year's Eve celebrations.

Like Ben, she'd tried to call her own plays, and they'd blown up in her face. She thought she knew best when, really, she only knew the Astroturf under her feet for that particular moment. God saw the entire game plan—and made his calls for good reasons.

On the sidelines, Lucas pulled Ben into a quick hug, then slapped his back and sent him running back onto the field. Tears pricked the back of Kat's eyes. God was giving her a sign, all right, right there in vivid Technicolor. And it was about so much more than her dreams; it went so much deeper.

Because as Lucas and Ben demonstrated, it only took one more chance to get it right. One wake-up call could be enough to refocus and win the game.

She wasn't disqualified at all.

It was just that perhaps God had a different dream in mind for her. And for the first time in her entire life, Kat breathed in the hope that perhaps that new dream would come with a victory she couldn't accomplish on her own.

And that was more than worth playing for.

twenty-eight

*L*ucas jogged after Kat across the nearly deserted school parking lot, streaks of light from the poles above breaking up the shadows between cars. But not enough for his liking. He hated that she hadn't waited on him like she usually did after his games and was walking by herself out in the dark. Did she really think that much had changed between them?

Had it?

It was like they were going to have to reset all their defaults.

"Kat, wait up." He didn't holler, didn't want to scare her. But she jumped a little anyway, turning and flipping the edge of her scarf over her shoulder. Even from this short distance, the color of the scarf brought out her eyes.

She waited beside a dented Ford that had rusted out. "Good game."

He caught up to her quickly, then stopped a few feet away, suddenly not sure what to do with his hands. He wanted to hold her. So he held on to the strap of his coach's duffel bag instead. "What do you mean? We lost."

She shrugged. "Was still good. Rachel nearly made me go deaf, screaming in my ear." A grin flickered across her face, then mellowed into something more serious. "I saw what happened on the field with Ben."

Lucas hitched the bag higher on his shoulder. "You mean, you saw him call his own play." He still couldn't believe the boy's nerve. But he knew the motivation behind it, recognized that panicked desperation Ben had felt. The teen had to decide between going with his gut and going with his instructions. It wasn't wrong to question authority sometimes.

But in this instance, Ben had chosen wrong, and it had cost them dearly.

"I saw how you handled it too." A passing car's headlights briefly shone across Kat's face, highlighting those features he'd come to love, the ones he used to be able to read like the pages of his favorite sports magazine. Lately, though, trying to read her was like trying to decipher a code.

And rarely did she let him linger long enough to study properly.

She twisted the edges of her scarf around her fingers, looking everywhere but directly at him. "You didn't lose it with him. I'm proud of you."

That soft comment went straight to his core. Lucas struggled to focus on the real topic of their conversation, when all he wanted to do was wrap her in a hug and demand that everything go back to normal. But normal wouldn't be enough, not after all they'd experienced together.

Not after those kisses.

He took a deep breath in an effort to redirect his thoughts. "Ben's a good kid. Just needs to know when to obey and when to challenge."

"Doesn't everyone?" Kat raised her eyebrow at him, and he had to agree.

"We're not so different. I told him that, too, after the game." Ben had taken his discipline well, and felt so lousy he even bargained for a harsher sentence. But Lucas knew better. It wasn't needed.

It was pretty hard to punish him in the first place when every word out of Lucas's mouth during his lecture had pierced straight into his own heart.

You've got a lot of people counting on your decisions.

What you do affects those around you and can either hurt or help.

What kind of man are you going be?

"I waited for you, for a little while." Kat stepped a foot closer, and his heart hitched. "But you seemed preoccupied with the guys, and well . . ." Everything she didn't say sounded even louder than the words she'd just spoken.

She'd waited.

But she'd left.

Which meant more?

Didn't matter. She was here now, and he needed to make the suggestion he'd been debating ever since Darren had pinned him down with the truth last week.

She let out a long sigh, staring somewhere over his shoulder at the stadium. "It was a really good game. An eye-opener."

For her too?

But first things first.

"Kat, we need to talk." Just not at either of their places. Not after that night last week, and not with Lucas's own raw emotions boiling under the surface. He wasn't entirely sure how the impending conversation was going to go, but it needed to happen somewhere safe. For both of them.

Because he might not even be able to get through it without choking up.

She nibbled on her bottom lip, then finally nodded. To her credit, she didn't immediately start quizzing him on the topic. Probably just assumed the worse, like he'd have done if the situation had been reversed. "Sure. Let's just go sit in my car."

Maybe they were still on the same page to a degree after all. Did she not trust herself completely with him anymore either?

And was it bad that the thought made him just a little happy?

They walked to her car, where she unlocked the doors before he slid into the passenger side, dumping his bag at his feet. He scooted the seat back to make more room for his legs. "I had an idea."

Her slightly pinched features settled into a relaxed, neutral state at those words, and she reached to turn down the radio that blared when she'd started the ignition. "What's that?"

"I've been thinking about the show, and the way all that went down, and—well, it's not right. Not fair. And I know you don't feel led to do anything about it, and maybe our options aren't really great in that regard anyway, but . . ."

She shot him a look, turning the dial to blow the heater at their feet. "Lucas. Just spit it out."

Yeah, really. Since when did he babble? Probably since he was dreading the words he needed to speak. But despite the fear of them, he knew deep down in his core that Darren had been right, and this had to happen. For Kat. And for himself, in a sense. He needed to test his own heart for her. He'd been so caught up in his own selfish ventures that he hadn't treated her nearly in the way she deserved.

If he could really do this, could really let her go—then he'd know that she truly had his heart.

Of course, at that point, it'd be too late, but the guilt and the regret would be gone, at least. He would be free of those.

Miserable and depressed, but free. More important, Kat would be doing what she wanted to do, and she would be happy. That was all that mattered.

He held his breath. "I want to be your first investor."

"Investor? In what?" She angled to face him, a parking lot lamp cutting a shadow diagonally across her face, hiding her eyes.

"You should start your own business. You have what it takes; you just need the boost financially." He swallowed hard, hoping his face hid what was happening in his heart. "So, you pick wherever you want to go. New York. Los Angeles. Dallas. Just name it, and I'll get you started. Interest free."

He wouldn't even accept loan payments from her, not at first. Not until her business became somewhat steady and was making a profit. That lump of money was sitting there now, waiting on his land. He hadn't needed it for anything else, so it wouldn't hurt him to give her more time to get going.

He wasn't going to need it once she left, anyway. Not for a long time.

Because buying his own dream meant nothing without Kat in the middle of it.

"Interest? Lucas. What are you even talking about? You can't give me a business loan." She laughed, short and hollow, like she thought he might be teasing her. "That's crazy."

"I'm serious, Kat." He leveled his gaze at her until she finally looked back, confusion and hope and wariness filling her blue eyes. "I believe in you. I want you to do this."

She opened her mouth, then shut it, looking away. Looked at him again, and shook her head. Tried to speak again, but no words escaped. Suddenly she leaned over and pressed her forehead against the steering wheel.

Was that a yes or a no?

He waited, sensing he shouldn't push. Or speak at all. Or maybe not even breathe. He hated when women didn't play by the rule book. He'd expected excitement, maybe happy tears, or a little shriek of joy. Something. Even her getting offended by his offer would be better than this mysterious silence, broken only by the faint sounds of Dean Martin drifting from the radio.

Just when he thought he was going to have to change the station to country, she sat up. "This is a big deal."

She had no idea. This venture was costing him a lot more than cash.

He reached over and took her hand where it rested on the

gearshift—no, where it was clenched in a death grip around the gearshift. He threaded his fingers through hers, raised their linked hands to his mouth, and pressed a kiss against the back of her hand. "I know."

"I mean, so big that I can't give you an answer right now." She shook her head again, her hair swishing against her scarf. "I need to think about it. Pray about it. I'm just . . . overwhelmed."

So was he. But she'd say yes. Once she got over the shock and realized he was offering her a one-way ticket to her dreams, she'd be on Google Maps faster than he could say *cupcake*.

Speaking of . . .

He let go of her hand and unzipped his jacket pocket, where he'd stored the gift he'd been carrying around for days, waiting for the right moment to give it to her. "You know how you always tease me about never being able to pull off a surprise or keep a secret?"

"Only because you threw me a surprise party last year for my birthday and included me in the guest list."

"Well, surprise." He reached into his pocket and let the gift inside drop down and dangle between his fingers. The cupcake necklace they'd seen while window-shopping in LA.

"Lucas! How did you—when did . . . ?" She broke off with a surprised little laugh.

There was the smile he'd been hoping for. "Went back and got it while you were trying on shoes."

"Shoes?" She stared blankly, as if racking her brain for the memory to fill in the gaps. "Oh, that night on Main Street? Those pink open-toed pumps?"

"Uh, sure." Whatever they were, they'd looked good on her. "I whispered to the sales clerk to keep you distracted with boots until I got back from down the street. Worked like a charm—no pun intended."

He undid the clasp on the necklace and motioned for her to twist around. She turned in the seat, removing her scarf and lifting her hair, and he fought the urge to plant a kiss on the back of her neck as he latched the chain.

"Thank you." The words whispered from her lips as she straightened in her seat, reaching up to pat the charm hanging over the top of her sweater.

"I hope it reminds you of the good parts of the trip." There had been some, despite it all.

"It already does." The wistful smile she offered made his stomach tighten. He had to get out of this car before he did something foolish, like retract his offer to send her away.

Or push her up against the panel of the car door and kiss her until reality meshed with his hopes.

☙

"I can't believe you made cupcakes." Rachel hip-bumped Kat out of the way of the sink and rinsed her hands free of vegetable shavings.

"You can't believe a cupcake chef made cupcakes for a party celebrating her TV debut on a cupcake show?" Kat deadpanned, nudging Rachel back as her friend began lining the chopped veggies on a platter.

"No, I can't believe a girl who makes cupcakes for a living made even more cupcakes to feed a bunch of people coming over to watch her on a cupcake show, where she just made five hundred cupcakes and got humiliated—" Rachel broke off her own sentence. "You know what I mean."

Humiliated. That pretty much summed it up, even though no one at the viewing party would know the whole story except for her, Lucas, and Rachel. "No, I see your point." Kat held up the plate of mini red velvets. "I think I just baked these on autopilot."

"I'm not saying they won't get eaten." Rachel plucked one of the minis from the plate and grinned, red-dyed crumbs oozing between her teeth.

"Classy." Kat laughed as she moved the desserts away from her friend and set them on the table in the dining room with the rest of the food. Everyone would be there soon—her entire family, Aunt Maggie, Lucas, the guys from the football team. Lucas had invited his good friend Darren, too, but he was on duty tonight.

She should have made more food.

She baked when she was nervous anyway, and thinking of everyone watching her lose on national television made her want to whip up a dozen cakes and a few hundred Snickerdoodles.

"Have you decided yet?" Rachel brought the tray of veggies to the table, pausing to dab a carrot stick in the pool of ranch dressing. "About Lucas's offer? Which, by the way, is the most romantic thing I've ever heard."

"Romantic?" Kat snorted, snatching a celery stick from the platter and nibbling on the end. "I hardly think him offering to pay me to go away is romantic. He's just being a friend—being Lucas." Protector. Provider. No different than he was to anyone who ever depended on him, though.

If he really loved her and wanted to pursue what had stirred between them in Los Angeles, he'd want her to stay. Wouldn't he?

He'd gotten her the necklace too . . . yet that could be a simple friendship gesture as well. The man was downright impossible to read these days. She used to know him better than the recipe for her favorite pumpkin scone cupcakes.

The timing of it all just gave her a headache. She'd had that specific realization about her dreams and her future at the football game last week, prayed, and immediately after, was offered funding to do exactly what she'd always wanted to, interest-free. Was that a sign of an answered prayer or was it merely a temptation she was supposed to avoid?

She wanted to accept. Badly—especially because Aunt Maggie had to sell Sweetie Pies and leave Kat potentially without a job. She wanted to take the loan and start a shop that would give her enough profit to pay Lucas back—and then some—and prove herself. Live her dream.

But her dreams lately felt so hollow away from him.

Just knowing he believed in her that fully filled a hole in her heart she hadn't completely realized existed—at least not to that depth.

Which sort of rivaled the bottomless pit in New Mexico's Carlsbad Caverns.

She grabbed a carrot stick, turning pleading eyes to her friend. "What do I do?"

"That's easy." Rachel gestured with her own carrot, her expression serious. "You pass me a brownie."

"So helpful." Kat handed over the plate of chocolate desserts. They did look therapeutic. She took one for herself.

"I'm kidding. Actually, I'm not, I do want one." Rachel grabbed one off the plate and took a bite before answering. "What's the real debate here?"

"I told you what happened at the game, the epiphany I had." Kat nibbled on the side of her brownie, leaning her hip against the table laden with food. "I just don't want to make the same mistake again. Don't want to dive in to something that I'm trying to control or make happen, moments after I commit to God to stop doing exactly that."

"Well, sure. That's a good thing to be cautious about." Chocolate crumbs dropped from Rachel's brownie to the floor as she pointed her finger at Kat. "But this isn't you controlling it this time. You didn't force Lucas to offer you thousands of dollars to invest in you or your business. You never even would have thought of asking."

"Of course not." She still had no idea why Lucas even had that much money set aside, anyway. How could one person's savings plan be that good?

"I'm just surprised he can afford it, with him about to be buying that land and all."

The brownie bite lodged in Kat's throat. "What land?"

"The ten acres, with the old farmhouse on it—you know, that place off Highway 169." Rachel stared. "You didn't know?"

"How did *you* know?" The man who couldn't keep a surprise a secret sure seemed to have a lot of them suddenly. How was this possible? And why wouldn't he have mentioned it to her sooner? He'd always talked about wanting to plant deep roots in Bayou Bend and find somewhere to spread out. This was good news for him—so why the secret?

It stung a little, to be honest.

"You know Adam works at the bank." Rachel's husband. He'd probably processed the loan paperwork or handled something with the mortgage transfer on the property. Figured. Probably the whole town knew.

She could ask them all in a minute. Ugh.

It still seemed impossible for her to not have heard a word about this. "Lucas is buying land? Really?"

"Uh-oh." A mask of realization stretched across Rachel's face. "Probably not now."

Huh? Not now?

Then it hit her too.

His investment.

twenty-nine

The episode was halfway over, the party in full swing, and all Kat could do was hide in the kitchen, load the dishwasher with all her mixing bowls and cooking utensils, and try not to think about how the last ten minutes of the episode would likely put a huge damper on the big get-together.

If her own bad mood didn't do it first.

There had to be thirty people crammed into her living room. The football players, her family, a few people from her father's church, Amy from Sweetie Pies and her boyfriend . . . they'd all turned out to watch her fail. Not that they knew it was coming, but surely they had an inkling by now. Her aunt was right—she wasn't nearly in a good enough mood since returning from LA to be about to launch her dream.

Lucas must have sensed the dark cloud of gloom over her head, because he kept hovering in the kitchen, stalling, asking questions like did she have more potato chips for the guys or taking ten minutes to get a glass of water for her dad, who was more than capable of getting it for himself and didn't want that much ice anyway.

No, Lucas wanted her to give him an answer, and now. Now?

285

How could she? He was trading his dream for hers—yet sending her away at the same time.

With so many mixed signals in that, she felt like a traffic cop.

"Are you sure you don't need help?" He was practically pacing in front of her sink, his shoes tripping over the edges of the floor rug.

"No, I've got all this." She waved her hand at him in dismissal, avoiding eye contact, afraid if she looked directly at him she would explode.

Turn down his offer.

Or worse—accept it.

Should she? If he didn't have any intentions for them if she stayed . . . why stay? If he was willing to send her away, if she wasn't going to have a job in Bayou Bend anyway . . .

No, it wasn't right. It just didn't feel good in her stomach.

Neither did the fact that half the town was about to collectively watch her lose a baking competition on national television—losing while doing the only thing she was good at.

Maybe God just wanted her at square one, with nothing.

"I can't believe my sister is a TV star." Stella's voice rose above the others mingling in the living room, and Kat paused at the dishwasher, tilting her head. Had she heard that correctly? "She looks great, doesn't she?"

A sincere compliment from Stella? In front of people?

Who knew.

She loaded another bowl into the bottom compartment of the dishwasher. Maybe she should get back in there after all.

"Of course she does." Aunt Maggie's voice sounded above the din of the sudden car commercial blaring from the TV. "And what a cute apron too." There was a slight pause, then the older woman's tone turned borderline protective. "Though I do hope that Piper girl gets what's coming to her."

They must have aired the scene with Piper ruining her decorations.

She hadn't been able to watch the majority of the episode with everyone, not after the first round, anyway. She made excuses about playing hostess and stayed out of the room, knowing she'd have to sit down after everyone left and watch/cry her way through it on her TiVo. Alone.

She loaded a large spoon next, trying not to make any clanking sounds. The compliments and defense from her family were nice. More than nice—and more than a little shocking. Maybe she'd stressed herself into a different dimension.

"Well, it's for certain. She did us proud."

Kat stiffened, one hand in the dishwasher, the other reaching back into the sink for the pile of forks.

That was her daddy's voice.

Tears welled. Her dad, proud? Of her baking? She swallowed hard, wishing he'd elaborate, yet somehow at the same time afraid he would and that in doing so the magic would somehow disappear.

But the room remained silent, hushed even by a pause from the television, as if the technology itself recognized the validity of the moment.

Her dad was proud of her. Her aunt and sister were complimenting her. All with sincerity.

And they didn't even know she could hear them. Did they talk about her like this any other times when she hadn't been there? Had she just missed it somehow?

Just when she thought she might explode with the possibilities and foreignness of it all, Lucas came up behind her and tugged her free of the dishwasher. He spun her around, her back pressed against the edge of the counter, and leaned in close, trapping any potential attempts of escape on her part.

"I need an answer, Kat. I've been waiting for days and giving you space, but this is a big deal—you said it yourself. There's a lot riding on your decision. So just make it already." His mouth was inches from hers, his eyes sincere, and she wanted to kiss him so badly. Wanted to punch him in the stomach for even putting her in the position to have to choose.

Wanted to lasso her dreams close and will them into existence.

She closed her eyes briefly. *God, I surrender. Again. All of this to you.* She opened her eyes, fresh clarity filling her empty resolve tanks. The dream was nothing without the Dream Giver, and if she wasn't following his steps for her life, then she didn't want to walk at all.

Somehow, she just knew those steps didn't include leaving Bayou Bend right now. Not like this. Not with Aunt Maggie's health declining and Kat's options so limited. No, she'd lost the competition on *Cupcake Combat* for a reason, and while it was sweet of Lucas to try to save the day, this time she couldn't allow it. Couldn't depend on him.

She already had a Savior.

And it wasn't Lucas.

It was time to prove in whom her faith really lay and give Lucas's shoulders a break from her burdens.

"Oh, hush, everybody. It's the final decision!" Stella's voice sounded with excitement. The volume was cranked up, and suddenly Sam's voice boomed from the living room, his final words blending with Kat's as she looked at Lucas and said something she knew he would probably never understand.

"The answer is no."

⸙

She'd turned him down.

Lucas absently piled plastic cups on top of paper plates, compiling a small tower before tossing the lot of it in the trash. It was almost full, which hadn't taken long with the number of people who had shown up to support Kat.

A room full of people who loved her, and she'd almost missed it, almost missed the pride and sincerity in her parents' eyes, the joy in her sister's face, the pleasure in her aunt's smile—all because of her jaded preconceptions.

Was that what she was basing her decision on with him too?

She hadn't even said why.

And his heart couldn't decide if it was more disappointed or relieved.

Everyone was gone now, after oozing condolences and assuring Kat she was still their favorite cupcake chef—next to Maggie—despite the loss. Kat had glowed under all the compliments, her icy wall of defense slowly thawing out as she basked in the warmth of their approval. Under the thank-yous, he saw the humility in her heart, the surprise, the gratitude. She couldn't be more grateful for their kind words.

So why hadn't they bothered to give them to her before now?

Some puzzles took longer to solve than others, though, and right now, he just wanted to know why Kat had returned his puzzle without even taking the pieces out of the box.

The answer is no.

The words burned the back of his throat as he gathered another armful of trash. Was she staying in Bayou Bend and turning down his offer because that was what she wanted? Or because of pride? Or fear?

Because of him?

So now what? He was supposed to just buy the land anyway and move forward with his plans, like they hadn't all revolved around Kat in the first place?

He didn't want his dream without her.

It'd be more like a nightmare.

So . . . they were both left with nothing? That hardly seemed fair. He guessed the old adage was pretty true after all. *All's fair in love and war.*

They'd certainly seen both in Los Angeles.

"Why didn't you tell me about your land?"

Uh-oh. He turned to see Kat standing, hands on her hips, a sponge clenched between her fingers. Last he'd seen her, she'd been scrubbing at a stain on the floor under the table, effectively avoiding him as she'd done most of the evening. She must have found her courage under there, because the fire that sparked in her gaze looked like it had ignited off a long fuse.

Darren had been right.

"Kat, I didn't mean to keep it from you. Not like that." He leaned against the counter, hands up in surrender. "I didn't want to say anything because it wasn't final yet, and for a while, it looked like it wouldn't be." He couldn't tell her the whole truth—that he'd intended for the land to be for them, that he couldn't tell her about it without proposing at the same time.

He shrugged, stalling. "Then my bid was accepted, and it snowballed pretty quickly." And his agent had had a legal mess trying to get him out of the offer without penalty. They still hadn't figured up all the details, and now, he wondered if he could undo the undo. Get his land back.

Did he still want it?

"That's the money you were offering me, isn't it? Your land money."

He swallowed, wishing he could lie, knowing he couldn't, realizing she'd see through it even if he had the nerve to try. She deserved the truth, anyway. But would she explode? Collapse? Would she see it as he meant it, or distort it like she seemed to be doing to all his motives lately?

Why did all his best-laid plans backfire so violently?

"*Isn't it?*" She stepped closer to him, pointing at him with the sponge, ignoring the drops of water that slowly dripped from the soggy edge.

He exhaled loud and long. "Yes."

The phone rang from its cordless station on Kat's counter. He was closer, and she was still breathing fire, so he grabbed it. "Hello,

Kat Varland's residence." Probably her sister remembering her gloves that lay forgotten on the entry table.

"Yes, hello there, I'm calling from the Food Network."

The professional male voice wasn't one he recognized from their trip, and Lucas frowned. "Yes?"

"I need to speak with Kat Varland, please." There was a pause and a shuffle of papers from the other side of the line. "It's urgent."

Must be, to be calling at nine p.m.

Just so long as it wasn't Thad.

He extended the receiver to her. "You should probably take this." And maybe a tranquilizer, too, as evident from the holes she kept trying to burn into him with her eyes.

She snatched it, not even pretending to hide her frustration at being interrupted, and glared at him as she pressed the phone against her shoulder. "Who is it?" she whispered.

"The Food Network."

Surprised registered in her eyes, dousing a bit of the flames, and she turned her back to take the call. Lucas really wished they'd talk to him first, let him screen whatever news they had in order to protect her, but he knew because of the confidentiality agreements, it would be a fruitless argument.

So he'd just listen from the other receiver.

He ran and grabbed it up from the station in her living room just as she spoke for the first time.

"This is Kat."

Lucas tilted the mouthpiece away from his lips so they wouldn't hear his breathing.

"Hello, Ms. Varland, this is Mason Reynolds from the Food Network. I just wanted to personally call and apologize to you for the mix-up regarding the just-aired episode of *Cupcake Combat* you participated in."

Apologize? For what? Lucas sat on the edge of the couch and leaned forward, bracing his elbows on his knees.

"I . . . we just watched it, but I don't understand. Why the apology?" Kat sounded as confused as he felt. At least she didn't sound angry anymore.

"I was told you were disqualified unofficially from the competition because of an issue with one of the male judges, and to be discreet, a decision was made to end it as if the Icing Queens won fair and square." Reynolds sighed, his breath rattling the line. "However, it was brought to the network's attention just today that what was represented as fact was, indeed, quite wrong."

"Wrong how?" Suspicion clouded her tone, and Lucas fought the urge to fist pump. *Good girl. Don't assume or give them an inch yet.*

Lucas knew before Reynolds spoke the words, though, exactly what he meant. He shook his head as the truth emerged—a little too late.

"It appears the producers were mistaken about Mr. Holson's innocence in your . . . encounter with him." He coughed. "I apologize for that, as well. There is no excuse. This is a professional industry, and I can assure you that he will no longer be acting as a judge for this or any other show on our network."

Kat was silent for about seven surprisingly incessant pounds of Lucas's heart. He didn't get it. The apology was nice, sort of—but what was Reynolds saying? What was the point?

"It was too late to stop the show from airing, due to the last-minute notice we received of the truth, but we feel terrible at Food Network for everything that happened."

Lucas frowned. Reynolds's voice sounded sincere enough, but what good was the apology when she hadn't won what she came to LA to get in the first place?

"Because of the mix-up, and the nature of the disagreement, we want to offer you the first place prize—on the condition that you'll agree to keep this situation quiet and between us." Reynolds didn't sound nearly as professional now, more along the lines of desperate to keep his job and the positive ratings for the show. "So at your official acceptance, you can now receive the same prize as the other winning contestant—a one-year baking contract at Bloom."

"At Bloom." The words echoed and dangled from Kat's mouth like a noose, and Lucas reeled back. *What?* Was she even actually considering this madness?

Lucas jumped off the couch and hurried, still clutching the cordless to his ear, into the kitchen. Kat stood by the refrigerator, half-twisted away from him, one arm wrapped around her stomach and her other hand clenching the phone like it might kick her in the jaw if she let go.

He waved his arms, eyes wide, using every ounce of sign language he could to indicate this was not a good offer, but she didn't see him. Or was ignoring him.

He sagged in frustration, stopping just short of going over and shaking her out of the stupor. They were going to apologize for the wolf's behavior, and then send the lamb into the wolf's den for a year? How did that make *anything* that had happened right?

She finally managed to squeeze out a response, something Lucas had been wondering as well. "How did you find out? Did . . . did Mr. Holson confess?"

Honest question, but one they weren't guaranteed to answer. Would he? Lucas held his breath.

"He did, only after being confronted with a testimony from one of your fellow contestants." Reynolds shuffled more papers. "I suppose there's no harm in telling you that it was the winning contestant herself."

"Piper?" Lucas mouthed the same name that Kat spoke, her voice a notch above incredulous. "How did she . . . why would—"

"Most unusual. She approached the producers after the charity cupcake gala and told them she'd overheard the entire exchange between you and Holson in an alley outside, as well as learned after the fact from the show's host that you had been disqualified because of the misunderstanding." Reynolds laughed. "It doesn't happen often in Hollywood, ma'am, but maybe the guilt got the best of her and prompted her to do the right thing."

The right thing. Piper? Lucas shook his head. After all that . . .

But sending Kat to New York to work at Bloom with Piper and Thad wasn't the right thing at all. Indignation began a slow burn. Maybe Piper had had a change of heart, but Lucas would bet his NFL signed football that Thad hadn't. There was no way he was letting Kat go up north to work under that slimebucket.

"I know this offer is still a lot to consider, so feel free to give me a call back tomorrow. I'll give you my number." Reynolds flipped back into professional mode on the phone, and it flipped a switch inside Lucas. "I will need an answer by then, however."

"I don't think so." Lucas gripped the receiver tighter.

Kat jumped and spun around, having just realized he was even on the line in the first place.

"You can take that offer and tell the network bigwigs that it's insulting. How can you apologize for a man's inappropriate behavior and then offer a prize that puts her at his mercy for twelve months?" The slow burn morphed into a steady blaze.

"Who is this?" Reynolds's voice sounded half-confused, half-defensive. "This was a confidential phone call, sir."

"I was there. I was Kat's assistant in the competition and witnessed everything." Lucas raised his eyebrows at Kat, silently asking if she was okay with his continuing. She sank against the edge of the counter and nodded, pinching the bridge of her nose.

Permission. Good. He probably would have kept going anyway. He squared his shoulders. "We don't accept the offer. Final answer."

Reynolds stuttered in surprise. "So you're turning down the network's compensation?"

He hesitated, wondering how far he could push this and then deciding to go for it. He used the firmest coach voice he had, the one Kat had told him numerous times was impossible to argue against. "No, I'm suggesting they change it into cash compensation."

Kat's eyes widened. She nearly dropped the phone but caught it just in time and returned it to her ear.

Lucas turned away from her so he could concentrate. "A fair amount that will help Kat get started with her own business." Just like he had tried to help her do. Maybe Kat would accept money from someone else if not from him, especially when she had actually won and deserved a prize.

His heart sank a little at the realization that she might take it. This must be God's will for her, if things were happening so suddenly and outside of his control. The fact that these people had even called in the first place was huge.

Clearly, God wanted Kat elsewhere.

And he and his broken heart weren't going to stand in the way another minute longer.

Reynolds started to speak, but Lucas wasn't done. He might be projecting his frustration and anger a little at this point, but regardless, he kept going.

For Kat's sake.

"And I suggest you be generous." He waited to give his next words plenty of room to sink in deep. "It'd be a shame for this indecency to go viral."

A long silence filled the line, and when Reynolds finally spoke, his tone was a mixture of both defeat and admiration. "Consider it done, sir. My people will be in touch."

thirty

She was actually going to miss this place.

Kat folded another packing box into shape, then sealed the bottom with tape. Her ponytail was coming undone, again, and loose hair swished across her face. She brushed the strands from her eyes with the backs of her dusty hands. So far, she, Aunt Maggie, and Stella had discovered several unexpected surprises while packing up Aunt Maggie's belongings in the shop, including a dangly earring, a measuring cup Aunt Maggie had been searching for more than a year, and an entire unopened pack of designer cupcake liners.

Plus a CD of the Backstreet Boys that had to be Amy's. Or Aunt Maggie's, on second thought.

"Do these stay or go?" Stella carefully backed out from under the kitchen counter and turned, her arms full of mixing bowls.

Kat looked toward the little office off the kitchen, and from her desk Aunt Maggie rolled the chair she was sitting in to peek through the doorway. She'd wanted to help pack, but the girls insisted she save her energy and not breathe in all the dust they'd be sure to stir up. She'd compromised by agreeing to clean out her desk instead, where she could still see what they were doing through the door when she needed to direct them.

"Those stay." She rolled back toward her desk, her voice rising from inside the office. "But pack my rolling pin with the marble handles. That's a memory that's going home with me."

This whole shop was a memory, at least for Kat.

How many hours had she spent mixing batter, icing cupcakes, and bantering with customers at the front counter—the stay-at-home moms' group, her father's secretary, the guys on the football team. How many days had she unlocked that front door and flipped the sign to Open? How many dollars had she touched and traded at the register, exchanging currency for culinary treats?

And why had she taken it all for granted and complained about every minute and inch of it until now?

You never know what you have until it's gone.

Sort of like what her friendship with Lucas seemed to be turning out to be. He'd left shortly after the phone call from the Food Network the other night, abandoning their argument, and they'd yet to talk since. She knew they would eventually, knew he wouldn't let things go unfinished between them, but the end of it all seemed so inevitable. She'd be going somewhere—anywhere—with that large check she'd gotten special delivery yesterday, and after that . . .

No one knew what would happen.

Yeah, she wasn't in a particular hurry to have that conversation with Lucas, either.

And she still didn't know what it meant that he had offered to trade his dream for hers.

She took the bowls from Stella and tucked them into the nest of Bubble Wrap inside the cardboard box. No more thinking, just packing. It hurt less that way. Aunt Maggie would be starting chemo next week. Several buyers were interested in the shop, too, but so far, nothing concrete had been offered—and unfortunately, none of them wanted to keep the business running as a cupcake bakery. Just in case, though, Aunt Maggie was leaving several key pieces behind that she could sell in a package deal.

Apparently Kat wasn't the only one having a hard time letting go.

"So where will you go, Kat?" Stella knelt back on the floor, looking more casual than Kat had ever seen her in an oversize college sweatshirt and jeans, hair tucked behind her ears like a little kid. "New York? Give Bloom some competition?" She winked, yet there was a distinct sadness behind her expression that surprised Kat. Would her sister actually miss her? Or was she just jealous that Kat might be moving to a popular big city, when despite all her pageant success she was still here in Bayou Bend?

One thing was certain. "Not New York." If she was turning down the offer of Bloom—which she totally agreed with Lucas's train of thought that he'd made perfectly clear to Reynolds—it seemed risky to set up shop somewhere as expensive and competitive as the Big Apple. She had some decent money to work with, yeah—but it wouldn't last forever. This was finally her one shot, and she needed to be wise.

Which was hard, because the cry of her heart these last few days kept her feelings on an emotional roller coaster, and she had yet to figure out how to bail from it.

"Dallas?" Stella pulled out several cupcake tins from the drawer under the industrial-size oven.

Kat took the tins and began wrapping them in Bubble Wrap. "Maybe." That was still a drivable distance away, so she could easily visit on holidays and to check on Aunt Maggie. But not so close that she would feel stifled.

Though looking around Sweetie Pies, she couldn't remember why she'd felt that way in the first place.

Someone knocked at the front door, and Kat set down the tins. "I'll get it." Probably a customer who hadn't heard they were shutting down, or maybe another townsperson who saw their cars out front and wanted to offer their regrets to Aunt Maggie. They'd already had two of those pass through today, despite the Closed sign.

Kat made her way to the front, and she was halfway to the door before recognizing the dark form on the other side of the glass.

Lucas.

Her heart hitched as she turned the lock, clarifying that she wasn't angry with him anymore. Maybe she'd been using the anger at his offer to defend against the way it touched the recesses of her heart. She was afraid what the offer really meant, afraid to take it the wrong way and make it mean more than it did.

Afraid to hope it meant anything other than him having no trouble at all in sending her away.

"Can I come in?" Lucas was lacking his usual lumbering confidence. This man before her seemed almost . . . broken. Did he hate the awkward disconnect between them as much as she did? The thought made her feel a little better. At least it wasn't just her.

Or maybe misery just loved company.

"Of course. We're just packing." Kat locked the door behind him, noting the purple bakery box in his hand. "Is that a—"

"Cupcake? Yeah." He set it on one of the nearby tables, then shrugged out of his jacket and draped it over the top, like the mysterious box was of little consequence.

"Hey, now. Are you cheating on Sweetie Pies?" She put her hands on her hips, mock-glaring at him, but knew short of going to Walmart and buying one from the bakery there, there wasn't much opportunity for that.

"I'd never." He grinned, but it didn't quite reach his eyes—which still wouldn't look quite at her. He seemed . . . nervous. Antsy.

Scared.

No. Not Lucas. That was her territory.

He swiveled toward the back of the store, where Aunt Maggie and Stella, currently unseen yet never unheard, were loudly debating the pros and cons of leaving behind Aunt Maggie's eccentric oven mitt collection.

"You guys need any help?"

"I think they've got it." She waited until his gaze finally landed on her, then flickered away. She reached up and touched his chin, directing his face back toward her. He looked as surprised at the bold move as she was. "You didn't come to wrap baking utensils, Lucas. Why are you here?"

He turned away, then raked his fingers through his hair before pulling his hands away and turning back to her. "I miss you."

She stiffened. *No, don't do this* . . . "I saw you just a few days—"

"No, Kat. I *miss* you." Lucas paced in front of her, his dark hair sticking out in stressed tufts. "None of this is okay. Ever since Los Angeles, things have been different, and I can't do this anymore."

The words stuck like a knife to her stomach. This was it. The conversation she'd been dreading for days—weeks, really. But he was right. It had to be done.

They had to say good-bye.

She swallowed hard, standing straighter and determining not to go down without some level of dignity. But one look at the torment in his eyes, the torment that had to be mirroring her own, nearly undid her. Tears sprang with traitorous abandon, and she softly forced out the words she knew to be true. "I can't either."

Maybe being nothing was better than this awful, unspoken, unending conflict between them. Whatever the tension was, they couldn't live in it any longer. Nor could they pretend it didn't exist.

Her fleeing the state would be her only saving grace.

"Good." Lucas seemed to breathe out a sigh of relief, smoothing his hair straight as if just realizing he'd rumpled it. "So you agree?" Hope shone in his eyes, and confusion rocked Kat back a step. He was relieved she felt the same? How did that make sense?

Maybe he'd actually lost it.

She crossed her arms, guarding her heart. "I guess I do."

He let out a whoop, grabbed her by the waist, and spun her around before setting her on top of the table with the cupcake box.

She stared, her hands still gripping his shoulders in surprise, heart racing with adrenaline and confusion.

Now she *knew* he'd lost it.

"All this time, I thought I needed some grand gesture to win you over. That's why I signed you up for *Cupcake Combat* in the first place." Lucas shook his head with a short laugh. "I wanted you to know how much I believed in you." He hesitated, reaching up and touching her cheek. "Loved you."

Loved her?

She held on tighter, knowing she needed to let go, needed to protect her heart, but she just wanted to touch him, hold him, breathe him in one last time. "I—I love you too." And she did, from the core of her soul, all the way up and out, over and under, forever and ever.

"I don't know how this is going to work, but I'll do whatever it takes, Kat."

Wait. *What?* This wasn't a good-bye speech.

What was this?

"If you want to move, start over somewhere in a big city with your prize money, then I support you." Lucas brushed her hair out of her eyes, the look in his gaze so tender it made her stomach hurt. "I can't move with you, at least not right now, but we can make long-distance work. I'll do anything to make it work."

"Lucas . . ."

He was rambling now and she still had no idea what link she'd missed in the conversation. "We can visit. Drive back and forth. Or even fly if you go somewhere far away."

"Lucas!"

He kept going, oblivious. "There's always holidays and the vacation time off from school, and of course, we have unlimited minutes on our cell phones—"

She shut him up the only way she knew how. Cupped his face in her hands and kissed him.

He kissed her back, silently, and then rested his forehead on hers, a little grin tilting the corner of his mouth. "Sorry. I'm assuming you want to talk too?"

She pushed him away just enough to see his face. "What are you talking about? I thought you came here to . . . tell me good-bye. End this drama. End . . . us." She motioned between the two of them. "I'm a step behind here. What do you mean you signed me up for the show to tell me how much you loved me?"

"That was the plan all along, Kat. The show, the ten acres, everything." He pulled out a chair from beside the table and sat down, clasping her hands in his and resting their joined fingers on her jean-clad knee. "It was all for you. For us."

"The ten acres?" He was still talking in code.

"That's the real reason I didn't tell you about my offer on the land. I wanted it to be a surprise, because I wanted you to live there with me." He squeezed her hands, and she squeezed back for dear life. "I was going to tell you about it when I proposed. But it didn't seem right yet. You were so . . . so lost. It wasn't the right time, and when the competition opportunity came up, I thought maybe then you'd start to believe me. Believe in yourself."

He'd done all of it for her. The realization sank in deep, along with the recognition that he hadn't been trying to send her away. He'd been trying to set her free. He had put her interests and desires above his own—twice—first with his offer to invest in her and then in convincing the Food Network to make her prize cash so she could go wherever she wanted.

"I get it now." Her words came out a whisper, and tears welled once again. She'd been so off. So wrong. So selfish.

So foolish to think she'd ever find happiness anywhere long-distance from Lucas. As a friend or as more. They were part of the same recipe, for better or for worse.

'Til death did them part?

"I don't want to move." The truth slipped out, growing larger the moment it was set free from her lips. "I don't want long-distance, Lucas. I just want you."

He stood, leaning over her, the love in his eyes nearly tangible as he smoothed back her hair and cradled her face in his calloused hands. "You don't have to sacrifice for me. We'll figure this out. I promise."

"No, I'm serious." Kat pulled back, standing beside him as she gestured around the empty bakery. An idea sank in, planting roots that buried deep and began to immediately flourish. "I've been here packing all day, and wondering why on earth I have no desire to leave anymore. I want to use my prize money to buy Sweetie Pies." She laughed at herself, at the shock and joy in Lucas's eyes, at the desire budding—blooming—in her heart, at the feeling of *right* that had been absent for so long. She could feel the Lord agreeing with her in her spirit. Yes. *Yes.* This was the right decision. A new dream—straight from the Dream Giver.

She said it again, with more certainty. "I'm going to buy Sweetie Pies. This is home. You're home, Lucas." She hesitated, reaching once more for his hand. "All this time, I thought I had to leave to be free, to be happy, but I don't anymore. I don't know why, but it's different."

"You might have thought you lost in California, Kat, but you found yourself out there." He wrapped her in his arms, pulling her against his chest. She snuggled against his heartbeat as he continued. "You're stronger now. All those insecurities about your ability, all those fears that kept you from believing in yourself—they're gone, Kat. That's why everything is different now. Your vision is different." He grinned down at her. "You're not afraid anymore."

He was right. She tightened her grip around him, breathing in his familiar scent, basking in the strength of his arms. She wasn't afraid. Or maybe she'd just finally realized there were things she feared losing even more than what she had originally feared.

"I guess there's only one thing left to do." Lucas was grinning now.

Kat stepped back as Lucas reached for the little bakery box. "Celebrate with a cupcake?" She laughed. "Good thing, since all the ones here are gone for the time being."

But not for long. Once she officially bought the shop from Aunt Maggie, she'd still sell vanilla, chocolate, and strawberry cupcakes. Oh yes. Right beside a giant display full of pumpkin scone cupcakes and raspberry lemonade torte cupcakes and Mexican hot chocolate cupcakes and . . .

Lucas opened the box and knelt in front of her, presenting her with a cupcake that looked homemade.

With a white-gold diamond band nestled atop the pink icing.

She brought her hands to her mouth and gasped.

"Kat Varland—I don't want to ever make another cupcake again. At least not without you." Lucas winked. "Will you marry me?"

She pulled him to his feet as he plucked the ring from the icing. "Yes. Yes!" Joy bubbled up and over in her heart.

He slipped the diamond on her finger, and she held it up to sparkle in the overhead lights. Perfect. But it could have come from a Cracker Jack box and been just as beautiful.

Her admiration of her new piece of jewelry was interrupted as Lucas kissed her so intensely her feet lifted off the floor.

He set her back down but didn't let go, pressing his mouth against her ear. "Hey, fiancée?"

She shivered at the husky sound in his voice, burrowing closer into his chest. "Mmmhmm?"

"I'm thinking I don't want a long engagement."

A slow burn crept up her neck and into her cheeks. She was in complete agreement. She edged slowly away from him, reaching for the cupcake abandoned on the table. "Well, I guess now there really *is* only one thing left to do."

"What's that? Celebrate with cupcakes?" He mimicked her earlier response.

"Something like that." Then she reached up and smashed the cupcake straight in his face.

He stood, blinking, frozen, icing dropping from his face in chunks. "Not fair, Varland. Not fair." He wiped his eyes, then grinned, licking his lips.

She edged over in front of him, laughing, and pulled a portion of iced cake off his neck. "Come on, now." She tossed him a flirty look as she popped the piece of cake in her mouth. "You know what they say . . ."

"What's that?" He pulled her close, rubbing his face against her own cheek and hair and transferring the icing, making her squeal.

She leaned back to smile in his face, barely getting the words out before he interrupted with another kiss.

"All's fair in love and cupcakes."

Kat's Raspberry Lemonade Torte Cupcakes

For the cupcakes and filling:

3 cups flour
1 tablespoon baking powder
1/2 teaspoon salt
2 cups sugar
1 cup unsalted butter, room temperature
4 eggs, room temperature
2 teaspoons vanilla extract
1 cup buttermilk
2 tablespoons lemon zest
2 tablespoons fresh lemon juice
1 to 1 1/2 cups lemon curd

Preheat the oven to 350 degrees. Line 24 muffin cups with paper liners. In a medium bowl, sift together the flour, salt, and baking powder. Set aside.

In the bowl of a stand mixer (or using a handheld electric mixer), cream the butter and sugar. With the mixer on low, add the eggs one at a time, along with the vanilla. Stir in the flour mixture in two batches, alternating with the buttermilk, lemon zest, and lemon juice. Beat just until combined. Do not over mix.

Fill the prepared pans with the batter, filling each cupcake liner ¾ full. Bake in preheated oven until toothpick inserted into the center comes out clean, approximately 20 to 25 minutes. Let cupcakes cool in pans for about 10 minutes before removing them to a rack.

Fill your cooled cupcakes with lemon curd using a pastry bag, fitted with a tip big enough for the filling to pass though. Insert the tip about 1 inch deep into the cupcake. Squeeze the pastry bag, filling each cupcake with approximately 1 to 2 teaspoons of lemon curd.

For the raspberry buttercream fluff and garnish:

    1 cup butter, softened
    4 cups confectioner's sugar
    1/2 teaspoon vanilla
    1/2 cup seedless raspberry jam
    1 (13 oz.) jar marshmallow crème or fluff
    Fresh raspberries
    Striped paper straws, cut in half

In the bowl of a stand mixer, cream butter until light and fluffy. Add vanilla. Slowly beat in the sugar, 1 cup at a time. Beat in raspberry jam. Once fully combined, gently fold in marshmallow fluff. Pipe onto completely cooled cupcakes and garnish with a fresh raspberry and a striped paper straw.

KAT'S TIP: If you don't have buttermilk on hand (and who does?), you can make your own! Just pour 1 tablespoon of bottled lemon juice into a 1-cup measuring cup. Pour milk over the lemon juice, filling the measure. Allow the mixture to rest for about 5 minutes, and *Voila!* You have 1 cup of buttermilk.

Discussion Questions

1. Kat felt stifled in her work at Sweetie Pies—yet at the same time, she held herself captive while complaining about being trapped. Have you ever let fear keep you from breaking out and taking a risk in relationships or your career?
2. Lucas loved Kat enough to sacrifice his dreams in order to help her accomplish hers. Has anyone ever done that for you? Have you done that for someone else? What was the result?
3. Kat had strained relationships with her family, especially her sister, for various reasons—namely, jealousy and miscommunication. How do you think Kat could have worked through those issues with her family members sooner than she did? Have you ever been in a similar position with a sibling or parent? What happened?
4. Because of growing up with a single mother, Lucas carried a burden of always feeling like he had to take care of everyone in his life—his family, his best friends, the kids on his football team. He didn't realize that sometimes being too invested in someone's life tends to hold them back, rather than propel them toward their goals. Have you ever let a circumstance of your childhood shape you negatively as an adult?

5. Would you ever compete on a reality TV show if given the chance? Why or why not? What theme would it be if you could star in a show?

6. Who are you most like? Lucas—the realistic Protector for those in your life? Or more like Kat—the afraid-to-leap Dreamer?

7. Kat loves baking, but deep down, was searching for her identity in something more. What do you feel like defines you, whether intentionally or unintentionally? What labels do you wear?

8. Kat and Lucas both kept waiting on the other to make a move and reveal their love for each other beyond friendship. Who do you think should have taken the lead there and why/when?

9. Kat tended to describe people in terms of cupcake flavors. What cupcake flavor best describes you?

10. Do you think Lucas's big gesture of signing up Kat for *Cupcake Combat* was a good way to reveal his feelings for her and show his support of her dreams? Why or why not?

11. At one point in the story, Lucas—out of his love and desperation—was torn between helping Kat win the competition and taking the opportunity to sabotage her efforts so she wouldn't win and move away from him. Have you ever wanted to do a bad thing for what seemed like a good reason? What happened as a result?

Acknowledgments

*I*t doesn't just take a village to write a book, it takes an army—an army of well-prepared, heartfelt warriors who are amazing at what they do!

Many props to my editor, Becky Philpott, for her editing prowess, her genuine friendship, and her sincere heart—I couldn't have done this without you! Your support and prayers for me during the writing of this novel will never be forgotten and never taken for granted.

To Jodi Hughes and the entire editorial and marketing team at Zondervan—you guys are so fun, and I loved your vision for this book from the start. Thanks for getting me, and being so great at your job!

Also special thanks to my agent, Tamela Hancock Murray, who is a rock in the ever changing publishing industry. Thank you for always covering me in prayer when the waves crash, and for your constant cheerleading and encouragement. You are a blessing!

Thanks to Lori Chally, Katie Ganshert, Anne Prado, Sarah Varland, Georgiana Daniels, Jenn Knight, and Krystle Trudell, who have taught me that friends are like cupcakes—you can't ever have too many, and the sweeter the better! You girls are such a blessing to me, you have no idea. Cupcakes on me!

To Jacki Amanda and Rebecca Melton—"Are you ready?" "NO!" Thanks to you ladies for swinging with me right out of my comfort zone and for making memories of the heart that can never be erased. Our mansions in heaven better be on the same block.

To Bobby, Christy, and my entire Authentic ministry family— God sent you to me in a big ol' giftwrapped package, and I am eternally grateful. We can't stop. We won't stop.

Special thanks to my mama, for being the world's best nana and babysitter for this mama who needed to write. And to Audrey Elise, the sweetest kindergartener this world has ever known, my heartbeat, my gift in life . . . I don't deserve you, but I wouldn't want to watch *Cupcake Wars* with anyone else.

To all my readers—this cupcake's for you!

And to Jesus Christ, the Author and Finisher of my faith, the one from whom all blessings flow—my best friend, the inventor of cupcakes, and the one who kept holding my hand even on the days when I let go . . . I love you.

About the Author

Betsy St. Amant has a heart for three things—chocolate, new shoes, and sharing the amazing news of God's grace through her novels. She lives in Louisiana with her adorable storytelling young daughter, a collection of Austen novels, and an impressive stash of Dill Pickle Pringles. A fiction author and freelance journalist, Betsy is a member of American Christian Fiction Writers and is multi-published in contemporary romance. When she's not reading, writing, or singing along to a Disney soundtrack with her daughter, Betsy enjoys inspirational speaking and teaching on the craft of writing and can usually be found somewhere in the vicinity of a white-chocolate mocha.

Visit her website at www.betsystamant.com
Facebook: BetsySt.Amant
Twitter: @betsystamant